P Back Please
J enc

GW00691470

ABOUT THE AUTHOR

Peter Gray has been writing in various guises since he was twelve years old and he has never been able to stop. From plays to magazine articles Peter has produced a plethora of work.

His first Sam Series book 'A Certain Summer' has had excellent reviews, one from TV presenter and ex England soccer coach Bob Wilson who grew up in the same area and could easily identify with the character in the book.

With many short stories, articles and celebrated Mummers Plays plus many touring productions under his belt. Peter is always busy writing something or other. He has also acted in and directed some of those productions and one such production played at Warwick Castle for six full seasons. He has also written several scripts for advertisements, mostly with a humorous theme as well as several live shows for the stage. He has now embarked on a new series of Adventure Novels of which more details can be found on this website at www.petergrayauthor.co.uk.

He lives in the Highlands of Scotland.

Plague Witch

by
Peter Gray

Tricky Imp Publishing

Plague Witch

First edition first published December 2020

Tricky Imp Publishers
Caithness, Scotland.
Email: books@trickyimppublishing.co.uk

A CIP catalogue record for this title is available from
The British Library.

ISBN 978-0-9572668-8-9

Cover design & artwork by the author.

More Information at:
www.petergrayauthor.co.uk
www.trickyimppublishing.co.uk

Printed and bound in the UK by 4 Edge.

[Latin: Tendimus huc omnes; metam properamus ad unam. Omnia sub leges mors vocat atra suas.]

'We are all bound thither; we are hastening to the same common goal. Black death calls all things under the sway of its laws.'

Publius Ovidius Naso (Ovid)

Chapter One

Detective Sergeant Ross automatically lifted his hand to his face. He gave a quick glance to the fingers expecting to see blood, but there was none. It was a reaction to the rush of pain he felt an instant after the man had attacked him. It had done the man no good of course. Ross had moved quickly enough to turn the man around and slam him into the car he was trying to steal. This, in turn, had brought blood from the man's face, and a renewed attack. By now however, Ross had him in a vice like grip and was seriously thinking of breaking the man's arm, but DC Rutherford had arrived and lifted the protesting man off his feet, bringing him crashing to the floor before he was trussed up with zip ties as if ready for posting off to some address or other. Even his legs were secured. He was then bundled into the unmarked police car, before the two detectives returned to the front seats. Ross pulled down the sun visor in the driver's seat to avail himself of the mirror behind it.

'Don't worry,' growled Rutherford, glancing over to Ross from his cramped position in the passenger seat. 'It hasn't ruined your good looks.' Ross was examining a deep scratch across his left cheek, which was showing promise of blood.

'I ought to kick the shit out of the little bastard,' hissed Ross, raising his handkerchief to the graze.

'Don't get too much blood on your hanky, you may need it later,' nodding to the body sprawled on the back seat. Ross turned in his seat and frowned with disgust.

'Shite,' he exclaimed, 'the bastard is bleeding on the seats. Let's get him to the station.' Ross put the handkerchief away and started the engine. Rutherford picked up the radio and messaged headquarters.

'Can we have someone up here on the bookmaker surveillance, we have to bring a perp into the station?' he announced. After a second or two, a reply insisted,

'There's no one to replace you, can't it wait?'

'No, we have injuries to the perp,' he replied and gave a passing smile to Ross, who was still trying to look at his injury in the rear-view mirror now and then.

'Okay, you'll have to come in then,' replied HQ, and Rutherford replaced the handset, trying to find a comfortable position for his oversize frame, in the undersize seat. The two men had become tired of the surveillance anyway, three days of waiting for a bookmakers assistant who had done a runner with the week's takings. He hadn't shown, and though he wasn't considered the most incandescent Roman candle in the firework display, he had been careful enough not to show at his girlfriend's house. The sight of a nervous young man looking up and down the street before trying to break into a new car had been a welcome distraction for the pair of them. The fact that the man attacked Ross as he was apprehended wasn't a surprise, but the ferocity

of the attack had taken the detective aback somewhat. It made Rutherford wonder, if the 'perp' had some previous offences, but that would come to light once they knew who he was. Ross was still concerned with the mark on his face and hadn't planned any further than depositing the man in the cells, and then breakfast with a cup of coffee.

'It will just be our luck for the little toe-rag to show while we are away,' sighed Rutherford. Ross glanced over to him for a second with a frown.

'Who?'

'You know,' replied Rutherford with sarcasm, 'the reason we were out here?' He sighed again, 'the person we are looking for, Thomas Serle?' Ross understood and nodded.

'Probably,' he replied and touched the mark on his face. This time there *was* blood. 'I still want to kick the crap out of this shite,' he insisted, pointing his thumb behind him. Rutherford slowly shook his head and looked out of the window onto a grey, cold morning.

At the Inverness police station, the man from the back of the car was taken to the cells and Rutherford began making out the paperwork for the arrest. Ross was in the toilets examining his wound. Rutherford had returned to the Cave, the office that C section operated from. He was alone. Most of the team were out on their own investigations, but he knew DS Wilson was still in the building somewhere. He was probably in a meeting with the DCI, as Wilson and DCI Croker had never really communicated well enough for them to regard either, with any sort of trust. Rutherford was bright enough to realise that Croker regarded DS Wilson as a competent officer who did as much as he was required to do, but nothing more. This wasn't due to any resentment or ulterior motive, Gordon Wilson simply valued his home life. He would never let any of his team down however, and if a job needed finishing, he was always there to do it. He just didn't compromise his relationship with his family. On the other hand, Croker knew Wilson wasn't ever going to do a detective inspector's job, on a detective sergeant's pay for any extended length of time. This was not the first time Wilson has been expected to run C Section in a temporary capacity, but Croker had long realised that Wilson simply didn't want to be a detective inspector. The value he placed in his marriage overrode his commitment to his job. He was dedicated, but all the team knew, if Wilson had to decide between police work and his wife, police work was going to lose. That said, his knowledge and experience, plus his dedication to the work, ensured he was the first choice as second-in-command, and he had previously run the section. In the interim period after DI Avalon had left, until DI Brown had taken over, he had taken temporary command. Now he was in that same position due to DI Brown being in hospital after an accident during a holiday abroad. That was something else that had got on Wilson's nerves, if not all the team. DI Brown had taken over C Section, but after just eight months, he had taken a holiday for two weeks. DS Wilson hadn't taken more than three days off in the last ten months, and Rutherford couldn't remember his last holiday since joining C Section. This hadn't gone down well, and when it was known that Brown was in hospital with a broken leg and complications to his spine, most of the team had their spirits lifted. Brown was capable, he was even good at

12

his job, but he wasn't a people manager, and a successful DI had to be just that. Even Croker didn't have any real confidence in the new DI, and when he knew DI Brown was to be off for some time, he was relieved to ask DS Wilson to resume his running of the section until a new DI was found. DCI Croker knew Wilson wouldn't do more than he needed to, but Wilson knew the team, and he knew how to get the best from them. He also knew Wilson would make a good DI too, but he couldn't force him.

Rutherford looked up from his PC screen as the door to the Cave opened.

'Sorted out your makeup?' he asked. It was DS Ross.

'That little shite nearly took my eye out.'

'The scratch is on your cheek, not your eye,' explained Rutherford returning to his report.

'Close enough,' replied Ross, passing his fingers over the mark, 'I don't think it will scar, what do you think?' Rutherford completely ignored the question and asked instead,

'Have you cleaned the car out?'

'I got one of the mechanics to do it. He owed me a favour, anyway.'

'I bet they love you down there, having to skivvy for you,' groaned Rutherford.

'They do actually, particularly Robbie,' replied Ross, walking over to the large monitor screen fixed to the wall. The monitor was switched off and the reflective black screen was being used as a poor mirror. 'I get his lad cheap computer games.'

'You're joking, right?'

'No,' frowned Ross, turning from his dark

reflection for a moment. 'Why would I be joking? I get them from my cousin who works for a software company.'

'Everything's downloaded these days. Who the hell buys CD's?' frowned Rutherford, staring at Ross.

'People who live up north and have shite broadband,' insisted Ross, returning the frown and leaving the monitor for his desk. Rutherford thought for a moment. Ross had more than a passing distaste for anywhere north of Inverness, and the 'up north' description caused Rutherford to wonder where his dislike of the extremities of Scotland came from. He shook his head and continued with his work, totally disinterested in the internet problems of the Northern Highlands. Ross went back to his reflection, this time through the black shiny screen of his phone. After a few moments of caressing the mark on his cheek said,

'I bet I won't be able to shave with this.' Rutherford closed his ears to Ross's ramblings.

The next person through the door was DS Wilson. He was carrying a folder and was about to walk to the glass booth at the end of the room, but stopped as he noticed Ross. He slowly walked up and studied the mark on his cheek, theatrically scratching within his ginger hair.

'That's gonna scar,' he said, shaking his head.

'No, it won't, it's just a graze,' replied Ross, unconvinced. 'We collared a little shite trying to break into a new car.'

'I know, I heard he's pressing police brutality,' answered Wilson entering the booth. Ross looked over to Rutherford and then followed Wilson.

'You serious?'

'Yeah,' nodded Wilson sitting down and casting the folder onto the desk. 'You need t' go downstairs and get your face photographed.'

'Proof I was attacked first, you mean?'

'No, not really,' explained Wilson glancing up at Ross, 'I was going tae have et blown up tae A4 and put et in my garden to keep the next door's cat from pissing on the flower beds.'

'Everyone is a comedian in this office,' scowled Ross as he returned to his desk. Rutherford had finished the report and saved the file. He then stretched, yawned and stood to look out of the windows.

'Soon be Christmas,' he said with a sigh.

'Aye, too bloody soon,' scowled Ross. He wasn't a fan of Christmas. In truth, no one in C Section was particularly interested in that time of year. It meant someone would have to cover the holiday period, and something usually cropped up about that time.

'Tom Murrey was talking about having another party around New Year,' offered Rutherford.

'Some hope, it's rare that many people can actually make those things. I'm not interested either way,' insisted Ross slumping back into his chair.

'Och man, the scar will have healed by then,' the big man replied, still staring through the glass.

'It's more to do with the *themes* Tommy and his wife organise. Why not just have a piss up, without pretending it's something else?'

'Jesus,' exclaimed Rutherford, turning to the DS, 'not everyone lives your shallow life. Some people like to spice it up with some sort of fantasy.'

'Aye, well,' shrugged Ross, 'that sort of thing is okay for the bedroom but away from there, it's just a mental illness.' Rutherford shook his head once more and returned to his desk. He put an earphone in his left ear and set his phone to play a mix of 90s rock music. He then moved the earpiece to the other ear, the one closer to Ross. DS Wilson came out of the booth and walked up to Ross and Rutherford.

'I'm supposing that you didnae see anything of the bookmaker's assistant?'

'No,' replied Rutherford sullenly, 'if he saw us leave he may have sneaked in.'

'Who's up there?' Wilson asked.

'No one,' replied Ross with a shrug, 'there was no one to take us off.'

'So didn't et occur to you that this attempted car theft may be a set up?' asked Wilson, raising his eyes to the two men. It hadn't, but neither of them admitted it. They glanced at each other, and then Ross said,

'It makes no odds. This little shite we brought in was bleeding. He fought back as you can see,' replied Ross, once again making an issue of the graze on his cheek.

'Aye, well,' frowned Wilson and then paused and looked up at the clock, 'maybe someone needs tae find out ef 'this little shite' as you call him, has any connections to the bookmaker case then.' He then turned and left the office. Ross looked at Rutherford and said,

'I've lost my appetite for breakfast, let's get a drink and find out who we have in the cells.'

'So who is he?' asked Rutherford. He was speaking to PC Munton, a saggy faced man of about thirty. He was always dour and quietly spoken, but he was well known for his fantastic memory, and his apparently inexhaustible ability to answer questions on general knowledge. It was said, that he was a whiz at his local pub, where his quiz team always won. Ross amused himself now and then by asking him obscure questions to see if he knew the answers.

'He refuses to say, says he wants his lawyer with him,' replied the sardonic PC.

'Who won the men's Wimbledon in 1984?' asked Ross to Rutherford's complete surprise. The PC considered this and looked to the ceiling as if he was scanning records.

'McEnroe, I think he defended his title against...' a slight pause, 'Jimmy Connors,' came the reply.

'Has the brief been sent for?' asked Rutherford, trying to get back onto the subject at hand.

'No, he couldn't give us a name for a lawyer, so we told him one would be provided when he needed it,' insisted Munton.

'Which single spent the most time at number one in 1997?' asked Ross, as if he hadn't heard any of the previous conversation.

'Easy,' replied Munton, not even looking up from his desk, 'Candle in the Wind, Elton John.'

'Anything in his pockets?' asked Rutherford. Munton reached under the desk and pulled out a box which was labelled up and looked ready for storage.

'Just this,' announced Munton. Ross tried to come up with a trick question as the big man searched through the few worthless items.

'How long did the hundred years' war last?' This time Munton looked up at Ross and gave a short smile.

'One hundred and sixteen years,' then he looked back down to his desk.

'Nothing in here to say who he is, a few coins, a bit of wire, a lighter, two house keys and a car key.' offered Rutherford, and he pushed the box to Ross who put his hand in, and with a cursory glance shoved it over to Munton.

'How many times has Scotland won the Cal-?' began Ross, but Rutherford interrupted.

'How can I get this knob to do some work?' he asked Munton and turned to push Ross out through the door.

'Forty,' called out PC Munton as the two men left.

When they were in the corridor, Rutherford looked at Ross and asked,

'Have you any interest in completing our tasks for the day?'

'Yeah, lead on, I'll follow. What you got planned?'

'Nothing, but testing the brain of Britain in there is not going to get us anything,' growled Rutherford.

'Then let me suggest we go and have a slow drive around the streets, near the spot our man in the cells was pretending to break in to the car.' Ross was grinning and holding up the car keys.

'You're not just content with breaking the man's nose, you steal his property too,' frowned Rutherford. 'Are you trying to instigate disciplinary action against yourself?'

'You know, for a big fat man, you're a bit of a Jessie when it comes to risks,' announced Ross as he headed off to the car park, adding, 'How the hell did Munton know my question was about the Calcutta Cup?'

'Fat? Who you calling fat?' asked the indignant

DC. 'You're the guy who eats three more spuds than a pig,' and he followed on behind Ross, pulling in his stomach as two women officers passed him in the corridor.

It took no time at all for them to get a result. The second street they drove down had quite a few cars parked in front of the identical semi-detached houses, some with extra vehicles in the converted front gardens. They knew they were looking for a Vauxhall, as the key was marked as such, so, as they slowly drove past each Vauxhall car or van, Martin Rutherford activated the key's remote control button at each one. Ross stopped as he heard the trill sound of a car unlocking. It was a Corsa, painted in a nondescript red colour. They parked a little further down the road and walked back to the car.

'So, what's your theory?' asked Rutherford, thinking that he had understood Ross's idea. Ross gave the Corsa a quick look over, but didn't touch it, then said,

'Well, think about it, Gordon was probably right.' Ross knew from past experience that DS Wilson was quick-witted and usually saw situations from different perspectives. 'His comments made me think about the situation,' continued Ross, 'that prick we arrested will claim he wasn't breaking into the car. After all, no tools were found on him, but because he had car keys, I realised he must have driven here. Who drives their own car to go and nick another?' Rutherford nodded at this. 'He'll then claim he was defending himself, thinking he was being attacked, after all,' Ross put on his best ironic voice, 'how could he know they were police officers?' Rutherford thrust his hands into his jacket pockets.

'So we were set up?' he asked.

'Looks like it,' nodded Ross, 'but when I saw the car keys in the box, it gave me an idea.' He narrowed his eyes and then began to explain. 'Thomas Serle gets one of his mates involved. If the bookmaker was telling the truth, Serle has made off with around twenty grand. So, he rings this mate, offers him five grand to distract the cops and get them out of the way. His mate jumps in his car, drives close by and parks up, then creates a fuss so as to get us off the street. He spends a day in the cell, bail, off home in time to watch Coronation Street in the happy knowledge that he just earned five smackers.' Rutherford frowned. 'So, I thought,' continued Ross, 'when he's released, he'll ring Serle's girlfriend, she'll pick him up, drop him off at his car and pay him from the money that Serle will leave with her. Then, he goes off on his travels.' Rutherford shrugged as he noted the registration number of the car. He then phoned through to Inverness, to find the owner of the red Corsa. Ross carefully opened the vehicle and looked inside. There was little of interest and the car smelled damp as if it let in water. Rutherford soon finished the call.

'Maybe you were right,' he nodded, replacing his phone in his jacket pocket. 'The vehicle is registered to Andrew Connor. It's currently on SORN and hasn't been taxed for six months.'

'I've heard the name, I'm sure of it,' Ross frowned.

'Probably. He has previous,' shrugged Rutherford. 'According to records, receiving, breaking and entering, two cases of assault and it seems the local plod know him because the nice Mr Connor beats up his girlfriend too. Interestingly, he *is* known to have connections with Thomas Serle.' Ross nodded.

'That helps with the arrest then,' he said as he looked at the car, 'and if we call for a truck to tow this away to the compound, it gives me an excuse for lifting the key.'

'By the book next time,' scowled Rutherford, 'I'm not going to cover your arse, you know that.'

'Stop whining, let's get back to the car, it's pretty obvious Serle has seen his girlfriend by now.' As they drove back to the station, Rutherford sighed and then said,

'It's a pity that Gordon won't take on C Section permanently.'

'He never took the exams. Anyway, he doesn't want it.'

'I suppose they would move him, it's not usual to leave a DI in post where they were DS's,' added Rutherford.

'That, and the fact that he has a fairly staid and comfortable existence,' mused Ross.

'How's the old boss, DI Avalon going on?' asked Rutherford, changing the subject slightly.

'I don't see him much,' replied Ross turning off the roundabout, 'he's away quite a bit with the job.'

'I noticed I hadn't seen him around the station,' nodded the big man, 'but wasn't that post temporary or something?'

'Yeah, a six-month contract,' replied Ross, 'he then went for some training.'

'Training, what sort of training?'

'I don't know,' scowled Ross, 'I'm his drinking mate, not his mother.' Ross paused a little then said, 'he did say he would be going away for several weeks at a time though.' He paused again. 'I'm sure he mentioned it finishes at Christmas.'

'Then what's he doing?'

'Don't know,' shrugged Ross, 'he was talking of taking another post with the SCD but I can't see that.'

'Why not?'

'He won't move from Inverness,' he replied as he stopped the car at the station. Rutherford heaved himself from the vehicle and leaned on the roof, his arms resting in front of him. Ross locked the car and glanced at Rutherford, who was now deep in thought. 'Why, you thinking he'll come back to C Section?' Ross was smiling as he turned to walk to the rear entrance. Rutherford came from his thoughts and followed.

'It would solve a problem for both sides, wouldn't it?' he asked. Ross typed in the security number to open the door and swiped his card. The door opened, and they entered. Inside, Ross glanced back at Rutherford.

'He'll not do that, he thinks like me in that respect, never return to the scene of the crime,' and he strode off down the corridor.

'Does he still see Sarah Underwood?' Ross didn't answer. He turned and walked up the stairs, heading towards the restroom and the terrible vending machine there. He pressed the button for black coffee and then the one for coffee with milk. He kept the black one himself, and passed the other to Rutherford. They then sat on the closest seat. The room was empty as it usually was. Rutherford had added a comment on how *he* would like to spend a few minutes with Miss Underwood.

'A few minutes is probably pushing it for you, isn't it?'

'A good-looking woman like that is going to suck

the lifeblood out of you if you take longer,' smiled Rutherford. He sipped his coffee and then added, 'Well?'

'They meet up now and then, but you know Jimmy boy, he never tells you anything.'

'They seemed pretty close last New Year in the Tavern as I remember.' Ross nodded at this as he remembered that Avalon was going through some sort of patch. He decided to say little about it.

'It was New Year's Eve, you know what it's like, you'll kiss anyone with a few beers inside you,' he paused and remembered something else. 'If my memory serves me correctly, you were committing some very perverse acts in the pub too.' For a moment, Martin didn't know what Ross was talking about and then it became clear.

'Me and Megan you mean?' he smiled, 'yeah, that was the spirit of the night, I like her though, she's got character.'

'She also carries several diseases too.'

'So why don't you like her, what is it between you two?' asked Rutherford.

'We get on fine,' replied Ross taking a drink of the rank coffee, 'it's all show, that's all. I suppose I like her too but we never admit it to anyone, or even ourselves.' He took another drink and then asked, 'So did it go any further?'

'With Megan?' asked Rutherford with surprise, 'no, it was just that evening, I would find it embarrassing to be with any woman I had to lift up so that I could kiss her.' Ross nodded at this and gave a slight smile. There was silence for a few moments, until Martin asked,

'So, is Miss Underwood still unattached?'

'You thinking of giving it a go?' laughed Ross.

'No, just interested in Jim's welfare.' There was a touch of resentment in Rutherford's face.

'Like I said,' repeated Ross, 'he tells me nothing. I only know that since the New Year, he's been away quite a bit with this training, and of course, Sarah is always busy. I don't think it's a serious relationship.' Ross thought for a moment. 'To tell the truth, I haven't seen him since...' he tried to remember the last time he had seen Avalon. 'I think it was last month, we went to the Tavern. One of the regulars had a bit of a birthday bash. That was the last time I saw him.'

'It's longer than that for me,' nodded Rutherford, 'I saw him chatting to Croker in the summer, oh and I waved to him in the car park a couple of months ago.' They both sat reflecting on their memories until Ross looked at his watch.

'Right, we had better go and give Mr Andrew Connor a going over.'

The following Monday morning, DS Wilson made an announcement at the weekly meeting before any of C Section left.

'I had a meeting with the DCI last week, and we discussed several subjects, including the Christmas coverage.' There were a few audible groans. 'Before I pass the sheet out, I wish et tae be known that I left the rota to the DCI, I had little or nothing tae do with et.' He then handed the rota sheets around and there were a few sighs but nothing untoward. 'The other subject we talked about was the situation concerning DI Brown. The Chief thinks that et's doubtful the DI will be returning anytime soon, and has concluded that, due to the needs of the section, DI Brown will be reassigned when he recovers.'

24

'So who's taking over?' asked Rutherford.

'I'm coming t' that Martin,' replied Wilson, leaning on a desk. 'The Chief es going to press the Superintendent tae find us a new DI, or at least allow him t' appoint one.'

'Can't he make you up Gordon?' asked Rory. Rory had only just got used to calling Wilson by his first name. His upbringing and training did not allow him to be informal easily, and once Wilson had taken over the section, it had seemed wrong to call him by his first name.

'He asked me ef I would take the job ef offered, and I will tell you what I told him.' Wilson paused for a moment, looked at the floor and then back up to the team with a tiny smile on his lips. 'Not bloody likely.'

'Why not? You're doing the job anyway?' continued Rory.

'I'm not designed for such a thing. I like what I do and I enjoy et. Doing a DI's job would take that from me. I don't want a desk job quite yet.' Rory shrugged at this and nodded slowly. He knew it didn't *have* to be a desk job, it just was, due to the amount of paperwork.

'And his wife won't let him, added Ross with a grin. There were a few laughs. Most people knew Wilson's wife, and they knew her to be both fiery, and what is generally called, 'a party animal'.

'And my wife won't let me,' nodded Wilson with a smile. He let the smile drop and then added, 'so for the time being, you'll just hae t' do with me and we'll wait to see who DCI Croker or the Super can come up with.'

'Didn't Tom Murrey take his exams a few months ago?' asked Rutherford. It was Ross who answered.

'He was going to, but he had an ulterior motive. He was considering moving to Stirling, but they've just bought a new house outside Inverness, so I'm guessing their plans have changed.'

'I thought Tom was a close friend of yours,' asked Wilson, 'didn't he tell you?'

'He told me about Stirling, but I haven't seen him privately for some time,' shrugged Ross.

'Is this something to do with...' began Rutherford, but the instant glare from Ross made him remember something, and he stammered an unintelligible answer. This wasn't lost on Rory Mackinnon or Megan Frazer, who had been quiet all through the meeting.

'So,' continued Wilson, seeing that Rutherford and Ross were to say nothing else, 'as et stands, we have t' wait, and hope that we don't get another DI who bows out after a few months.' He stood upright and asked, 'You are out this morning, Rory?'

'Yeah,' nodded the young DC, 'me and White are in court for that drunk driver case.' White was in the room, but as usual the newest recruit to the section hadn't said a word. 'We should be back later. I think it will be adjourned.' Wilson nodded, and he looked at White who was staring into space. Wilson's frustration with White was clear as he sighed, and pushed his hand through his ginger cropped hair.

'Any other business?' he then asked, 'no? Carry on then.' As Wilson walked to the booth, Ross shot Rutherford a deep frown, Rutherford looked back pushing out his bottom lip and made an exaggerated shrug. Again, both Mackinnon and Frazer saw this, but neither reacted. Frazer continued with her work instead,

26

but Rory was soon on his feet and pulling on his jacket. He raised his brows to Frazer and then turning to DC White, said,

'We better get off White, I don't want to be late.' White was a real problem to the section. No one liked him, no one wanted to work with him, and yet for some reason, DI Brown had seen him as an asset. Even Rory couldn't bring himself to call him by his first name, and that was unusual. The rest of the team had taken to calling him 'AI', mainly from the computer gaming world where non-player characters are called AI, meaning artificial intelligence. His nick-names had been many and various, including, Mr Out-to-lunch, DOA and Zombie. The latter inherited from his short time in B Section. He wasn't stupid, he seemed highly intelligent and was, if anything, over-qualified, but he had no interest in interacting with humans, and that was quite a drawback for someone working in the police force. DS Wilson detested the man. He cited his dislike as not the fact that the man was tedious, or matter-of-fact, but due to the reasoning that White must have changed his character through his career. He maintained that White could not have made it to the position he was in, without being less antagonistic. He simply would not have remained in the force. Some previous officer would have marked him down as being unsuitable. So, with this in mind, Wilson had done some research. He found what he was looking for but told no one what he had discovered. Unfortunately, knowing that White was not naturally the way he was, did nothing to appease Wilson's dislike of the man. In truth, it had made him abhorrent to the DS, and he rarely allowed him to work on anything other than minor cases.

With Rory and White on their way to the courts, and DS Wilson in his booth, The Cave seemed quiet, and it wasn't long before Frazer had built up enough boredom of the report she was writing up, to turn slowly around to Rutherford who was just perceptibly nodding his head to the sounds coming from his phone and through his earpiece. She then looked past him to Ross, who caught her eye watching him. He frowned instantly. He knew Frazer didn't miss a thing, and he thought he knew what she was up to.

'Sooooo…' began Frazer, dragging out the single syllable so it resembled a whole sentence, 'is that to do with, what?' Rutherford removed the earpiece noticing she was staring at him, and asked,

'Pardon?' and he frowned.

'You said to Rossy earlier, 'is that to do with?' I'm just wondering what it *is*, that it's to do with.' It seemed a complicated question, but Ross knew exactly what she was getting at.

'Keep your nose out of it, Frazer,' scowled Ross.

'Never mind,' grinned Frazer, 'I got my answer,' and she turned back to her report before adding, 'Rossy has a woman… poor thing.'

'That's the problem with this office,' insisted Ross with annoyance in his voice, 'no one can keep their noses out of other people's private lives. If they can't find anything, they'll just invent it.'

'I'm just wondering what the poor thing has wrong with her to be desperate enough,' smiled Frazer without looking back to him.

'Do you know how rude it is to ask people about their personal lives? It has nothing to do with anyone in this section.' Ross had replied as if he was talking to

28

himself, but the statement had prompted Frazer into further action.

'You should talk,' she demanded pointing to him, 'I remember you finding out that the young PC who was with us on the Culloden house break in case some months ago, was going out with his first girlfriend.'

'Yeah,' nodded Ross, 'I liked him, he was very shy, and I wanted to give him some encouragement.'

'But that's not what you did, is it?' frowned Frazer, almost in an angry tone.

'I believed I showed an interest in his predicament, that's all,' insisted Ross frowning back.

'Predicament? You probably scarred him for life.'

'Nonsense,' insisted Ross, 'he seemed to take it in his stride. I was trying to help, that's all.'

'How does asking some shy young PC, 'have you shagged her yet', constitute helpfulness?'

'That was just banter,' frowned Ross. Frazer was about to begin a tirade at Ross, but Rutherford stood and began to move all the small items from Frazer's desk. She cut short her reply to Ross to ask Rutherford what he was doing.

'Damage limitation,' he replied without giving her eye contact, 'I remember the shit this office got in last time you two fought.' It was true, and Frazer remembered it, the time she threw a paperweight at Ross. DI Avalon had been in charge at the time and the office had gone into meltdown over the affair. Frazer still blamed herself. She still wondered if Avalon had ultimately left the section because of the incident. She kept her gaze on Rutherford, who calmly sat back in his seat, and continued what he had been doing previously, pushing the earpiece back in his ear. Frazer glanced at

Ross, and then picked up her jacket and went for a walk. Rutherford continued to tap the keys of his keyboard as if nothing had happened, with Ross watching on.

'You can't fathom a woman, can you?' he asked, though it wasn't really meant as a question. Rutherford stopped typing and turned to Ross with a neutral stare.

'You know,' he began calmly, 'I don't throw paperweights, I throw these,' and he held up one of his massive clenched fists, 'I find they do more damage,' and he continued typing. Ross had no fear of other men, he knew he could handle himself, but as he looked at Rutherford's massive frame hunched over his desk, he hoped he would never have to put Rutherford's claim to the test.

Chapter Two

It had been such a long time since Avalon had actually travelled on a train. He had forgotten quite how inconvenient they were. It was almost impossible to travel from Inverness to Birmingham unless you wanted to do it overnight, and then you had the choice of between one, and four changes. If he wanted to make the journey earlier, he would have to fit in with what the train company wanted, rather than what was convenient for the passenger. The cost was pretty inconvenient too, and so there wasn't a great deal of deliberation. It would be the airport for him and just over a one hour flight, rather than the 'up to fourteen hours' that the railways wanted him to undertake. He didn't really want to go to the conference anyway, but as DCI Croker had pointed out, they had to send someone to this event and Avalon's tenure in his post had ended and even his training was drawing to an end. It was true, he had been six months with the Specialist Crime Division, and that had given way to training for the Major Incident Team. He had been pointed to the SCD post by Croker, who knew he wanted out, but had considered that Avalon just needed time to gather his thoughts. For all his faults, Croker knew a good officer when he saw one, and he didn't want Avalon to leave the force, just because exhaustion had taken its toll. Avalon had agreed the post might be what he needed, and had become part of the Safer Communities Support & Co-ordination team. It meant he would have to travel, and would be away from home some of the time, but he thought the change would be good for his health. He was placed within a small team which would travel to Schools and colleges giving talks and demonstrations on a wide range of prevention and intervention subjects, including violence and harm reduction. Knife crime was a big part of his remit, and for a month or so he enjoyed the new post. Gradually though, the travel, the endless cycle of events, the same uninterested audience, and the repetition got to him. He had begun to wonder what would become of him after the contract was over. There was a chance he could join the Specialist Crime Division as a full time DI, but that meant moving from Inverness. That wasn't ever going to happen, and so he spent his evenings in hotel rooms wondering what he could do. He had heard of a job within the SCD, working with agencies tied to vulnerable groups, such as the Scottish Government, Victim Support. Crimestoppers, the Scottish Business Crime Centre and other similar organisations were also involved. He had considered this, but in the end, he knew that he would miss the cut and thrust of the investigative side of the job. Croker had been clever. Avalon could see that the DCI had coerced him into a position where he would want to return to something like his old job due to the tedious nature of the contract. It had been fortuitous in the end however, because Avalon had heard from one of the SCD officers that the

MIT were looking for several new investigators for the team. Luckily, the Highlands was one of the areas they were needed. Avalon applied and was accepted but he then had to travel once more. Over a couple of months he attended week-long training sessions, most of them with the Strathclyde branch, but for the most part, he enjoyed it. The training was to end just before Christmas and in Avalon's mind, that's why Croker had phoned him with the chance to go to the conference in Birmingham. He wanted to know what Avalon would be doing after the training. The conference was just an excuse. It was to be a four day conference, supposedly on policing the borders after Brexit. The theme of these conferences didn't matter, they were all basically the same, and Avalon had attended enough of them to know exactly what they were about. Most people would attend several of them and yawn their way through pointless talks and films, and come out the other end no wiser or richer for the experience. There was a benefit for most officers however, something that the organisers or the senior officers would never understand. Yet, it was something that those who attended, knew all too well. Avalon had benefited himself. His post to Inverness had come directly from such a conference. He had gone from Birmingham to Edinburgh to a conference and ended up working in Inverness. Was this an omen he thought? Coming from Inverness to Birmingham could see him moving again. The thought was amusing. He wasn't leaving Inverness even if he was offered a Police Commissioner's post. Maybe, being part of the MIT would help with his future anyway.

He had agreed to Croker's suggestion though, and as the DCI had said, there was no one else to send.

There was also the fact that Avalon knew Birmingham like the back of his hand. Fine, the conference was to be at the National Exhibition Centre, and somewhere at the back of his mind, he decided that a trip back there wouldn't be too stressful. He might even arrange to meet his ex-wife Carol, although he would only be there for four days with just a single afternoon free. The conference was described as making better integration with the police forces of Europe after Britain left the EU. That was a laugh indeed. The politicians not being able to organise Brexit properly meant most of the coppers working in the industry would probably be retired by the time it actually happened. To make things worse, the man who had been in charge of Brexit for the Tories, the man who had resigned because of the workload, had now been made Prime Minister. That seemed perverse to Avalon. The man who couldn't undertake a minor role in the government was now in charge of the whole thing. Either way, he decided it might be worth a trip, if only to walk the streets of Birmingham again. He would be with two other Inverness personnel, a DS from the Press Liaison office and a civilian working from the Inverness Police Station. He would, however, be meeting them there as they were sticking to plan 'A' and travelling on the underperforming railway network.

The flight was quick, convenient and pleasant. He called for a taxi to take him straight to the hotel as it wasn't far, but he had his luggage with him. He could then unpack and have a preliminary trip over to the city. Firstly, he was struck by the noise. Even in the centre of Inverness there wasn't anywhere near the volume of sound that assailed his ears in Birmingham, and the second feature of the city was the smell. It wasn't as he expected. He knew there would be a distinct lack of fresh, clean air but it was more of the commercial odours of the place that struck him, and the lights. Yes, Christmas was close but the amount of seasonal lights in the city was incredible. He was so used to the sensible approach to festivities in the north, but this chaos of lightbulbs and neon signs, was extraordinary. As he walked down the street, there was a constant change from the smells of clothes shops, pubs, restaurants and takeaways, to the overpowering reek of diesel exhaust fumes as trucks rolled by. Even though it was still daylight, the shop window Christmas lights, and brightly lit advertisement signs were everywhere. For the first time in his life, Avalon saw the stupidity of using so much electricity on a medium to sell things that people didn't really need. The content of the advertising also struck him, the way that the posters showed goods that no one needed, the way they prayed on the sort of people that just aimlessly upgrade what they already have, to keep in step with their peers. He shook his head slightly and made his way back to the hotel. He decided that a city that he once enjoyed being in, had become something he didn't understand any more, and once again, he became homesick for Inverness. As he walked to find a taxi, he did a double take at a car showroom window. He stopped and returned to look at a car that sat behind the glass. Even *he* was amused that he would ever look at a car in a longing way. He felt a little uncomfortable looking at this car, as if it was slightly pornographic and thought about walking away. Instead, he found himself inside the showroom. The car was silver, and he could tell it was a Mercedes Benz, if not the name of the model. He went closer and slid his hand along the edge of the car, tracing its lines and feeling the curve of it. He looked inside and saw the car was a luxury model. He stood back and only then felt the presence of the salesman.

'She's an older model sir but with very low mileage,' the man announced with a broad West Midlands accent, 'would you like to sit inside?' Avalon nodded, and the car seemed to fit him like a glove. He was unlucky with cars. A Saab that he had purchased had been wrecked the previous year in a pursuit with another vehicle, and since then he had bought something as a make-do. The problem was, the make-do had become his permanent vehicle. The car he was now sitting in, had been the first ever car in his life that had called to him.

'So, what is it?' he asked. The man looked a little bemused at the question. 'I mean, I know it's a Mercedes, but what model?'

'It's an S class sir.'

'Okay, can you write that down for me?' asked Avalon getting out of the car. 'The model, the year and the price,' he then added, as the man was still looking a little puzzled. He was thinking something along the lines of, 'what sort of goldfish can't remember Merc S Class?' but then he considered he might wish to research the cost of the insurance.

'We can deliver it for you if you wish,' smiled the man handing him a business card with the details written on the reverse.

'To Inverness?' smiled back Avalon.

'Really?' asked the man, raising his brows. 'Well, I suppose we could, at cost of course,' he nodded, trying to imagine how far Inverness was.

'I'll think about it,' smiled Avalon once more, holding up the card with the details, and he left, not before glancing back at the vehicle.

Fortunately, the hotel was reasonable, and had a small bar, which would serve his needs if he didn't feel like wondering at night. He returned to his room and had a quick glance through the conference brochure that he had, with the itinerary of the proceedings. There was a list of speakers and other important attendees, but little of interest, and he sought out a biro so that he could cross off the subjects and speeches he considered that he could miss. It left him with five he would have to attend to prove he had done his bit. Fortunately, three of those were on the same day, the others on separate days, but it would leave him with space to manoeuvre, and he began to plan his own, more interesting itinerary. Phoning Carol would be a priority. She would never forgive him if he had gone all that way and not called her. He would also go for a walk past his old nick in Wolverhampton. He didn't know why, it was probably just inquisitiveness to see how he would feel. He also wondered about going to see the old house, but he dropped that idea as there were both good and bad memories from that location, and he wasn't sure he wanted to be reminded of either. After all, he hadn't seen those places for… how long ago was it? It was four years. Could it really be that long since he drove from Bilbrook in Wolverhampton, to Inverness to start a new life? Plenty of polluted water had flowed down the Shropshire Union Canal since then, that was for sure, and he began to think of other times and other places he had lived. His life was going so fast, it seemed like no time at all since he was making the move from Lincolnshire to the West Midlands and before that, his time in Norfolk seemed not all that long ago. He had been in his late thirties when he first moved to Scotland, now he was in his forties and the flow of time was speeding up, he was sure of that. Well, there was nothing he could do about it, all he could wish for was that the change of pace didn't become any quicker, and he got to enjoy his time a little more. With that in mind, he scanned the internet looking if there was any entertainment on that might interest him. He saw that there was a rock band on in the St Peter's Park area but his recollection was that the district was almost a no-go area for the police. He decided to stay around Solihul instead.

The first day at the conference was to be the usual mix of pleasantries and explanations about the following few days. Avalon had sent texts to the two people from Inverness he had to meet and told them he would see them at the entrance to the conference. The representative from the liaison office was a thirty something officer called DS Robert Pearson, and the civilian was Andrea Crum, a fresh-faced woman who looked like this was her first such conference. She was plain and quiet but had a look of expectation about her. DS Pearson looked more worldly wise and had a thin, pleasant face with almost black eyes. This was accentuated by black hair and deep eyebrows. He seemed fine to get along with and Avalon wondered if he should suggest they all do their own thing.

'I don't know quite what your orders are on this trip,' he began, 'but personally, there are only a few items of interest for my department.' He waited a second for a reaction. There wasn't one. 'I think under the circumstances, it might be better if you two look at what you need to attend, and then plan your own itinerary.'

'Aye, that suits me fine,' nodded Pearson. Alison just nodded. He added that they could get together one evening to discuss the conference, but in truth, he wasn't all that interested. They stayed together for the time being.

By lunchtime, it was obvious a few people were finding excuses not to return to the auditorium for the afternoon session. Avalon did, simply because he had no plans for the day. As he sat and listened to some civilian rant on about how the people on the street had fears about the level of policing after Brexit, he considered what he was going to do that evening. He even jotted down a few ideas on the factsheet on his lap. It must have seemed to onlookers that he was taking the whole thing seriously. In truth, he was trying to decide if he should stay in and watch Pain and Glory on the TV, or go out for a drink. He heard the speaker say,

'...and in that respect, the people on the streets are right to be afraid of what might happen.' He looked up and gave the woman a quick glance. It took time to focus, and he was beginning to wonder if he was going to need spectacles soon. The woman was dressed in a powder blue suit and looked nothing like the sort of person who would know or care anything about the 'people on the streets.' He returned to his notes and decided he would go out for a drink and check on the internet for a decent pub locally. At the back of his mind, he was also trying to tie in a visit to the National Motorcycle Museum, which was close by.

As he was leaving the conference centre, he followed along with most of the others and made his way back to the hotel, taking care to look for a reasonable venue for the evening. Things had changed around Birmingham, but the local area was Solihul, and it was fairly much the same as he remembered it. The hotel was close enough to walk, and though the sky was grey, he considered the exercise would be good for him. Others had decided the same, and so a loose procession was heading towards the hotel, and he struck up a conversation with another CID officer from Nottinghamshire. The conversation was simplistic and mainly about general comparisons, but it gave Avalon the idea that he could bump into people he knew, people he had worked with previously. Thankfully, anyone he had known from Wolverhampton would be going home rather than to a hotel. The odds of meeting previous colleagues though, were remote, as there were several hotels housing people from the conference, so it would be doubtful he would be unlucky enough to meet anyone he knew.

Avalon woke the following morning to another grim day, and from his room he saw it was raining. He showered and shaved, and then went down to breakfast, nodding casually to the people already at their tables. Fortunately, there was no one he knew. Even his two fellow Invernessians were absent. He then returned to his room and dressed for the conference. His attire was casual but smart. He resisted the typical look of CID for something he was more comfortable with, and the rain had slowed enough for a showerproof jacket to be good enough for the walk to the centre.

By the time he had reached the building, the weather had brightened and though it was cool, it was quite pleasant. Inside, the foyer was busy. He had two presentations to see that day. Both were important in the respect that he would have to be able to give a talk to his colleagues when he returned. One was how policing policy could change through Brexit, and the other was specific to Scotland and how borders might be managed. He looked around him and then at his watch. He was a little early for the first presentation, and he wondered about a drink and headed to one of the café's, it would give him an opportunity to look for one that did vegan food. He wasn't exactly what other vegans would call vegan, but he had changed his diet substantially in the last year and he felt better for it. He just hadn't done it for the same reason as Sarah Underwood, and he didn't share her views on the subject. It hadn't caused arguments, far from it, she had valued his input, but on one of the few occasions they had been able to meet, she had led him to a vegan café she knew on the edge of Inverness. He had been critical of the establishment, and she had tried to defend it. To Avalon, an argument was when two people offer opposing or contrary views to debate a particular subject, mainly for the elucidation of both parties. Based on his own criteria, he didn't think what had happened in that café had been an argument. He couldn't really describe what it *had* been. She had called him a snob, in an amused way because he had been less than complimentary about the establishment. He had insisted that it wasn't so much a vegan café, more of a hippie café. Sarah had laughed about it to begin with, but as Avalon had continued to point out the lack of systems to cater for hygiene, such as tables that

41

were constructed in such a way as to be impossible to clean properly, or poorly maintained toilets, she had become less tolerant. She had finally pointed out that maybe *he* ought to suggest the next place to visit. If there was to be a next time. In point of fact, there hadn't. Not for any particular reason, mainly as they never seemed to be available at the same time. They had, however, both agreed that they would spend some quality time after Avalon's tenure with the SCD had finished and his training was complete.

Avalon had been daydreaming, as he sipped his coffee and perused the menu in the pleasant café he was now in. He then happened to glance up, and for a second he saw someone he thought he recognised. He looked again to make sure, and for a moment, he doubted it but then he heard the voice. There was no doubt. It *was* his old nemesis, Detective Sergeant Paul Staunton. He and Staunton had rarely seen eye-to-eye, and Avalon had left Wolverhampton with Staunton in a bitter mood towards him. Avalon glanced quickly to be sure it was him. It was. He was with three other people, one female, and they were sitting at a table not twenty feet away from him. Avalon smiled to himself when he remembered the way he had left the office in Wolverhampton for the final time. It brought a warm feeling to him. It was a far off memory of a moment before his life had changed. He finished the coffee and decided to leave before Staunton saw him. He had no wish to embarrass either of them, but the problem was, as Avalon stood to leave, Staunton also stood to fetch a spare spoon after dropping his. Their eyes met and to Avalon's surprise, Staunton gave a glimmer of a smile.

'Holy shit…' exclaimed Staunton, then paused,

'if it ain't DI Avalon.' The comment meant that Staunton knew he had been promoted, therefore he probably knew a little about Avalon's career too. There were more surprises to come. Staunton made his way the few steps towards Avalon and held out his hand. His grip was firm but there was no hint of malice. 'Alright mate? No need to ask how you're doing,' he said, 'made up to DI, so I have been told.' Avalon nodded and gave back a brief smile. Though four years had passed, Staunton, working from that big office in Wolverhampton, was still awaiting promotion. His accent seemed broader than he remembered, but that could be down to not hearing it for some time.

'So how are things at Wolverhampton?'

'Ah y' know, nothing changes, same old shit, different knob jockey in the saddle,' replied the burly Staunton. He looked older, much older. In those four or so years, Staunton had aged at least ten. His hair was grey and his eyes were dull and static. He was more animated talking to Avalon, and his old brashness was still there, but something had gone. Maybe that's how Avalon seemed to him too, certainly older. He knew he had changed out of all proportion since leaving the West Midlands. Staunton had turned to the people at his table and without regard to whom he was with or where he was, he called back,

'Hey mates, this is DI Avalon, he used to work in our office. He's gone north to become a porridge wog.' Inwardly, Avalon cringed, but he nodded back to the people at the table. They, in turn, nodded or waved as Staunton turned back to him. 'You should call at the office before you go, mind,' he said as an afterthought, 'not many of them left now. All new faces except for

Crossley and Ellis.'

'I might do that if I get time,' nodded Avalon, knowing it would never happen. He wanted to ask what had happened to Green, but he didn't. Green had particularly been hated by Avalon, but over the past few years, he realised he really didn't care. They shook hands again and Avalon left for the auditorium considering that his theory on not meeting people he knew had quite a flaw.

It had been a long day, not necessarily in hours, but the tedium had made it seem much longer than it actually was. Back in the hotel room, he thought about giving Carol a call. He picked up his phone and dialled, glancing to his watch. It was four-thirty, so she may still be at work. There was no answer, so he thought about food and decided to have something light in the hotel restaurant, and maybe a glass of wine. He wondered about meeting DS Pearson and Alison Crum, just to be sociable.

They did meet in the hotel bar, just for a casual chat, and after a few notes on the conference, talk moved to the usual things. They asked each other about their jobs and a little about their lives. Pearson had moved from Perth to take the post, which he enjoyed. In that respect, he was the opposite of Avalon who hated dealing with the press. Pearson liked the contact with the public though, and he suggested there were worse places to work on the force. Alison was very quiet, until she had a couple of glasses of wine. Then, she was all too eager to tell them she had worked in the communications section for two years, before working with the Child Protection System, primarily with the Child Protection

Improvement Programme. She explained that there was some concern that once the UK left Europe, that the agency considered, child-care would become a backwater. Avalon nodded and smiled now and then, but realised that Alison would probably never stop talking now she had started. He wondered if someone would have to slap her face to make her stop. She was rambling on about a new charter being presented ready for April next year, when Avalon felt his hand twitch. Had he just imagined that he wanted to slap her? He had to act before his subconscious self, took over.

'Are you married, Alison?' he asked on one of her brief breaks for breath. She looked taken aback at first.

'Yes, I was married just a month ago, as it happens,' and she smiled. 'I know what you're thinking,' she quickly added, 'and no, I don't have children, and I think that's exactly why I wanted to work in that sphere.' It hadn't worked, but Pearson accepted Avalon's lead and asked,

'So where are you from, originally I mean?' Once again, she looked surprised anyone would ask the question.

'I was born in Fort William but moved to Inverness when I was ten years old. I live near Dingwall now.' The two men nodded, but before she could continue, Avalon stood and asked if they wanted another drink. He went to the bar and noticed Pearson leave for the toilet. This was what they needed, some space to break her train of thought. By the time they had both returned, she had become a little quieter, and the conversations returned to normal. Pearson asked about Avalon's career, which he skipped over, and then at last, they said goodnight, leaving for their own rooms. Avalon rung Carol's number as he lay on the bed watching some nondescript TV show. There was still no answer. He picked up his watch from the bedside table. It was eleven thirty. He wasn't worried that Carol wasn't answering. He knew nothing of her life now, and though it was out of character for her not to have the phone by her most of the time, he realised there could be many reasons for the silence. He mentally shrugged and turned off the TV, which he hadn't really been watching. He decided on a quick shower and then to bed, but almost as soon as he turned on the water, his phone rang.

'Hello,' he said without checking who it was.

'*Hello, have you been trying to call me?*' It was Carol.

'Yes, nothing important, I was just catching up,' he replied, waiting to test the water before committing to anything.

'*Oh, that's nice, we haven't spoken for some time, how are things?*'

'Pretty good,' he replied, 'and you?'

'*Fine, I'm up your end at the moment, I'm staying with mum and dad until the New Year.*' That explained the delay in answering. He laughed. '*What is it?*' she asked.

'Guess where I am?' he replied with an obvious irony in his voice.

'*Well, either Edinburgh, or...*' she paused as the possibilities ran through her mind, '*oh, don't tell me you are in the West Midlands?*'

'At this very moment I am in a hotel room in Solihull, just at the side of the airport,' he said.

'*Isn't that just typical? Don't tell me you're*

46

moving back south?' It was put as a question.

'No chance, here for four days with work,' he paused for a second, thinking that it got him out of trying to find time to go and see her. 'I was going to visit you, but there isn't much point now. How are your parents?' he asked, trying to change the subject.

'They're fine, dad's been under the weather for a few weeks but he seems good now.'

'He loves Christmas, that's bound to perk him up. Send them both my love,' he added.

'Yes, he does, and I will,' she replied.

'Okay, have a good time up there, and look after yourself.' The conversation wasn't intentionally being cut short. It was the nature of things since their parting. They had grown gradually further apart, and they found hardly anything in common with very little to talk about.

'You too,' she replied, *'and if you get time, come down and see us. I'm here until the third of January.'* Avalon said he would if he had time, he didn't know what he would be doing after the Christmas period. He didn't even know if he would have a job. He continued with his shower, smiling at the fact that she had gone north just as he had come south, but knowing in the back of his mind, he probably wouldn't go and visit them.

The following morning was a little less inclement, and it promised to be a reasonable day, weather-wise at any rate. There was little at the conference for him that day and so his plan was to go to the motorcycle museum in the morning, and call at the conference centre for half an hour in the afternoon to show his face. After breakfast, he walked to the museum and drooled over the fabulous machinery there. Deep inside, there was a pang of regret. These lovely bikes, sitting quietly, looked like caged animals. They seemed preserved in aspic without use or purpose, waiting for the day they would be allowed to come back to life. He left the museum thinking that he really ought to ride his own treasured Triumph Thunderbird more often.

He made his way back to the conference rooms and found a café that looked suitable and ordered his lunch. As he sat there, he amused himself by thinking what would have happened to him if he had stayed around Birmingham. Life was so complex, many options are open to every person, but the only route you can ever experience, is the one you actually take. Avalon thought that it would be interesting to be able to play the routes you didn't take like a video game. Maybe not, there could be regrets from such knowledge. He stood and left the café feeling refreshed and passed by the entrance to the conference centre, but decided not to enter, then as he turned away, he heard a voice mention his name. There were many people around, so he wasn't sure who it was, and then he heard it louder.

'My god it is. Jimmy Avalon.' He looked around with surprise. It was some considerable time since anyone had called him Jimmy in a pleasant way. He saw a woman of around forty years old, wearing a black skirt with a dark wool jacket. She wasn't particularly pretty, but neither was she unpleasant to look at, a sort of unusual look to her features, and he knew he recognised her. He just didn't know from where. He tried to portray a neutral expression. He hated these moments when you ought to know someone, but don't. The way you have to circumnavigate the conversation to get hints of their name, or why you know them. 'I thought it was you, but you have changed so much,' she added. This gave him a clue, though there was no accent at all. She was from his distant past, he knew that but... Then, it suddenly came to him. When he had known her previously, she had short hair, now it was over her shoulders and blonde, rather than the mousey brown of those years ago.

'Liz Marriot, is that really you?' asked Avalon with a broad grin. He had a recollection that she had a nick-name when he knew her but that, and exactly where he knew her from was just beginning to be computed in his brain. She smiled back and held out her hand. She was so different, older of course, but slightly thinner and with a confident aura. It was coming back to him.

'It certainly is,' she replied with a genuinely pleased look in her eyes. 'But I'm...' there was a hint of a pause before she continued with, 'Elizabeth Cumberland now.' They didn't exactly shake hands, it was more of a connection being made again.

'A great name for an author,' smiled Avalon. It had all come back to him now. When Avalon was a beat copper in Norfolk, Lizzy, whose nickname had been 'fry-up' for a short time, he never found out why, was on his patch. They knew each other socially as well as professionally, and Lizzy would drink as much as the men in those days. There were about eight of them who would go around together, all PC's, all just starting out and eventually, Avalon had left to join the motorcycle training scheme. He hadn't known of Lizzy's future from there.

'And you,' she continued, 'you look so different from way back then. Two thousand and four, was it when you left Norfolk Constabulary? God, it's an age ago.'

'So obviously you're married,' continued Avalon still smiling, 'are you still with the firm?' He looked at the features in her face, the crow's feet lines around her eyes actually suited her. In her youth, she had looked somehow sullen, even though that was not her personality. Not many women improved with age, but Lizzy had.

'Yes,' she nodded, 'I'm guessing you are too, being here.'

'Yeah, I work for Police Scotland, Inverness.'

'Oh, right, *that* far away,' she said, raising her brows, 'I'm with Thames Valley, based in Oxford. CID of all things.' Once again, Avalon broke into a smile.

'Really? I'm CID too.'

'That is so weird,' she laughed, 'who would have thought? I'm surprised either of us stayed with the firm, never mind moved into CID.' She paused and looked deeper into his eyes. 'How far did you climb then?' He knew she was speaking about his rank.

'Detective Inspector,' he shrugged, 'I've been working on a contract for the SCD, it's just about over actually, so if you can put a good word in for me…' He didn't know why but he didn't mention the MIT.

'Not me, I'm a lowly DS, you wouldn't want to work in Oxford anyway, it's a bit of a hellhole for crime at the moment.'

'I thought Inspector Morse had cleaned up Dodge City?' smiled Avalon once more.

'Oxford is nothing like that load of crap they portray on the box, there are streets that are just not safe to be on. Just a few weeks ago, a girl was knifed in the neck in broad daylight.' Avalon dropped the smile as he nodded.

'Yeah, I heard about that up at our nick.' He paused for a second then added, 'I'm happy where I am, something will crop up.'

'Are *you* married?' she suddenly asked.

'You mean, other than to the job? I was, but it didn't last. I could blame the job, but that's not the whole story,' and he sighed, making it clear that he wasn't about to add anything to the statement.

'So, have you got anything on? We just *have* to go for a drink and catch up.'

'No, this is a free day for me,' he replied. He thought that with Carol up in Scotland, he had nothing planned for the evening, and it would be good catching up on old times. 'I'm not doing anything this evening if you are free.'

'Okay,' she smiled and pulled out her phone, 'give me your number and I'll text you later.' This done, they parted company, vowing to meet once both of them had done what they had to do.

They finally agreed by text to meet at her hotel. It had a good restaurant and a decent bar, so Avalon phoned for a taxi. Lizzy met him in the foyer and he was surprised to see she had made a real effort. She was wearing a figure-hugging dress in dark blue. It looked expensive and was cut just above the knee with a deep vee-neck showing off her none-too-shabby cleavage. She greeted him with a kiss, just a peck on the cheek, and he was taken aback by how good she smelled. Her perfume must have been expensive too, as it was subtle, but effective, and he thought he recognised it. They walked to the restaurant and sat, but as they looked at the menu, Lizzy was surprised to find Avalon was vegetarian and almost vegan. She explained that she had been a vegetarian before getting married, but it had lapsed. Avalon paid no attention to the subject and changed it quickly. He knew from his experience with Sarah that it was a political minefield. They then talked about the old team as they ate dinner.

'What happened to Kev Grundy?' asked Avalon as he cut into something called a 'spanakopita' that he had never tried before.

'I don't know where he went from Norfolk,' she replied, 'but I bumped into an old boyfriend a couple of years ago who knew him. It seems he's working somewhere in the Thames Valley, but I haven't come across him yet.'

'Wasn't he the one who set himself on fire?' grinned Avalon.

'Yes, I was told he was trying to…' she suddenly realised someone at one of the other tables may hear them and lowered her voice. She then leaned forward, 'He was trying to light his farts and something went wrong. I heard he jumped up,' she paused to stifle a laugh, 'and knocked something over. It was at that point they managed to set the curtains on fire.' She couldn't hold back and she laughed so much, she put her cutlery down and covered her mouth with a serviette.

'You weren't there then?' Avalon asked, also laughing.

'No, Nicky Pocock told me about it after. It was one of the few weekends I didn't go around the town with them.' Avalon shook his head as he remembered those times. They had been brief but fun, and he had almost forgotten about them.

'They are great memories,' he nodded as if still

back there in his mind.

'We were all good mates, everyone was just out for some laughs,' she agreed, 'it couldn't happen these days I suppose.'

'To be honest, it was touch-and-go back then,' insisted Avalon returning to his food. 'A bunch of beat coppers by day, and a pack of wild animals at night.'

'But it was all just honest fun,' she nodded, and Avalon saw the smile evaporate as if modern life was returning to her mind. 'We never bothered anyone, and we all got on well.' They paused and then the subject was changed yet again, as each of them gave an abridged version of their life since the Norfolk Constabulary. Avalon enjoyed his meal and when they had done, they went into the bar and sat in two easy chairs. Avalon noticed her legs for the first time. They were shapely and lightly tanned. He looked at the rest of her too and saw such a difference from the hard drinking party girl of fifteen years ago. As she relaxed with her legs crossed, holding her drink in her hand, he began to find her quite attractive. Her personality had a great deal to do with it, but she was also good to look at, if not a stunner. He thought she noticed him looking, though she didn't react to it. They then got onto the subject of the conference, but that subject was quickly exhausted. Eventually, Lizzy asked him if he thought marriage was a bad thing for a copper.

'Not as such,' he offered, 'and I see plenty who can balance work with a private life, but sadly, it isn't the majority.'

'I know,' she frowned. 'I think it has to be a special relationship for it to survive.'

'So how are you?' he asked tentatively.

'Oh, fine,' she smiled, 'this is my second time. The first was with another copper and that *was* a disaster.'

'So, Mrs Cumberland is a new thing?'

'Not new,' she replied, 'five years in March, the first one lasted fourteen months.' She smiled at him. 'I made sure it was right this time. His chat up line was, 'do you like Cumberland sausage,' so I wasn't immediately impressed. I asked him if he was a copper, he said no, he was a brewer, and I thought that sounded good to me.' Avalon could sense she was joking, yet he could also see there was truth in the basis of the story.

'And he's fine with *you* being a copper?'

'Well, as fine as he can be.' She gave him a grin. 'We live our own lives and he's away quite a bit with business, so we have our own space, I think it's that, the freedom that makes it work.' The grin became a coy kind of smile. Avalon was wondering if she was flirting. If she was, how did he feel about that? She suddenly changed the subject.

'Now I think back to our time in Norfolk, I don't remember any of the chaps having girlfriends.'

'Erm…' Avalon paused as he tried to remember, 'I think Johnno had a girl, you remember, Johnno Clarke? He was going out with that really good looking girl from Wroxham.'

'You seem to have no problem remembering her,' she smiled, and she took a drink but her eyes watched him over her glass.

'I also remember that *you* had a nickname,' he returned the smile, changing the subject. 'I also remember what it was, but not why.'

'Fry up?' she laughed, uncrossing her legs and

reeling forward. 'Yeah, I had that name all the time I was there.'

'So?' asked Avalon. She ceased laughing but still kept a cheeky grin as she re-crossed her legs and sat back once more. This time she left the glass on the table. Avalon wasn't sure, but the skirt seemed to have been moved slightly, and she was showing more of her legs. He did everything in his power not to look.

'It's nothing profound,' she began. 'I once went out drinking with two of the boys and a new woman PC, *she* didn't stay long as it happened. We went out into Norwich and I had too much to drink. When they were walking me back to my flat, I kept insisting I wanted a fry-up, over and over again. I want a fry-up, I want a fry-up. Eventually, someone, I'm not sure who it was, said we could probably get a pizza if I was hungry.' She looked deep into his eyes to try to gauge his reaction, but Avalon had spent too many hours in interview rooms to reveal his thoughts through his expression. She eventually continued. 'A fry-up not a Pizza, I insisted, but they took me to the pizza takeaway. Just as I reached the door, I began to say, Fry-Up, but it came out as fry-ugh, as I was sick.' She looked back to him and he was smiling. It was clear she was slightly embarrassed about admitting it to him. 'Not the pinnacle of my life, and to make things worse, I hate fry-up's and I had a very serious hangover the next day.'

'Well, that explains the name,' smiled Avalon.

'But…' she added, 'they began calling me *throw up*. Only after I threatened to get revenge, they agreed to change it to *Fry-up*.' Avalon nodded with a subtle laugh but, as if to make an effort to push her past aside, she added, 'It's difficult to imagine me like that now. I probably take life a little *too* seriously.' He felt her eyes looking through him. She still had a trace of a smile on her lips, but there was something else, or was he reading something that wasn't there? She looked to her watch, quite openly and with an obvious gesture.

'Yes, it's getting late, I suppose-,' he began, but she quickly interrupted him.

'Oh, no, I'm not clock watching,' she looked slightly alarmed. 'I think I do it automatically, it's the job I suppose.' He nodded a smile.

'But, you probably have to be up early?'

'No,' she replied, 'I have to be there after lunch, but nothing in the morning. How about you?'

'No, I was going to go to the late morning session, but I'm seriously thinking of skipping it,' he replied.

'Well, how about we get another drink and...' there was a hint of a pause before she added, 'well, we could go up to my room?' She then frowned, 'Oh that sounds wrong doesn't it? It's just that these shoes are new and they are pinching a little.' She reached down to the shoes with her left hand and kept the right hand on her knee. It gave Avalon an excuse to look at her legs. The shoes, dark blue high heels, did indeed look new, but there was an exaggeration to the way she let her hand run up her leg as she sat back in the chair.

'I'm not sure it's wise, even if it's just to take your shoes off,' and he raised his brows questioningly.

'It's perfectly innocent, is it the married woman scenario you're worried about?' she asked.

'Sort of,' he replied, but he was also thinking of his relationship with Sarah Underwood. Did they even have a relationship? Yes, it was true that a romantic

56

couple of evenings had been undertaken, there had certainly been kissing and on one occasion some heavy petting, but there always seemed to be something wrong. For Avalon, the best memory was almost a year ago, when he had returned to the Tavern pub to meet her. They had kissed totally and passionately, and Avalon had revelled in a moment he had often dreamed about. Kissing her, smelling her, and feeling her warmth. After that moment, everything had stalled. Every time they managed to get some quality time together, something interrupted them or something wasn't quite right.

'I understand,' she smiled, 'but we were friends so many years ago, we know each other enough. I think we can trust each other, don't you?'

'The correct term is 'knew',' smiled Avalon. 'Those days are so long ago, we have both changed enough over the years for us to be strangers, we're both very different to who we were.'

'Outwardly changed, yes,' she nodded, 'but do people change that much inside?'

'Some do,' he admitted.

'Well, the offer stands,' she smiled, and gathered up her small handbag.

'I didn't say I wouldn't,' added Avalon, widening his eyes a little. She stood and made her way to the bar, tugging down her skirt as she walked. He followed and stood at the bar with her. She ordered two glasses of wine and charged it to her bill. She passed one glass to him and held up her own.

'The way I see it, as we are both in the CID, we are almost related. Cheers.' She gently touched his glass with hers. She took a sip and then headed for the stairs.

At the door to her room, she handed Avalon her

glass as she reached in her bag for the key. She opened the door, stepped inside, and he followed as she closed the door behind them, placing the bag on an occasional table. He offered her the glass back, but she stepped inside his arm and reached up to kiss him, placing her hand behind his head to hold him to her. With both hands holding the wine, he was helpless, and he allowed himself to be forced against the door as her tongue explored his mouth. When she came up for air, she took her glass, sipped two or three times staring into his eyes, and then placed the glass on the table by the bed.

'I thought you wanted to take your shoes off?' he asked.

'I did,' and she kicked them off, 'but you're too tall for me to reach without them.' She gave him a conspiratorial grin and reclined on the bed. 'We're both the same height on this,' and she patted it fondly. Avalon questioned the moment for a few seconds as he sipped his wine. Back in Inverness, he was in some sort of 'friendship' with a woman he considered was one of the best looking in Scotland. Here was a pleasant, fairly attractive, but in some ways an ordinary-looking woman, who was married, but responsive to him in a way that brought out all the primeval instincts in him. It wasn't just because she wanted him that Avalon was so aroused. There was some sort of chemistry going on, that had never happened with this woman when he had first known her. Back then, to his knowledge, she had never had a boyfriend, and none of the friends he went around with had ever shown any sign of wanting her in that way. He walked to the bed and placed his glass on the table with hers. He sat, and she immediately began to remove his jacket and open his shirt. She then thrust him to the bed and hoisted her skirt to straddle him. She kissed him as if she had waited her whole life to be with him, and yet a few hours ago, she had forgotten he had existed. This outpouring of passion hadn't come from something nostalgic, not even from repressed feelings from the past. It was passion and lust from the chemistry of the moment. Twelve months ago, Avalon would have made his excuses and remained downstairs, he still had the excuse, she was married, *he*, had a girlfriend. Over the past year he had changed. He knew he had to, and the person he was now, differed greatly from the self-analytical man he had been previously. He rolled her over onto her back and he felt her give way to his command. He forced open the neck of the dress to reveal her bra, but for a second he felt a tensioning. Maybe it was that expensive dress? He half rolled her and undid the fasteners. She helped him pull it up and over her head to reveal a remarkable body, a body that looked younger, and taught. He gently kissed her all along it, right to the end of her toes and back up, ending at her breasts and removing the cups of the bra to allow access to her nipples. She whimpered like an animal caught in the gaze of a predator. It excited him, it drove him on. He removed the bra and then slowly slid down her panties, looking eagerly at what was revealed. He knew he had to take things easy, moments like this had come very few times in his life, and at the back of his mind was the thought that it could be over far too quickly. He moved on top of her, and her whimpering took on another pitch and she writhed, closing her eyes and clutching the pillows with her varnished nails. Avalon felt a tingling down his spine and in an effort to hold on to the moment, thought of unpleasant memories. It didn't work, and it felt perverse, so he abandoned that tack and let things take their own course. He looked down at her and almost laughed. There was no reason for it, it was just a collection of emotions flooding out together, emotions that had become intermingled and corrupted by each other, to the point that a laugh was the overriding total. He suppressed it behind a grunt, as the wind left his thrusting body, and a sound came from the pocket of his jacket, now crumpled on the floor. He knew it was his phone, but even if it was the Secretary of State for Scotland himself, he was not getting in touch with Avalon tonight.

Chapter Three

Christmas came and went, but luckily nothing big came in for C Section, though there was still a great deal of work due to being short-handed once again. Even their old DI came to visit them one afternoon, to bring a few gifts for his old friends. It had been odd for him to walk back into the Cave, particularly with DS Wilson sitting in the seat within the booth. He had entered to see Ross, Rutherford and Mackinnon chatting around a desk by the windows, and DS Wilson in discussion with Frazer within the booth. They all smiled with genuine pleasure as he entered, all except Ross who had known he was arriving. Avalon dropped off his small parcels by the worn out, fake Christmas tree, brought out of the store cupboard for the few days it was needed, and then sat with the main group.

'So are you coming back to plague us?' began Rory, but he paused. He was so used to calling Avalon 'Boss', it had put him off his thread. He eventually ended the question with, 'DI?'

'No, nothing doing,' smiled Avalon, 'I've had enough of you lot for a lifetime.'

'So what are you doing?' asked Rutherford, 'your

61

contract is over now isn't it?'

'Yes,' nodded Avalon, 'and at this moment, I've no idea.'

'You know what he's like,' cut in Ross with a playful frown, 'he won't tell us anything, blood out of a stone comes to mind.' Frazer and Wilson joined them.

'Hello Boss,' smiled Frazer.

'I'm not your boss, that's Gordon's job.'

'Not for long,' smiled Wilson, looking genuinely relieved.

'Do you know something?' asked Rutherford.

'Not much,' replied Wilson, raising his brows, 'but the DCI says the Super has finally agreed that we need a DI.'

'And extra hands?' asked Rutherford.

'He hasn't gone that far, but ef we get a DI, I can get on with my own job,' shrugged Wilson.

'So we're going to continue even more understaffed than usual,' complained Ross. Avalon looked around the desks. He could see two of them currently used as dumping grounds for various boxes and office equipment.

'So is this full complement?' he asked. He had spoken to Ross on many occasions, but Ross being Ross hadn't really commented on the situation in the office except for a casual 'Aye, it's fine, usual shite,' and so Avalon knew little about the inner workings of the section.

'More or less,' nodded Wilson, 'there's A.I. but I gave him most of Christmas off, nobody wants tae work with him anyway.' Avalon knew A.I. was the current name for DC White, through what little Ross had told him.

'I can't believe he's still here,' added Ross.

'DI Brown saw something in him, I don't know what, but that's why he's still here,' explained Frazer. It then occurred to Avalon that DC Boyd had left some months ago. He didn't hear it from Ross, but from PC Olivia Kirk, who he had spoken to some time ago about it.

'So you didn't get a replacement for Alison?' he asked.

'No,' shrugged Wilson, 'Croker said he'd asked for another officer, but that's as far as et went.' He looked at Avalon for a moment. 'There was a time when we all thought they were running the section down for a reason.' Avalon kept a neutral expression at this. With so few personnel, it would make sense for DI Lasiter in B Section to take over C Section and integrate it as one. It was probably Lasiter who had stopped it however, even if it had been suggested.

'Well,' sighed Avalon at length, 'I can tell you that isn't the plan at the moment.'

'Go on,' insisted Rutherford.

'One of the posts DCI Croker offered me was my old job back.'

'And you said no?' asked Frazer with surprise. At this point, Wilson helped Avalon out.

'Croker has promised that we will have a new DI by the middle of January, the end at the latest,' he insisted.

'Do we know who?' asked Mackinnon.

'Nope,' replied Wilson, shaking his head. Frazer was still stinging from the fact that Avalon had refused his old job back.

'So why don't you want to come back to us?' she

asked. She sounded as if she had just been told her husband of twenty years had left her for a younger woman. Avalon looked across to her. She had changed her look again. The makeup had gone and her hair was without any style, making her seem harsh. She looked much older too. He had seen her now and then around the station over the past year, and he had noticed the gradual change. Only now, when he was closer to her did he see that she looked more like she did when he first met her.

'Many reasons,' sighed Avalon, 'but the main one is that things have changed, for me and for C Section.' He went no further than that, and Frazer continued to wonder if the real reason for him going, and not wanting to return, was the problem associated with the incident between her and Ross. She knew that Avalon had tried to protect her. She also knew he had gone against policy to keep her in position. Did he now think that she was a liability? In her mind, she saw it as her fault entirely. She wanted to explain that she had changed, that she was different, and she had a different approach to the work. What she didn't know was that Avalon could have said the same thing. He liked these people. He didn't want to become their boss once more, for they would get quite a shock. The only person that had an idea about the truth of this was Ross. He and Avalon had spoken briefly about it, and though Ross didn't think it would be a problem, he understood Avalon's thinking.

'I heard that Alison left to start a family?' asked Avalon to change the subject. He knew the whole story from Kirk, *they* didn't know that, however.

'Aye, but it wasn't a planned thing,' smiled Rutherford.

'She didn't know she was pregnant,' nodded Rory, 'I think it was more a shock to her than to us.'

'She was terrified she was too old,' added Wilson, 'but these days et isnae that important. I took her tae see the missus and they had a talk about et.'

'Is she coming back after?' asked Avalon.

'PC Kirk knows her a bit, added Rutherford, 'she says she's not. It seems odd to me to get this far with a career then throw it up in the air.'

'That's 'cos you're not a family man,' smiled Wilson. Avalon noticed Ross had not just been quiet, but had totally ignored the conversation.

'So what have you been offered?' asked Ross, seeing Avalon's eyes on him.

'Not much,' shrugged Avalon. It was the truth, Croker had a few holes he had to fill, but he couldn't make posts up for Avalon to try. 'He more or less told me that I can have a DS position in any of the sections.'

'Ouch,' groaned Rutherford, 'that's a kick in the pay grade.'

'That doesn't worry me as much as how it would look on my record. I don't mind being a DS, but what commanding officer is going to believe it was a voluntary move?' That wasn't the whole story, and most of the experienced members of the team knew it, but they also knew it would be sticking point if Avalon was to try to climb higher in the future. There were many reasons Avalon, or anyone else for that matter, wouldn't make such a move. They, and he, knew his options were limited.

'So are you waiting for Lasiter to keep to his promise and retire?' asked Ross, raising his brows.

'Lasiter will never retire. They'll have to push

him out of here in a bath chair,' grinned Avalon. Everyone except Ross saw that even with the threat of nowhere to go, Avalon was upbeat. This made them suspect he *did* have plans, and he knew exactly where he was going. Only Ross knew that Avalon was reaching a dead end. They had spoken about it briefly on the phone and Avalon had changed the subject then, as he was about to do now.

'Well, I have to move on and let you lot do some work for a change.' He stood and after wishing them a good New Year, he left.

It was soon January, and he found himself still in more or less the same position. He knew that Croker was losing patience with him after he lost his composure for a second and told him how he felt.

'You either want to come back to the CID or you don't,' Croker had insisted. In Avalon's mind, that meant, 'last chance'. The thing that no one seemed to understand, Avalon wasn't bothered either way, he truly didn't care. The last year had given him plenty of time to think, and twelve months ago, he didn't suspect he would still be in the police force, never mind the CID. Giving him ultimatums or threats was like water from a duck's back. He knew that there were so few detectives in the force, just as everyone else did. He could walk into a job anywhere, particularly now he had MIT training. Yes, it would mean moving and yes, it could mean a drop in pay, but he would have a job. Those thoughts were not comfortable for him though. He wanted to stay in Inverness, he wanted to be a detective, but he didn't want to make his life a misery once more.

In the middle of January, two things made him

re-assess his situation. One was a command from the Detective Superintendent to go and see him. Avalon had been kicking his heals in the drugs section for a couple of weeks, helping out in the office and working on follow-up calls, and Avalon wondered if the Super was going to ask him to stay in drugs. The second was a news report about a mysterious virus in China, a virus that the World Health Authority was highly concerned about. This was something close to Avalon's heart. He and Ross had discussed something like this when they were at a loose end one evening in the Castle Tavern. There had been a few people knocking about a theory or two on how the human race might go extinct. Being a pub discussion, some outlandish theories had been submitted, such as global tidal waves, alien invasion and even beings from another dimension. Meteorite strike had been popular, as was something catastrophic happening to the sun, but both Ross and Avalon, plus two others, had suggested a global virus. Not only that, the two of them had agreed on China as being the start of the plague. He decided to keep his ear to the ground on the reports as he readied himself to meet the wrath of the Super.

As it happened, the Superintendent had summoned him for something totally unexpected. He had been asked to sit on an internal investigation down in Dundee. It was to be for three or four days only, and as the Super had said in a derogatory tone,

'I picked you out DI Avalon as you seem to be the only one who doesn't have a place at this moment.' Avalon took that as a direct criticism and tucked it away. So it was, four days after the Foreign Office advised against travel to China and the same day British Airways ceased flights there, Avalon was once again leaving Inverness as he took the train to Dundee.

The internal investigation at Dundee was a protracted affair and almost as soon as he arrived, he knew it would take longer than 'three or four days'. He wasn't part of the investigative team, he was part of an independent, three-man team sifting through the information and reports to ready a case against two Police Officers accused of taking bribes. Avalon, and most of the other officers hated this kind of investigation, but it had to be done and was always undertaken by outside police forces, or independent officers. He kept a close watch on the virus which the papers and news channels were calling 'Corona Virus', as by the end of the month, two cases were reported in the UK.

Though Avalon went back to Inverness for a week, to his dismay, he had to return to Dundee as the investigation wasn't going well. By the tenth of February, there were eight cases of the virus in the UK and the news channels were flooded by the subject. It wasn't long before the first British death was reported, and, by early March, the British Government held an emergency COBRA meeting. Avalon had returned to Inverness by then as the Dundee investigation had stalled. It was unlikely he would be returning, and he was again summoned to see the Super. This meeting was much different to the first. It was quick and to the point and Avalon left the office feeling that the virus was about to change the way the police worked. He also sent a text to Ross.

'Do you recall the virus discussion in the pub?'

he wrote. There was no answer

'Well, I don't see how we can continue tae do our jobs under these restrictions,' insisted Wilson.

'Neither do I Detective Sergeant, but this has come from the top,' explained DCI Croker. 'I'm not happy about it and to a degree I think it's a knee jerk reaction because they don't know what to do.' Wilson shrugged and went back to the Cave to tell them the news.

'This virus epidemic…' he began, but he paused, not sure what he was supposed to say. The pause was so long that Rutherford told Wilson to continue, and though the DS looked up from the floor to him, he still looked vague. 'We're supposed tae take some measures t' allow us tae work with this social distancing bullshit.'

'How are we going to do that?' asked Mackinnon.

'Christ knows,' sighed Wilson, 'I think essentially, et's going tae mean we shelve everything.'

'We can't do that,' scowled Ross, 'they said there was a leaflet coming out, what happened to that?'

'You know, and I know that the leaflet won't even be big enough tae wipe ye'r arse with,' growled Wilson, 'ef we have tae keep two metres from each other and the public, we don't have a job anymore.'

'Well, we don't take notice of it then,' shrugged Rutherford, 'do it when we can but judge it by the situation.' Ross nodded to this but Wilson was adamant.

'We're the bloody polis, we're the once who's gonna end up enforcing this in the end.' He pushed his hand across the top of his red hair. 'I just don't know how the senior officers expect us tae work this,' he added. A few of C Section were already thinking that for the first time since they had known him, Wilson seemed stuck. He almost seemed in a panic. For now, they let it go, but certainly Ross and Rutherford, who glanced to each other, wondered if Wilson was going to be up to a crisis like the one that seemed to be gathering.

Just one week later, all public gathering had ceased, the public were panic buying and there were over fifty deaths from the virus reported. Then two days after, DCI Croker went home feeling unwell, it was announced that he had contracted the virus. It sent a small wave of panic around the station and further measures were introduced to protect themselves. A one-way system had been implemented at the station, so people didn't have to pass in narrow corridors. Rooms with two doors had an in and out, and the restroom was closed. In the Cave, the desks had been rearranged to make as much space as they could manage, though two metres were impossible for everyone, even with the understaffing.

With the Chief out of action, and lacking a dedicated Detective Inspector, more responsibility fell on the senior DI, John Lasiter. Lasiter, not being a man to suffer fools gladly, could be difficult to work with, particularly when he was under pressure and that was certainly the case at that moment. The Detective Superintendent also came under pressure to secure a replacement DCI, and he had spoken to Lasiter about him being 'made-up' to acting DCI. Lasiter had resisted this as Detective Inspector Cook from D Section or even DI Mescari from the Drug Section had as much experience as he did. Lasiter even suggested that the uniform section Chief Inspector could take over the duties. As it happened, there was a Senior Investigating Officer at Aberdeen that could be seconded for a few weeks to cover the DCI's post. The Superintendent announced this to Lasiter, who passed on the news to the relevant section heads.

By the middle of March, the new DCI was in place and C Section, was still struggling with balancing their job, and keeping two metres apart. It was difficult, and sometimes impossible, but when they could, they stuck with the recommendations. It was going to get tougher still. DS Wilson had met with the new chief and found that Acting Detective Chief Inspector Lindsey Duncan, was even more severe than Croker.

'So, what's she like?' asked Rutherford as Wilson returned after a briefing. Wilson stopped and thought for a moment. He looked at the floor and then up to Rutherford.

'I suppose she's a cross between DI Lasiter on a bad day, Croker on a good day, and a ghost.' This caused a few puzzled looks from the rest of C Section.

'What's the ghost part in there for?' asked Frazer, still confused by the analogy.

'You'll see when you meet her,' frowned Wilson.

'I was more concerned about the Lasiter part,' frowned Ross. Wilson nodded and was about to enter his booth, but he stopped and looked back into the room.

'Oh, I forgot to tell you. The new DI will be joining us in a few days.'

'Anyone we know?' asked Rutherford.

'I have no idea, the *Chief*,' Wilson put emphasis on the word, 'doesn't know anything yet. She got a memo from the Super. She wasn't going to mention it, I had to ask,' he frowned and then sat at his chair. Ross sighed and said to no one in particular,

'I'm betting it's DI Mescari.'

'That's no' a bad thing, Mescari is a good guy to work for,' offered Frazer.

'Aye, there are worse I admit,' nodded Ross, 'but I'm not sure someone who has worked in the drugs section for eight years is going to fit in C Section that well.'

'A good detective is a good detective,' insisted Rutherford.

'We'll see,' shrugged Ross and looked back down to the computer screen as he searched for news concerning the virus.

A few days later, on a pleasant Monday morning, Ross arrived a little late to the office as usual and walked over to his desk. He pulled down a blind on the window, as the sun was streaming in through the smoked glass and onto the monitor screen. As he began to remove his jacket, Rutherford said,

'Don't get comfortable, were off to a meeting.'

'What meeting? I was under the impression we had stopped meetings?' replied Ross, pushing his arm back into his jacket sleeve.

'New DI,' shrugged Rutherford, 'he wants us in the conference room.' Ross raised his brows. He had only been in there twice in his life. Once when he started with the department, for a talk and a film on detective policy, and once to watch a demonstration on the use of the latest scenes of crime kits. It was one of those medium-sized rooms, fantastic for small presentations, but useless for anything else. The banked seating was in a curve that surrounded a small stage with a screen behind it. It was rumoured that the sound system alone cost the tax payer eighty thousand pounds. Ross didn't think even the best cinema would pay that much on a sound system. As the team gradually made their way into the room with its wood-cladded walls and blue PVC seating, its own particular smell invaded their noses. It was the smell of lack of use, as if the room had just been built. Each of them sat with at least two spaces between them and tried to get comfortable on the badly designed seats. It was easy to see why the new DI had chosen the venue. Everyone could see the stage, the natural sound quality was good, and though it didn't have a large seating capacity, the depleted staff of C Section could make as much space as they wanted between each person. Wilson was the last to enter and he was carrying a pile of leaflets. He took them to the small table at the stage and then found a seat.

'You might have closed the door behind you Gordon,' frowned Rutherford. The door was to the side of the auditorium and beyond it was a large window facing the sun. The rays were throttled at the aperture to fan out in a blinding beam of light. Ross, being the nearest, stood and fought his way through the bombardment of photons to close the door and bring normality to the room.

'He's like Jesus Christ,' offered Ross, nodding over to Wilson.

'Ready to be crucified you mean?' laughed Rutherford.

'No, born in a sodding barn,' frowned Ross.

'It was a manger,' insisted Frazer, always ready to correct Ross.

'So what the hell *is* a manger smartarse?'

growled Ross.

'A rack of sorts that holds cattle food, you simpleton,' replied Frazer with a calm voice.

'So the Son of God was born in a hay-net?' mused Ross, leaning back in the immoveable seat.

'Not quite,' laughed Rory as he saw the image of an infant with its arms and legs poking through the holes of the net. Ross sighed again and decided to stir the room a little before the DI arrived.

'I'm surprised DC White didn't point that out sooner, or did you want to explain that there is no evidence that Jesus Christ ever existed?' White, who was sitting near the front, turned slightly to gaze at Ross, but without any reaction, turned to face his front once more. With White not reacting, Ross became impatient and looked at his watch.

'Whoever he is, he's late.'

'We weren't given a time Rossy,' insisted Wilson, 'so button et. The email from the DCI just said, first thing.'

'This *is* first thing, so he's late,' insisted Ross.

'How the hell would you know first thing?' laughed Frazer, 'I think it was Jubilee year, the last time *you* arrived first thing.' Ross was about to berate Frazer, just as the door opened, and the golden rays burst into the room as if a volcano had erupted. For a split second in time, with the dark figure in the centre of the light, it looked like a scene from a science fiction movie. The scene where the door of the UFO opens, and the alien walks from the searing light inside. The figure was tall and slim, and as eyes adjusted to the vision, a man with short hair in a very well-fitted suit could be seen. The door was closed, and the light went out, revealing a

74

character face with a glimmer of a frown and a look of purpose in his features. He quickly took in the room, scanned the gathered faces and strode to the area of the stage. When there, he glanced once more at the faces and picked up one of the leaflets Wilson had brought in earlier, placing it on the lectern at the front of the stage. His face remained impassive, as if there was nothing, and no one who could make any impact on this man, and nothing could prevent him from doing what he had to do. At least one of C Section saw something in the features that almost made them swallow hard. The suit he was wearing did not look like the usual suit of a detective. It wasn't from Matalan, and it wasn't off the peg. It looked handmade and was of a greyish green fabric, cut in a modern, yet classical style.

'I know you were expecting someone else,' announced Avalon, 'but this is what you get.' He looked again at their faces as if daring them to speak. They didn't, not a murmur. 'I have a lot to get through so I will start straight away as I know you are all busy.' He paused, still silence. 'Firstly, I do not intend to change the systems DS Wilson has implemented, the only changes will be in our approach to the virus. I will stress, however, I take this very seriously, and once virus countermeasures are implemented, I will come down heavily on anyone not sticking to protocol.' He paused again, this time for breath. 'I also intend to reassess the layout in the office,' more than one of the team noticed he did not use the name 'Cave' in his sentence. 'If we cannot set the desks to provide minimum distances, then we will be split into two teams and find another office. I know how you feel about this, but we have no option.' He looked at a few of the faces before continuing. 'As

75

you probably know, the public lockdown, as it is being called, begins today and a tougher stance over social distancing is being implemented. I hope that the CID will not be brought in to this area of policing as from what I can gather from our legal teams, this is not written in law and so can only be enforced by local council by-laws. It's a legal minefield and I hope it doesn't affect us. More government money has been promised, and I hope that virus testing can be expanded for the police force. If not, I will make steps to ensure this section gets testing equipment, even if I have to acquire it myself.' This time he paused and looked at a few of their faces, but continued quickly. 'I have been informed that DCI Croker has been confirmed as having the Covid virus and I'm sure we all hope he makes a full recovery, however, I have already made some inquiries to how he may have contracted it, and if it may have been spread here. From what I can gather, the likely source is from within his own family, as his sister-in-law has been on holiday in Italy recently. I will, however, ensure that everyone here gets tested so as to put your minds at rest.' He picked up one of the leaflets and held it up. 'These information leaflets have a great deal about the virus and cover everything we know about it. I want all of you to take several and make sure you read them. If you have any suspicion at all that you have any of the symptoms, I want no heroics, just let me know, straight away.' He paused, and this time there was a sigh. 'These are odd times. At some stage, this will be part of history, and in the future someone will read about it and wonder what life was like. We have to live through this first, and we have to continue to do our jobs. People who break the law, criminals, will take no notice of this lockdown.

They will more likely see it as an opportunity, and we are here to stop them taking advantage of the situation.' He looked at his watch. 'So, if there are any questions about this or any other subject fire away.' He expected Ross to be first with some kind of quip but it wasn't him.

'I know you said some weeks ago you wouldn't take the job,' said Rory, 'but what changed your mind?' Avalon nodded and then replied.

'The Superintendent,' he replied emphatically. 'Don't get the opinion I *wanted* to come back, DS Wilson was doing well enough. I was told that there was no option.' He looked around the room. 'Or rather, the only option was to get my arse out of Dodge.' This was the first glimmer of humour, yet there was no smile. Rory nodded and then added,

'Welcome back Boss.' There were no 'here, here' comments, no spontaneous applause, nothing.

'Thanks,' nodded Avalon, 'but you may not be saying that in a few weeks. This is going to hurt. It won't be easy and I'm not even sure if things will be the same when it's over.'

'If this is what I think it is,' chipped in Ross at last, 'nothing's ever going to be the same.' Avalon looked at Ross. Maybe this was alluding to the text that Avalon had sent him some time earlier, about the pub conversation they once had.

'I agree,' nodded Avalon, 'any other questions? No? Okay, as we are all here, we may as well conduct other business here too.' Avalon pulled up a seat from the rear of the stage and sat, crossing his legs and pulling his notepad from his jacket. 'Firstly, are there any big cases being worked at the moment?'

'Nothing big,' replied Wilson, 'but we have a few

court appearances from the smuggling case at the end of last year.'

'I think it likely that some of those could be put back due to the restrictions,' suggested Avalon.

'Yeah, et's likely,' agreed Wilson, 'just a bucketful of less serious stuff then. Housebreaking, shop breaking, and two assaults. There es also an old case which DCI Croker wanted looking at, but I suppose that could be shelved.'

'What was it?' asked the DI.

'A missing person from four years ago, et seems someone found a shoe in a disused boat that could have belonged to the missing person.'

'Do you think it could be from that person?' asked Avalon.

'On the surface, yeah. Et fits the description of the clothes she was wearing,' nodded Wilson.

'Is the boat near, or in water?' asked Avalon.

'The boat was half sunken in some thick reeds near Loch End,' explained Wilson.

'We better get the area around the boat dredged, or at least get a diver or two in there,' suggested Avalon. 'Anything else?'

'Nothing that can't wait,' replied Wilson. Avalon nodded but seemed in thought. He looked back to Wilson and then said,

'Okay, we're not getting any more staff, but under the circumstances, it wouldn't help us all that much. Have any of you been regularly teamed up?' Wilson answered this too.

'Ross and Rutherford have been working together and Mackinnon and Frazer, I have kept DC White at base with me.' Wilson wasn't using first names.

He too must have felt the negative energy from Avalon.

'Then that's how it will remain,' nodded the DI. Wilson's shoulders perceptibly sagged and Avalon noticed it. 'So let's return to the office and see how we can space the desks a little better.' This they did, and after rearranging the furniture once more, a good six feet could be measured between each person, though DC White's desk was close up to the glass petition of the booth. Avalon had noticed that there was a new cupboard on the whole of the far wall of the booth.

'Who put this in?' asked Avalon.

'DI Brown. He said he wanted tae keep current files in there, but I dunna think he ever used et.' replied Wilson.

'Did he remove the coffee machine?' Wilson nodded again. Given the contact restrictions, Avalon thought it best to forgo a new machine.

Wilson had already moved his things from the booth and was taking up his place at the rear of the room once more. Avalon lifted up the box he had brought into the room and opened it. It contained a hand-sanitiser which he placed on the shelf which had previously supported the coffee machine. There were already a few hand-sanitisers around the building, but now C Section had their own. He then sat in his old seat, which wasn't his old seat as such, but a new modern one, and then considered his second move. He was supposed to go and see the new DCI as soon as he had settled in. He decided to speak to the only person he knew who had met her. He walked to the rear of the room and leaned on the wall.

'What's the Chief like?' he asked. His expression wasn't as harsh this time, and Wilson saw he wanted the nitty gritty, not the official stance.

'Temporary Acting Chief,' corrected Wilson, raising his brows. 'DCI Lindsey Duncan, seconded from Aberdeen where she has had several roles including the DCI of their drugs section. From what I found out from records, she's forty-eight and divorced with two grown-up children. Born en Macduff in Banffshire, now lives en Inverugie near Aberdeen.'

'I can find that out myself,' frowned Avalon, 'if I know you at all, you found a contact at Aberdeen and asked a few questions.' He said this in earshot of everyone else, and so Wilson relaxed a little and considered that Avalon may have been just making an impression.

'Well, I suppose I found a few things, but I had a wee bit of a meeting with her too,' shrugged Wilson. 'She has a reputation of a problem solver for her commanders,' he began, 'and a problem causer for those below her. Takes on difficult cases happily and cracks the whip more often than et's needed. She earned the nick-name of 'Ice Maiden' over there, and I can see why after meeting her.' Avalon jutted his bottom lip out a little and nodded.

'And how did she seem?' he asked.

'Like her legend,' frowned Wilson. 'She was matter-o'-fact, without character or any human qualities that could be regarded as a 'positive trait', but...' he paused, 'that's just my opinion.'

'Okay, I have to speak with her so I thought it may be wise to find out what I could,' shrugged Avalon, as he stood upright.

'Don't expect et tae be a long visit,' added Wilson.

Chapter Four

Avalon could hear a voice as he reached Croker's office. He waited and listened. It sounded like DCI Duncan was on the phone as there was no other voice but hers. He knocked lightly and carefully opened the door. She looked to him and motioned to the seat opposite her desk with her biro, as she listened to the phone. Avalon carefully closed the door and sat.

'Yes, well, that isn't any concern of mine, I just want him to know that I have asked and would like him to react to it,' she said in answer to someone on the other end of the phone. Her accent wasn't as pronounced as he had expected. The Aberdeen area had its own dialect and even its own words. She had very little accent, as if her education had been away from where she grew up. As she listened to the voice on the phone, she stared at the side wall and occasionally jotted something down on a pad. It gave Avalon time to assess the woman the Aberdeen nick called, the Ice Maiden. She was pale, very pale and wore no make-up, or very little at least. Her hair was lifeless and brown, though most of it was streaked with grey. It was clear that she was just forty-eight from her record, but she looked older. She dressed plainly and had a way about her that was probably designed over the years to allow her to compete with the men in her profession at an equal level. Away from the office, she was probably different. Either way, by all accounts, she wasn't well liked by her subordinates back in Aberdeen.

'Yes, if you would, he has my number,' she insisted to the phone, 'thanks, bye,' and she placed the phone back on the receiver. It wasn't the usual phone that Croker had, that was probably in the cardboard box on the floor with all the other items of Croker's. The desk was now clear of everything except for the computer screen, an office phone, a mobile phone and the jotter she once more quickly wrote upon. 'Sorry about that,' she said and looked up to him, 'you must be DI Avalon,' and to his surprise, she softened her gaze and reached over to shake his hand.

'With all due respect Ma'am,' said Avalon with a blank expression, 'given the circumstances, I think that it's best we forgo the handshake.' She paused and thought it through as she resumed her position.

'Yes, quite,' she answered, but Avalon was thinking that it wasn't the best of starts. She seemed to look through him for a moment and then folded back a few pages of the jotter to find something she had obviously written previously. 'You have been working away, I believe, with the SDC?'

'Yes,' nodded Avalon, and he was about to explain more about his training period too, but she continued.

'I also understand from the Superintendent that you are returning to a post you had previously abandoned?' Though outwardly she seemed personable, the way she constructed her sentences and the words she chose proved to Avalon she was a firebrand. It was clear, the use of the word 'abandoned' meant she was on the offensive.

'On a temporary basis only,' informed Avalon.

'So you intend to abandon it again in the future?' There was that word again, and Avalon was tired of her already.

'You will have to speak to the Detective Superintendent about that,' replied Avalon, keeping to strict protocol on the subject, 'as I am not aware exactly how much he has divulged.' She frowned at this and held his gaze for some moments. It looked like it was war, and not a single weapon had even been drawn. She looked down at the jotter and read something before saying,

'Then I'll leave you to it Detective Avalon,' and she gave him a look that meant he was free to go. He stood and left, but in the corridor he smiled to himself and shook his head steadily.

'I told you,' smiled Wilson as Avalon entered the Cave. The DI raised his brows a little, as he headed to the booth with the remnants of the smile still playing on his face. As he was about to enter the booth, he called to Wilson.

'Gordon, you got a minute?' Wilson met him in the booth and sat in the spare seat. There was less room in there with the new cupboard, and so it was difficult to make the two seats much more than five feet apart. 'Is there anything I need to know about the section?' asked Avalon quietly. White was still in the Cave writing up a report or something similar.

'Nothing much,' shrugged Wilson, 'most things

are as they were before. Morale es a bit low due tae various things like workload and lack of staff, but...' he trailed off as Avalon noticed his eyes flit to one side.

'DC White?'

'Aye,' nodded Wilson, 'he's a wee bit of an issue, I admit.'

'Not much I can do about him,' frowned Avalon, looking across to the man. 'I'm surprised he's still here.'

'DI Brown considered his analytical brain an asset, so he's clung on by his fingertips.'

'I mean, I thought he would have got fed up of the gybes,' explained Avalon.

'He's a thick-skinned bastard, that's the problem,' added Wilson. Avalon nodded and sat back in the chair.

'So nothing I need to know?' repeated Avalon.

'No, nothing changes around here, you know that well enough.' Wilson stared at Avalon for a moment, and the DI could see there was something on his mind.

'Ask away,' he said, raising his brows.

'So why *did* you come back?' Avalon nodded and then smiled.

'I was telling the truth,' he said, 'I was told in no uncertain terms that I had to take on C Section. It's only temporary though, until this crisis with the virus is over, or they find another DI.'

'Or until you retire?' smiled Wilson.

'We'll see how it goes,' replied Avalon, returning the smile. He wanted to ask how Ross and Frazer had been. He wondered if anything had gone off between them. Was that the reason Frazer has returned to her previous look? But at the back of his mind, he knew it wasn't that important. If there had been another incident between the two, Wilson would have probably reported them. He liked a joke and a bit of fun, but people had to do their job, and do it well. 'I'm guessing DC White isn't going to be very happy to see me?' grinned Avalon.

'Tae be honest, I don't think he gives a shite about anything,' explained Wilson. 'I have fed him all the mundane tasks, but he just carries on and minds his own business.' Avalon nodded.

'Okay,' he said, 'I know no one else will have thanked you, but you did a good job of looking after the section.' Wilson gave a knowing nod.

'Aye, nothing to et,' and he winked at the DI as he stood. As Wilson returned to his seat, Avalon glanced at White once more who seemed oblivious to his surroundings and then sighed, stretching his legs under the table. So, this was it. Just over a year ago he left that booth, and now here he was, back in the driving seat as if nothing had happened. He switched on the computer screen and checked any news about the virus. It was depressing reading. There had already been over 100 deaths in the UK and it had only just begun, Avalon switched off the screen and tried to think of something more positive.

It took Avalon much longer than he had expected to settle into the running of C Section. It was the following Monday during the morning briefing that he felt reasonably comfortable with his position. There were many reasons for this, the main one being the year he had been away from the routine of an office that runs a certain way from day to day. The mundane routine of the daily systems took some getting used to, and only on major cases was the daily tedium altered. He had now abandoned his good suit too, and returned to the cheap, off-the-peg jacket and trousers that he normally wore. It felt more comfortable, and he didn't have to worry if it got ruined.

He didn't know what he was going to say at the meeting, but he had a few things he needed to resolve. There had been a few items on the news which he wanted to bring up, but his main priority was the safety of the team. There had been promises of regular testing for the covid virus, but he knew promises from Governments were on paper and not real. With that in mind, he had spent some time working out a few systems to keep his team, and the general public safe. Luckily, most of his team lived alone, DS Wilson was married however, and he understood that Rory Mackinnon was living with a girlfriend, so those two had more to lose. He had also heard rumours that Ross was seeing someone, so he would need to find out more information. He stood near his booth to begin the meeting with everyone else seated at their desks.

'It's going to be a quick meeting this morning,' he began, 'I just want to cover a few details concerning the virus.' He paused to look down to a piece of paper he had quickly jotted notes on. 'As you probably have heard by now, both Prince Charles and the Prime Minister have been confirmed to have the covid virus, and while this probably has no great interest to you, it may be an argument to the general public to flaunt the lockdown. It's likely they will use the fact that there is one law for those with power, and another for the common man. I bring this up as it could cause some disturbances to our uniform brethren. It is also the case that the sad news of a nurse dying from the virus has reached us and with around a massive, ten thousand people in hospital, more could succumb.' He paused to look around their faces as he pushed the notes into his pocket. 'Safety of the team is paramount. I have taken the decision to keep those who live with partners in the office unless we are pushed. Those living alone will be the front-line troops, and I include myself in that. My plan is that DS Wilson will coordinate all outside teams from here with the help of DC Mackinnon. DS Ross and DC Rutherford will make up the other team and will attend any incidents in separate cars. The second team will be myself, and DC Frazer. DC White will be back-up for both teams.' Avalon glanced over to White, who seemed impassive at this information. 'As to ongoing cases, I see nothing that will cause us any problems at the moment. I know B Section is busy helping the Major Incident Team with an old case, and they have some breaking and entering cases at commercial properties too. Other than that, people seem to be taking the lockdown seriously, and the usual petty crime has all but ceased. Drug related crime and alcohol abuse is likely to increase however.' He looked up as he took in a deep breath. 'Any questions?'

'Do we all have to take separate cars from now on?' asked Ross.

'Yes, where possible. Pool cars will be made available for this,' nodded Avalon.

'How is this going to affect Scenes of Crime and forensics?' asked Rory.

'They will have their own policy, but I expect it will not impact too greatly on anyone. Vehicles are being made available for Scenes of Crime teams and if any major incidents come in, we will react to them as normal, we just have to adjust our methods slightly.'

'Wouldn't it be easier for those of us working together to use the same car?' asked Ross. 'I mean, we're working here together, we'll be out on a case together, what's the difference?'

'The difference is distance,' insisted Avalon. 'You have to maintain two metres where possible. The more contact you have with people, the more testing we will need.' He paused, 'unless you want to live together for the foreseeable future of course,' he added. Ross looked at Rutherford, who winked at him.

'No thanks, I'll take option one,' nodded Ross. It was at that moment that Avalon recalled hearing from someone, he didn't quite remember who, that Ross was seeing someone. Had he moved in with her? He didn't know, and he made a mental note to try to find out. If it *was* the case, he may have to treat Ross as married, and keep him back from the front lines. It wasn't going to be an easy question to get around to asking however, as it was likely to spark a similar reaction from Ross. He would probably want to know if Avalon and Sarah Underwood were serious. That almost made him smile. It wasn't much of a relationship when he thought about it, but maybe that was best. They had seen each other over Christmas. They had been out for meals and a drink on two occasions, but on both, they had gone their separate ways after a brief kiss. On one occasion, Sarah had actually stayed over at Avalon's house. Instead of going out, Avalon had provided the venue and the food and Sarah supplied the wine. It had been a pleasant evening and after, they had watched a DVD, snuggled into the large sofa, and both enjoyed the closeness of each other. It hadn't been what could be described as passionate. They had cuddled, they had kissed a little, but Sarah had fallen asleep and after, they had slept separately. On that occasion, it had been Avalon's decision. Sarah had said they could both go to Avalon's room, but it was clear she was exhausted and Avalon didn't want any sort of compromise. Neither did he want to put Sarah under any pressure. In the end, that night of cuddling besides the fire, watching a DVD that Avalon could not now remember, was probably all either of them needed from the relationship. Neither of them had anyone to share their joys, their sorrows, or their excitement with. They had no one to tell their worries to, no one to turn to when doubts troubled them. Maybe that was all their relationship would ever be, until one of them became bored with it.

Back in the Cave, the questions were over and Avalon had a few words with Ross and Rutherford about the Bookmaker case. They had released Andrew Connor without charge, as it was obvious nothing could be proven, and Serle was still at large after a month on the run. Serle's girlfriend had been brought in for questioning but released too. Surveillance had been put on her, but everyone knew it was probably pointless. With the lockdown, it was unlikely she would move about anyway, and the act of surveillance had become problematic with no one on the streets.

Avalon cast a glance towards White once more as he stepped back into the booth. His face couldn't be seen from the booth, even though he was close. Fortunately, he was obscured behind his computer screen and Avalon had moved his own screen for a little more privacy. He had decided that he would make no concessions with White. He would place him in the firing line and if he didn't perform, he would move him on. The new Chief didn't seem like the sort of person to suffer a slacker and so he would leave the problem with her. For now though, he would give White another chance.

Four days later, the month of April was already upon them and the year was passing quickly for Avalon, if not for the rest of the country forced into lockdown. Deaths in the UK from the virus had quickly risen to just over four thousand, and were still rising. To add to multiple theories and stories about the pandemic, there were many worries from the Police Force in general, that they were not getting the support from the Government. They were not alone. Even the people who had to deal directly with the virus, the health workers, were getting neither the help nor the equipment to protect themselves. It was worrying, and every time anyone had to go out, there was an extra pressure placed on the officers. There was a pressure out on the streets too. The Government had promised that eighty percent of their wages would be paid to most people who stayed at home, but there were many that the system wasn't helping. Self-employed, those between jobs and those with low income businesses. Many people were going to lose their jobs, their businesses, and their loved ones. That meant angry people. That meant crime. Avalon was also aware that if something went wrong in the communities, the police would be prompted to use heavy-handed tactics. He hoped that those in charge would use common sense, but it wasn't a great time to be back in charge of a section. He found himself constantly watching his staff, trying to assess their moods and needs. The job was going to be tough, and each day he tried to second-guess what the next few days would bring so that nothing took him by surprise. One thing that did take him by surprise was an envelope that arrived that afternoon.

'Avalon,' he said into the desk phone in response to it ringing.

'*Hello Detective, et's PC Kirk downstairs,*' responded the female voice. '*There's a letter, well something,*' she added with doubt, '*an' et's addressed to you, shall I bring et up?*'

'No, thanks,' he hesitated, 'given the restrictions, I'll come down for it,' he replied, and he had set off to pick up the missive from the front desk where each section has its own box. He had called through the corridor to thank PC Kirk and then retreated back to the office. On the way, he had realised it felt like a card, a birthday card or similar. The address was typed however, onto a sticky label but the postmark was Inverness. As he now sat with the unopened card on his desk, the detective inside him was still working away at the mystery of it. Did everyone examine their mail so intently? Probably not. The cream envelope looked like the sort that would be supplied with the card, and so he pulled his penknife from the drawer and slit the top of the envelope. He pulled out the card which said on its front, 'Good luck in your new job.' He frowned, not only was it a little late, he didn't think it could be classed as a new job. Neither could he imagine who the hell had sent it. He opened it to find out and saw the inscription,

'*I hope this isn't too late, I just thought about it. Love Sarah.*' The frown left his face and became a smile. He didn't know why, but the message really cheered him up. As far as he could remember, no one had sent him anything like that before. But then again, a lovely carving still stood in pride of place in his living room that was a gift from people at the nick when he moved into his new home. He then had the problem of where to put the card. Should it go on show? Should it stay in the office or should he take it home? For the time being, it sat on the desk at the side of his screen. He looked up. Most of the team were in the office, and only Ross and Rutherford were out, tying up a few things on a minor case they were working on. Wilson was still typing up all the reports he hadn't had time to do previously, and Frazer was helping Rory Mackinnon with a couple of unrelated burglary cases. White was... What was White doing? Avalon looked at his notes Wilson had given him. The list said White should be working on two missing person cases and several reports from three weeks ago that Croker had asked for. Rather than antagonise White, he decided to pick his way carefully through the room to ask Gordon for clarification on those reports. Wilson agreed that they weren't all that important, and so on his way back, the DI glanced down at White's screen. He was indeed busy, but it was clear, he had something else on his mind. Avalon returned to his desk just as the door to The Cave opened. It was the new DCI. She didn't enter the room, she just asked,

'DI Avalon, have you got a minute?' Avalon was glad he had just read the notes from Wilson. It was a reminder of what they were working on, and it was likely that the DCI wanted that information. The door to her office was open, but he moved just inside the doorway so as not to be too close.

'Sit down DI,' she said, seeing him there.

'If you don't mind Ma'am, I'd rather not break the two metre rule.'

'Do you think it will make a difference in this

job?' she asked, keeping her eyes on her screen.

'I'm not in a position to comment, I'm just trying to lessen the risk to myself and the team,' he replied, in the friendliest tone he could muster. She made no further comment but looked up to him.

'I see the bookmaker case has stalled.'

'Yes,' nodded Avalon, 'Serle is still in hiding and the girlfriend has been uncooperative.'

'I have just been going through the case again and as I read the report on the arrest of Andrew Connor,' she announced, 'I wondered about the handling of the arrest. I suppose you had your doubts too?' He remained silent. 'Do you think it was handled correctly?'

'I do,' he nodded, 'I think they had to act as soon as the man looked suspicious. If they had sat by and let it happen, they would have been criticised for doing nothing. As it was, the man attacked one of the officers without provocation.' He paused, but she showed no sign of adding anything. 'Both the officer and Mr Connor were injured in the altercation, so they had no option but to arrest him and bring him in.'

'But he wasn't charged with anything?'

'No,' replied Avalon, 'it was seen as, not in the public interest to take the issue to court.'

'Because this man wanted to press charges?'

'I don't think that was a deciding factor, but you would have to contact the Sherriff's court,' he replied as pleasantly as he could under the circumstances.

'And the person who they were looking for managed to slip by without anyone seeing him?' she asked, knowing the answer.

'That has been assumed,' he replied, 'but we don't know that for sure. He has had ample opportunity to do that since.' She gave a single nod and looked back at the screen, then asked,

'So you consider their actions to be correct under the circumstances?'

'I see nothing to suggest they were in error,' he replied calmly. She nodded again but kept her eyes on the screen, she was obviously reading something. 'Is there something I need to know?' he then asked, still keeping his voice calm.

'I just wanted your opinion on the report,' she replied, this time glancing up at him, 'and I wanted to let you know that there will not be extra staff allotted to your section,' she added. She looked at him this time as if expecting some kind of reaction. He kept his gaze the same. 'Given the circumstances...' she paused, 'with the virus.' He still didn't bite. Instead, he raised his eyebrows and gave the slightest nod.

'You could have sent me an email to say that,' he thought, but instead he said,

'We couldn't fit anymore in the office, given that we are keeping minimum distance,' this time he paused, 'as was the advice we were given.' She didn't give him any indications of what she was thinking, but Avalon sensed an aggression in her, probably not intended. It could easily just be the way she was. Aberdeen called her the 'Ice Maiden'. Maybe that was what everyone felt that met her.

'I think it's a good decision DI, let me know if you need anything,' she eventually said, Avalon turned and left without any comment. He thought a simple nod would suffice. He couldn't ever remember Croker coming to the office to summon him, if she was to call at the room every time she wanted to speak to him, it was going to become annoying, particularly if the reasons were to be as banal as this little talk. Back in the office, Wilson was on the phone in the booth. Avalon stopped some distance away and listened.

'So, can you find out, it doesnae make any sense until we know a bit more?' he said into the phone. 'Aye, I know that fine, but we need to know more before we can react to et.' Wilson paused as he felt Avalon's presence. He raised his brows as he looked over, 'Aye, do that,' he suddenly continued, 'and tell him to contact us on this number direct.' He put down the phone. 'Sorry about that, et was ringing,'

'No need to apologise, problems?' asked Avalon, aware that everyone still seemed a little 'jumpy' about his return.

'I don't know yet,' replied the DS with a shake of his head looking down at the phone, 'there are reports of a body been found in a quarry but at the moment, all we know es that bones have been found.' Avalon nodded at this. 'I dinnae want to mobilise people until we know ef et's not just some chicken bones.'

'Do we know where?' asked Avalon, 'I mean which area?'

'Not yet, but-' the phone rang and Wilson moved to answer it but hesitated.

'You deal with it Gordon,' insisted Avalon nodding to the phone, 'I'll go and warn the others, just in case,' he paused then said, as Wilson lifted the phone, 'and find out if it's in our area or not.' As Wilson answered the phone, the DI went to tell the others to wrap up what they were doing just in case. He looked back to the booth and Wilson nodded to him. Avalon nodded back and looked down to Frazer.

'See how many cars are free, I can take mine but we need enough transport for four of us,' he paused and then added, 'and make sure there is a Scene of Crime team on alert.' He walked back to the booth where Wilson was still on the phone.

'And has he confirmed that the area hasn't been dug recently?' he asked. There was a long pause and then he asked, 'Then can you get something tae put around the area, something tae stop anyone going through there?' he paused again. 'Okay, that will be fine, we'll get someone there straight away,' and he replaced the phone.

'What have we got?' asked Avalon, still not ready to throw resources in yet.

'The guy at the site says they were clearing an area that hadnae been used for an age, when the driver of the machine went for a pee. He got out of his cab and saw some bones, he thought they looked human.'

'How could he tell?' asked Avalon.

'Well, you know yourself, everyone is an expert with all these crime serials on TV.' Avalon blinked. 'But he had a look around anyway, and he saw some discoloured sand and had a poke around with a stick.'

'Great, probably a compromised site,' frowned Avalon.

'I'm not so sure,' replied Wilson, 'that's another feature of the TV serials, he said his driver knew to be careful as not to make a mess, ef et was a body. Then he says he found a skull in the sand.'

'Well,' exclaimed Avalon, 'that is something that is identifiable by most people.'

'That's what I thought, and the foreman took a look at it too,' nodded the DS, 'he's convinced it's human.'

'Okay,' nodded Avalon, 'stay put here and sort out the SOCO team, I'll get over there, where is it?'

'Near Balnafoich, do you know et?' Avalon shook his head but Frazer said she knew the area.

'Megan, you and Rory get down there, I'll follow in my car, DC White,' he looked down to White. 'Get in touch with Forensics, just to let them know. Contact the uniform section. Tell them to get anyone they have close to get down there if they haven't already, and we could do with a few extras if they have anyone spare.' For a second he stared at the man to see if he was taking it in. He simply didn't know. 'Then follow on yourself.' Avalon looked back at Wilson.

'If Ross and Rutherford come back, keep them here just in case.' Wilson nodded and then Avalon went to find a scene of crime kit as his car didn't have one, then he left.

'Where is everyone?' asked Rutherford as he entered The Cave. DS Wilson was alone, manning the phone in Avalon's office.

'You're going to have to sanitise that booth before the DI comes back,' insisted Ross. Wilson ignored Ross and spoke to Rutherford.

'We had a shout, a possible body in a quarry. Well, remains at any rate.'

'Where?' asked the big man.

'Near Balnafoich.'

'That's not our area is it?' asked Ross.

'Not really,' shrugged Wilson, now looking at Ross, 'but we're not all that busy and the other sections have their own problems.'

'I'm surprised the Wicked Witch of the West is allowing us to work on a major case,' smiled Ross, 'having a new DI too.' Wilson narrowed his eyes.

'If you're tryin' tae get her a new nick-name, you're too late, B Section have beaten you to et. And secondly, I'm sure the DCI knows all about the Boss.' It was the first time anyone had used that name for Avalon since his return.

'So what's the name?' asked Ross.

'I don't recall,' sighed Wilson, 'and I don't much care, I just know DI Lasiter has had a few run-ins with her already, so B Section are not flavour of the month with her.'

'She must be a stoater if DI Lasiter is having problems,' smiled Rutherford.

'So what do we do?' asked Ross, parking his backside on the edge of one of the desks.

'Nothing yet, the DI wants you to stay here ef you can, just en case.' It was then that the door opened and after a quick look around, the DCI came in.

'Do we know anything yet?' she asked, looking directly at Wilson.

'No Ma'am,' he replied, 'but I'll keep you posted as soon as I hear.' She nodded, gave a cursory glance at the other two then turned and left.

'I can't help wondering,' began Ross still looking at the closed door and folding his arms, 'why she didn't just ring, or email?'

'Hmm,' sighed Wilson, 'I think before this es over, we're all gonna be hoping DCI Croker recovers quickly.'

'Well,' smiled Ross looking at Rutherford, 'I never thought I would say this but yes, the sooner The

Toad comes back to his Lilly pad, the better.'

'Do we know how he's doing?' asked Rutherford.

'Well, he's still alive ef that's what you're thinking,' frowned Wilson.

'It did occur to me,' nodded Rutherford, leaning on the frame of the booth. 'This virus seems pretty deadly and Croker is knocking on a bit.' Ross unfolded his arms and made his way to his desk adding,

'I think it'll take more than a Chinese virus to kill off our Toad.'

'For one, et isn't a Chinese virus,' called back Wilson, 'and two, et seems you don't have tae be old or ill tae succumb to et.'

'Course it's Chinese, they're all Chinese,' insisted Ross sitting down and switching on his screen. 'That's what comes of eating mice, rats and bats. They probably eat their own children,' and he paused as if thinking for a second, 'or is that Perth?' Wilson shook his head and looked at Rutherford, who was frowning deeply.

'Is he ill-informed, or es he just stupid?' asked the DS.

'Just a knob,' shrugged Rutherford, and he went to his own desk.

Chapter Five

Avalon was following Frazer, who was in a pool car as he wasn't quite sure where the quarry was. Unlike some of the other officers, Frazer was a steady driver, and being in a car she wasn't used to, seemed to slow her down even more. His own car was an older Volvo estate, which was supposed to be a stop-gap after his own car was wrecked in a chase, but as was usual with Avalon, he still had the vehicle. It didn't have a police radio, so he couldn't even tell her to get a move on. If it had been PC Kirk driving the car, he would have struggled to keep up. They were on the A9 going south and so he decided to overtake and try to find the place himself from his satnav. There was no other police equipment on the vehicle either, so 'lights and horns' were out of the question.

Avalon eventually pulled his car onto the quarry site, which seemed to cover a large area, and he was stopped by a uniformed officer to ask who he was. The officer then told him where to go and he took a winding track until he saw several vehicles. There was a white van, several contractor's vehicles, two excavators and two marked police cars. He also saw Rory Mackinnon there talking to one of the contractors. He parked up and went over to Rory. As the DC saw him, he said to the man,

'Oh, this is Detective Inspector Avalon. He'll be in charge of the investigation.' Avalon nodded at the man and gave a brief smile. 'This is Mr Dean. He's the foreman of the site.' He then looked around and saw the uniform officers had taped off several areas by connecting warning tape with rope pins and traffic cones.

'Are you the man who found the bones?' he asked.

'No,' replied Dean shaking his head, 'that was Davey, Davey Rose. He's the lad standing by the truck drinking tea.' The man pointed to a short man in his thirties who looked unconcerned by the affair.

'So, you're not on lockdown at the quarry then?' asked the DI.

'Oh, yeah we are. It would normally be busier than this. There's just me and two drivers left,' explained the man. 'The site manager wanted the get the new road levelled.'

'New road?' asked Avalon.

'We're expanding. The back end of the site is finished and the area over there,' he pointed to some open fields and several copses of bushes, 'is going to be opened up for working.' He looked back to Avalon. 'We have to drive an access road through and the manager wanted to level the road before the birds nested in the trees and shrubs.'

'Very admirable,' thought Avalon, but he doubted that was the real reason. Either way, they now had a body unearthed.

'Will you ask the driver to come and see me please?' and he turned to Rory. 'What have we got?' Rory pointed between some bushes and led Avalon up a slight rise as he spoke.

'It's like we were told. The driver, Mr Rose, was levelling this area to allow a gravel road to be laid. He got out of the cab to urinate, and he saw the bones. I tried to stay away as much as I could, but the bones look scattered. I think the machine may have cut through the site. I can't quite see the skull though from here,' and he stopped by the yellow tape.

'Did you speak to the driver?'

'Yeah,' nodded Rory, 'he's easy to talk to, he's worried he messed up the site for us.' Avalon nodded, looked over the area and said,

'Wait here for Mr Rose, I'm going to take a quick look, just to make sure,' and he gave Rory a weak smile. In the sand, he saw streaks of different colours, remains of shrubs and grass with a few rocks here and there. It looked like this area had been sitting dormant for years. He saw a few bones but nothing he could identify, then away to his left he saw footprints and a stick lying by what looked like the side of a skull. Closer inspection showed clearly it was indeed a skull, probably an adult, but it looked old, as if it had been there for some time. He looked around and indeed, the place it was found in, looked as if it was some considerable years since anything had been done there. Thirty or so feet away sat an old oil drum. It was partially covered with sand, and it was almost rotted away. He backtracked the way he had come and went to speak with the man who had arrived, along with the foreman.

'Tell me what happened,' insisted Avalon.

102

'Not much to tell,' replied the man with a shrug. 'The foreman told me to start clearing the site, ready for levelling for the new access road. The manager is a bit of a birdwatcher and didn't like the idea of coming back after lockdown to find all the greenery full of nests.' He pointed to his machine and then the area he spoke of. It was now surrounded by tape, including the machine. Avalon considered that the quarry manager might be a little optimistic about how long the lockdown was for. 'I'd moved some loose rocks from over there and then started on this bit. I was going to dig into this sandy area and flatten it. I got out to take a piss, and that's when I saw a bone. As I looked around, I saw others.' He then pointed to an area where Avalon had seen the skull. 'When I saw that dark bit of sand, I had a look for some other bones and thought I saw a skull sticking out of the sand, so I got a stick and cleared some dirt from round it. I thought I had better take care just in case.' He spoke that part more quietly and looked at Avalon. 'I could see it was a skull, and I thought it looked human.' Avalon nodded. 'Did I do right? Is it human?'

'Yes, you did right, Mr Rose,' nodded Avalon again, 'but don't broadcast this just yet until we know what we have here. As far as we know it could be an ancient burial.'

'I doubt that,' frowned the man, 'it wasn't very deep.'

'I doubt it too,' agreed the DI, 'but nevertheless, until we know more details, I wish to keep it quiet.' The man nodded and Avalon looked over to the foreman. 'How long is it, since this area was used?' he then asked. The foreman pursed his lips, shrugged, and then scratched his head.

'I'm not sure exactly,' he finally announced, 'there were some large rocks somewhere here a few years ago, but it's been more or less wasteland for ages.'

'So no work has been done here?'

'Not to my knowledge,' he shook his head then added, 'it looks like sand was stored here at some stage but I can't remember that.'

'How long have you worked here?' asked Avalon.

'About ten years on and off,' said the man doubtfully, 'but I sometimes work at the company's other sites.'

'Do you have records of what work is done, and where on the site?' asked Avalon as he saw Frazer and White walking towards him.

'Not really, not with any detail,' replied the foreman, shaking his head. He thanked the man and asked him to stay close by and was about to speak with Frazer, but the foreman stammered, 'Er… can we bring the machine out of there now?' He pointed to the yellow vehicle with a large bucket on the front.

'Not until it has been examined by the forensics team, we need to go over it thoroughly and the area it has been working,' insisted Avalon. The man frowned as Avalon turned to Frazer. 'We had better get the pathologist out, I know we'll probably find little from the remains, but we still need him here.' She nodded and pulled out her phone. Avalon then turned to White. 'That man over there is the driver of the machine, ask him exactly what happened and write it down. I've questioned him already, but I want a detailed version.' White nodded and went to talk with the man. Soon after, the Scenes of Crime team arrived and had a quick look at the site.

'It looks like the digger skimmed the top of the grave, so it's likely some remains will be scattered,' Avalon explained. The SOCO officer nodded and went to change and speak to his team. He then explained to Avalon they would first check the whole area and then try to find the point where the body was. Avalon knew from experience they would cover the spot with a tent to allow forensic work to be completed more easily. They would probably place lights in there too. As he stood watching the site springing to life with the various comings and goings, he began to think that the body had been there for some time, possibly even years.

'Pathologist will be here as soon as he can,' explained Frazer closing in on him, 'and Rory says the Forensics team has arrived.' Avalon wondered if it would be Sarah, but it was soon clear she wasn't there, and Hendry had come instead. Hendry was an experienced and knowledgeable technician who was always as helpful as he could be, but the DI couldn't quite work out if he was disappointed it wasn't Sarah Underwood. Hendry soon came up to Avalon and had a smile on his face. He automatically held out his hand and then thought better of it, retracting it and standing a little way from the DI. Hendry wouldn't be able to access the site until the Scenes of Crime team had examined and identified all points of interest. He could already see small markers being placed in the newly turned sand, tiny numbered tags placed everywhere something could be seen or identified. Hendry, however, was ready to start as soon as he could and was wearing his white coverall.

'Glad to see you back on the job, DI Avalon,' and he pulled on his mask.

'Nice to *be* back,' Avalon nodded and noted that Hendry and his team were probably the best equipped to repel any virus, as they constantly worked with masks and protective clothing. He also considered that his colleague, Sarah Underwood, was one of just five people that knew he was returning to his post. She must have told him too, as Hendry certainly wasn't surprised to see him there.

'So,' continued Hendry looking at the site, 'what exactly do we have?'

'A set of remains, certainly looks human, but it has been disturbed by the digger. I'm not sure how far they are scattered, but the skull is there.' He pointed. 'The priority is to find out how long they have been there. I'm convinced they aren't ancient, looking at the ground, so the pathologist is en route.' Hendry nodded as the rest of his team gathered close by with equipment. There were just two of them. A younger woman he had seen before, and another male he couldn't identify under the mask.

'Once a path has been cleared, we'll try to find the main source of the remains. I'll get soil and sand samples too.' Avalon thought Hendry was saying this for the benefit of his team, but then he turned directly to Avalon. 'It… could take some time,' he hesitated and looking around, 'but we'll do our best to finish before dark.' Avalon nodded and then moved back towards the car beyond the bushes. The rest of his team had been busy interviewing the staff at the quarry and getting statements. Even White seemed to have done what was asked of him. Avalon looked at the exposed site and saw one of the first problems the virus brought them. An incident vehicle was practically useless if people were to stay any distance from each other, and this meant everyone sat in their own vehicle if the weather turned inclement. That in turn meant no discussion, no ideas being bounced around, and so little interaction concerning the case. It was going to be next to impossible to keep to the social distancing routine. He returned to his car and removed his jacket, then replaced it with a warmer, quilted coat. The weather had been pleasant enough, but it was an open site and it would probably become even cooler as the afternoon grew long. He then sat in the car and thought his way through the process of what was looking like the beginning of a major case. He knew he would have to phone the new DCI soon to let her know what he had found, and he wasn't looking forward to that. In some ways, this investigation could be what C Section needed to bring them together under Avalon once more. He knew there was something uncomfortable in the air, and the chance for them to work on something big could steady everyone's nerves. Unlike fiction, a single detective doesn't solve a crime, a team of detectives are involved and sometimes hundreds of them are brought in for major cases. This can only be done if the team works well together and they are headed by a strong and competent officer. A single detective rarely becomes famous. The likes of Jack Slipper and Tommy Butler found their way into the newspapers because of the nature of the crime they investigated, not for any other reason. They worked on the Great Train Robbery, which was unique at the time. It caught the imagination of the public, and the names of the detectives appeared in the news a great deal. Generally, the only time you see the name of a detective in the news is if they get something wrong, or if the crime is different or unique. Other than that, a few lines may appear as a statement, and then it may not be a detective that actually worked the case. Most detectives preferred it that way. It is in their interest to stay anonymous, and certainly Avalon wasn't keen on seeing his name in print. It was more important that a good team came together on a case, rather than an individual, and that was what Avalon had to do. He had to once again, hone them, lead them, and form them into a well-oiled machine, capable of cracking cases as quickly and efficiently as possible. The trouble was, he was different now, and they were different. He knew that it couldn't be like it was, but the job had to be done and either way, it would get done. He saw a man approach and so he wound down his window.

'Are you Inspector Avalon?' Avalon nodded and got out of the car. 'I'm the site manager. I was told what had happened.' He was a small man, thin with a constant expression of doom. Avalon was going to question him about why they were still working at the site but, he thought better of it.

'Do you mind making a statement to one of my officers?' he asked instead.

'Not at all,' he shook his head, pushing his hands deep into his coat pockets.

'I'm particularly interested in the area where the remains were found,' asked Avalon.

'So there is no doubt, it is a body?'

'No doubt,' nodded Avalon solemnly.

'Well, I can't tell you much,' shrugged the man, 'we are expanding the site and we have to run a road for the haulage vehicles. That is the obvious way through.'

'And what was it used for previously?'

'Nothing really,' shrugged the man again, 'it's just one of those places, it has no particular use. I think it held topsoil for a few years, and I recall when we dug the north pit, the vehicles were parked there at night. Nothing specific.'

'Has there always been easy access to it,' asked the DI, 'I mean, in the respect of the asphalt road that runs close by?'

'Yes,' came the answer, 'I suppose so, even before it was improved, there was a gravelled road through here.' He paused for a moment. 'I've worked for the company since two thousand and three, and there has been a service road there since that time.' Avalon gave a nod.

'I may have to ask more questions later, but I would like you to tell one of my officers this too so we can get a record of that area.'

'Yes, of course,' the man agreed and then followed Avalon towards Rory Mackinnon. Even taking statements in the open was difficult, but they had to protect themselves and the public from the potential of the viral threat. He hoped they could improve on writing notes over the bonnet of a police car, with interviewer and interviewee each side of it however.

Avalon walked back to the secured site and saw that the SOCO tent had been erected, and Hendry could be seen just inside it. Around the site, there were several white suited people, some on all fours examining the sand. One was taking photographs of both the finds and the vehicle that had unearthed them. To his right, the foreman was looking apprehensive, and the driver was watching the proceedings with interest. When the site manager had given his statement, he asked Avalon if the foreman and the driver could continue with their work. The DI informed him that work on the new access road would have to stop, the vehicle was not to be moved and they should observe strict social distancing. Other than that, yes, they could continue. Of course, they had to remain available for further questioning.

Avalon hadn't worked with the pathologist before, and he seemed young for the post. Doctor Ewan Forbes looked no more than in his mid-thirties and had film-star looks. His hair was dark and lush, and he sported a neat beard and moustache. This appearance was only marred by the fact that he was a short man, but nevertheless, well-built and muscular. He also looked older at close quarters. That aside, Avalon considered that this police pathologist was probably popular with the fairer sex. The man nodded to Avalon as they met and smiled warmly. He then made a quick appraisal of the site and then moved over to the taped off area. He looked back and asked,

'Was I correct in thinking the remains may have been here for some time?'

'Yes,' nodded Avalon, joining him at the tape, 'some bones have been scattered by the excavator but the forensics team think the area within their tent is the main point of the grave.'

'There's probably little I can tell you then,' added the man. His accent sounded English despite his Scottish name, yet there was a remnant of an accent Avalon couldn't place.

'I understand that, but as we have to try to identify the person, I thought that you may be able to at least tell us the age and sex of the remains.'

110

'Of course,' nodded the doctor, 'we'll try our best,' and he looked around the site before asking, 'is it alright to go in there?' Avalon nodded and led him to the tent where Henry and his team were busy trying to excavate the rest of the bones from where they had originally been buried. Hendry looked up for a second but ignored the new visitor.

'Hmm,' exclaimed the doctor, 'I suppose I could take a look at the skull,' and he went back outside. He bent down by the skull, and using a pencil, tilted the skull to one side. 'I'm guessing female,' he eventually said, 'I'll know more when I see the rest of the skeleton and I would say…' he paused tilting his head to one side and then withdrawing the pencil, 'between thirty and forty-five years of age at death.' Avalon knew a good anthropological pathologist or forensic scientist could determine age and sex from a skull, but this man was confident enough after simply casting his eyes over it.

'Based on the wear of the teeth?' asked Avalon, genuinely interested.

'Mostly,' nodded the man standing, 'but I can tell more when we find the lower jaw and the rest of the bones.' He was still holding the pencil, and he pointed towards the skull with it. 'The lack of a brow and rounded crown suggest a female, but the lower jaw will throw more light on the sex,' he glanced towards Avalon, 'and of course the pelvic area.' Avalon was already warming to the man. He was freely including the DI in on his thoughts. This information would allow the team to begin looking for missing persons that could possibly fit the details of the bones.

'I don't suppose you can tell how long the remains have been there?'

'Correct,' smiled the man, 'I'll leave that to the forensics teams, but from what I have seen, I would guess years rather than months.' Avalon thanked him and went to find Frazer.

'Call Gordon and ask him to look for a missing person, female, around thirty to forty-five years of age,' he explained, 'probably been missing for at least a year and in a surrounding area of about thirty miles of Inverness.' Frazer nodded and walked a few steps away to make the call. He then looked at Mackinnon and White and said,

'You two better get back to the office, Gordon is going to need help finding the ID of this person.' The two of them walked to their vehicles and Avalon returned to the taped off site where two new PC's arrived to take off the two that had been the first on the scene. One of them just happened to be PC Dowd. The man nodded to Avalon, with a simple,

'Afternoon, Detective Inspector.'

'Hello PC Dowd,' he gave a slight smile to the officer, who then asked,

'Anything particular we need to know?'

'Not really,' shrugged Avalon, 'with a bit of luck we should be away before dark,' and he walked back to Frazer.

'Got any thoughts?' he asked her.

'Well,' she began, 'I'm guessing et's foul play.' Avalon raised his brows. 'Shallow grave in a remote area,' she explained, 'et doesn't look like an accident does et?'

'I accept that. No, it doesn't.'

'Other than that,' she continued, 'I wouldn't like to say. The skull looks intact, the only damage I've seen

112

to any of the bones seems to have been caused by that digger.' She nodded towards the yellow machine on the rise. 'My only question would be at the moment es, why here? Doesn't a quarry seem like an odd place to dump a body, particularly as quarries are dug up a great deal?'

'Maybe,' nodded Avalon, 'but if what the foreman says is correct, this place may have been just a bit of waste ground previously.' Frazer considered this, but then she shrugged and with a sigh said,

'Well, ef that's true, these bones could have been here some time.' And that was what Avalon had been thinking. It had also run through his mind, that the body could have been put here by someone who had previously worked at the quarry and knew the area. It wasn't an unreasonable hypothesis, but he would have to wait for some results. Any post-mortem would be little more than an examination of the bones to see if the cause of death could be ascertained. Other than that, they would be dependent on what forensics could find.

As the light faded and the sky began to grow less defined to the east, Avalon looked up from his position in his car seat to see Hendry walking towards him with his mask removed. He was removing the bright purple forensic gloves and was walking with a purpose. Avalon pushed his door open and stood.

'I'm pretty sure we have all the bones from the grave,' said Hendry, as he closed in, 'and the team is packing them ready for the pathologist.'

'Do you think you have it all?'

'I can't confirm every bone is there, but it looks like a complete skeleton. It was partially folded in a sitting position, it's likely whoever put it there couldn't be bothered digging the hole large enough to take the whole body.'

'Not an ancient burial then,' nodded Avalon with a hint of a smile, 'I'm guessing we have photographs?' he asked.

'Yes,' nodded Hendry, 'at every stage. We've also taken soil samples at each stage of the recovery and we have collected most of the debris close to the skeleton so we can sift it for study at the lab.' Avalon nodded and closed his car door.

'What about the excavator?'

'We've taken samples from the blade and from the material in the bucket,' Hendry explained as the two of them walked steadily to the site, 'and I suspect, the damage seen on a few of the bones will have come from that source.' As they reached the taped area, he turned to Avalon and said,

'Oh, and I hope you don't mind, I told DS Frazer that she could send for the pathologists van to collect the remains.'

'Not at all, where is she by the way?' asked the DI as he looked around the site.

'She has gone to find one of the PC's to let them know what is happening.' Avalon nodded and crossed the tape to peer into the tent. There was a two to three feet deep crater inside with a black box at the edge of it, which probably contained the bones. He left the tent and looked around once more as Frazer walked towards him. She could see him thinking through something.

'Problems Boss?' she asked. For a second, he didn't react and then, as if coming out of a dream, he looked up and stammered,

'No, no, I'm fine,' but his face showed that wasn't the case. Frazer looked at the sand below their

114

feet and thought she knew what he was thinking.

'But...' she paused, as if unsure if she should say anything, 'you're wondering ef there are other bodies under here?' He looked at her with a glare that made her wince inwardly, but then he asked in a level tone,

'Is that what you are thinking?' She paused a moment and then nodded. Avalon sighed and looked back at the sand and then across to the tent where Hendry was speaking with his team. He then glanced back to her and asked,

'What did you tell the uniformed officers?'

'I said the forensics team had finished, but I didn't know what your plans were. Dowd told me that their shift is over in thirty minutes.' Avalon crossed his arms and thought for a moment.

'Right,' he suddenly said, dropping his arms, 'tell Dowd that I want the site securing overnight, then ring Gordon to see if he can arrange to get one of those mini-diggers out here in the morning, as early as possible. I'll have a word with Hendry.' He found Hendry by his vehicle, packing his equipment and clothing into the rear of the van he had arrived in.

'I'm ordering an excavation of the surrounding area in the morning,' he said. Hendry nodded and replied,

'Not a bad idea, I think it's some time since that area has been disturbed. We had to brush around some of the material it was so compacted.'

'Yeah,' nodded Avalon, 'I'm hoping there's nothing there but you never know.' Avalon hesitated. He wondered what Hendry knew about his relationship with Miss Underwood. 'I thought Sarah might have been involved on this one?'

115

'She's working on a bit of a difficult case in Fife,' he replied, 'it's her speciality so she was the first consideration.' Avalon nodded knowingly, but inside he recoiled. She had a speciality, and he didn't even know what it was. Of course she did. Most forensic scientists had some sort of specialist area they work in, and he hadn't even thought to find out what hers was. There was hardly any wonder he didn't understand what their relationship was about. He didn't know anything about her, but then again, she wasn't the easiest person to extract personal information from. As he said goodbye to Hendry and walked back to the uniformed officers, he wondered if *he* was any easier to get along with. He doubted it. He was still stinging from the revelation of not knowing about Sarah's life as he explained his plans to the rest of those gathered. They waited for the unmarked van to take the remains away, and then they left.

Avalon stayed in the office the next day. A new major case was always the best way to galvanise and motivate the team, but he would have preferred that he had a little more time to settle in. There was still a great deal to do at base, and so he had sent Mackinnon and Frazer to oversee the excavation of the burial site. Avalon had given them a rough area to remove the sand from which was a square, some distance from the place the body was buried. The actual grave hadn't been deep and didn't go into the earth below the sand. This meant whoever had buried the body had decided not to go deeper than the soft part. This allowed Avalon to consider the perpetrator would likely not dig deeper for any other bodies he or she had placed there, if indeed they had.

As he waited for results to come in, he set DS Wilson and DC White on several tasks relevant to the investigation. White was continuing to check for missing persons matching the bones found, and Wilson was contacting the owners of the site to try to build a chronological history of the place the body was found. He was also gathering a list of employees past and present. Other than that, Avalon would need to wait for anything the pathologist and the forensics team could find. He knew it could be some time before they had anything definite, so he continued working on his task of going through the previous cases that C Section had dealt with in the past year. He already knew some of the more important cases through Ross, but he read through them nonetheless.

To Avalon's surprise, Dr Forbes rang him as soon as he had finished the examination of the remains. The DI was impressed with the man's enthusiasm and could see a good working relationship with him. Unfortunately, there was nothing he hadn't already guessed.

'*The damage to the bones was undoubtedly caused by the blade of the machine skimming the top of the grave,*' he announced. '*There is some evidence of damage to the right radius which is indicative of a very old injury, probably very early in the person's life. There are no signs of other injuries or trauma, and nothing to suggest how the person died. I'm sure the person was female and around the twenty-five to thirty-five age bracket. Probably had a child or children and was reasonably healthy in adulthood. There are signs of dental work, but I would guess this wasn't a person who had a regular check-up.*' He paused. '*I know it isn't*

117

much, but I'm sure a forensic anthropologist will shine a great deal more light on this.'

'Are all the bones there, Doctor?' Avalon asked.

'Yes, everything. The forensics team didn't miss a thing. Do you want me to arrange for the remains to be collected?' The doctor was being as helpful as he could. Avalon said he would be grateful and then informed Wilson and White of the pathologist's findings. The door to the Cave suddenly opened, and the DCI stood there looking at Avalon, not before glancing around the room. She asked him if he had a moment and then shut the door. Avalon had nodded, but he was finding this habit of hers tedious. He was sure the rest of the team would find it irritating too. He knew she wasn't actually checking up on them, but it was certainly counterproductive. He would ask DI Lasiter if she did the same to B Section. For the time-being, he pulled on his jacket and went to see her.

'Take a seat DI,' she said with the hint of a smile. He now knew it wasn't a real smile though. It was something she did, and it meant nothing. He looked at the seat, and this time decided that even though it wasn't the required distance, he would acquiesce. 'How are you going with this quarry case?'

'I did make a report last night,' he said as light-heartedly as he could.

'Yes, I have seen it, but I wanted your opinion,' she insisted, looking across from her screen. Her paleness was accentuated by the dark spectacles she wore, with slightly tinted lenses. It gave her a look of illness, or at least of being unwell. She was far from subdued however. Her piercing eyes were as sharp as thunderbolts under those lenses.

118

'At this stage,' he shrugged, 'I don't have an opinion, and I'm still waiting for the remains to be tested by forensics. I have a verbal report from the pathologist who says that the cause of death is unknown.' She nodded and looked back at her screen. Avalon guessed she had his report and was reading it, checking for any inconsistencies.

'I think that this may have to be handled by MIT,' she began and gave him a quick glance, 'after all, they have primacy in murder cases.' Not so long in the past, Avalon would have become angry and shown it. Now he was different. A year is a long time in a person's career, and he had changed a great deal. The comment hadn't stopped him from being angry though, he just dealt with it differently. He looked at her calmly and assessed the woman a little more. If the Major Investigations Team were brought in, it would mean *his* team may be off the case, which would do nothing to lift morale. It could make it look as if Inverness were not capable of solving larger cases. Avalon knew that wasn't why she was suggesting the MIT. He knew she was covering her own back. She was in the post temporarily. As soon as DCI Croker was recovered, she would be back off to Aberdeen and so she didn't want a major investigation around her neck. Avalon suddenly realised that she didn't have any idea what he had been doing for the last few months leading up to Christmas. If she had, she wouldn't have simply suggested MIT, she would have asked his opinion. He had several choices. He could shrug and accept it and let her go ahead. After all, he hadn't even had time to warm his seat up in the office. Or, he could simply go around her and speak to the Superintendent, though Avalon wasn't keen on that. He had the ear of the Super at the moment, but no detective wanted to be too involved with high-ranking officers more than they needed to be. It was best to be anonymous, as was normally the case. Being known meant being a target. Neither was he keen on being taken off the case. Being brought back into C Section, only to find them pulled off a case would seem to the team that it was Avalon's doing, morale would drop even more and his credibility would be damaged. He went for a third option, to tell her about his training with MIT. Firstly, he decided to play it cool.

'We don't yet know this is a murder case,' he said calmly. She removed her spectacles and frowned.

'What other option can you think of when someone hides a body?' she demanded.

'Involuntary manslaughter for one,' offered Avalon, still as calm as if it mattered little.

'It amounts to the same thing as far as an investigation is concerned,' she replied, still frowning.

'I didn't say it wasn't a crime,' insisted Avalon, realising he was pushing his luck a little, 'but we don't know this is a *major* crime yet.' She didn't reply straight away, but he knew this wasn't due to her accepting his theory. He knew she was angry and was trying to calm herself before replying. This was confirmed when she replaced her spectacles and sighed.

'So, find out what it is and then we hand it over to the MIT,' she replied. Avalon began to wonder if she knew what the MIT was. He had recently worked within the SCD, albeit in a minor capacity, but he had a broad knowledge of how some branches of Police Scotland worked. Yet, until he had direct involvement with MIT, he hadn't known very much of how it worked, mainly because his area wasn't a regular major incident area. There were many criticisms of MIT, his, and many other officers' main complaint, was that most policing decisions were coming from the Borders. How can someone living and working in Dundee or Glasgow understand the needs of the officers or the public of the Highlands and Islands? Quite simply, they cannot. More and more, Scotland was becoming Lothian and Borders. The Highlands was a separate nation. PC Dowd had once said, jokingly, that the Chief Constable thought Inverness was in England. It wasn't such a joke anymore. Small police stations had closed and if a traffic incident happened in the north of Sutherland, officers would have to travel from the nearest base in Dingwall, over two hours away. In the south, that would be unthinkable. It was like a car being sent from Dundee to attend a problem in Ayr. But, in the Highlands, it didn't seem to matter. In a time when many Scots were talking of independence, the Highlands already had it, simply because no one gave a damn about them and they seemed excluded in many ways. But, he was a copper first and any political opinion he may have must give way to his job.

'I'll keep you informed,' he eventually said as he got to his feet, 'but I think a call to Detective Chief Inspector Liam Robertson of Strathclyde CID may be of interest.' She looked up and frowned. He wasn't being awkward, and neither was it his fault she didn't know enough about her officers. He just thought he should drop a hint. It was something he had become used to. He would carry on and do what he could to solve the mystery. He returned to The Cave to tell everyone not to plan anything for the weekend.

121

Chapter Six

Saturday morning arrived with the news that the death toll for the UK had risen over five thousand, but back at Inverness Police Station, the good news was, there was no second body to report. The site at the quarry had been excavated and nothing had been found. Though the cordon had been removed from the area, DC Frazer had informed the site manager not to fill in the hole until they heard from DI Avalon. Now, they were just waiting for reports from the forensics labs on the bones and the soil samples. Hendry had confirmed that nothing else was found with the body, no ligature and no jewellery. There were a few insect remains, and they were being examined for further investigation. Twelve possible missing persons had been identified as being a similar age as the skeleton, and that was going back two years. It was just a waiting game. Avalon knew Hendry would inform him as soon as anything was known. This reminded him of Sarah Underwood's specialism, and he tried to think of a way of finding out without a direct question. It was possible that he could work out a way to bring it into conversation with Hendry, or then again, he could just ask her. The phone rang and Avalon answered it, expecting Hendry's voice. It wasn't. It was PC Kirk informing him that some evidence bags had arrived back from the courts that had been used on one of DS Wilson's previous cases. He replaced the handset and wondered how long he would have to wait for news. Possibly days if nothing was showing up on the remains. The rest of the team were in The Cave, all except DS Wilson and DC Mackinnon, who were out assisting with the dredging of the area at Loch End near the sunken boat. Avalon wondered if it was a good time to find out about Ross's relationship, though he wasn't sure how he would broach the subject. He walked into the main part of the office and beckoned Ross over. Ross sat in the spare seat and asked,

'What' is it?'

'Nothing, I was wondering how the bookmaker case is going.'

'It stalled, you know it did,' he shrugged, 'we brought Serle's girlfriend in again, but we just got the usual crap.'

'The DCI asked me about it,' explained the DI leaning back in his seat.

'Really?' he asked with surprise, 'I suppose she's on the warpath?'

'Not really,' replied Avalon, with an unconcerned expression. 'She actually asked me what I thought. It felt like it was me under scrutiny rather than you two.'

'She's going to be a pain in the arse,' nodded Ross, 'no wonder she's got a new nick-name so quickly.' Avalon raised his brows. Somehow, she had acquired a new name at Inverness,

'Oh?' he asked.

'Lasiter's mob gave it her. It seems the DI and his

team have had problems with her already,' explained Ross.

'Well,' sighed Avalon, 'DI Lasiter won't take kindly to her interference.'

'No,' replied Ross, 'but I hear a few others around the place are none too pleased either.'

'That's usual,' shrugged the DI, 'no one likes change, and DCI's always bring change.' He paused for a moment. 'So, what have B Section Christened her?' he asked.

'The Plague Witch,' he replied, interlocking his fingers behind his head.

'Harsh,' shrugged Avalon.

'Aye, but it fits.'

'I suppose it does,' shrugged Avalon, 'she looks positively anaemic close up.'

'Well, I'm not sure I want to be that close to her, but I had to laugh when I heard it for the first time. A witch brought in during a plague.' Ross leaned forward and gave a short laugh.

'It's a good enough reason not to be a DCI,' nodded Avalon, 'they never get anything nice as a nick-name.'

'Well, you already have yours,' replied Ross, glancing over to him, 'Auld Clootie isn't so bad.'

'But at another nick they would find a new one,' insisted Avalon.

'I suppose so,' shrugged Ross, resting his elbows on his knees, 'but the worst you could get is Miserable Bastard.'

'That's a bit unfair, I don't think I'm miserable.'

'We haven't seen much of you at the pub over the last few months,' insisted the DS sitting up straight once more. 'Too infatuated with the girlfriend?'

'I haven't seen her for ages,' admitted Avalon with a slight frown, 'what with us both being away...' he trailed off. 'And while we are on the subject,' he added, 'I hear you have found someone to take pity on you.' Ross frowned deeply, then it subsided as he realised that it was difficult to keep such a secret. He leaned back in his chair, rested one leg across the other and nodded. 'So why the secrecy, you never mentioned it?'

'Like I said,' frowned Ross, 'if you had been to the pub, maybe I would have brought it up. I'm not likely to mention it here am I?' Avalon shrugged and waited for Ross to tell him more. Ross stared back for a moment and then gave in. 'Her name is Trisha, and I actually met her in the pub.'

'So she's local?'

'Not really,' replied Ross shaking his head, 'she was visiting her brother, she lives near Nairn.'

'What does she do?' asked Avalon, genuinely interested.

'Does it matter,' shrugged Ross, 'it's just my luck to find someone I get on with just before a lockdown.' Avalon had his answer. They weren't living together, so he could consider Ross still single.

'It's bad luck I admit,' shrugged the DI, but many people are in the same position.' Ross saw Avalon as he used to see him, as a mate, a friend.

'She's a dancer,' he said quietly, 'but keep it to yourself, everyone would take the pish out of me if they knew.' Avalon was struggling to know how a dancer could make a living in Nairn, but he kept quiet and just nodded. Ross could feel the question Avalon was aching to ask, and so he helped out. 'She has a small dance studio, mainly for young girls, you know the sort of thing,' he explained. Avalon didn't, he just watched Ross with a blank expression. 'She enters competitions and does…' Ross had run out of steam. It was clear even he was struggling with a suitable explanation. There was a long silence. 'She's a…' another pause but this time shorter, 'pole dancer.' Ross waited for a comment. There wasn't one. Avalon simply sat with a glassy stare. 'She dances… with a pole,' added Ross, but Avalon just stuck his bottom lip out a little. 'Nothing to say?' asked Ross, sick of the silence.

'Some Polish people are lovely,' he said.

'Not Polish,' spat Ross, 'she dances with a pole, or rather around one,' added Ross with a hiss, trying to keep his voice quiet.

'I know what a pole dancer is Rossy,' it was Avalon's turn to pause, 'but it sounds a little…' this time *he* ran out of steam, he couldn't quite find what he was trying to say and didn't want to say the wrong thing.

'I know what you're thinking,' nodded Ross slowly, 'because that's what I thought.'

'I'm not sure what I'm thinking,' replied Avalon, furrowing his brow.

'You're thinking it sounds like she works in a strip club or something.'

'In Nairn?' spluttered Avalon.

'Well, I got the wrong end of the stick too at first,' admitted Ross. 'I think I got confused with lap dancing, but when she showed me a video of what she does,' he slowly shook his head, 'it's amazing. I was truly impressed. It's like it ought to be in the Olympics,' he insisted. 'It's a mixture of strength, beauty and dance, just fantastic to watch.'

'You like her don't you?' smiled Avalon.

'Yeah, she's alright,' shrugged Ross as if it was of no consequence, but Avalon smiled deeper. He could see the animation that Ross was holding back in describing what she did. He was trying so hard to keep calm, but his eyes betrayed his true feelings.

'I'll have a look at this on the internet when I get home. It sounds intriguing,' said Avalon resting his chin on his hand.

'It'll impress you if you find the right video, it's one of those-' the phone rang.

'Avalon,' the DI said as he picked it up. 'Go on,' he added, and then there was a pause as his face became more serious. 'I don't suppose I can come over, can I?' he asked. 'Right, I'll come straight away,' and he put down the phone. 'Forensics has something for us,' he said as he stood and pulled on his jacket.

'What about the lockdown?' asked Ross.

'Hendry says it's fine, it's a lab after all.'

Avalon was taken into the main laboratory after he had donned the white suit and a mask. The skeleton was laid out on a rubber-covered bench, and all the bones were placed in the anatomical positions relative to each other. A bright light hung above the bench.

'I'm not sure it's quite PC, but we've named her Sandy,' said Hendry tentatively. Avalon shrugged. Was it any worse to give a dead person a nick-name rather than a live one? 'She was a white female,' continued Hendry, 'around a hundred and sixty-two centimetres tall with brown hair and brown eyes. There is an injury to the right radius, which may have been acquired when she was younger. We know she lived in Scotland most of her

127

life and was probably local to Inverness.' Hendry paused at this point to pick up his notes.

'So, she was about…' Avalon wasn't great with metric measurement, 'five feet four?' Hendry was the opposite and worked it out on a calculator.

'Yes, around five feet four, give or take an inch.'

'How do you know where she lived?' asked the DI.

'Mainly due to the minerals found in the bones from the water she would have consumed. We are finding other items in there, but we have limited resources here.' Hendry explained, 'we can find most trace elements but we can't always say what they are. I think samples will have to be sent away for further analysis.' Avalon nodded.

'What else?' he asked.

'I think a forensic anthropologist could make a better guess, but with the report from the pathologist and what we have found, we are rounding her age down to thirty-six, with a three-year error each side.' He pointed to a few clues, including the ends of the long bones. Hendry looked down at his notes again. 'She may have been pale skinned but further tests should give a more accurate assessment,' he concluded, and then frowned. 'The thing that puzzles me, is what I found in the remains of the bone marrow.' He showed Avalon to a slide image on a computer screen. 'These cells look wrong,' he paused, 'I'm not sure what has happened to them but this is something that took place Antemortem.'

'Before she died?' asked Avalon. Hendry nodded.

'She may have had some rare disease, and if that is the case, she should be easier to identify.'

'Could this be what killed her?' asked the DI with

a frown.

'Possibly,' nodded Hendry, 'but why bury her if it was a natural death?'

'It could be something introduced into the body,' suggested Avalon still examining the image.

'You mean poison?' Avalon nodded at the question. 'Then we have the perfect person arriving back tonight,' Hendry smiled but Avalon couldn't see it behind the mask.

'You mean Sarah?' he asked.

'Well,' nodded Hendry, 'toxicology is her subject.' Avalon had his answer to Sarah's specialism without even asking. He nodded and said,

'Of course, and she's back tonight?'

'Yes, I spoke to her earlier, she's thinking of sending Sandy to Dundee.' Avalon sighed a little. That meant more delays in finding the truth of the remains.

'Well, thanks for showing me this,' said Avalon, 'it tells us more about her. What about the time period she has been in the ground?'

'That's more complex an issue,' replied the technician. 'We have examined the insect casts, but there are few of them and in poor condition. Most have disintegrated, which suggests she's been there some time. But we do have enough pollen to suggest she was put in the grave around June or July.'

'We just don't know which year,' added Avalon.

Avalon left the building and drove back to the station, wondering if it was a good idea sending the remains to Dundee. He would ask Sarah what she had in mind, but for now, they had slightly more idea of what Sandy may have looked like. Back in The Cave, he placed his jacket on his chair and then stood at the front of the room.

'I have just got back from forensics,' he looked at their faces, there still wasn't a spark in the team yet, 'and we now have more information. The woman was more likely to be thirty-six years old with a few years error either side. She was around five feet four inches tall, with brown hair and brown eyes. Caucasian, with a pale complexion, and she is likely to have lived locally for most of her life. There is a healed injury to the right radius that was probably received when she was younger.' He paused and looked around them once more. 'It isn't much, but we can narrow things down a little more accurately.'

'Was she a mother? I mean, was there evidence of her having children?' asked Frazer.

'It looks so, but I'll get that confirmed later,' nodded Avalon.

'When did she die?' asked Rutherford.

'That we don't know yet, but push the search back to ten years.' He knew that would bring up many more results, but now they knew more about her, the search would be easier.

'Anything on cause of death?' asked Ross.

'No,' replied Avalon, folding his arms, 'and there is no trauma to the body or the head, but…' he was guessing now but he thought he should tell them just in case something cropped up in the search. 'She may have had a rare or unusual bone disease,' he then added, 'equally, she may have taken, or had administered, some toxic material. The lab will let us know as soon as they can isolate what it is.' He unfolded his arms and raised himself from his leaning position, 'any questions?' There were none and so he returned to the booth as they searched through the endless missing person reports, now going back ten years. He was a little impatient, but he knew Sarah well enough to know she would be eager to get back to her work first thing in the morning. He would call her to find out what her plans were for further tests.

A little later, DS Wilson arrived back and went to Avalon to explain about the dredging he had attended and informed him that they found plenty of scrap but no links to the missing person. He suggested that the shoe was likely to be a coincidence. He then turned to start on his report but Avalon asked,

'Have you got a minute?' Wilson shrugged and sat. Avalon rested his folded arms on the edge of the desk and asked in a low voice, 'any ideas what to do with DC White?'

'What do y' mean?' asked Wilson with a puzzled look.

'You've had more dealings with him,' sighed Avalon, 'he's doing his job but...' he seemed lost for words. Wilson knew what the boss was getting at, but he didn't know what to tell him. He nodded and then sighed, looking down at the floor.

'He's got a past,' he eventually said. Everyone had, but when someone like Wilson makes a comment of that sort, there is something particular he is referring to. He paused for some seconds and then looked up to Avalon. 'I didn't like the little tosser anyway,' he whispered, 'but he got on my nerves so much a' decided tae have a look into his past.' He looked into Avalon's face and continued. 'Et struck me that he couldna have got this far as he es, so he must have changed along the way.' He paused again, and Avalon saw that Wilson didn't know if he should share the information.

'Tell me the short version,' shrugged Avalon, 'I haven't much interest in him either.' Wilson thought for a moment and then continued.

'His record says he did his time on the beat en Sheffield, moving tae Glasgow when he passed his exams, or was et the other way around?' Wilson faltered on this detail before continuing. 'Anyway, he was doing pretty well there for a while, and then he seemed to drop off the map.' Wilson raised his eyes and sighed before saying, 'as y' know, I have some contacts over there and so I made a few calls. It seems DC Angus White was the protégé of DI Donald Fisher, he was his blue-eyed boy.' Avalon didn't know who he meant but it was obvious Wilson saw him as important. 'But, something went wrong. DC White was involved with a long-term case involving two children that had been groomed for crime. White was known for his intellect, but et seems he was also very ambitious, and pushed the boundaries of his skill, substituting facts with intelligent guesswork and intuition. Ultimately, et backfired, and he was dragged over the coals for et. He got emotionally involved too, and so he was put on office duties and that was the end of his ambition.' Avalon was silent. He took a deep breath and glanced over to White sitting behind his computer screen. As he exhaled, Wilson continued. 'So not only has et taken away his expectations, he now wants to punish everyone else for his errors, as ef et's our fault.' Wilson's distaste for the man was clear, but Avalon suspected there was also something else in the detail of the story. Either way, the DI could see that Wilson saw DC White as a coward, giving up, and just doing what he had to do, nothing more.

'So why haven't you tried to get rid of him before then?' asked Avalon, seeing a little of White in DS Wilson. Wilson frowned and then glanced behind him through the glass of the booth. White didn't react, he just kept on looking at his screen.

'A part of me feels sorry for him, I suppose,' sighed Wilson looking back to his boss. 'From what my mate at Glasgow nick told me, he was a scapegoat. His hunches had been right, et was just the way he went about et. He was dumped in the shite, and someone else got the credit. Maybe, from then on, he decided tae take all compassion from his psyche and deal with facts, nothing but facts.' Avalon sat silent again, seeing Wilson beginning to look guilty for his distaste of White. 'But that doesnae change a thing,' replied Wilson, suddenly slapping his thighs before standing up. 'So, what are y' gonna do?' he then asked, looking down at Avalon.

'I was going to give him a second chance, but after what you have told me...' Avalon shrugged as he trailed off. Wilson nodded and returned to his desk to write up his report. Avalon thought for some minutes. He wondered if he should admit to White that he knew something of his past. Maybe, he certainly had to sort *something* out. He stood and leaned his head around the glass and said,

'DC White, a moment of your time,' and he sat back down. White slowly made his way to the booth and stood waiting. 'Sit down,' announced the DI. White paused for a moment. Avalon had spoken with him before, it hadn't been at all friendly and now he was expecting a similar conversation. His thin face was blank and straight away, Avalon was finding it difficult to see anything positive in keeping him on.

'I told you some time ago that I want full co-operation from my team. That hasn't changed, and I need to put my cards on the table.' He paused for a moment. White's expression remained fixed. 'I know about your past, your time at Glasgow.' Still nothing. 'You probably came to Inverness to get away from that past, but it's caught up with you and we need to sort something out.' A slight frown began to etch its way onto White's brow. 'Your past doesn't matter a damn to me Detective Constable, I'm only concerned with the here and now and, to that end, I need you to become part of the team, or leave.' There was still little reaction. 'Do you understand?' Avalon didn't say the final part in an angry tone, more as if he was checking that White was still awake. White nodded. 'At the moment, you are universally disliked,' and Avalon held up his hand in anticipation of interruption, 'and before you say that you don't care, hear me out.' Avalon paused again. 'I'm not saying you need to be liked, but you need to integrate. The character you have built for yourself is your business, but here, in this office, and out in the field for that matter, you have to be part of the team.' White blinked a few times and Avalon wondered if he was getting through. 'I understand you were a good enough detective and I can see after what happened, you feel resentment.' The DI didn't wish to get embroiled in White's career or seem to be sympathetic, and so he remained vague.

'Yes sir, a little,' was White's understated reply, but Avalon began to think he was getting somewhere.

'So,' he continued, 'I'm going to leave this with you, but I want results straight away or you will force

134

my hand.'

'I can't just change overnight,' replied White, 'even if I could, they would think I was schizophrenic.' He had nodded his head towards the main room. Avalon saw that the man may at last be considering what he had offered.

'Agreed,' nodded Avalon, 'and I'll leave it with you to work out how you go about this transformation, but don't take too long.' Avalon tapped a few keys on his keyboard, he wanted White out of his hair now, his patience was nothing like it had been eighteen months ago. 'For now, I want you to help Frazer with her missing persons search.' He then looked back at White and gave a curt nod. White got the hint and returned to his desk. Avalon wasn't too concerned about the decision White would make. It would just make life easier if he didn't have to go to the DCI and complain about him.

Sunday came around all too soon and as Avalon entered the office, he had a feeling that it was going to be a busy day. Mackinnon and Wilson were having the day off, but everyone else would probably be tied up one way or another on the quarry case. The DI knew *he* was certainly going to be busy, and his first call would be to the forensics lab and a conversation with Sarah Underwood. This was to be the first time Avalon had spoken to her in a professional role since their relationship had begun. He lifted the phone with a certain degree of forethought, and he was conscious that he needed to keep the conversation short, and to the point.

'*Hello?*' came the questioning voice at the other end. He wasn't sure he recognised the particular female.

'It's Detective Inspector Avalon, I-' but before he could complete his question she replied,

'*Oh, just one second,*' and the phone went quiet, except for a few background noises. When sound came back, there was a shuffle and Sarah came on the phone.

'*Hello, you don't waste any time.*' Her voice sounded playful, but he still looked up at the clock on the wall to be sure he had got the time right. A glance at his watch confirmed it was two minutes past nine.

'Sorry,' he said, 'you usually start at eight-thirty don't you?'

'*It was a joke,*' she replied, '*so, what can I do for you Detective Inspector?*' There was a slight hint of sarcasm evident.

'Have you had time to look at the results from the remains found at the quarry?'

'*Yes,*' she replied in a flat tone. Avalon had overdone the normality. He realised he hadn't even said 'good morning', or 'how are you'. Further comment wasn't forthcoming and so he relented and said,

'I'm sorry, you're probably tired, how did your trip work out?'

'*That's the second time you've said sorry,*' she replied, '*but it went well enough, though I got stopped by some of your lot to see where I was going.*' There was an amount of frustration in her voice now, particularly when she said 'your lot'. He took it to mean the police.

'Well, the lockdown is being taken seriously, we're all taking this one step at a time.' He tried to sound upbeat, but he wasn't. 'Oh, and thank you for the card, it made me smile.'

'*You're welcome. Anyway, back to the subject at hand,*' she sighed, '*I haven't spoken with Phil, except by phone and email and he's off today so I'm stuck with the reports he's made. There is something he's found in the cells within the bone tissues. Most of the osteocytes show signs of the material, though the quantity seems low. I suppose this could be due to the body being in the ground for some time.'*

'Ideas?' was Avalon's simple question.

'Poison, without a doubt,' she replied, *'but I can't say what, at this time.'*

'So she was killed?'

'I didn't say that,' she insisted, *'we all have poison in our bodies, it's the amount that is the critical factor.'*

'Paracelsus,' sighed Avalon.

'How do you know about a Swiss physician that lived over five hundred years ago?' she laughed, *'did he write poetry?'* Avalon wondered if this was sarcasm.

'I don't recall any of his poetry,' he replied flatly, 'but he did say that, *'all things are poison and nothing is without poison, only the dose makes a thing not poison.'* Or at least something like that.'

'Yes,' she said in a more agreeable tone, *'you've just about summed up his theory.'*

'He was someone I came across when I worked with SOCO,' he explained.

'Oh yes,' she replied, *'I was forgetting.'*

'And I didn't realise until a few days ago,' he began, 'that your specialist subject was toxicology.'

'Didn't I say?' she asked, *'I suppose it isn't something that comes out in social chit-chat.'* She paused and then spoke in a middle-English voice, *'What a wonderful wine bar this is, oh and did you know that everyone has Polonium 210 in their bodies?'* Avalon

had considered that the conversation had been stuffy and matter-of-fact. He even thought that the invisible barrier between them could be felt on the phone, but to his surprise, she seemed animated and even, dare he say it, ebullient? He had never known her to make a joke, not a real joke at any rate, and here she was making dark humour in an English accent. Maybe she was just taking liberties with his own accent. Maybe not. Either way, the conversation was taking longer than it ought, and soon someone in the office would be wondering why he was taking his time.

'So, when might we know something?' he suddenly asked. There was a pause, and she replied in her normal tone.

'*Later today I would think,*' there was a pause, '*do you know who she was yet?*'

'No, it's a difficult one because we have no idea how long she was in the ground, so we have no clue how far to look through the records to find her.'

'*We are looking at the soil and sand samples,*' she offered, '*that could give us something but we are so busy at the moment.*'

'I understand,' he sighed, 'we'll wait for something to crop up.' He thanked her and was about to hang up, but then thought of something. 'Oh before you go,' he began, 'you may be able to help with something else.' He paused but she was silent. 'A mate of mine went on holiday to Cornwall late last year and got a mysterious swelling all over his body.'

'*Go on,*' she said tentatively.

'He phoned and asked me what he should do. I told him to visit the Tourist Inflammation Centre.' He put down the handset and still looking at it said, '*That's* a joke, just not a very good one,' and he stood as he pulled on his jacket.

He walked into the main office and told them that there was still nothing further on the quarry case, but they were to keep trying to find possible matches. Frazer told him there were one hundred and seventeen possible missing people, but they had managed to eliminate over twenty of them with medical records, as neither having an injury or living around the area most of their lives. Several others had been discounted due to further information not being applied to their files, so when the counting was over, they still had eighty-nine missing females over the last ten years. This didn't take into consideration the hundreds of people who go missing more than once, and the ones related to mental illness. Many of the missing people are found, only to go missing again, and so to keep the search numbers down, some of those groups would only be investigated when all other possible names were exhausted. It was a constant problem for Police Scotland. Tens of thousands of people go missing each year, but around sixty percent are found, with a quarter of them going off once again. Hundreds of thousands of man-hours are wasted every year on the process, but luckily, only a small percentage of them stay missing. Avalon looked through some of the records and shook his head at the amount of others they would have to sift through if 'Sandy' wasn't identified. The door of the office opened and in came the DCI with a frown. She looked at Avalon and then asked,

'Anything on the quarry case yet?'

'No Ma'am,' replied Avalon as calm as he could be, 'I would have let you know if we had, we're waiting for forensics I'm afraid.' She nodded, gave a quick glance around and left. Avalon turned back to Frazer, who he had been talking to, and saw the rest of the team either smile, or shake their heads before continuing with their work.

'I think the DCI has haemorrhoids,' said Ross in a low voice.

'That, or a spring is sticking up through her chair,' suggested Rutherford.

'She's trying to impress someone,' added White, but the shock to the rest of the team was such, it was as if he hadn't spoken. Everyone ignored it, just in case it was in their imagination. The DC was still looking forward at his screen and it seemed unreal that he would have joined in with a conversation, particularly one so banal. Ross eventually gave a sly glance to Rutherford who just raised his brows, but Avalon feeling the discomfort of the silence added his own tilt to the comment.

'Possibly, I just don't think she wants to rock the boat, and a major murder investigation might ruin her time here.'

'But ef et were solved quickly, wouldn't et be a feather en her cap, so to speak?' questioned Frazer.

'But if it isn't,' replied White, 'it'll go against her.' Ross looked at Avalon with a deep frown, it was clear that White had spoken, his South Yorkshire accent couldn't be mistaken for anything else.

'Maybe,' nodded Avalon. White still hadn't turned around, 'I still think she's just keeping her head down.'

'But with respect Boss,' began White once more, 'that doesn't fit with her previous posts and it seems to be at odds with her character.' The whole room was stunned, not just because White was adding something to the discussion, but because he had called Avalon 'Boss'. Avalon expected several retorts from the team, but there was nothing. Even Ross was silent. It was left to Avalon to engage with White, which was difficult because in truth, he agreed with White's theory.

'So you know about her?' he asked. White had been watching the room through the misty reflection of his screen, but now, he turned to face Avalon and rested his left arm on the back of the seat.

'Only from what I heard DS Wilson say just after she arrived,' he explained. 'She's a problem solver, if that's correct, she isn't going to balk at a major investigation. That means, she's either trying to prove a point, or, cementing her reputation by putting in her own input.'

'So as to take the credit?' asked Rutherford after finally getting over the shock of White's input.

'I would assume so,' shrugged White and he turned back to his screen.

'Well,' sighed Avalon, walking back to the booth, 'we'll soon see how she reacts once we get something back from the labs.' He picked up his phone and dialled the pathologist's office to ask about the results. He was told the pathologist wasn't there, but the report had been sent. He checked his emails but couldn't find it. He would have to wait.

It was late in the afternoon when Avalon finally got the information that would push the case along. He had been reading through the pathologist's report that had finally arrived. The part that he was looking for was clear. The pathologist had confirmed that it seemed quite

141

evident that the woman had given birth to at least one child. He looked at the phone for a moment as it rang before answering. He then glanced up at the office through the glass as he picked up the handset.

'Avalon.'

'*It's Sarah.*'

'Have you got anything?' She had only said two words, but he had the feeling there was something wrong. The way she had spoken those two words had an air of trouble about them.

'*Yes…*' she paused, '*quite a bit, but some of the results don't make a great deal of sense.*' He glanced at his watch and then up to the clock.

'Should I come over?' he asked. She paused again then said,

'*It's probably best that you do, this is going to take some explaining.*'

Chapter Seven

Avalon got out of his car as Ross's car pulled in beside him. Ross clambered wearily out of his vehicle and leaned on the roof.

'So why have you dragged me along?' he asked, 'I could be doing something interesting with the rest of my Sunday.'

'Like what?' asked Avalon, raising his brows.

'There are loads of options,' shrugged Ross, 'watching TV repeats, ironing my shirts for Monday morning, wondering what to cook for tea, try to work out how to use the dishwasher, look for-'

'You didn't have to come,' admitted Avalon, turning towards the door of the labs.

'I could even have stood staring aimlessly out of the window,' frowned Ross, this time pointing at Avalon, 'wondering what the hell life is about.' Avalon pressed the doorbell on the building and waited.

'I want to talk to you about something,' explained Avalon.

'Fire away,' nodded Ross, 'I normally keep my lovemaking skills to myself, but I'm sure I can give you a few pointers.' Avalon glanced at him and raised his brows. 'I may have to try out Miss Underwood for myself before I formulate a-'

Ross was interrupted by a click as the door unlocked. They entered and walked into the foyer. Sarah was there to greet them and she gave Avalon a pleasant smile. He knew it wasn't her stock smile, the one she gave to colleagues, it was her genuine smile.

'Hello,' she said and then looked at Ross. He got the stock smile. 'DS Ross,' she added. She turned and entered the lab, and the two of them followed. There was only one other technician who was working in the glass cage known as the 'samples room'. The skeleton was still on the rubber-topped table. The light was off and she led them to a desk with a computer screen already showing an image of a cell in microscopic detail.

'Your message sounded a little confused,' said Avalon, looking at Sarah.

'We'll get to that point in a minute,' she began, 'for the moment you need to look at this,' and she pointed to the screen. 'This is a better image of the substance we found in her bones. I'm not sure quite what the percentages are yet, but I think this would certainly be what killed her.' Avalon looked at the image. He didn't really know what he was seeing, but he assumed they were vastly enlarged cells.

'So I'm guessing you know what it is?' asked Avalon.

'I suppose you know what ricin is?' she simply asked. Avalon thought immediately of a famous case.

'The Georgi Markov case?' he questioned.

'Wasn't that the Umbrella Murder, the one the Russians were supposed to have carried out?' asked Ross, slightly bemused.

'Yes,' nodded Sarah, 'Markov was injected with ricin.'

'So you're saying that...' he paused and nodded slightly towards the remains on the table, 'Sandy was killed with ricin?'

'But how would someone get hold of ricin?' frowned Ross.

'Easily, it's made from castor beans,' replied Sarah, folding her arms.

'The same stuff castor oil is made from?' asked Ross, still by no means sure he understood. Sarah nodded again.

'How much would it take to kill a healthy adult?' was Avalon's question. Sarah uncrossed her arms and leaned on a bench.

'That would depend on which method was used to apply it,' she insisted. 'Of course it can be injected, but it could be ingested or inhaled, either way could be deadly with a very small amount.'

'Is there any way that someone would use this to commit suicide?' was Avalon's next question.

'It's possible,' Sarah replied, tilting her head as she nodded, 'but anyone knowing how to make it, or obtain it, would presumably know enough about the poison to know what a horrible death it would be.' Avalon considered this. It was unlikely that this was anything other than foul play.

'You mentioned on the phone,' asked the DI, considering the conversation they had earlier, 'when we spoke of Paracelsus, that we all have toxins in our bodies.'

'That's correct,' she agreed.

'But you mentioned Polonium,' he said, 'were

145

you serious?'

'Yes,' she smiled, 'I was, and I only mentioned it because it's the obvious eyebrow raiser.'

'And this comes down to Paracelsus's theory? It's there, but not in a great enough quantity?' he asked. She nodded again.

'It does. Polonium is used in industry for antistatic purposes mainly, even on antistatic tape,' she explained. 'It's everywhere and some of it enters our body. Fortunately, it has a short life, and it dissipates quickly.' She thought for a second, 'Except in smokers,' she added. 'People who smoke, retain much more of it than people who don't, and in most cases it's the Polonium which causes the lung cancer.'

'Jesus,' sighed Ross, 'I'm glad I stopped when I was young then.'

'It was a good idea,' smiled Sarah, 'for several reasons.'

'But could it be a similar case with ricin?' asked Avalon, trying to get back to the topic.

'No,' she shook her head. 'Absolutely not, ricin isn't found just hanging around, and it has few other uses.' Avalon glanced back to the bones and then to Ross.

'So she was administered this and died a horrible death.'

'That's going to piss off the Plague Witch,' Ross grinned.

'Pardon?' asked Sarah.

'Just Ross's cruel humour,' frowned Avalon, and changed the subject quickly. 'So do we have any idea how long she has been there?' Sarah took a deep breath, crossing her arms again as she did.

146

'We are never going to be very close on that subject.' She paused and looked at the floor. 'My best guess is that these remains have been in the ground for some time, but further tests are needed to extract DNA.' She looked back up to Avalon.

'I was told you may want to send them to Dundee,' he said. She nodded but knew that Avalon would be less than happy as it could take time to get results. 'Give me your best guess,' he said. She gave him a blank stare for a moment, then unfolded her arms and stood straight.

'I know you won't want to hear this but I think around twenty years.'

'Christ,' he groaned as he turned to Ross, 'that's going to change the pace of this.' Ross shrugged.

'It could be more, these are dry bones and...' she went silent and when Avalon looked at her, she had a deep frown and her lips were pinched.

'So there's more bad news?' he asked. She exhaled as if she had been holding her breath.

'I think I've explained before how we check oxygen levels and Ph. levels in soil for clues about how long a body has been in the ground?' He didn't nod, he just sighed. 'Well, we tested soil from around the area and got little from it except for three samples close to the body,' she explained. 'Two of those samples showed similar results, which indeed point to the remains lying there for some considerable time.'

'And the third?' asked the DI, guessing that there would be something to tax the team even further.

'The third sample, which was from directly under the body, hinted that it had been there longer,' she gave a sheepish look, knowing it wasn't good news.

147

'How does that work?' asked Ross, 'I mean, what does it mean?'

'We're not sure,' she fidgeted a little, obviously unsure about their conclusion. 'We wondered at first if the results were corrupted, but we did more tests and found that the results were correct. We even wondered if the body may have moved and then taken back, but...' She left the two detectives to mull over that one. Avalon couldn't visualise the situation and needed something tangible to work with.

'Can you draw where the samples were taken from on a bit of paper or something?' he asked. Sarah took them to the small office, which had a whiteboard on the wall similar to the one in The Cave. There, she picked up a black marker and drew a 'U' shape to represent the hole they had excavated to remove the remains.

'Phil and his team took samples from the whole area and most of them showed nothing more than we expected,' she said as she drew. She then picked up a blue marker and began to draw small crosses at points just outside the 'U' shape. 'They took samples all around the body, these two,' she paused as she drew two more crosses near the base of the shape, 'were the best two results for calculating how long the body had been there,' she explained. 'But here,' she picked up a red marker and drew. The cross was right in the base of the 'U' shape, 'is where the differing sample was.' Both Avalon and Ross could see why they had considered the theory the body had been moved. That just didn't add up, and Avalon discounted it. He pressurised his mind in to thinking of an alternative, but he couldn't think of any reason why the results would be so different.

'I have to ask this,' he said to her, 'is there any way, any reason at all you may be getting something wrong here?'

'We can never be absolute on these things,' she shrugged, 'but with my, and my team's experience, plus several computer models, we would all have to be in error.' Avalon nodded, then, he glanced to Ross, who was still looking at the drawing. Ross was holding his chin, and he gradually turned his head to Sarah.

'So,' he began, 'these tests use the surrounding soil to analyse it for Ph. and stuff like that, which gives an indication...' he stopped as he had an idea, but wasn't sure how to put it across. She tried to help him.

'Yes,' she nodded, 'there are many tests on each sample, such as oxygen levels and such, but it's a known science. Though, it can be affected by outside influences.'

'And are those samples,' he continued, 'or the surrounding ground, affected by the leaching of the body fluids during decomposition?'

'Yes, to a degree, and that is part of the process,' admitted Sarah, 'but the earth in the vicinity has a high concentration of sand, and that comes with its own set of problems.'

'So what's your theory?' asked Avalon, seeing that Ross was passing something through his mind. He shrugged but still stared at the sketch on the whiteboard.

'I'm not sure, I'm still struggling with the idea, but if this is the only point...' explained Ross pointing to the red cross on the board, 'is it possible...?' he trailed off with a deep frown as Avalon caught up. He could see Ross's theory, and it wasn't pleasant at all. Avalon stepped to the board and picked up the black marker, looking directly at Ross.

'You don't want to say it do you?' said Avalon with a blank stare. He turned to the board and drew a similar sized circle under the 'U'. He then put the top on the marker pen, and dropped it on the table, turning to leave as he did. 'Come on, we have to move quickly.'

'Care to explain?' asked Sarah, looking at the whiteboard and then to Avalon with a puzzled look. Avalon stopped and turned.

'This is just a theory of course,' explained Avalon, 'but one we can't ignore.' He pointed to the board. 'What your red mark is saying, is that the body has been there longer. It has, but not that body. There could be another one underneath.'

'But you excavated all around the area, didn't you?' she asked.

'Yes,' nodded Avalon with concern, 'but we didn't go any deeper. We excavated at the same depth only.'

Sunday evening wasn't the best time to organise an excavation on the site, and so, by the time Avalon and Ross had telephoned the site foreman, organised the team for the excavation for Monday morning and returned to the site to tape it off once more, they were the only ones left in the office. Avalon looked at his watch and Ross, seeing the movement, glanced at the clock.

'There were times,' sighed Ross, raising his brows, 'that we would have gone for a jar at the Castle Tavern.'

'Those days are gone,' replied Avalon, stifling a yawn. He stretched his arms instead and then added, 'we

150

can't do much more, we'll just have to wait for the morning. Let's go and get some sleep.' As they both stood, Ross asked,

'So what did you want to talk to me about?'

'What?' asked Avalon, stopping in his tracks.

'You said that you had asked me to follow you to the labs so we could talk about something.'

'Oh, yeah,' nodded Avalon, 'I forgot all about that,' and he perched on the edge of a desk. 'It was about the team, I was thinking that as we aren't going to get any more staff, and as we only have two detective sergeants, I will have to take a more hands-on role.'

'So what's that got to do with me?' asked Ross leaning against the wall, 'it's you that it'll affect.'

'I know, it's extra work,' shrugged the DI, 'but I want to know how everyone gets on.'

'You mean as in, who gets on and who doesn't?'

'Exactly,' nodded Avalon.

'Well,' began Ross folding his arms, 'I'm fine with the big man at the moment and Gordon gets on with everyone except White. You know Rory is fine with anyone and...' Ross shrugged, 'let's not beat about the bush, the only fly in the ointment is White. And that is made worse by the fact that he actually said something today.' Avalon nodded as he thought through the best options. 'Have you spoken to him?' asked Ross with a frown.

'White?' asked Avalon, 'of course, I have to speak to him.'

'About his attitude, I mean.'

'I think White knows how I feel and I'm sure he realises that under the circumstances, we need everyone to pull their weight.'

'That hasn't answered the question,' grumbled Ross, 'and anyway, it never bothered him previously.'

'I'm giving him his last chance,' answered Avalon, 'but the point here is that no one wants him as a partner.'

'You've got that right,' grinned Ross.

'Okay,' nodded Avalon, 'everyone will be in for the morning meeting, I'll give it some thought before bed,' and they left for home.

Monday morning meetings had always been traditionally the most important. Avalon didn't like sticking too closely to a format, but there were things he had to sort out.

'I've been thinking about the teams,' he announced as soon as they settled into their seats. He leaned on the frame of the booth and glanced to where the coffee machine once stood. He was missing that availability. 'We won't be getting any further staff and so we have to make a few changes, and with Gordon back at his desk, this seems a good time to implement those alterations.' Reorganisation of the teams could be a very contentious issue, and he had considered his choices carefully. Officers had to be happy with their working relationships if they were to operate efficiently. 'As we only have two sergeants, I will act as the third DS. Rossy and Martin will stay as previous. Gordon, you will team up with Rory.' Gordon nodded and looked over to Mackinnon who gave a brief smile. They would make a good team and got on well. Since Alison Boyd had left, Wilson had been without a regular partner. 'Megan,' continued Avalon looking across to Frazer, 'I think your separate skills will be required now and then by the other teams and so for the time-being, you'll be the floating third team member.' Avalon suddenly realised he had given Ross a chance for a jibe, but Ross sat quiet and impassive. 'I also know that you are invaluable behind the scenes and so I want you to work with me on the background to the quarry case.' She didn't look thrilled by the decision, but she nodded. 'Angus, you will be with me,' and White looked surprised for a moment but nodded too. There was almost a palpable sigh as everyone realised they wouldn't have to work with White, and Avalon hoped he wouldn't regret the decision, which was why he was keeping Frazer by his side. He then looked at Ross. 'Still nothing on the bookmaker case?'

'Not yet,' he replied, 'unless someone comes forward with some information...' He trailed off with a shrug. Avalon nodded and turned to Wilson.

'Have you got anything on?'

'Aye, plenty tae do but we can give you a hand ef y' need et,' replied Wilson.

'No,' said Avalon, 'not at the moment, stick with what you are working on until we need you.' He then looked back to Ross and Rutherford. 'You two make your way to the quarry. The excavation is due to start at nine-thirty. I'll follow on.' He let them leave and then spoke to Frazer. 'There isn't much point in carrying on with the missing person search. If Sarah Underwood is correct, we might have to go back twenty years.' Megan nodded once more.

'So what shall I do?' she asked.

'Forensics are doing more tests on the soil samples this morning, I need to know what they find, as they find it, so keep in touch with them. I also need to

153

know if there have been any incidents in the past with a poison called ricin. If anything crops up, I need to know.' She raised her brows and began tapping keys to research ricin before she did anything else. 'DC White,' announced Avalon, 'meet me at the quarry. We have a long day ahead of us.'

By the time Avalon had arrived at the quarry, the early clouds had cleared and it was turning into a sunny day. A breeze was rising from the southwest however, and so the team had begun the excavation without the tent. They were well underway by the time Avalon arrived and, as per his instructions, they were attending the area where 'Sandy' had been found. He walked over to the spot to where White and Rutherford were closely watching the proceedings. Three of the forensics team, including Sarah, were carefully sifting through the sand with tiny trowels and brushes. It looked more like an archaeological dig than a crime scene.

'Where's Ross?' asked Avalon, looking at Rutherford.

'Back at his car, he's on the phone,' and he nodded towards the BMW. Avalon made his way towards the car and the open door, but as he got closer, he could tell from the way Ross was speaking, he was in conversation with his girlfriend. Ross saw him and holding the phone to his chest asked,

'You want me?' Avalon shook his head with a wry smile and returned to the dig. It was an anxious time, Avalon hoped there wasn't a body there at all, as, if there was, someone had met a terrible end. But on the other hand, he didn't want them to be wrong. In the hole, one of the technicians, he couldn't tell who, was still moving small amounts of debris away, and gradually, they could see the colour changing as they reached the level under the sand. They would stop now and then to take samples, placing them in small containers to be labelled. Avalon sniffed the air as Ross joined them at the scene.

'Girlfriend?' asked Avalon. Ross nodded, and then as if to change the subject asked,

'So they've not found anything?'

'Not yet.'

'How deep are you going to dig?' he then asked.

'Not far,' replied Avalon, 'I wouldn't have thought the soil sample would have been contaminated unless a body was close to it.'

'You think we got it wrong?' asked Ross, still looking over to the dig.

'Probably,' nodded Avalon, looking up at the blue sky. 'It's likely that it's just an anomaly from the fluids mixing with the sand.' He shrugged. He didn't know the science behind it all. He would just wait and see what turned up. Ross's phone rang. Avalon wondered if it was the girlfriend ringing back and so did Ross, as he turned away and said,

'DS Ross.' He was silent for a moment until Avalon heard him suddenly say, 'really, where was this?' There was another pause until he eventually added, 'okay, I'll get DC Rutherford to come and sort it out, thanks for letting me know.' He put his phone away and turned back to Avalon with a grin on his face. 'They've got Serle, the bookmaker thief.'

'Who's got him?' asked Avalon, wondering who else was working on the case.

'An ambulance was sent to an address near

Culloden. It seems he had an argument with the girlfriend and she stuck a knife in him. One of the uniform lads recognised him, so they arrested the girlfriend and put a guard on him at the hospital.'

'He's not dead then?'

'It seems not,' smiled Ross, 'loss of blood from an arm wound. The girlfriend sent for the ambulance because she thought he was going to die.'

'Obviously she doesn't realise that if you stab people you can hurt them,' replied Avalon with disgust. 'Okay, you better get off,' he added.

'Martin can deal with it, I'll stay here,' replied Ross and then as an afterthought, 'if that's okay with you?' Avalon didn't answer. He just looked back at the dig. As Rutherford was leaving the quarry in the pool car he had brought, there was a discussion in the hole and Avalon heard his name mentioned.

'DI, we have something.' Avalon stepped over the cordon and moved to the dig. The top of what looked to be a skull was showing. Someone was taking photographs, and Avalon sighed.

'Okay, let's see what we have,' and he watched as the team carefully removed soil and shale from the area. Gradually, it became clear it was the forehead part of the skull, but as it was unearthed, they got a shock. The skull was small, very small, and everyone could see they were dealing with the death of a child. Avalon swallowed and knew the case had suddenly taken a darker turn. It would now become a much more difficult case. He wondered if they were dealing with a serial killer and that was daunting. It was something he had never worked on before, and he stared for some at the little skull before it was covered temporarily with a forensic sheet. The team

156

would now want to surround it with their tent and it would take time to secure. He looked to his right and stared blankly at Ross, who was also thinking through the situation. He looked over to Avalon and, for a second or two, there was no expression. The DI didn't want to talk about what they had found at that moment, and decided to cross the barrier and speak with the dig team. He explained that the whole site would have to be excavated at that same depth, and he then returned to his car. There was a great deal to do. They would need a small excavator, and some means to move the spoil. Most of the work would probably have to be done by hand, but the heavier work could be accomplished by a machine. He also needed to ring the site manager and explain that the area was to be out of bounds. Ross walked slowly back to where the cars were parked and asked simply,

'What do you want me to do?' Avalon wasn't sure what they could do until the site was cleared.

'You better get back and help Martin,' he said, 'we can't do anymore here until the site has been thoroughly searched.' Ross nodded solemnly and left. He then set White on sorting out the excavator, and then he rang the DCI.

'*Shit!*' was her first reply to the news. '*So I assume you're digging the whole area?*' she then asked.

'Yes,' replied Avalon, 'God knows what we're going to find here.'

'*Okay,*' she sighed, obviously troubled by the news, '*I'll get in touch with MIT, this could be big, very big.*'

'What about press?' asked Avalon, unsure if she had the same aversion to the newspapers as DCI Croker.

'*For now,*' she said, '*I'll just inform them that we have found a body, no details yet.*' She was about to end the call when Avalon thought of something he had told her once, but he considered it was only fair to remind her.

'Oh, did you contact Detective Chief Inspector Liam Robertson at MIT?'

'*Haven't you mentioned him before, what's this about?*' she asked in an impatient tone.

'It's just that he knows me, I didn't want you-' but he was interrupted.

'*I'll sort MIT out DI Avalon. You concentrate on finding out what else is in that ground.*' And she ended the call. Avalon sighed and sat in the driver's seat, wedging the door open with his foot to allow the sunshine into the car. It was still breezy, and though it gave the dig-team a little trouble putting up the tent, it wasn't as strong as it could have been on that exposed site. He leaned back onto the headrest and tried to clear his mind. A child's body had been found buried below a woman's body. The child had died previously to the woman, that was obvious from the soil samples, but could they have been related? If they were, then this probably wasn't a serial killer. The more he thought about that, he knew that wasn't what they had. A serial killer usually follows patterns. In the killer's mind, there is a reason. A serial killer would choose women, or he may even target children, but both? It seemed unlikely, but Avalon couldn't quite grasp any other situation that might cover this. They would have to wait until the site had been fully searched, and that could take some serious time. He looked up at the blue patches of sky between the wispy clouds and then down to the sandy ground where the open door cast a shadow. He watched a tiny ant scurrying along, making short work of the obstacles in its way. He wished he was more like that ant, determined and resolute, coping with whatever life threw at him. But he wasn't such an animal, and emotions, the very thing that made him human also caused him problems. Seeing the skull of a child had brought him up against a checkpoint. He knew, of all the things that a detective would see in his career, the death of children affect them the most. It didn't matter that they didn't have their own children, although it must trouble those that did, even more. It was just the utter futility and waste of a life that was never able to achieve, or learn, or experience what it is to live a full life. He found he was staring at the shadow on the ground, and he could see it moving. That surprised him. He had never considered it before, but yes, he could just make out the shadow of the car door creeping along. The sun above seemed almost static, and yet here on the floor, it was moving. It suddenly made him feel very aware of his mortality, and he considered that watching that shadow scurry along like the ant, time was running out. The body in that grave had never had the chance to think those thoughts. It probably never even considered its mortality before someone snuffed out its life. He shivered and shook himself free from the thought. He knew people who had done so much with their lives, and yet he had done so little. He was well over forty, fast approaching fifty and he had done nothing important with his time. He was sitting in a desolate quarry, watching a shadow become longer by the second, waiting for yet another set of bones to be excavated in the hope they could catch the person who had committed the crime. Certainly, some people would say it was worthwhile, some would even say honourable, but at that moment, to Avalon, it seemed dead-end. Not just dead-end, it seemed pointless. There was always another person ready to take life, why? Because society allowed it, and they allowed it because people like him would dirty their hands and their minds for the good of the populous. He suddenly felt tired and for some reason, he began to get a headache. He climbed out of the car and took a deep breath of air. He knew he did the job he did because it felt natural to him, to analyse it was never going to solve problems. He knew these moments came with certain cases, and he also knew he just had to work through the pain barrier and get his second wind. His phone rang.

'Avalon!' his reply was harsher than he intended.

'*Boss, et's Megan,*' came the reply, '*I've found something interesting to do with this ricin poison.*'

'Go on,' he said in a lighter tone.

'*Someone called Christopher Joyce,*' she replied, '*he was accused of poisoning his neighbour's dogs. A vet confirmed that ricin was used.*'

'When was this?'

'*About fifteen years ago,*' she replied, '*but the charges were dropped as there was no proof.*'

'I see,' sighed Avalon.

'*But,*' continued Frazer, '*it wasn't the first time either, he had been accused of the same crime, or similar at least, two years before that.*'

'Does he live locally?'

'*Somewhere up north, from what I can gather,*' was her vague reply.

'We'll have a look at that later, for the moment,'

insisted Avalon, 'I'm stuck down here, and we have another body.'

'*Shite,*' she said. '*Another female?*' She was also wondering about a serial killer.

'We don't know yet,' he replied, omitting further details, 'but I'm going to be here some time. I've sent Rossy and Martin off to sort out the bookmaker case.'

'*Do you want me to do anythin' else?*'

'No,' he said, 'just stay available in case I need something following up.' She told him she would follow up on Christopher Joyce while she waited. Avalon placed his phone back in his pocket and went to find DC White.

On the face of it, White seemed fairly unmoved by the sight of the small skull in the ground. He was sitting on a rise in the ground some thirty feet away, glancing around the area.

'Anything happened?' asked Avalon as he closed in. White stood.

'I think they have most of the body uncovered,' he replied and then glanced over to the white tent.

'Let's take a look then,' and they once more crossed the tape and walked to the tent. There wasn't much room inside, and so Avalon pushed his head around the flap.

'How's it going?' he asked. Sarah wasn't there and the Scenes of Crime officer was working in her place. The man was new to Avalon but seemed thorough and quick.

'We have everything exposed, just collecting samples for forensics, Detective Inspector,' he said from within the mask. Avalon nodded, 'another half hour should see us finished,' he added. Avalon couldn't help glancing down at the pathetic skeleton in the base of the trench. He withdrew and turned to White.

'We better tell the pathologist we're ready for him,' he said.

'Do you want me to do it?' asked White. It seemed he was at last doing what he was paid to do.

'Yes, I'll have a word with forensics,' sighed Avalon, 'let's hope this is it.'

'It will be sir,' nodded White.

'You sound sure of yourself,' said Avalon, as White was dialling the pathologist's office.

'It's not likely to be a serial killer,' he frowned. Avalon was seeing that he wasn't the only one looking at that as a poor option. 'It doesn't fit the MO of that kind of killer,' he added.

'So do you have another theory?' he asked, but White got through on his phone.

'Pathologist's office? It's DC White, Inverness CID.' Avalon left as White continued the call and he went to find Sarah. He didn't get to hear if White had a theory or not, for as he closed on Sarah sitting in the back of the forensics van, she asked him a question.

'So, what do you make of that?' Avalon looked at the sky again.

'I have no idea. It doesn't fit with anything I have experienced.'

'Could it be a serial murderer?' she asked. Avalon shook his head.

'I doubt it. I can't offer an alternative though, and that worries me.'

'A child makes it much worse, it's going to be a strain on everyone,' she added.

'Yes,' replied Avalon softly, and he glanced down to her. They waited, silently. Sarah, sitting on the ledge of the rear of the van, and Avalon leaning on a car beside it. She eventually looked up to him and he could feel her eyes on him.

'Isn't it odd?' she began, 'we can meet here for work purposes, but we can't meet for social reasons.'

'I was thinking that myself,' he said with a blank expression. 'I suppose this is a unique situation,' and he glanced down to her.

'We've been promised regular testing,' she sighed, 'but I suppose nothing will come of it.'

'That will only tell you if you have the virus, it won't stop us catching it,' replied Avalon.

'I realise that, but this could go on for some time,' she protested. He could tell there was some strain in her voice. He crouched, leaning against the vehicle, and looked into her eyes.

'Given your job and your experience,' he said with concern in his eyes, 'how long do you really think this could go on?' She blinked several times. It was obvious she had already given it some thought.

'While I was down in Fife,' she eventually said, 'I had a conversation with a very highly regarded doctor in the viral field. It was his opinion that a vaccine for this kind of virus could take ten years to refine. We could be entering a new era of social change.' Avalon gave a slight nod.

'So what you're saying,' he asked, 'is that we may have to live with this for some considerable time?' He looked hard into her face and added, 'years in fact?' She gave him a vague expression.

'It's possible,' she began. 'All these viruses come from the same source. China, and while they continue to eat wild animals, this will continue to happen.' She paused for a moment then added, 'and one day, we may see a super virus.'

'Another reason to be vegan,' nodded Avalon emphatically.

'Yes,' she sighed, 'these viruses never come from plants, but unfortunately, we can all die from it once the epidemic starts.' He stood and thought deeply about it. 'I'd better get back to work,' she said, and gave him a sullen glance as she passed.

As Avalon drove back to the office, he was thinking through the case to get his mind off the subject of the virus. He looked at what he knew about the case as it stood. The pathologist had examined the site and commented that the second skeleton was indeed of a young child, but he would only make a guess about its age based on measurements. He had also said that the body had been 'cast' into the hole as it wasn't laid out carefully. That fit with the first body and was already beginning to look like a similar burial. So, from Avalon's perspective, a child was either killed, or had died, and was unlawfully buried by someone who had little regard for the infant. Sometime after, an adult female had been killed, probably poisoned, and had not just been buried close by, but right over the first grave. That body too, seemed to be dumped in a much shallower grave. Could the two bodies be related, genetically or otherwise? Both were likely. The pathologist had also agreed that, as in the case of the adult, there was no obvious cause of death for the child. He also wondered that if DNA was proving to be difficult to extract from the first skeleton, it was likely that the second one would be even more difficult. Old-fashioned police work would have to come into play, and that would take time.

As he pulled into the car park of the police station, he was suddenly aware that he had heard someone saying, he couldn't remember quite who, that B Section was looking at new information that had come to light on a very old case. He would have to see DI Lasiter to find out if their cases were linked. As he entered The Cave, he glanced automatically at the clock and checked his watch. It was becoming a habit.

'I've got all the info on Christopher Joyce ef you want et.' It was Frazer and she was holding a folder. The records must go back some time if there was still a paper record of it.

'Bring it with you,' he called and nodded to the booth. 'So what have you found?' he asked as they both sat.

'He's got a record, but nothing serious,' she explained. 'He has appeared en court four times, once for the incident with ricin, twice for assault, and once for a breach of the peace. All old cases, nothing recent. He seems to be one of those people who would rather throw a punch than say hello.'

'Does he seem like a poisoner?'

'Not really, but that doesn't mean anything. After all, it's likely he poisoned his neighbour's dogs.' she shrugged. Avalon cast his eyes around the room as White returned. It was quiet as everyone else was out.

'Sounds like a nice sort. Well, we better send someone to talk to him either way,' nodded the DI.

'It seems DI Lasiter knows about him, his name appears several times on his record,' added Frazer as an afterthought.

'I have to see the DI, so I'll ask him about it,' and

he reached into the folder to find a photograph of the man.

'Et's a pretty old image that,' announced Frazer, but Avalon stood and said,

'It's probably how he looked the last time the DI saw him.'

B Section's office was even less populated than The Cave, with just DI Lasiter and DS Murrey going over some details on their whiteboard.

'Allo Jim, what can we do y' for?' Avalon placed the photograph on the desk in front of them, but it was Murrey who was the first to comment.

'There's a face from the past,'

'What do you know of him?' asked Avalon and gave a weak smile.

'Only two things,' admitted the quiet speaking Murrey, 'Christopher Joyce isn't his real name, and he's a hard bastard.'

'He's not so hard,' disagreed Lasiter, 'yeah he's apt tae start swinging, but he's usually provoked.'

'It sounds as if you have some...' Avalon trailed off, looking for the right word, 'respect?'

'Not respect,' frowned Lasiter, 'but I do think he's a wee bit misunderstood.' Lasiter seemed happy enough with the explanation and looked down at the photograph. 'So what's the interest en him?'

'The poison called ricin,' explained Avalon. 'We think the body found at the quarry may have connections with the substance.' Lasiter pursed his lips and then folded his arms.

'Y' know, nothing was proved that he had anything tae do with that?'

'Yeah, right,' nodded Avalon, casting Lasiter an ironic frown. 'Whether he poisoned dogs or not, it's something I have to check on. Do you know where he lives now?'

'I heard he retired, somewhere up north on the coast.'

'Retired?' asked Avalon, 'retired from what? His record says he was a welder.'

'Aye, he was a welder,' nodded Lasiter, 'a good one by all accounts. Learned his trade on the ships en Glasgow. He's a bit of a recluse though. Hates people with a passion, so I doubt you'll get a warm welcome.'

'I'm not planning on having tea with him, I just want to rule him out,' Avalon squinted at Lasiter, 'or rule him in to our investigation,' Avalon paused. 'You say it isn't his real name?' he then asked.

'That's right,' nodded Lasiter, unfolding his arms and sitting on a desk. 'His dad used tae knock his mother around when he was a wean, and when he grew big enough, he beat his dad t' a pulp for et. He would have gone down ef et wasnae for the circumstances. He and his mother left, and he got a job near Perth. He hated the old man so much, he decided to get rid o' his name. He did et all official too. Joyce was his mother's first name.'

'His original name was Jarvie, Christopher Jarvie,' added Murrey. Avalon nodded and then got to the next subject.

'You're working on an old case with a missing person, I was wondering if there may be a connection with the bodies at the quarry.'

'Bodies plural?' asked Lasiter with a surprised look.

'I'm afraid so. We found a second body of a child

167

this morning.'

'Hmm,' exclaimed Lasiter, 'et already occurred to us that et fit. We have a suspect but we don't know where the body es, and on the face of et, there are similarities.'

'We're just looking for one body though,' explained Murrey, 'and the age of the victim doesn't match.'

'We'll keep an eye on et though,' added Lasiter, and he gave the name of the victim so that Avalon could look at the file and compare it with what they found.

As Avalon walked back to the office, he was struck by the similarities of the two cases, but either way, there was enough to make them very separate investigations. As he entered the office, he glanced at his watch. The time was racing by. He heard Frazer's voice.

'Oh, wait a minute, he's just come en.' She held the receiver to her shoulder and added in a lower voice, 'Et's a DI Robertson from Strathclyde CID,' and she placed the phone on the desk. Avalon took a deep breath in and exhaled slowly. He then picked up the receiver and said,

'Hello Liam, it's the wrong time to be booking a holiday at Porto del Inverness-shire.'

Chapter Eight

'*Porto del Inverness-shire is it now?*' laughed DI Robertson, '*if I had time for a holiday, it would be somewhere warmer than Inverness.*'

'So if I can't book you a holiday, what else can I do for you?' asked Avalon with a broad smile on his face, remembering the affable nature of Robertson.

'*Well, it's these bodies you found, I was wondering if you could fit this in?*' asked the man. '*We have two other MIT officers up there, but we're all pulled out at the moment.*' Avalon wondered if Robertson realised how odd his words sounded. He had spoken as if Avalon had found a gold broach down the back of his sofa, not two bodies in a quarry. '*Can you drop onto it?*' he added.

'I'm working on it at the moment, but yes, I would like to keep with it.'

'*You're already on it, that's odd?*' mused Robertson.

'Odd, why?' asked Avalon.

'*Well, I've just spoken to one of your DCI's and she didna mention you were already on it.*'

'She's standing in,' admitted Avalon, 'and we

don't exactly see eye to eye, and…' he paused. Robertson had already witnessed Avalon's playful character at first hand, so he guessed what was coming.

'*So, you never told her you had been with us for a few months? That's why she rang us then.*' Avalon smiled as he thought about the DCI speaking with MIT.

'That about covers it,' added Avalon.

'*She mentioned one set of remains are of a child.*' Robertson spoke with an amount of sadness in his voice.

'Yes, we found them this morning,' admitted Avalon, 'I had the whole site excavated, just in case.'

'*Aye, okay, it sounds like you have it all covered then,*' replied the DI and Avalon could hear another conversation going on in the background. '*Do you need other officers or is there someone there you can borrow?*'

'I've been put back in charge of my old team, they're a good bunch. I'll keep it with them if that's okay.'

'*Aye, no bother,*' replied Robertson, '*I'll let you get on then, and Jim, let me know if you need anyone, it's busy but I'm sure I can round a couple up from somewhere.*' Avalon thanked him and replaced the handset. He decided to go straight to the Chief and get the confrontation over with. The DCI was typing as she motioned to the chair. Avalon sat this time and waited for her to speak.

'I have been in touch with the DI you mentioned,' she began looking at him over her spectacles, 'he told me you have had recent training with MIT.'

'Yes, I did almost four months on and off,' nodded the DI.

'And you chose not to tell me?' He sensed anger in her tone, though she seemed outwardly calm.

'I did ask you to contact DI Robertson, and I wasn't sure if they would sanction me heading the investigation,' he explained. She stared at him for a moment, then, as she pushed her spectacles up the bridge of her nose she said,

'I still do not see why you didn't inform me.'

'I'm sorry Ma'am, in hindsight, maybe I should have,' he said, and to get quickly off the subject, he added, 'I came to see you about the quarry case.' He paused to let it sink in. 'We have found another body at the site as you know, but, it was under the spot where the first one was found.' She furrowed her brows a little. 'The second set of remains are confirmed as a child, we don't know what age yet, but they have been taken to the forensics lab.'

'Dear god,' she said, and removed her spectacles. For the first time Avalon saw her eyes. They were puffy and slightly red rimmed, not as if she had been crying, more the look of someone who didn't sleep a great deal. He considered that if B Section saw her now, they would be calling her The Vampire and not the Plague Witch.

'I have had the whole site excavated and fortunately, there are no other remains. We have yet to establish cause of death or how long they have been there.'

'Do you have any leads?' she asked, replacing the glasses.

'A few tenuous ones, but we need to establish the identity of the female first,' explained Avalon. 'Forensics wants to send at least parts of the skeleton to Dundee for further analysis and I was considering letting them do a facial reconstruction.' The Chief nodded at this.

'The press are going to be interested when they learn a child is involved,' she frowned.

'I would say so, yes,' agreed Avalon, 'the bones of an anonymous woman who died twenty years ago, are probably of passing interest to them, but the child makes a difference.'

'Indeed,' she replied, beginning to type on her keyboard. 'I'll speak with the press office, in the meantime, if you need anything, let me know.' Then, ceasing her typing and looking straight at Avalon, she added, 'and I wish to be kept informed at every stage DI Avalon.'

'Yes Ma'am,' he nodded, then stood and left.

Tuesday morning brought the news that there were over seven thousand deaths from the Covid virus in the UK, and at last, they had confirmation that regular tests were being implemented for his staff. It was one of the many issues he would have to deal with during the course of the day. Firstly, he had to set out the important tasks for the team.

'How are you going on with the bookmaker case?' he asked as he walked up to Ross. He had read the reports Ross and Rutherford had filed, but he asked anyway.

'It's all over but the shouting,' replied Ross, 'Serle is still tight-lipped but the girlfriend was co-operative and we got her to sign a statement. She even told us where the remainder of the cash is hidden. We just need the search warrant and that should seal it.'

'The warrant should come through soon,' said Avalon, and then added, 'I could do with someone checking out on a lead concerning the quarry case.

'Check our diary Martin,' replied Ross, 'have we got time to fit this in?'

'We have to be at Lady Charlotte's place for cocktails later, but I would think we can manage it,' smiled Rutherford.

'Christopher Joyce, no serious previous but he is handy with his fist and doesn't like visitors,' explained Avalon.

'Sounds like my sort of person,' smiled Rutherford again.

'He was once accused of killing a neighbour's dogs but the case was dropped due to lack of evidence,' added Avalon, 'the connection is ricin.'

'That's the poison found in the remains, so he used ricin to kill the dogs?' asked Ross.

'As I said, the case was dropped, so you will need to tread carefully. Check his case notes before you go. DI Lasiter seems to think the man isn't the ogre his record says but knowing John Lasiter...' he trailed off though both Ross and Rutherford knew what the DI was getting at.

'So, have we got an address?' asked Ross. Avalon did have an address. Based on Lasiter's comments, he had checked Local Council records and found where Joyce lived, and he knew it wouldn't please Ross. He wrote the address on a scrap of paper and handed it to him, changing the subject as he did.

'I'm going over to the forensic lab this morning, I want to see if anything has been found on the new remains.' Ross nodded knowingly until he read the address on the paper.

'Shite,' he exclaimed, 'why do I get all the trips

173

up north?' Rutherford leaned over to read it.

'Och man, it's a lovely day again, it'll be a nice wee jaunt. Better than being in the office,' he grinned. Rutherford was correct, in Avalon's opinion. It was yet another pleasant day and in some ways, he was a little jealous. He was going to be inside a lab, looking over some human remains, and wishing he was somewhere else. At least he would get to see Sarah.

An hour later, he was indeed at the lab and Sarah was explaining what they had found out about the tiny skeleton laid on the inspection bench.

'As the pathologist had said, there is no obvious cause of death,' she began, 'and also like the pathologist, we don't know the sex of the child.'

'So you don't have any ideas about that?' asked Avalon.

'Not really,' she admitted, 'sexual dimorphism isn't pronounced on pre-adolescent children. The best I can offer is a wild guess that wouldn't be any use to you. The acetabulum, that's the socket in the pelvis from which the head of the femur is secured, is usually larger in males, but without a similar sized, and known example, I can't say. You would need a forensic anthropologist for that.'

'So, another reason to send them to Dundee,' he sighed and Sarah nodded. 'Okay,' he added, 'let's get them over there, I would like a facial reconstruction performing on Sandy too.'

'I was going to suggest that,' said Sarah. The two of them were silent for a moment and then Avalon asked,

'I'm guessing you didn't find ricin in the child's bones?'

174

'No,' she replied looking around to him, 'nothing to suggest any type of poisoning, but I have my suspicions that this child wasn't as healthy as it ought to have been.'

'You think it was neglected?' he asked, raising his brows.

'I don't know, maybe not neglected, probably just ill. There's nothing concrete, just a few little anomalies,' she frowned, 'but the bone expert in Dundee is one of the best in the world. They have tests that can even detect ink from tattoos in lymph glands.'

'How long do you think it will take?' he asked.

'I suppose that will depend on the workload they have.' Avalon nodded, it was a stupid question anyway. It would take as long as it took, and he knew that. He looked down at the small set of bones and he felt a wave of sadness that this poor child had been denied a normal life. The tiny ribs were perfectly formed, even though they had been in the ground for so long. Their growth stopped, like a broken watch, telling the same time forever, and no one would know who this person could have become, how it may have influenced the world, for good, or ill. He sighed deeply.

'Have you got to get back?' came Sarah's voice, pulling him from his thoughts.

'Why? Have you got something else for me?' She frowned at this, and Avalon was confused. She tilted her head to the office and walked away, he followed. She walked through the office and opened the door to the outside and waited in the tiny car park.

'What is it?' asked Avalon, unsure what was happening, and she closed the door behind him so they were alone outside. She glanced up at the CCTV camera and moved towards the vehicles to be out of its gaze.

'This lockdown is getting to me a little,' she said, casting him a glance that he didn't quite understand.

'Is this to do with the conversation we had yesterday?' he asked, but she didn't reply. He then added, 'I admit, most of us are having to change our lives,' he agreed, but he could offer little else. She leaned on the rear of his car and he walked slightly to the side and rested his arms on the roof.

'Given what we spoke of, this could be semi-permanent,' she frowned, 'and that could change…' she paused, and Avalon could see something in her eyes that wasn't a common sight in Sarah, doubt. She had her doubts from time to time, he knew that, but rarely did she show them.

'I'm not sure what you're getting at,' this time *he* paused. He thought he knew, but didn't want to jump the gun. 'Are you… are you talking about us?' She gave a small sigh and then the briefest of nods.

'I was thinking about our conversation last night. No…' she suddenly amended the statement, 'I was thinking about *you* last night,' It made Avalon's stomach flutter a little. 'I really wanted to come round and see you.' He tried to keep his features impassive.

'That would have been nice I have to admit. It's just with this lockdown…' more pauses.

'I know in my position I shouldn't say this but… I bet you can't stay two metres away from your team, can you?' He shook his head.

'No, it's impossible. We just do what we can to get the job done. Every day we walk into someone, or pass something across and touch hands. As many have already said, it's impossible to stay with it all day.' he

176

admitted.

'Same here,' she said, 'and I am quite aware that the risk of spreading the virus takes president but...' she paused, hoping he was guessing what she was saying. He wasn't sure he should continue down that route. He wanted to take her in his arms, even without her saying she wanted to be with him. It then struck him as odd. For this past year, she had built an invisible wall, or at least he thought she had. A barrier that stopped them linking as they should have. Only now, during a lockdown, when they were supposed to stay separate, did she seem closer to him than anytime previously.

'I don't know what to suggest, we're not the only ones. There are a few at the nick in the same position.' She looked at the floor and Avalon had the impression he hadn't told her what she wanted to hear. 'We're not even getting the amount of virus tests we were promised,' he added.

'What did you expect? They talk and talk, and the public believe it, I'm not one bit surprised. We already have one of the highest death rates in the world from this virus, it all makes me sick.' Avalon was taken aback, not from what she had said, he agreed with her. He was more surprised that she had even voiced an opinion, and with such venom. It was the first time he had heard her give any opinion about politics at all.

'It's getting to us all,' sympathised Avalon, 'but it won't be forever, we just have to toe the line until we know more about it.' He was trying to make her feel better, he didn't really believe what he was saying, and she knew it. Their conversation the previous day had seen to that. His distrust of the government was absolute. He had spent too many years in the police force not to know panicked rhetoric when he heard it. 'Do you need to talk?' he asked, wondering if something else was troubling her.

'No,' she sighed, 'I'm probably just being selfish,' and she stood upright and pulled her lab coat closer around her. Avalon didn't want the conversation to end like this. He could tell she was about to go back into the lab, and it would mean them parting without resolving anything. He moved towards her.

'Listen,' he began, 'we both live alone, we have no family living close to us.' He wasn't sure where he was going with it, but he continued. 'If we were married, or even living together, we wouldn't give it a second thought.' He was formulating an idea, but he could just perceive a tiny frown creasing the corners of her eyes. 'Come round, come to my place,' he said, and wondered if he was moving a little too quickly. 'I'm not suggesting you move in permanently, and I'm not saying we should consider that it's living together, just staying at the same house.' His pause was just to take breath. He needed to explain his idea fully before she put a stop to his plan. 'There's plenty of space there, as you know, and you could have your own room. Let's call it, a temporary marriage of convenience.' She was staring at him. 'At least think it over,' he added as he examined her features. She had grown her hair over the past year, and it had gone darker. He didn't think it suited her quite as much as other styles she had worn, but she still looked fabulous to him. She was dressed more casually than usual too. Under the lab coat she wore a tee shirt with jeans, not her usual working attire. He looked at her makeup too and noticed it wasn't as pronounced as normal. She said nothing, and he wondered what she was thinking. He had gone out on a limb and he had done his bit. It was up to her now and as a final gesture, he leaned towards her, gently taking her head between his hands and kissed her softly.

'I don't care about the consequences,' he smiled, think it over,' he smiled again and got into the car, watching her through his rear-view mirror. As he pulled out of the car park, he saw her standing stock still. She didn't even wave to him, and he wondered if he had done the right thing. Just for a second or two, there was doubt. Then he smiled to himself. He didn't care. It was what he felt was right, and he could still taste Miss Sarah Underwood on his lips.

Ross pulled into a layby on the narrow lane just off the A9. He turned off the radio which was playing one of the usual songs that the station, like every other station, played over and over again. He got out of the car and breathed in the cool air as Rutherford pulled in behind him in a pool car. The weather was fine, that was true, but he hated anywhere north of Inverness. He didn't even know why. He just knew that there was a lot of land in the Highlands, and anywhere he had to go was always hours away.

'Is this it?' asked Rutherford, pulling on his jacket as he locked the car.

'No,' growled Ross, 'I just stopped to take photos of the nothingness.'

'What is it with you and the north Highlands?' asked Rutherford, 'I love it.'

'Can you hear that?' asked Ross, holding up a finger. Rutherford listened for a moment and then said,

'I can't hear a thing.'

'And doesn't that freak you out? 'cos it does me,' frowned Ross.

'It's just peaceful, no traffic, no pollution-'

'No reason to come here,' interrupted Ross.

'Let's speak to this Christopher Joyce before you get a panic attack,' said Rutherford, shaking his head. Joyce's house was hidden away behind trees in a large plot of land with landscaped gardens. As Ross walked up to the double gates, he saw a man snipping away at a small bush with gardening shears. He was thick-set and was wearing a wide-brimmed hat, which looked incongruous given the rest of his casual clothing.

'Hello,' called out Ross as Rutherford stood close to him, 'we're looking for Mr Joyce, Christopher Joyce.' As the man turned, the bright sun glinted off the blades of the shears. He gave the shears a little shake, which opened the blade, and then he held them as if they were a weapon. 'We've got a live one here,' whispered Ross out of the side of his mouth.

'Not the best choice of a weapon though,' answered Rutherford in the same kind of whisper. The man slowly approached.

'Who's looking for him?'

'Detective Sergeant Ross, Inverness CID.'

'Well, you can piss off,' he answered aggressively, and he continued to close the distance. Ross almost smiled, the situation was ridiculous, but he managed to hold it back.

'We need to speak to Mr Joyce, it's a matter of urgency,' explained Ross.

'That's your emergency, not mine,' glowered the man. Ross could see this was indeed Mr Joyce, he was somewhat older than he was in the photograph in his file, but it was certainly him.

'It won't take a minute Mr Joyce, just a couple of questions,' insisted Ross. Rutherford was continually amazed by Ross, the way he could change from being an antagonistic buffoon into a professional police officer in the blink of an eye. It was incredible to watch. The man stopped at what could probably be measured as two metres. He still held the shears in a menacing way, but he didn't answer. 'We've come a long way to speak to you Mr Joyce and we have a long journey back,' continued Ross, 'and I'm sure it's easier to talk here rather than you coming down to Inverness.'

'You'll need a warrant to get me down there,' he scowled.

'We would, and we would have to make this journey again, but...' Ross shrugged as he trailed off. He sighed and began turning.

'What's it about?' asked the man suddenly.

'Well,' began Ross turning back towards him, 'we would like to ask you about a compound,' he thought it was a better word than poison, 'called ricin.' For a second, the man looked puzzled, and then the penny dropped.

'So you're going to dig that shite up again?' asked the man with a deep frown. His accent was a mix of Inverness and borders, similar to Lasiter but not as pronounced.

'We just want to ask you about...' Ross paused. What did they want to ask him about? If he asked the man if he had killed people as well as dogs he may as well turn around now. He thought in a split second of a reasonable question. 'Well, about the acquisition of this compound.'

'You do know I was acquitted over that incident?' asked the man, Ross nodded. 'So what makes you think I would know anything about it?'

'We have come across it in another case and we are obliged to follow up on everything we know about it,' explained Ross. 'As you can imagine, not many names were flagged, but yours was one of them.'

'So someone's dog has been poisoned and you want to know if I did it?' asked the man shaking his head. He turned and began to walk away. Ross looked at Rutherford and shrugged.

'Not a dog, Mr Joyce,' called Ross, 'a woman, and it was about fifteen years ago.' Ross decided to leave out details about the second body and he didn't have facts about the date, but he thought it would resonate with the man. It did, and the man suddenly spoke and turned around as he did so.

'I was born in a rough part of Glasgow in a society that was so toxic that I'm amazed I survived it.' He paused and looked around him. 'You smell that?' he continued, 'that is the start of the Rowan blossom. Some people don't like it but I love it. Mainly because it doesn't smell of dockyards, steel mills, of decay. I love the smell of it because I can stand here and smell it whenever I want,' the tone of his voice became harsher as he continued. 'And you think I would compromise that, this freedom just to snuff out someone I didn't like? By Christ, it would have to be a better reason than that.' The man ceased and Ross felt relieved. He thought he was about to hear the man's life story and he didn't have the patience.

'I wasn't accusing you of anything Mr Joyce, but you must understand, we have to rule you out of our investigation.' He walked back towards the two detectives, a little quicker than he left.

'And with that statement you are making it clear, that you and your brethren down in Inverness don't see me as innocent, so it doesn't matter that nothing was proven, I'm still guilty.'

'You must understand, Mr Joyce,' replied Ross calmly, 'we are investigating a murder, possibly a double murder, and our records show one name when it comes to the use of ricin. If only to eliminate you from-'

'Do you know what innocent means?' growled the man. Ross said nothing. He simply looked casually at the man. 'It means, not guilty, it means not involved with the crime.'

'That's a dictionary definition,' cut in Rutherford, 'in legal terms it just means, nothing can be proven.'

'Who's the ape, has he got a growing disease?' spat the man at Ross without looking at Rutherford. Ross sighed, the big man's input hadn't helped much and then Rutherford continued.

'I'm normal size,' he frowned, 'everyone else is small.' Joyce looked up at Rutherford for the first time. For some reason, he seemed to calm and there were a few seconds of silence before he looked back to Ross. Slowly he said,

'If you come again, bring an arrest warrant,' and he turned and walked up the drive. Ross looked at him for a moment and then without a word, he turned and walked away. As Rutherford caught him up he said,

'That went well, what we gonna tell the boss?' asked Ross.

'Tell him the truth, we'll get nothing out of him,' replied Rutherford.

183

'I hate coming north,' spat Ross, 'it always seems a waste of time.' He stopped and looked at Rutherford. 'So how did you think that your comment would help the situation then, hot shot?' Rutherford thought for a few seconds then said,

'I got sick of the arsehole in half a minute. It was either that or punch him.' Ross glared at him for a moment and shook his head.

'And you had the audacity to tell me to do things by the book,' said Ross, shaking his head. 'It was obvious that this was going to be a wasted journey,' he continued, 'Anyone could be involved in this. Joyce has no connection to the quarry or that area.'

'I had a quick look on the internet before we came,' announced Rutherford, 'and you can find out how to make ricin there.'

'So did I,' admitted Ross, 'it's not rocket science.'

'Rocket science isn't rocket science,' replied Rutherford with a frown.

'What?' frowned Ross.

'Well, it isn't is it? Confine explosive materials, light blue touch paper and stand well back.'

'I think you'll find,' squinted Ross, 'getting a man to the moon was a little more complicated than making a Roman candle.'

'Getting a man to the moon has nothing to do with rocket science,' insisted the big man.

'As I recall, they used a rocket,' announced Ross, 'or was it the case that when you were at school they told you that they used a large catapult so you could understand it?'

'Rockets were used to break the earth's

atmosphere,' insisted Rutherford, 'but the journey itself used planetary gravity and hydrogen boosters.'

'Yeah, so the science is complex, lighting the blue touch paper isn't at all accurate, is it?' frowned Ross searching his pocket for his keys. Rutherford began to smile as he thought back to his youth.

'That reminds me,' he said, 'when I was little, we used to-'

'I don't want to hear it,' interrupted Ross, 'and you were never little.' He thrust one hand into his trouser pocket and the other jangled his car keys as he walked away. Rutherford raised his brows, sniffed the air and followed on, determined to drive back more slowly than Ross.

Late in the afternoon, Avalon got an email that the bones were on their way to Dundee, and though it would be a few days before they expected results, Avalon was hoping there would be a positive outcome. Sarah had also hinted that the bones could have been in the ground even longer than they had first thought. It wasn't what Avalon wanted to hear, but the bonus was, the further back they were confirmed to have been in the ground, the lesser amount of records they would have to trawl through. This was due to the fact that they could discount anyone who had gone missing after that particular date. The problem that would come with a longer time period, was more to do with people, and possible witnesses, moving out of the area, or in some cases being deceased. Ross and Rutherford had returned and told him that, as expected, Mr Joyce had been less than helpful and so glancing up at the clock, he considered that he may as well go home as there was little more he could do.

Not so very long ago his drive home would have been filled with self-doubt during a new case, thoughts of whether he had done enough or not. That was the case no longer. He always had doubts about his ability, but they no longer wore into his free time as they had once. Nevertheless, this new case was certainly causing him some consternation somewhere in the back of his mind. The waiting was always the worst part of any case, and as he pulled into the drive of his house, he was already aware that he was spending too long in the office. That could be partly due to the lockdown, which wasn't helping, after all, there was little to do back at the house. It was late and as he entered the kitchen, he decided that a quick sandwich was probably all he needed. He ate at the table in the kitchen, washed his few pots and plates, then retired to the lounge. How his life had changed. He scanned the room that was once his bolt-hole, now it was his prison, or so it seemed. He was better off than many people, that was true. At least he could still get out to work. He looked across his bookshelves, knowing that he hadn't read any poetry for some considerable time, or any of the classics that he once regarded highly. The guitar had been consigned to the loft and he couldn't remember the last time he had played any music. He had changed a great deal and his life had changed. Since working away so much, a local woman had done his cleaning, a task that he had disliked, but one he didn't balk at. He would have to take on that task himself once again now though. Another indulgence that had ceased was his occasional dram of whisky. Where once had stood four or five single malts, just a single, half empty bottle could be seen and he wasn't even sure where his rare glass was. Only the laptop was used, mainly to watch an odd movie these days, but looking at it across the room, an idea came to him. Maybe he and Sarah could link through it at night, she in her house, he, in his. A virtual candle-lit dinner was how he was seeing it. He would send her a text and suggest it. The text sent, he booted the machine up and sat at the desk to see which software would suit best. He wasn't on Facebook, so it would have to be one of the other packages out there. Once he found what he was looking for, he stared at the screen and in the back of his mind, the case popped up several times. It was bound to. He knew that, particularly a case that was proving to be rooted so far in the past. To force the subject temporarily from his mind, he opened the draw and pulled out a dog-eared business card and read the back. It was the name of a car and he typed it into the internet to see what popped up. It brought up a car that had a recommended retail price of over seventy four thousand pounds. He amended the search by typing in the year of the car he had seen in Birmingham. To his surprise, there was nothing that old for sale in Inverness. There were newer ones, but they didn't look the same, it was a car of a particular year that had made him stare. The newer ones didn't appeal to him. He wondered if a person could have the same taste in women as they do in cars, as younger women just didn't appeal to him. He laughed and shook his head, then decided to turn on the radio. Once again, this medium wasn't one he chose often. He found it difficult to find a station that he could leave on for any length of time. He had tried most stations but for one reason or another, he couldn't get used to the inane advertisements or the same twenty or so tracks they played over and over. At the moment it was tuned to Radio Two, as there were no adverts, but once one show was finished and a new one started, they would recycle the same tracks and he would turn it off. For the moment, it was a female presenter he didn't recognise and the song playing was by David Bowie, not his favourite but it was fine in the background. He then went back to the internet and searched to see if he could find a Triumph Thunderbird for sale. He wasn't thinking of selling his, but he was curious to find out what it was worth. As he was examining one particular example, his phone rang.

'Avalon.'

'*Good evening, I just received your text.*' It was Sarah.

'Oh, hello,' he stuttered, turning away from the laptop. 'I just thought it was a good idea. We could talk together and even see each other...' he paused, 'if you have a laptop or something.'

'*I could do it on my phone, but the laptop would be better,*' she admitted.

'So, shall we arrange it? I know it's always going to be if we can both make it, but this way, we can arrange it for late evening.'

'*Yes,*' she replied, '*it sounds good to me.*' Avalon nodded, even though she wasn't able to see it. She also seemed hesitant, as if she had something to tell him, but didn't know how to begin.

'Is there something wrong?' he asked, wondering if she had become sick of the sham relationship they were having. He reached over and turned off the radio.

'*No, nothing wrong,*' she said, but he still felt something. '*I just rang to say that it's a great idea, that's all, oh and...'* she paused. Here it was. The crunch part of the conversation. *'I was thinking earlier in the day, didn't you break the law by abandoning the social distancing policy?'* Avalon frowned, what was she about to say?

'It's not law, just a guideline,' he replied suspiciously.

'Oh, I suppose that's good then, seeing you are a policeman,' she replied, and though he detected a playfulness about her, he was still unsure where the conversation was going. *'So does that mean that if I break the lockdown, I can't be arrested?'*

'Well,' he drew out the word to give himself time to think. 'Strictly speaking, no. You could have the threat of a fine, and I suppose if you refused to comply with a request to return home, or refuse to give your name and address, there is a vague possibility of arrest.' He paused, 'but even then, you could probably hire a good lawyer to prove the arrest itself wasn't legal.' He had spoken slowly, and with a touch of irony in his tone, unsure where the conversation was going. He wondered if she had put any thought into the question he had asked earlier in the day, or had she just dismissed it? He didn't want to ask her again. It seemed better to leave her with the option.

'I see,' she said without conviction.

'So what is it you're planning to do?'

'Do?' she asked.

'The thing that you thought might get you arrested?'

'Oh, nothing,' she sighed, *'I think you've convinced me not to anyway.'* She paused for a second and then added, *'so when shall we do this virtual night*

out then?'

'Tomorrow?' he suggested, not knowing if either of them would be available.

'*We could try it, why not?*' she replied.

'Okay,' said Avalon, 'I'll make the food, you bring the wine.'

'*Time?*'

'Oh, when we can both make it, I suppose.' They said their goodbyes and Avalon sighed a little. He would enjoy her company right now, at that very moment, but at least they may get time tomorrow. He looked around the room again but decided that a shower and an early night would be in order. With luck, the morning would bring them a new lead.

What the morning did bring, was a break in the weather as the clouds had gathered and the showers had begun. It also brought notification that his team were scheduled for virus testing during that day. Other than that, nothing of note came in concerning the quarry case, but the doctors had pronounced Serle fit enough to be interviewed, as long as virus countermeasures were taken. Ross and Rutherford went to see him, but he was still not talking. He wouldn't even say why his girlfriend had stabbed him, though she had provided her own statement on that score. She had explained that she had found out that he had just been using her, as he didn't have a place of his own to stay. When she had asked him how much he had stolen, he had lied and an argument ensued. It was during that argument that she had stabbed him, but she maintained she hadn't meant to hurt him, even though she wanted nothing more to do with him. She had also added that she would give evidence against him for leniency regarding the stabbing. The case was all but closed. The rest of the work would be in the hands of the courts, but that could take time, given the lockdown. Most of Avalon's day was spent going through paperwork and putting his own systems in place for C Section. Just after lunch, he noticed two tradesmen working on one of the offices and he was curious enough to find out how come they were allowed to work together. They told him they had been altering the interview rooms before the lockdown, and now they wanted to get the new office ready so they could work separately. It was then he asked a question.

'I don't suppose one of you can dismantle a cupboard in my office, could you?'

'Give me a mo. an' I'll come an' av' a look,' replied the man, he had an east London accent. Avalon told him where the office was and he waited for him in the booth.

Twenty minutes later he appeared and looked at the cupboard and the small area of the booth.

'Yeah, I can do that, shouldn't take long,' he nodded. He then looked at the open side of the booth. 'Did they not get around to finishing this?' he asked, nodding to the spot where Avalon was standing.

'To my knowledge, it was supposed to be opened ended.'

'Do you want it closing in?' asked the man raising his brows. Avalon had never considered it.

'It depends on how long it would take,' he said, unsure if it was the right time for alterations. It would also impact on the rest of the team.

'We could do it at the weekend,' suggested the man. In the end, they managed to formulate a plan to enclose the booth into a proper office and make more room in there. He just had to get it sanctioned. That could be an issue, given that the new DCI was not on the best of terms with her staff. Either way, he would try. He could always give her the excuse that it would help with the covid virus countermeasures.

Avalon then went to have another word with DI Lasiter about Christopher Joyce. Murrey wasn't there this time, but DS Douglas and a face Avalon didn't recognise were there. Lasiter invited Avalon into his cramped office and though they would have to sit closer than recommendations, he let it go.

'How are you getting on with the Plague Witch?' asked Lasiter with a grin.

'Not as well as you by all accounts.'

'Aye,' smiled Lasiter, 'she loves us here in B Section, I was thinking o' having some garlic hung over the door.'

'I believe that's for vampires,' smiled Avalon, 'though you can never be too careful.'

'So what can I do for you today?' asked Lasiter, leaning back in his chair.

'We went to see Christopher Joyce,' explained Avalon raising his brows, 'but he was unhelpful.'

'That's normal for him,' nodded Lasiter.

'So would there be any point in bringing him in?'

'I doubt et,' reflected Lasiter, 'he knows his rights, so he would give you nothing. He'll make you earn your wages, that's for sure. But you could try him, though I doubt he's your man.'

'Why do you say that?' asked Avalon.

'He's not a killer,' shrugged Lasiter, 'not of humans anyway.'

'But you think he poisoned his neighbour's dogs?'

'Et's possible, even probable.' Lasiter glanced to the floor and then back to Avalon as if he was trying to recall something. 'The thing with Joyce es, he has a twisted sense of morality. He thinks that es moral code es much more refined than anyone else's. He's so sure of et, that when someone gets on his nerves, an' he has tae break that code tae put them en their place, he feels, that en etself, es an affront to his person.' Avalon gave a blank stare. 'Et's complicated and some shrink will probably hae a fancy name for et, but essentially, that code would prevent him from being a killer in my mind.' Avalon nodded with an abstract expression.

'Sublime,' he simply said.

'Sublime es a good description of him,' nodded Lasiter and then added, 'but you're beginning tae sound like Para Handy.' Avalon's features changed to a mild, questioning frown. 'Aye, being English, y' wunna know who Para Handy es,' grinned Lasiter.

'I have heard the name, wasn't it a Scottish sitcom?'

'Before et was ever filmed,' said Lasiter solemnly, 'et was a series en a Glasgow newspaper.' A good natured expression came across Lasiter's face, for it could never be accurately described as a smile. 'Para Handy was as much a Scottish hero as the Bruce in my book. Aye, fiction true, written by Neil Munro, but capital, nonetheless.' Lasiter dropped into a strange accent that Avalon likened to west coast island dialects he had heard. 'Peter Mcfarlane waass the skipper o' the Vital Sperk, the smertest boat en the tred. An ef Dougie was here now, he'd tell y' so,' and at this, Lasiter broke into laughter. The sound he made was like a coughing camel, but it was a laugh in the strongest term of the word. Avalon left Lasiter reciting more of the newspaper literature to himself, and entered the corridor back to his office. The name Para Handy stuck in his mind however, and he decided to search online for a compilation edition as soon as he had time.

The afternoon became tedious as he completed some of the minutia of reports and other administrative paperwork, and then with nothing more that required his attention, he went home at a reasonable time for a change. It was raining heavier now, and this added to his gloomy aspect. When he arrived, he immediately thought of his virtual evening out with Sarah, which brought him from his mood. She hadn't phoned or texted to say she wouldn't be able to join in, but then again, neither had she confirmed she would. He decided to send a quick text to find out, and then he showered. As the soothing water massaged him, he wondered what he should make for the meal. There was only him, and after all, the food wouldn't be a great part of the evening. They would be talking, not eating. Wine would be a good idea, candlelight? Would that work on a laptop? As he dried himself, he considered Provencal, maybe with pasta, that way he could prepare it and then it would be ready to finish off just before they went online to chat.

Avalon wasn't a natural chef, and he didn't particularly enjoy cooking, but living alone for so long had taught him a few things. In Wolverhampton he had eaten take-away food most of the time, but since moving to Scotland and changing his diet, he had learned a great deal about cooking. Provencal was just another of those dishes that was a gem for someone who doesn't know when they will be back home, as it can be prepared earlier. He checked his phone, but there was no reply from Sarah. Nevertheless, he began the food and left it to cool, setting the table for one, and placing his laptop at the opposite side of the table. His phone trilled. It was Sarah, she said she would be able to make it and was looking forward to the distraction. Distraction? Is that what he had become, a distraction? Probably not the best use of the word, but he was beginning to see a very subtle side to Sarah. He had always thought that she didn't indulge herself with humour, but that wasn't true. Her humour was hidden, or disguised as something else. He supposed someone as intelligent as her was going to primarily, amuse herself, and if the surrounding people got it, that was fine by her. He then began to wonder if she was intelligent, or was she just highly qualified? It was difficult to know that from qualifications. Avalon knew from experience of fellow detectives, education and qualifications were no guarantee of intelligence. That came from your DNA and a hunger for knowledge, not colleges and universities. When he really considered it, he didn't know. In truth, he didn't know Sarah Underwood very well at all. That probably came from the fact that their time together came from them never being close for very long at any given time. Most normal couples sleep together, holiday together, and now and then just sit and enjoy each other's company. He and Sarah had done none of those things. They met, chatted over a meal, and then usually parted company. He nodded to himself. Wasn't that what suited them both? He was no longer sure about that. He had felt more connection, more energy on that night of lust with Lizzy

Cumberland, than he had ever felt with Sarah. But then, Lizzy was uncomplicated, she was easy to understand and empathise with. Sarah was complicated. He didn't think he would ever understand her. As he waited, he spun the laptop around and searched for a complete copy of Para Handy. Once found, he bought it online and looked forward to its arrival. It probably wouldn't be as essential reading as The Iliad, or Virgil's The Aeneid, but Avalon felt eager to open its pages. He reset the laptop to receive Sarah's call and turned it back to face into the table. There was a text on the phone, he hoped that was the message to say she was ready and he read it as he warmed his food. It was, the message read,

'*Five minutes and I'm ready.*' He quickly finished off the pasta and warmed the Provencal, then checked his internet connection to be on the safe side. He heard the laptop trilling an incoming connection, and he allowed it. There on the screen was Sarah with an apprehensive smile.

'Good evening,' he smiled back. She waved, but it shook the image, so he assumed she was using her phone. 'It's not easy to see you, but you look nice,' he added.

'*Well, I thought I should make the effort,*' she replied, the image a little hazy.

'You look as if you're in your car,' he said as he could see what looked to be the headlining of a vehicle. In some ways, he was a little disappointed. He had expected her to have put more thought into it.

'*Yes,*' she replied, '*just a moment,*' and he thought he heard her exit the car. He was now puzzled. The image steadied and she brought the phone closer to her face as it was dark. She seemed to be walking. '*That's*

196

better,' she eventually said.

'Where are you?' he asked with doubt on his features.

'*You know how you said I couldn't be arrested for breaking the social distancing rules?*'

'Yes,' replied Avalon, unsure what she was going to say.

'*Well, I thought about this and tried to come up with something you could get arrested for,*' she said, but he could see little of her, as if she was in a darker place. He was now wondering exactly what she was up to. '*It seems one of the lesser crimes I could commit is damage to personal property,*' she then added, and her face became clearer in the screen. Then she showed what seemed to be a plant-pot in her other hand. In one movement, she let go of the pot and it fell. There was a feint crash, and she grinned at the screen.

'What are you up to?' he frowned, 'Are you out in the rain?'

'*Criminal damage, that's what I'm up to,*' she replied, still smiling, and she showed the broken pot by her feet on the floor. Then the screen moved and showed her face once more, yet she seemed to be on the move again. '*Someone needs to arrest me,*' there was a pause, and though she was now stationary again, there was less light. She drew closer to the screen and said, '*have you got your handcuffs with you?*' just as the doorbell rang.

Chapter Nine

The sky was a pall of cloud as Avalon walked from the car to the entrance of the police station, but he still took in a deep breath of the air before he entered. This new day was another unknown quantity to him, but he hoped he may hear something that would move his investigation on. He was only too aware that this was his first case under the guise of MIT, and he didn't want it to stall. He greeted Rory Mackinnon and Frazer, who were the only two present, and made his way to the booth. He removed his jacket and sat, switched on his computer screen and looked into the main room. He then noticed the card Sarah had sent him, still at the edge of the desk, and he instinctively picked it up and placed it closer. He gave a little smile and then looked up as White entered with his usual blank face. The man spoke to no one and sat at his desk. Rutherford and Wilson entered next, chatting about something or other, and then Ross followed in some minutes later. He nodded at Avalon as he walked to his seat, and Avalon raised his brows. He then looked down to his computer screen and after scanning his emails, returned to the case at the quarry. He had thought a great deal about the reasoning why those two bodies occupied the same grave. Undoubtedly they were connected, and that would be advantageous in the respect of finding an identification of the victims. Their search of missing people now included women who had disappeared with a child. If they were wrong, it would clutter up their search, but the odds were that the two deaths were somehow connected. By early afternoon, Megan Frazer had found only two women who had gone missing with a child over the last twenty years. Neither of them seemed to fit. One was too young and in the second, the child was older than the bones they had found. Expanding their search over a twenty-year period had brought up a few more possible names however, and Frazer was busy checking and cross-checking all information on these new identities. Avalon looked through the file of Christopher Joyce once more, and brought up any relevant details about the man on the computer records. On the face of it, it didn't seem likely that he was connected with the bones from the quarry, but further digging into his past was worth pursuing, as he was the only connection they had with ricin. The problem remained, if they were to bring Joyce in, he would cause them trouble and Avalon wasn't keen on serving a warrant unless it was really necessary. The more warrants that failed to produce anything, the less the Sheriff's Office were likely to issue them. Avalon then had the idea of seeing what other police forces had, concerning ricin and set DC White on the task.

Waiting was always the hard part, and there was a great deal of waiting on cases like this. He decided to have another word with DI Lasiter, but as he reached the door to B section's office, he could hear raised voices. He carefully opened the door and peered inside. He saw

Murrey and Douglas at their desks, seemingly unperturbed by the commotion coming from Lasiter's office. Both men looked up to Avalon as he crept inside and Murrey raised his brows. Once inside, Avalon noticed two other officers in there, DS Nicholls was seated behind the door and a new DC that Avalon hadn't met was in the office with Lasiter. The office door was closed, but the glass window showed that Lasiter was not directing his tirade at the DC, but at the phone.

'Sounds serious,' whispered Avalon.

'Aye, it is,' nodded Murrey, glancing towards the office.

'Who's on the other end of the phone?' asked the DI.

'The Plague Witch,' answered Murrey sheepishly, and he went back to his work.

'The bitch has been interfering again,' added Nicholls without prompting, 'I thought the guv'nor would explode last time she stuck her hooked nose in, but this time he's thrown it all up in the air.' Avalon could hear what Lasiter was shouting, and it did indeed sound serious. Lasiter was apt to explode with anger now and then, but the wording he was using this time was a cut above anything previously.

'I'll come back some other time,' frowned Avalon, and moved towards the door he had just come through.

'Aye, probably best,' nodded Murrey, looking up from his screen.

Avalon plodded back to The Cave, wondering what the outcome to Lasiter's outburst would be. It was clear that the DCI had interfered with the running of the section, and it was likely that the new DC in the office had been the focus of her action. Avalon had clearly heard Lasiter ranting on, that maybe she should go and run the section. Seeing as Lasiter was approaching retirement, he was certainly throwing caution to the wind. It was also interesting that the argument was taking place over the phone, meaning that Lasiter had instigated it. It was more likely that the DCI would have made her way to their office if it was something she had begun. He walked to his booth and sat, wondering what the outcome would be, and if it would have repercussions for C Section. For the next two hours, he expected a visit from either Lasiter or the DCI, but it didn't come. Instead, late in the afternoon, he received a call from the Superintendent, asking him to see him as soon as possible. As Avalon walked the corridor to the Super's large office, he steeled himself for what would come. As it happened, it was an anti-climax. The Super had got wind of Avalon's involvement with MIT and wanted to explain to the DI that Inverness took president over MIT. Avalon had assured him that he agreed, and would share everything he found with the DCI, as he would with any local case. The mention of the DCI didn't seem to bring a reaction from the Super, and so after the short interview he returned to his office. Just before he left for home, he got a text from Sarah saying she would be going home to her house, as there were things she had to do, and Avalon wondered if that would be the last time she would go to his house in the evening.

Saturday was sunny once more, but as Avalon locked his car and headed to the main building, he could see that clouds were gathering, real and metaphorical. As he seated himself in the booth and checked his emails, he wondered what the outcome had been over Lasiter's argument with the DCI. He spent the rest of the morning trying to secure protective equipment for his team, but decided not to involve the DCI with his needs. He then asked Frazer and White if anything else had cropped up over the ricin subject, but nothing had shown itself to be connected. Two minor cases came in, one burglary in Kirkhill and a minor assault in Dingwall. The local police had all but solved the Dingwall case, and DS Wilson and DC Mackinnon drove out to Kirkhill around lunchtime. Avalon looked towards the shelf where the coffee machine used to stand. He was missing that device, not just for the coffee. It was the most casual way he could think of to assess the mood of the office. Rather than ask direct questions, sauntering up to the coffee machine and making the odd comment, was much more subtle. It was easy to ask how a particular lead was going, or introduce a particular subject as you poured a coffee. Now, if he went into the main room, it was all too obvious what he was doing. He wondered about finding a replacement, or even bringing his own from home. The phone rang. He wondered if it was an angry tone as he reached for it.

'Avalon.'

'*Hello, it's Sarah,*' came the reply, she continued before he could react. '*You probably need to come down here if you can get away,*' she said hurriedly.

'I can get, yes,' he replied, glancing up to the clock and once again confirming the time with his watch.

'*I had a phone call from Dundee this morning,*' she continued. '*We have something for you, but it's best you come over. It's complicated.*' As he walked to his car, he thought how he had needed more information on the quarry case, but with the tone of Sarah's voice, he didn't know quite what to expect. He told White to meet him at the labs as he thought it best to leave Rutherford and Ross to cover things while he was away. As soon as White arrived, Avalon pushed the doorbell and waited to be shown in. Inside, Sarah took them to the small office where he introduced DC White, as he didn't think they had met. Sarah said hello with a smile and White nodded.

'So what have you got for me, it sounds serious?' Avalon asked.

'It is, yes,' she agreed, 'but very puzzling too. She sat at the computer and opened an image. Avalon recognised it as DNA coding. 'The Dundee team has managed to extract enough DNA from both samples to confirm that the two bodies were indeed related. The child is male and was around seven years old at death. They are convinced, in Dundee, that this is mother and child.' Avalon became acutely aware that this was serious. The child had been the first to die and was buried illegally. Sometime after, the mother was probably killed and placed in a grave above the child. Did this mean that the person that hid the bodies had sympathy for the two of them and buried them together? That was doubtful as both bodies looked as if they had been dumped more like rubbish than people. He nodded to her and raised his brows.

'Yes, that makes it complicated,' he said. It was quite an understatement. 'Was any trace of ricin found in the child's bones?' he then asked.

'None,' she said emphatically, 'but nothing that would indicate a cause of death either.' He sighed and sat in a chair close by. He looked into her eyes and added,

'This makes even less sense than it did before.'

'I know, but there's more,' she replied, and he noticed the glimmer of doubt in her face.

'Somehow, I knew there might be,' he sighed again, glancing over to DC White. White was wearing his usual blank expression.

'The team at Dundee have done a whole raft of tests on both sets of bones and with the new data we have from the soil samples…' she paused, 'we think that the deepest body has been there around thirty years, and Sandy's body just a few years less.' Avalon didn't show a great deal of surprise at this.

'Well,' he said at length, 'at least we have the DNA. That should help.'

'Not that much though,' frowned Sarah. 'My colleagues at Dundee asked the local CID to run a search, but nothing cropped up.'

'That's understandable,' he shrugged, 'DNA profiling was in its infancy back then, but if we find a suitable match, it will help us to confirm we have the correct person.' He paused before adding, 'I'm guessing the facial reconstruction will take longer?' Sarah nodded, but Avalon could see there was something else she had not yet mentioned. 'You have more, something you haven't told me yet.'

'Yes, there is something else,' she nodded, 'but there is a tiny bit of conjecture over this one.'

'Go on,' he insisted. Sarah looked at the computer screen and then found an image that looked like a close scan of a bone. She pointed to the screen and continued.

'It's not easy to see in this image, but I have seen

the detailed images and they show variable growth in the bones of the child. The bone experts in Dundee are ninety-nine percent sure they know what causes this kind of marking.'

'Just a moment,' interrupted Avalon, 'when you say variable growth, what do you mean exactly?'

'As the bones grow, they leave marks, similar to annular rings in trees.' She waited to see his reaction. He nodded his understanding. 'In a normal, healthy child, these should be a constant. They should be even and regular. In this child, that wasn't the case.' Avalon frowned as White decided to speak for the first time.

'He had a few bad winters,' he said.

'That's a good analogy,' nodded Sarah, looking up to him. 'In a tree, a bad winter makes the rings smaller. There is less growth. The bones of this child show evidence of this happening, albeit over a shorter period.'

'And you said,' continued Avalon, 'that they know what makes this happen?' Sarah nodded gloomily.

'It is something they have witnessed before. They think that this child was put through an enormous amount of stress in the time before it died.'

'Or was killed,' added Avalon quickly. He looked down at the floor and back up to Sarah. 'Can we tell over what time period this may have happened?'

'This image,' she pointed to the screen once more, 'doesn't show very much, but I have seen the original scans as I mentioned, and the areas where growth stops or decelerates is pronounced. It would be almost impossible to make an accurate assessment, but we all think that the child was put under a great deal of stress over a twelve-month period, probably in short bursts, as normal growth appears to be there too.'

'Would this happen over a family breakup?' asked the DI.

'It depends on the child I would think,' replied Sarah, 'but yes, I imagine a particularly turbulent breakup would cause this.'

'But you don't think so in this case?' frowned Avalon.

'It isn't my field, but…' she paused for a moment, 'down in Dundee, they think something very stressful happened to that child on several occasions.' He nodded and looked down to the floor once more, leaning onto his knees. It was White's turn to speak.

'Is this detail of the bone growth known in legal circles?' he asked and, before she could reply, he amended his question, 'I mean, could we go to court with this?' Avalon was surprised that White was thinking that far ahead, but he had a point. They needed to know if it would be allowed as evidence if they ever sorted this case out.

'Yes, of course,' she replied, 'with the reputation of these experts, they would be taken very seriously in law.' Avalon gave a brief nod and sat upright. He looked at White, sighed again, and stood.

'Is there anything else?' he asked Sarah.

'No, but if I hear anything, I'll let you know.' He nodded to her and left, giving her his professional smile. He wanted to ask her if she would be going to his house or staying at her home, but he couldn't do that for many reasons. He would have to wait. In the mean-time, there was a great deal to do. Their missing person search would have to go back into the 1990s, and that would mean extra work.

As he and White returned to the office, Avalon thought about the covid virus once more and scanned his computer for any further news on the subject. Apart from the fact that it was clear the death toll would broach the ten thousand mark, there was little. He considered how odd the situation was, sitting there in his glass fronted booth, trying to find out how two people died and who they were. It would probably be an expensive case for the taxpayer and yet, out there, beyond those windows, people were dying by the thousand, and no one seemed to care. No one would be brought to book, no one would be found responsible and no one would be prosecuted, and yet, which was the greater crime? The truth of this caused him some anxiety, and he felt claustrophobic in his booth. He rubbed his eyes and then sighed deeply into his steepled hands, before looking to the shelf that once held the coffee machine. He would bring the one from home. He needed a coffee, but even the poor excuse of a vending machine in the restroom was now out of bounds. It then struck him where he could get a reasonable cup of coffee from. He picked up the phone and dialled an internal number. He just hoped there was a friendly voice on the other end.

'*Hello, PC Dowd,*' came that friendly voice.

'Neil, it's me, are you alone down there?'

'*Yes, why, is there a problem?*'

'Problem? Yes. Get the kettle on, I need coffee.'

'*No trouble, I'll meet you in the car park, I'll get PC Blackstone to sort out the desk.*'

PC Dowd carried two cups of coffee on a tray and even supplied some biscuits to accompany the repast. Avalon, who was sitting on the low wall by the entrance, enjoying one of the sunny spells of the afternoon, smiled. Dowd was a strange character for sure. He was so extraordinary and yet so ordinary at the same time. He sat the required distance away and pushed the tray between them, removing his cup as he did.

'I'm sorry DI, I couldnae find any doilies,' explained Dowd with a serious face.

'Coffee and biscuits are the important parts Neil, not the flim-flam around the edges,' replied Avalon, taking his cup and a single biscuit.

'Looks like you're having a wee bit o' trouble with the quarry case then?'

'Yes,' replied Avalon, crunching into the biscuit, 'the more we find out about this one, the more difficult it becomes.'

'So, I'm guessing,' began Dowd, 'you still have no idea who she, and the little one were?'

'Not yet,' replied Avalon, finishing the biscuit and leaning forward, cradling his cup. 'We do know they were related, probably mother and son.'

'Still no cause of death?' Avalon shook his head and sipped the coffee.

'The mother was probably poisoned with ricin, and the child was under a great deal of stress before he died. Not a pleasant case in many ways.' Dowd was quiet for a few minutes, then, he said,

'Ef et was the mother buried first, et would make you think the poor wee child had seen it happen, but as et stands, that canna be the reason.' Avalon agreed and then wondered if the same was true of the mother. Had she seen the child die, or known something about the death of her son and was killed before she could speak? It was doubtful, as she probably lived for a year or two after, maybe more. No, it seemed the truth was still hidden.

'So,' began Dowd questioningly, 'how do you know the child had been under stress?'

'The bone experts in Dundee can read our bones, similar to the growth lines of a tree,' explained the DI. 'High levels of stress can halt the growth of bones in the young.'

'Now that is something I didnae know,' nodded Dowd deep in thought, 'and I'm guessing that all this was happening just before the boy died?'

'That's how it seems,' nodded Avalon, 'the changes aren't visible with the naked eye, but the scans taken at Dundee show the whole story.' Avalon took several more sips at the coffee, then said, 'I have to get another coffee machine in The Cave. And thanks, you're a lifesaver Neil.'

'Och, don't mention et, I was late for my break anyway, an' I might have a spare machine for you at home.'

'Really?' asked Avalon as he stood.

'Aye, et's been en the garage a few months so et might not work, but I'll bring et en. We don't use et.' Avalon thanked him for the coffee and the offer of the machine, and feeling a little more relaxed, he returned to the office.

The first thing he did was break the news to Frazer that the bodies could have been in the ground since the late nineties. She jutted out her bottom lip and nodded, but then a frown came over her face.

'I'm thinking we may have to err on the side of caution and go back to nineteen eighty-five,' explained Avalon.

'That's a long time ago Boss,' called Rutherford,

who had been listening. 'I bet some of those records are still on paper.'

'Probably,' agreed Avalon, 'but anything major should have been put on the computer system, and the dates we're mainly concerned with are eighty-nine to ninety-four. That's the best guess from forensics.'

'I was two years old in eighty-nine,' sighed Rutherford.

'So you'd be no taller than six feet then?' chirped in Ross.

'Well, you wouldn't have been much older,' insisted Rutherford ignoring the jibe.

'I was…' Ross paused as he worked out the dates, 'about eight years old in eighty-nine and as I recall, I had a fight with my best mate over Guns n' Roses. He thought 'Child of Mine' was great, and I thought it was shite.'

'So you had no music taste then either?' grinned Rutherford. Frazer, who was quick fingered as always, had probed the internet at the same time as she was expanding her search.

'Talking of music taste, or lack of et,' she said, 'during Christmas of that year, Andy Stewart hit number four in the charts with Donald where's your Troosers?'

'An' people talk of the good old days,' laughed Rutherford.

'When you have finished with All Our Yesterdays,' interjected Avalon, 'can we return to the subject at hand?' There were a few sheepish expressions, and Rutherford apologised. 'If we examine between those years first and then expand either way if nothing crops up, maybe we can find something.' He saw Frazer was still frowning, which, with the exception of her comment about Andy Steward, had been the case since he had returned. 'Is there something on your mind?' he asked her. She looked up with a start.

'Oh, er...' she stuttered. 'Well, to be honest, aye, there es.' She shuffled through some tatty case files on the side of her desk. They looked quite old and she must have brought them from the archive. 'A day or two ago, I found an old case that I thought had some relevance to our quarry case, but as it was much earlier, I discounted et.' She couldn't seem to find the file and so, she returned to the computer. 'Most of et es on the database but I brought the records up to check through et.' She punched a few keys and then read a serial number quietly to herself. She then scoured through the old files she had on her desk once more. 'Here et es,' she sighed, and picked up the file to hand to Avalon.

'Tell me about it before I commit time to this,' insisted Avalon refusing the document. She placed it back on the desk and began to read from the computer screen.

'In 1992, Geoffrey Gibson was arrested en connection of the disappearance of Mary Anne Fenner, nee Munroe, and her nine-year-old son, Carl. The investigation went on for almost two years, but there wasn't enough evidence to convict Gibson of their murders, as no body had been discovered and no witnesses could be found to testify en the case.' She paused and looked to Avalon. His stare was unreadable. She continued. 'Suspicion had also fallen on her estranged husband, Stuart Fenner, who et seemed was the one who reported his wife and child missing.' She glanced up to him again before finishing with, 'but nothing could be proven that either man had anything to

211

do with her disappearance.'

'And why did you single this one out as probable?' asked Avalon, unconvinced.

'Call et a gut feeling,' shrugged Frazer. 'I've read through so many of these cases, this one doesn't have anything I can pick holes en, except for the date.'

'And so now the dates fit?' he asked, folding his arms and resting on an empty desk.

'Aye, they do,' she nodded.

'Knowing you, Megan, I'm guessing that you have read through the notes and found something else?' She nodded again.

'Like I said, et's a gut feeling,' she replied. 'The investigation was handled by Detective Inspector Mowat, and et's clear he thought *he* had the right man. After reading through the case notes, I'm not sure, but there es something wrong for certain.' Avalon looked at the clock on the wall.

'I've got nothing better to do at the moment,' he said, finding a chair, and sitting the wrong way round. 'Give me more details,' and he rested his arms on the back of the seat. Frazer glanced around the room at the others as if she had a little stage fright, but she exhaled and using the notes on the screen, began to relate the case.

'Stuart Fenner reported his wife and son missing, after getting no reply to phone calls from her when he tried to arrange to see his son. He told the police he had gone to the house but found no one home. The local officers checked the house and found from neighbours that Gibson and Mary Anne had left to move south. Gibson was eventually traced to an address en Stirling but insisted that he and Mary Anne had parted company when they left Inverness. En the meantime, Stuart Fenner had told police that he had asked to see Carl, but she had refused and he had become angry. She told him that she had been given custody, and that was that, but he insisted that the courts had said he was allowed to see his son once each week.' She paused and looked at Avalon. 'The first thing I noticed,' she continued, 'that during the trial, et became clear that previous to this, Fenner had not tried to see his son.' Avalon gave a shallow nod, so she returned to the notes.

'Fenner admitted at the trial,' she continued, 'that they had a blazing argument and Mary burst into tears. Fenner said he thought something was wrong, and he insisted that ef he didn't see his son, he would go round to the house and cause trouble. Fenner said that she panicked at this point and agreed to his request, but she said she needed time to arrange et. Fenner gave her a week. When she didn't contact him, he went to the house to find et empty.'

'Sounds suspicious,' nodded Avalon.

'Et does,' agreed Frazer, 'and Fenner thought so, enough to say at the trial that he thought something terrible had happened to Carl.'

'You said that suspicion also fell on Fenner,' interrupted Rutherford.

'Yes,' agreed Frazer. She was now quite animated. 'DI Mowat thought it was odd that Fenner sought out his son, only after the boy seemed to have gone missing, and so he considered he had information that he was keeping from them.'

'Maybe he found out they were planning to leave the area,' offered Rutherford, 'an' he didn't want to have to travel to see his son.'

'But that has no logic,' insisted Ross, 'this guy didn't see his son anyway, why would distance have any relevance?' Avalon nodded at this.

'I agree, I can see why DI Mowat was doubtful, we would be the same.'

'Fenner said at the trial,' added Frazer, 'that he began to feel remorse that he had left his son with a mother that was unfit to look after him.'

'Well,' sighed Avalon, 'we can discount that, it's pretty clear that the separation wasn't amicable.' He looked at the gathered faces. The only one he couldn't see was White, who was behind him. 'Does anyone have any thoughts? Could these be our missing identities?' He needed more information, that was clear, but he also valued input from his team. He would have liked Wilson's opinion, but he was out with Rory.

'You know my thoughts Boss,' frowned Frazer, 'this case prickled me before the dates even fit.' Avalon nodded and looked at Rutherford.

'It has potential,' agreed Martin Rutherford, 'there is nothing to say this isn't them.'

'Yeah, let's dig a little deeper,' shrugged Ross as Avalon's eyes fell on him.

'Angus?' asked Avalon without turning to look at him. White stopped working and leaned back in his seat.

'We need dates. The timescale needs to be analysed before I would commit to it, but…' he paused. 'For me, the crux of the matter is how long was it between them leaving Inverness to the point Fenner was found in Stirling?'

'Why so hotshot?' asked Ross with a hint of sarcasm. White turned in his chair to face Ross.

'It's quite simple,' explained White. 'If the time

214

between him leaving Inverness and the police finding him is months or even weeks, there is plenty of time for arguments and parting of ways. This woman and her child may quite simply have left to go elsewhere. However,' this time White gave a hint of sarcasm which was new for him. 'If it was just a few days, that would make me wonder why she would leave with this man if she intended not to stay with him.'

'Not game changing though, is it?' came back Ross.

'Got a better idea?' he paused and gave a cynical grin, 'hotshot?' This made Martin smile, and he gave a wink to Ross, who ignored him.

'Okay,' sighed Avalon, 'Angus has a point.' He paused and then looked to Megan. 'You and Angus make up a whiteboard with all the details we have. I want a chronological order for the evidence and the details of the investigation.' He turned to Ross and Rutherford. 'You two need to find out if we can trace any living relatives of these people, Including Mr Fenner. If we can find a willing relative, maybe they'll allow DNA testing so that we can solve who these bodies are. I also want you to try to track down DI Mowat, though he's probably retired by now. That shouldn't be difficult, at least. Any questions?'

Avalon sat at his desk, and brought up what they had on the computer on the Gibson case to see if he could find any loopholes. If he could, it would mean they had stalled. If it fit however, well, he just had to stay optimistic.

It was late in the afternoon when they had any results from their searches. Detective Inspector Mowat had retired some years ago and had bought a bed-and-breakfast just outside Nairn. He and his wife had run it for the last five years. Rutherford had contacted him and the ex-policeman had agreed to speak with them. Rutherford said he seemed disinterested in the case until he informed him that the bodies may have been found. It seemed the old detective in the man was not quite gone, and he offered any information he could supply. Gibson seemed to have dropped off the edge of the world. Neither he, nor any relatives could be traced. Stuart Fenner was easier. His name popped up on the police computer and it seemed the man had moved to Newcastle where he had been involved in two minor cases there. Relatives of Mary Anne Munroe, as she was before marriage, had been a little more difficult to trace, but just before he was about to call it a day, Ross found something. One of the recorded witnesses on the marriage certificate was a certain Charles Munroe. His address had been given as Scorguie and so Ross, as a last resort, checked council records to see if the name appeared. It did. A Charles Munroe still lived in the area and was registered as a plumber. It was late in the day however, and though he informed Avalon, they decided to leave it for Monday morning. It was Saturday, and though Avalon and most of the team would be in the office in the morning, he had decided that Sunday would be for research, report writing and any other work that needed to be covered.

As he left the office for home, he realised he hadn't thought about Sarah since seeing her earlier in the day. She hadn't hinted if she would be going to his house or not, so he was unsure what the evening would bring. The house was empty when he arrived, and after coffee and a shower, he heard the doorbell ring. It was Sarah carrying a holdall. Avalon took the bag from her and said,

'Why are you ringing the bell?' he ushered her into the kitchen, 'I gave you a key, have you lost it already?'

'No, well…' she stuttered, 'I don't know, it just feels strange to walk straight into someone else's house.'

'As I told you,' frowned Avalon but with a soft voice, 'treat this place as your own, that's what we agreed.'

'I know,' she smiled, 'it's just a little odd to me at the moment.'

'Do you want a drink… or something?' It was odd for Avalon too. It was years since he shared a house with someone and the whole experience was new again. He felt he was being over-attentive and so he tried to slack off somewhat. 'The shower is free, if you need it.'

'I may have a bath later,' she said. She looked tired, and Avalon was stuck for anything else to say. He decided to fill the kettle again. 'Hot drink?' he asked.

'Tea please,' she sighed and then, 'I think I'll take a seat,' and she walked into the lounge.

'Have you eaten?' he asked as he brought her the tea. She was reclining on the sofa with her shoes abandoned nearby and had her eyes closed.

'I had lunch, but I'm fine for the moment.'

'I could make something if you like?' he offered.

'James,' she said a little sharply, then paused. 'Sorry, I'm just a little tired.'

'I'll leave you then,' he said and placed the tea on the coffee table. She closed her eyes, and he was about to return to the kitchen.

'Look,' she said without opening her eyes. 'If this is going to work,' her eyes opened and looked at him, 'we have to get a few things straight. I'm not a damsel in distress, I don't need looking after and I still want to live my life the way I like.'

'Yes, as we agreed,' he nodded, 'I want that too.'

'So stop fussing over me,' she said a little softer, 'this is what I do every evening when I get home. I fall on the sofa, close my eyes until the metamorphosis into me, rather than a lab technician, is complete. I then consider food but rarely eat any, and after that I light some candles and take a long hot bath.' She allowed a little smile. He laughed, and though she didn't know him all that well, she could tell it wasn't his normal laugh.

'Times like these are always difficult,' he began, the smile still playing on his lips, 'that dark, grey area where people get used to each other's foibles and idiosyncrasies. I'm told it's a difficult situation, particularly for people who have lived alone for some considerable time. So, in mitigation, I'm not fussing, I'm just being me too.' He turned and left. She closed her eyes and sighed. It was a long, deep sigh, which accompanied a thought. That thought was,

'This is why I have stayed single all these years.'

Avalon sat relaxing on the sofa with the remains of a sandwich on a small plate by his side. His right hand cradled a glass of red wine and his feet were crossed on the coffee table. There was a CD playing quietly on the stereo. Not one of his, but one Sarah had placed on the cabinet when she had opened her holdall to unpack. It was by Nik Kershaw, and though Avalon knew who the artist was, his only recollection of him was something from way back in the eighties, and a half-remembered track from a film in the early nineties. This brought the case whirling back into his mind, and though he and Sarah had agreed that work should never be mentioned, he couldn't keep it from his mind. To break it free, he concentrated on the music. He was beginning to like it, though the tracks were each very different. A few of them sounded as if he had heard them before, though it was doubtful. He sipped on the wine as he sank deeper into the sofa. He felt tired and wondered if it was politic to have an early night, just as he heard a door open and a waft of softly scented air fell over him. It smelled of soap and flowers, Sarah appeared and smiled reservedly as she sat by his side. She was wearing pyjama bottoms and a pale blue cotton top with a stylised picture of an owl on it. This vision of the woman who had tempted just about every male copper at the nick was such a contrast in her nightwear. Gone was the perfectly positioned hair and designer makeup. Now it was just her. Crow's feet lines just visible, marks and blemishes in her skin and maybe even a wisp of slightly greying hair, tumbling over her face in a way she would never allow as 'daytime Sarah'. She even allowed herself a silly exaggerated smile to him as she saw the wine glass.

'I don't suppose I can drink that, can I?' she asked nodding to the wine bottle.

'It's vegan,' he nodded. She reached for the empty glass he had supplied and poured herself some. She made no comment but just leaned back and relaxed. 'But I doubt Rossy would approve,' he then added.

'He's not happy with vegans, you mean?' she asked.

'Not that,' smiled Avalon, 'believe it or not, Ian

Ross is a wine snob, and this wine having a screw top is way below his quality watershed.'

'How odd,' she frowned, 'DC Ross seems to the casual observer to have no quality control whatsoever.' Avalon laughed deeply at this, and it reminded Sarah of something.

'And I'm sorry for being sharp earlier,' she said, taking another sip of wine.

'It's nothing, forget it. Let's change the subject,' he insisted. 'How did you get into Nik Kershaw?'

'No, tonight isn't about me, let's talk about you instead.'

'It's a boring subject with little or nothing to tell,' he insisted. He leaned forward and topped up their glasses before resuming his relaxed position.

'There must be something that would interest me,' she smiled, 'I know you were married, I know you have no children, and that you came here from Wolverhampton. I also know you are originally from Norfolk too.'

'Then you know everything about me,' he smiled once more.

'Do you have family?' she asked.

'I have a brother, but we haven't spoken in years. We get on, but sort of drifted apart.' He thought for a space. 'I don't even know where he is or what he's doing at the moment.'

'So, where in Norfolk did you grow up?' she then asked as she snuggled deeper into the sofa.

'Near a little village called Thwaite Saint Mary, in the middle of nowhere, but we moved to Dereham by the time I was ten years old. I went to senior school there and moved when I started college.'

'But you don't have a Norfolk accent, do you?' she asked.

'I'm not sure I have an accent at all,' he shrugged, 'what with the constant moving about, I think I just picked up phrases and bits of an accent. Most people think I sound as if I'm from the midlands somewhere.'

'So, if you had stayed in Norfolk, how would you have spoken?' There was a hint of mischievousness in her voice and on her face.

'I'm terrible at accents, I have to warn you,' he frowned.

'Even your own?'

'All accents,' he insisted, and he sipped at his wine again.

'Go on,' she laughed, 'speak like a Norfolk native.' He frowned deeper to her, then smiled.

'I'll try, but I doubt it will sound authentic.' He thought about the accent of his childhood and tried to remember his friends, and how they spoke. Even his father had little or no accent, but his aunty had a rich, original Norfolk tongue, and he tried to recall it. He coughed and then gave it a go. 'Well,' he began, 'et would sorta sound like thess.' The attempt was shaky to begin with, but Avalon considered it was close. Sarah widened her eyes.

'It sounds like Somerset or something like that.'

'No,' replied Avalon, still in his accented voice, 'Somerset and the West Country accents are richer, with more tones,' he insisted, 'where I'm from, et es flatter, without the long ends.' She laughed as he ended.

'Well, you almost sound like a pirate to me.' She then paused and looked serious, putting her free hand to

221

her mouth. 'Oops, sorry, I didn't mean to laugh.'

'No need to be sorry, it sounds odd to me too,' he replied in his normal voice. He looked into her eyes. 'So now, I have a question.'

'I hope it's not about my accent,' she grinned.

'No, it's more about your secret life,' he said with a serious expression.

'Oh,' she exclaimed, the smile washing out from her face.

'Yes,' he continued, 'the Sarah Underwood that I know, doesn't seem to fit with a blue cotton shirt with an embroidered owl on the front saying 'I'm tired', nor does that image sit comfortably with jim-jam bottoms that have a printed teddy bear pattern on them.'

'So you expected my pyjamas to have little microscopes on them, is that it?' she asked, the smile returning.

'No,' he shrugged, 'but it's a striking transformation nevertheless.'

'I don't wish to disappoint you…' she began and then he detected that she was about to say something and then thought better of it. She looked into his eyes for some seconds before adding, 'this is who I really am.' He knew that wasn't quite what she had intended to say, but he let it be, and then he smiled and said,

'Then, I like who you really are, Sarah Underwood.' She sipped at the wine, not taking her eyes from his, and then leaned her head on his chest. He could hear her quietly humming along with the tune playing on the stereo. The track was called, You're The Best.

Chapter Ten

Avalon slumped into his chair with a slight involuntary noise. It was one of those noises that he had noticed old people make every time they begin, or cease some activity. He knew he would have to stop it before it became a habit. He looked up at the clock in The Cave and tried his best to stop another habit he was cultivating, that of checking his watch soon after. Ross wasn't as late as usual and Avalon noticed him sit, and then stare out of the window. There was something on his mind, that was clear, and Avalon thought he knew what it was, but he pushed it from his thoughts. It was Sunday. The day most normal people didn't go to work. Even Sarah was taking a day off. She was going to speak with her sister through the internet and Avalon had watched her getting ready for the day, just before he left. As he sat there thinking about the previous evening, and the way she had reacted when she had first arrived, he wondered if the professional Sarah was a character out of her makeup box. The more he thought about it, Sarah Underwood, the forensic expert, was applied along with her makeup, and not until the makeup was removed, could she be herself. He thought back to when he was a child, listening to an Alice Cooper interview on the radio. Alice had told the interviewer that Alice Cooper wasn't real. He was a character that the singer played on the stage as soon as the makeup was applied. It wasn't a fair analogy to drag Alice Cooper into the same thoughts as Sarah, but he did wonder if that was how she dealt with the pressure of the job. In some ways, he did the same. For him, it was the cheap suit and tie. He wouldn't dream of dressing that way in his own time. Then again, he didn't seem to have his own time. When he should be spending a leisurely Sunday afternoon with Sarah, he was stuck in the office writing reports. Ross came back into his thoughts and so he stood and walked to the edge of the glass partition.

'Rossy, got a minute?' he said and returned to his chair. Ross ambled to the booth, and sat in the spare chair and yawned. 'Did Martin make any arrangements to see ex DI Mowat?'

'No, I don't think so, why?'

'Do you fancy contacting him and seeing if he's available today?' asked the DI.

'On a Sunday?' frowned Ross, 'I'm sure he's got nothing better to do than speak to us, and anyway, I have to go out to Scorguie on Monday.'

'Weeell…' said Avalon, drawing out the word much longer than he ought to. Then, in a quieter voice, continued with, 'he lives out Nairn way, doesn't he?'

'Yeah,' frowned Ross deeply, 'which means it's another long journey into the middle of nowhere.'

'But on the bright side,' continued Avalon, 'it can't be far away from the one that dances with a pole.' Ross was about to add something and then a light came on behind his eyes. He dropped his frown, widened his

224

eyes and then took on a suspicious look.

'You serious?' he asked. Avalon nodded and sighed, looking to his computer screen, 'but...' he added, 'make sure DI Mowat is seen first, and make sure all proper distancing is observed.' Ross waited for a moment. 'Have you not got a call to make?' asked Avalon without looking up.

'Yes... yes,' stammered Ross as he stood and turned to leave.

'And don't be all day,' Avalon added. Ross simply gave him a cheeky grin and reached for his mobile phone.

Avalon continued with his report, including everything they currently knew about the quarry case. Not all the official documents had arrived yet, and the report from Dundee could take a few days to arrive, but the detail could be amended if needed. He had finished it by early afternoon and sent a copy to the DCI and another to MIT headquarters, so they knew how he was progressing. He then decided to have another trip to B Section, if only to see if anyone was there to update him on the progress with the so-called Plague Witch. As he entered, there were two officers, DS Murrey and the new face that Avalon didn't know.

'Ah, DI,' smiled Murrey, 'come to spectate on a bore event?'

'Same for me, paperwork all morning,' smiled back Avalon. 'Is John around?' he added, looking over to the small and empty office.

'No,' replied Murrey. 'He was supposed to be in, but after his little brush with the PW, he decided to take a day off. Just me and Kieran here.' He nodded to the new face, who gave a smile. 'Have you met DC Aitken yet?'

'I have now,' nodded Avalon to the young man. He looked young but was probably late twenties or early thirties.

'Nice to meet you DI,' said the lad with a confident voice, which sounded local. Avalon couldn't understand why, but he didn't think Kieran was a suitable name for a CID officer, and he was surprised that no nick-name had been proffered.

'I'm surprised that being in B Section, you haven't already been christened with a witty but disparaging nick-name?' It was Murrey who answered.

'You're welcome to try, but what can you make from Kieran Aitkin?'

'It's almost a tongue twister, I admit,' laughed Avalon. He then sat on a close chair and asked, 'So what was the tiff with the DCI about?'

'Yours truly here,' replied Murrey, nodding towards the DC. 'The DCI saw him downstairs and got him involved with carrying some box files to her office. Normally it wouldn't have mattered, but then she asked him to take some other stuff to her car, and Kieran told her he was busy with a job for the guv'nor. She told her that she had authority over the DI and he should do what she asked. He told her he would, but only after he had been to see DI Lasiter.' Avalon glanced round to Aitkin with a stifled grin.

'You've got balls DC, I'll give you that,' he said.

'Aye, but she went ape shit and told me that my time here wouldn't be long with that attitude,' explained the lad. 'Then she stormed off and when I came back here and told the old man, he went ape shit too and got her on the phone.'

226

'And you saw part of what happened next,' explained Murrey.

'Come back Croker, all is forgiven,' smiled Avalon.

'The guv'nor's exact words,' nodded Murrey. He leaned back in the chair and added, 'Did you need to see him or can I help?'

'It's just this Christopher Joyce, he's not playing ball,' explained Avalon, 'and I just wondered if there was any other way to get to him.'

'Nah,' sighed Murrey, 'he's well known for being difficult, but as the old man said, he's no killer...' he paused, 'not of people anyway.' Avalon nodded and returned to his office and continued with the tedium of the paperwork, in the certain knowledge that the DCI wasn't at work. Rutherford and White had been catching up on their own paperwork, and then both of them worked on any loose ends within the quarry case. Frazer was taking a rare Sunday off, as were Wilson and Mackinnon. Avalon knew that this major case could demand long hours at any time, and so he thought it prudent that they should take some time off before that happened. He had also decided that they would all leave for home at a reasonable time, as it was doubtful Ross would be back early that evening.

As he left for home, the weather was fine, but the day had been very unstable, and he could see heavy clouds on the horizon. As he pulled into the drive of his house, he was thinking through his future with Sarah. He wondered if this could be a lasting relationship and began to prepare himself for all the small, irritating habits that the other person might have. He had seen Sarah's home some time ago, and it was clean and tidy if a little random in the way it was furnished. He hoped she wouldn't turn out to be untidy. It was something he didn't like. He wasn't one for dusting and other tedious housework, but untidiness was certainly a pet hate. Then he wondered if he would have habits or things he did, that would equally annoy Sarah. He shrugged and tried the door. He didn't know if she would be in. She was, and to his surprise, he could smell cooking. He couldn't quite put his finger on what it was, but the smell and the feeling of homeliness was pleasant. It was almost like being married again, but he gave just the merest hint of a thought to his time with his ex-wife, Carol. In the lounge, the radio was on in the background and soon Sarah appeared from the door to the passageway.

'Oh hello, you're earlier than I expected,' she gave a smile.

'Yes,' he nodded, 'something smells good in the kitchen,' he then added.

'Just a vegetable bake, nothing fancy,' and she made her way to the kitchen to check on it.

'How was your chat with your sister? Is she well?' he called after her as he removed his jacket and tie, and slumped onto the sofa.

'Yes, she's fine. We had a long blether and talked about the past,' she said as she returned. She was dressed casually and with her hair loose, he thought she looked relaxed and in a good mood. 'She sent me some old photographs she found in her attic the other day. It's one of the reasons I went back to my house, to pick them up. I hadn't seen them for years, so it set us talking of the past.'

'Nice memories?' he asked.

'Some nice, some not so nice,' she smiled.

'Do I get to see them or are they private?' he smiled.

'Maybe later,' she replied, 'So, do you fancy trying this bake?' He wondered if she had deliberately changed the subject.

'Certainly, I'll take a shower first though if that's okay?' he stood and went to the bathroom. As the hot water revived his body, he leaned on the shower wall and realised that their relationship would always be a struggle, simply due to their working relationship. They had already made a cast iron rule that neither of them would speak about their work when at the house, but neither of them were much good at chit-chat, and with no common interests or hobbies. That left few subjects for conversation. They ate, and the food was good, then they retired to the lounge with the radio still playing.

'Shall I turn that off?' she asked as she sat opposite.

'No, it's fine,' replied Avalon, leaning back on the sofa.

'Oh,' she suddenly said, but then paused. 'This isn't directly about work, but I notice you have your photograph in the local paper.'

'Really?' he sat up surprised, 'I knew the press office had released more information but I haven't been near a photographer.'

'It was in Friday's edition,' she explained, 'I still have it,' and she left to fetch the paper. She returned and passed it to him before returning to the easy chair opposite. He glanced at the picture and then read the report, which announced that DI Avalon was leading the investigation.

'That photograph is ancient, I don't even own

that tie anymore,' he insisted.

'They use what they have, I suppose.'

'I know they do, but they might have used one with a neutral expression instead of something where I look as if I'm constipated. That one was during an interview a few years ago.' He was frowning as he added, 'up in Golspie as I recall.' Very fleetingly, he also remembered the woman he had met there and the little bothy he and Ross stayed at. He didn't know why, but every time some memory that was even remotely romantic shot through his mind, he felt guilty. He hadn't even slept with Julia. She had been a very different type of woman to Sarah, probably quite opposite in many ways. He put the paper aside and looked to her. She was watching his reaction and had a slight smile playing on her lips. 'And that reminds me, you have some photographs...' he trailed off, watching her reaction this time.

'They're not very good. Three of them are of me and sis at the wedding of a relation. They're too far from the camera and a bit grainy.'

'I don't mind that,' he smiled, 'you asked about my past, now I want to know more about you.' She bit her bottom lip in thought, then shrugged and said,

'Okay, they're in my bag,' and once again she retired to her room and fetched them in. This time she sat at his side on the sofa, but raising her leg to her side she sat facing him, scanning through half a dozen small photographs. She eventually pulled one from the set and handed it to him. He raised his brows after seeing Sarah much younger in a knee-length blue dress and a wide-brimmed hat. The hair that came from it was wavy and much lighter than it was currently. The image wasn't sharp, but her features could be easily seen.

'If that's your sister, you look nothing alike.'

'No,' she smiled, 'we're not much alike in any way really. She doesn't look like that anymore either. She's probably a few stones heavier and has very short hair.' The sister was a few inches taller than Sarah at the time, but about the same build. When she passed him the second photo, which was a little clearer, he could make out that the sister looked plain. Avalon wondered if one of them was adopted.

'You don't even look similar,' he said, raising his brows. She laughed.

'People used to say that then,' and she looked him in the eye, 'but I had started wearing heavy eye makeup that was popular at the time, and glossy, lined lipstick. She just kept with her usual light eyeliner.' She gave a little sigh, 'We look more alike now though,' she then added. Avalon looked back at the image. He could see the makeup was different but even then, a twenty-year-old Sarah completely overshadowed her sister in many ways. She hadn't offered any more photos, Avalon noticed.

'Is that it?' he asked.

'Oh, these are just my mum and dad some years ago.' Reluctantly, she showed two images of her parents. They were just ordinary people that he could have seen on any family shot. The mother had a pleasant face, a little overweight but with a genuine smile. She had probably been pretty when she was young. The father was handsome, but stern looking, as if the smile he was struggling with was costing him money. She then passed him another image. It was of a Highland terrier. 'That was Tyke. He was the dog we had when I was young. I don't remember much about him now, but it's nice to have a picture of him.'

'And the last one?' he asked, noticing there was a final image. It was smaller than the others, and Avalon considered that it was probably older.

'Not this one?' she smiled, but the smile had a serious side to it.

'Okay, is there any reason?'

'I don't like it, it's not one I ever show people,' she replied.

'Then why keep it?' he asked.

'I probably won't but when my sister gave it to me she laughed, and…' she broke off. There was something in her past that was troubling her. 'Well,' she continued and Avalon noticed the photograph was being closed in on itself and was about to be crushed, 'it was innocent, and meant nothing to her, but to me…' she broke off again. Avalon thought it could have been an old boyfriend of hers, something that stuck in her memory.

'It's fine if you don't want to show it me, but don't deny your past, just keep it until you're sure you don't want to see it again.' His voice was soothing and sympathetic. 'Then, if you still hate it, destroy it, but I can't imagine what could cause you to feel like that.' She looked down at the image she now had clamped in both hands. Without looking at him, she thrust the photo at him and slumped back on the sofa, staring into space. He took the image and let his eyes take it in. It was what looked like a school photograph of a girl around ten or eleven years old. She wore a gingham dress, had strawberry blonde coloured hair, which was neck length and extremely curly, even frizzy. She wore glasses and

232

her eyes seemed to be looking in slightly different directions. There was a subdued smile, but that smile did not extend to the eyes, and it was a troubled countenance in many ways. Though the face was totally unknown to him, he knew it must be Sarah. Why else would she have it, and why be so loath to show it to him? But he could see no resemblance to the woman now by his side. He considered how he should now react to the image.

'So...' he pondered a little, 'how old were you here?' Her head immediately shot round to him and for a terrible moment, he wondered if the image wasn't her, and he had misread it. Was it some lost friend or relation from her schooldays?

'So you see me in it?' she said abruptly.

'Sort of,' he shrugged, 'we all change from our childhood, but I suppose it couldn't be anyone else seeing as you didn't want to show it to me.'

'I was eleven,' she said, looking towards it, 'and at the height of my despair.' He looked at her, she looked as sad as he had ever seen her.

'So, do you want to talk about it?' he asked.

'Not really,' she shrugged, 'I exorcised that demon years ago, but I still feel sorrow for the desperate little girl in that photograph.' She spoke as if the girl was dead. He supposed in some ways she was. In Avalon's eyes, the girl wasn't disfigured or even ugly. She was actually pleasant looking, but the hair, the spectacles and the wayward eye would make a great target for disdain from other children, and he supposed that had been the main issue.

'Then, might you explain it to me?' he asked gently.

'There isn't much to tell, really. I was a bit of an

233

outsider at school, I couldn't see very well and so I was being left behind, and quickly becoming a figure of fun. I think that's why I was annoyed when my sister laughed.' She turned to him. 'She wouldn't remember it as I do, but all the boys were after her, she was pretty, she was clever, and for some of that time I was jealous of her. I was a figure of ridicule and she was admired.'

'I think most families have sibling rivalry,' he agreed, 'but I can understand that you were not playing on a level field.'

'Certainly not,' she nodded as she looked back into the middle distance, 'but my teacher saved me, I suppose. She went to see my parents to tell them that if I had corrective surgery on my eye, I would improve my schooling. She told them that I was as clever as my sister, but even at the front of the class I couldn't see. I was having terrible headaches too.' She swallowed deeply. 'I was also worried about the bullying from some of the other pupils, but she told them nothing about that.'

'So, I'm guessing you had the surgery?' he asked. She glanced round to him and then brought her knees up to her chin.

'Yes, but much later.' She spoke wistfully now. 'It wasn't that easy then, and my parents didn't have the money to go private, but...' she paused, 'when I was fifteen, I went to have what turned out to be a relatively easy operation and within two weeks, I could read without glasses of any sort.'

'And had your education suffered?' he asked.

'Yes, it had. But the biggest change was when I looked in the mirror and could see my face as clear as day. My sister made me up one day with her own makeup. She straightened my hair, and even bought me a

234

dress with some of her first earnings. Then she took me to a local Ceilidh, and the result shocked me. No one knew who I was. All the boys stared at me.' She turned her head to Avalon. 'Can you understand how that felt?'

'I think so,' he nodded. She rested her chin on her knees once more.

'After that, I became a problem child,' she added, 'but in a very different way. I had a power over men I didn't realise existed, and I was horrible with it.' She went silent.

'Does anyone else know?' he asked after a moment.

'No, not really,' and she turned to him, 'my family knew. They had to deal with my new problem.' She turned from him and dropped her feet back on the floor. She then took the photographs from him and returned them to her room. Then, she walked to the kitchen and brought them both a glass of wine. She sat opposite him again.

'I'm glad you told me that,' and he allowed a glimmer of a smile.

'I'm sorry to burst the bubble,' she said as she took a gulp of the wine.

'There *was* no bubble. We all have some skeleton tucked away. It just takes a brave moment to admit to it.'

'Even you?' she asked in an ironic voice.

'Even me,' he replied, raising his brows.

'So don't tell me, you're really Bible John.' She was referring to one of Scotland's most notorious serial killers. He had never been caught.

'Not quite that, but this isn't the time for it,' he insisted.

'I wish I hadn't told you now,' she said, pulling

up her knees again.

'I'm glad you did,' he smiled more openly. 'I think sharing those intimate things, bonds people in a way that even time doesn't.'

'But now, in the back of your mind, you'll keep thinking, 'what was it she did that was horrible?' and that bothers me.'

'Don't let it,' and he let the smile drop. 'I don't care, and to be honest, I've been a copper too long for anything like that to bother me. I'm just happy that you trust me enough to tell me.' She remained quiet this time and soon polished off the wine. She then stood and said,

'I'm going for a shower,' but as she passed he grabbed her arm. She stopped and looked down at him.

'I mean it,' he said, returning the smile, 'I'm really glad I know more about you.' She gave a nod and sighed, then went to the bathroom.

The year was passing quickly, and it was already halfway through April as Avalon stepped to the front of the office for the Monday morning briefing. He surveyed the faces of his team and began with DS Wilson and DC Mackinnon.

'Gordon,' he began, 'you and Rory will stay on the day-to-day business. There are two new breaking and entering cases, well, one is attempted but they need attending to.' Wilson nodded. 'As for the rest of us, we need to make hay on the quarry case, I don't want this dragging on while the DCI is on the warpath. So...' he paused as he scanned the jobs through his mind. 'Megan, chase up on any friends or relatives with the names we have and see if there are any dental records for either of the two missing people who could be tied to the bodies.

Angus, you help with that,' and he turned to White who nodded. 'Martin, I want you dig deeper into any ricin connections from longer ago or other poisoning cases.' He then turned to Ross. 'I know you have to go to Scorguie today, but I need you to tell me about your interview with DI Mowat.'

'I sent you an email,' frowned Ross.

'I know, but you know I like the personal touch.' He then looked up to the others. 'Carry on, and if anything crops up, I want to know.'

Ross followed Avalon to the booth and sat in the spare seat. Avalon removed his jacket and placed it on the back of the chair.

'What did you think of the retired DI?' he asked as he sat.

'Just seemed like any other B and B husband to me. Hard to imagine he was in the CID,' replied Ross, and Avalon smiled.

'Remember, that could be you in a few years,' he said.

'I hope not,' replied Ross with a grimace, 'he's got religion.'

'Really?' asked Avalon, surprised.

'Aye, not the genuflecting, rosary bead sort of religion,' explained Ross, 'the worse kind, politics.'

'Oh, I see,' and Avalon raised his eyebrows. 'Nationalism?' added Avalon.

'No, not really,' frowned Ross, 'you'd probably have to call it 'shireism' or something.' It was obvious that Avalon didn't understand but Ross wasn't keen on explaining further so he changed the subject. 'He seemed eager to give any help though.' Avalon nodded at this and brought something up on his computer.

'I've read everything I can find on the case. Was there anything he told you that isn't here?' asked Avalon, nodding to his screen.

'Not much,' sighed Ross, 'well, you know, the same sort of speculation we all make when cases fold.'

'Such as?'

'Well,' reflected Ross thinking back to the meeting, 'he's not sure that either of them are wholly innocent, he made that clear on several occasions.' Ross leaned back and interlinked his hands behind his head. 'He says that Stuart Fenner tried everything to damn Gibson. He thinks most of it was revenge on a man that stole his wife.'

'But the case notes say she left him because of his abusive nature,' insisted Avalon, 'not because of Gibson.'

'Yes,' nodded Ross, 'and Mowat thinks that was correct, but for the sake of the trial, Fenner played the spurned husband, probably for the sympathy vote. Or, as Mowat thinks, a hatred of Gibson.' Avalon showed a blank expression for a moment, then he looked back at the screen of the computer.

'I wonder if there's another reason for the hatred, or is it just a revenge trip as DI Mowat thought?'

'I don't know,' shrugged Ross, 'but Mowat is convinced that there is something that they both know, but won't mention.'

'You mean he thinks they are both involved with Mary and her son?' Ross nodded and sat forward again.

'But you have to wonder why this went to court without a body,' he said. Avalon looked to him and widened his eyes.

'In a strong case, you don't need a body, you

know that,' he insisted.

'But this wasn't a strong case,' insisted Ross, 'Mowat admitted he was getting pressure from above as they had several major cases at the time.'

'Nothing changes,' groaned Avalon.

'No, it doesn't, except for the fact that in this case, there just isn't enough evidence to point the finger as Gibson.' He paused and began to count the issues on his fingers. 'No real evidence of blood or violence was found at either address, in fact, nothing unusual was found by forensics at the addresses or in Gibson's car.' He pointed to the second finger. 'There were no witnesses that heard or saw anything unusual at either address, and at the address where Gibson was arrested, the neighbours confirmed they had never seen any female with him.' He stuck out the third finger. 'Even though both men and their addresses were examined, no evidence of either Mary or her son Carl, were ever found except at Inverness where the normal amount of fingerprints and fibres were found. Nothing suspicious.'

'What about the witness that said they saw Fenner's car near Gibson's house?' asked Avalon.

'Mowat told me that the witness was so poor, the prosecution never called her,' replied Ross in a high pitch. 'It was a backup but never taken seriously. The whole prosecution case revolved around the fact that Social Services didn't do enough to find out why the child wasn't attending school.'

'And that was a gift to the defence, as they stated the child was still at the address three days before they left,' added Avalon.

'But,' insisted Ross leaning forward, 'Fenner had insisted that the child hadn't been seen by him for

239

months prior to them moving from Inverness, and if that little body we found is Carl, Fenner could be right.'

'Except that the defence proved that Fenner hadn't arranged to see the child on any previous date,' added Avalon. Ross sighed with a nod and leaned back in his chair. Avalon noticed Frazer walking to the booth.

'Found something?' he asked as she leaned on the frame.

'Yes, Boss,' she said, but her face was hard to read. 'We've found Mary Anne Fenner's dental records, but there are no records for her son.'

'Have you arranged to have copies sent out?' the DI asked.

'Yes, I informed forensics that we're sending them over, but what about the child?' she asked.

'If we can't find records, there's nothing we can do,' sighed Avalon, 'but all we need is to confirm that Sandy is Mary Anne. We have DNA to connect the two sets of bones together.' She nodded and returned to her seat.

'Well, we'll know soon enough,' exclaimed Ross.

'Yes,' nodded Avalon, 'but Christ knows what we'll do if there isn't a match.' Ross stood and began to return to his desk, but he stopped and turned to face Avalon.

'Oh, and thanks, by the way,' he said.

'For what?' asked Avalon, pretending to forget about Ross's trip to Nairn. Ross smiled and continued to his desk. 'I just hope you were the perfect gentleman,' called Avalon.

'No one's perfect,' called Ross without glancing back.

Just over an hour later, it was confirmed that there was a positive match with the dental record of Mary Anne Fenner and the x-ray taken of the teeth of the skull they had been calling Sandy. DNA samples obtained from both sets of bones confirmed that the child was indeed a son of the woman. It was thought, as she had only one child, the bones must belong to Carl Fenner. Avalon looked at the old photograph of the woman that he had placed on the whiteboard. She had been plain and ordinary, her hair showing no signs of her being interested in styles of the time. The only photograph of Carl was when the boy was about three years old and bore very little resemblance to how he may have looked at the time of his death. They now knew who the bodies were, they just had no further idea of why they came to be buried together, and who had put them there. The odds were that either one, or both of the men were responsible for the deed, and it was clear that the two men would have to be interviewed, along with any friends or relations still living. They would also have to contact anyone heavily involved with the original case. Fortunately, Ross was already on his way to see a distant relative. There was little stored in the archive that forensics could examine again, but Avalon had it brought out of storage and sent to the forensics lab. Avalon looked out of the window and saw heavy cloud, and it reflected his mood. He still couldn't understand why the two bodies had been buried together at different times. He strolled to the front of the office and asked,

'Anyone got any ideas about this case?' For some moments there was no response.

'Are there still just the two suspects?' asked Martin.

241

'We're not aware of anyone else linked to this case, so yes, we have to consider that Stuart Fenner and Geoffrey Gibson are the two likeliest people to be involved.'

'So, looking at the time-frame on the board,' continued Martin, 'the husband only seemed interested in seeing the child a few weeks before the house they rented was vacated.'

'It seems that way,' agreed Avalon.

'So logic would say that Fenner somehow found out that they were on the move,' continued the DC, 'someone must have told him.'

'But no name was brought up at the trial and Fenner claims he felt bad about not seeing the boy,' explained Frazer as if it was all obvious.

'But that's the point,' insisted Rutherford turning to Frazer. 'He was lying about that, but who actually told him?'

'He could have been informed that Carl was missing from school by Social Services,' offered Avalon, 'he wasn't looking after the boy but he was still the father.'

'Then we need to fill in the gaps,' answered Rutherford.

'I agree,' nodded Avalon and he leaned on the booth frame. 'Let's put more work into this timeline and find any records, including anything that didn't get to the trial. Social Services got a caning from the court for not keeping records on the boy, so we can't go there. Try to track down anyone working for them around that time.' The Cave became a hive of activity once more, and several telephone conversations began almost immediately. The DI walked steadily back to the booth.

242

He was beginning to wonder if this was going to be beyond him, but he began to process applications to the Sheriff's Court to bring the two men back to Inverness for questioning. Later in the day, just after the moment that Avalon was wondering what the outcome with Lasiter and the DCI had been, the door to The Cave opened and the DCI looked in.

'Have you got a minute DI?' was all she said and then disappeared. Avalon entered her office and remained standing.

'You wish to see me, Ma'am?'

'Yes, take a seat DI Avalon.' Reluctantly he sat. 'I know there are no secrets when it comes to police stations, Detective Inspector, so I assume you heard about DI Lasiter's disagreement with myself?'

'I don't take much notice of gossip, Ma'am,' he said, 'but I have certainly heard about heated words.'

'Indeed,' she replied, looking down at the computer screen for a moment. 'It is unfortunate that it has come to this and it has caused a few problems to say the least, but I know I can still count on the other sections to continue regardless.' Avalon frowned a little. He didn't think the argument was all that serious, and though Lasiter could be aggressive to say the least, he didn't tend to hold grudges.

'With respect,' replied Avalon, 'I think every section at this nick does their job to their upmost capabilities, bar none.' She looked up to him but said nothing. After a few seconds and what Avalon thought was a slight sniff, she looked back to her screen.

'I have read your report of the quarry case and I wondered if you had made any further progress?' she asked.

'We are making some progress and we have now confirmed the identity of the woman in the grave.'

'Ah, good,' she nodded, 'and the child?'

'Due to DNA results, we are as sure as we can be that the child was her son.'

'Can I release that to the press?' she asked. Avalon was cautious. Yes, it was almost certain it was her son, but on a sensitive case like this, you rarely made assumptions.

'I would say that it looks likely,' he eventually said.

'Then I'll inform the press office, the papers are pushing for news and if we don't tell them something they will start guessing.' The DI felt like she was too talkative, too easy-going. Was she trying to find an ally? He knew for sure it wouldn't be him.

'Is there anything else?' he asked and stood. She looked up to him as if there *was* something else, then eventually said,

'No, no, of course, you must be busy.' And he left. It wasn't the first time he had left her office with a smile on his face, and probably wouldn't be the last, but he had to find out if there had been further developments between her and DI Lasiter. For now though, he had far too much to do.

When Ross returned from his interview with Mary Anne's cousin, the plumber at Scorguie, he had to admit that he had found out little.

'It *was* he who was the witness on the marriage certificate, but he and his cousin didn't see much of each other after that,' he explained. 'He did say that Mary had a habit of choosing the wrong sort of men, and when I questioned him about that, he said that Fenner would knock her about after drinking. He told me that the husband wasn't the first, as an old boyfriend had been abusive and though he understood Gibson didn't hit her, he said that the only time he came across the man, in his words, he said 'the guy creeped me out'. That's about it,' shrugged Ross as he completed the explanation. Avalon nodded and everyone returned to their work, disappointed that nothing had come from that source.

As he sat on his sofa that evening, watching Sarah reacting to a text on her phone, Avalon wondered if the Plague Witch, as people were calling her, would be any more destructive as the weeks rolled on. It wasn't unusual for new officers to create a little chaos. Even DCI Croker, who most people had become used to, tried to stamp his own style on the proceedings. In his case it had failed, but it left a bad taste in most people's mouth. With DCI Duncan, he wasn't sure if she was just arrogant or incompetent. She had a good record by all accounts, so it had to be the former. He looked back to Sarah, who was smiling at something on her phone. The rule on not talking about work at home had been a good one, but he soon realised that the two of them had so little else in their lives that there was nothing left to talk of. Did he need a hobby? Did he even have time for a hobby?

'What was that for?' she asked, not taking her eyes from the phone.

'What was what for?' he asked.

'That sigh, it seemed quite a meaningful sigh,' she said and her eyes, still smiling, flashed him a deep brown glance. Had he sighed? He didn't recall it.

'I…' he paused, 'I didn't realise I had sighed. I'm probably just tired.'

'Have an early night then,' she suggested, placing the phone besides her. 'You're probably going to need the sleep.' He smiled to her and gave a small nod. The thing was, that's not how he felt, and he thought back to why he had made an involuntary sigh. Was it another feature of growing old?

'Oh, I forgot to tell you,' she suddenly said as she stood. 'A small parcel arrived today, there was a note saying it was in the shed.' She left the room and returned a minute after. She was carrying a small packet, which she handed to him then left for the kitchen. There was a poor excuse for a shed at the side of the garage, and the postman left anything that was too large for the letterbox there. He felt it, and he thought he knew what it was. He unpacked it and found inside, the complete collection of Para Handy, the book he had sent for. Sarah returned with two glasses and a bottle of wine. She poured two drinks and sat opposite.

'A book?' she noticed. He nodded and turned to cover towards her. 'Para Handy?' she smiled, 'I would have thought that was a little…' she trailed off, not knowing which words to use. She shrugged instead.

'From what John Lasiter told me, this,' he pointed to the cover, 'is the greatest known Scottish legend since Rob Roy MacGregor.'

'I know as little of Rob Roy as I do of Para Handy,' she admitted, 'but if the reruns of the old Para Handy TV series are anything to go by, you may be disappointed.'

'So you never got behind Scottish history and legends then?' he smiled wryly.

246

'Not really,' she said playfully, 'the only thing I know about The Bruce is what I was taught at school and I've never even seen Braveheart. I leave that for the tourists,' and she gave him a look that he understood immediately.

'Ouch, that's below the belt,' he frowned then asked, 'Did you know that the name Braveheart was given to Bruce and not Wallace?' She didn't answer. She picked up her phone once more and glanced back. This time it was her turn to sigh. She then raised her brows and said,

'Did you know that the idea that the two sides of the brain work separately is completely false? And the so-called fact that humans use only part of their brains is untrue?'

'Well, if that isn't another dig at me, no I didn't, but then again, that doesn't take into account Chief Superintendents,' he replied. After a short pause he added, 'Did you know that goldfish have a much longer memory than people think? It's considered they can remember things over several months.'

'Read your book,' she smiled. He smiled back and opened the book. Here he was, sitting just five feet away from Sarah Underwood, and he was reading the tales of Para Handy.

Chapter Eleven

'I'm going to bring Joyce in,' announced Avalon to Ross. Avalon had sat in the booth considering his options on the quarry case, until he saw Ross glance over to him. He then nodded to the booth entrance and Ross, understanding the meaning of that subtle nod, sat in the spare seat.

'Okay, but we have nothing on him,' shrugged Ross.

'I know,' sighed Avalon, 'but we have to question him due to his connection with ricin.'

'I don't want to point out the obvious,' sighed Ross, leaning forward slightly, 'but I'm going to. Joyce will tell you that he was acquitted due to lack of evidence.'

'I know that too, but that case was a private prosecution and in truth, some of the laws in Scotland are somewhat behind the times when compared to the rest of the UK.'

'I'm not with you,' frowned Ross.

'Here,' insisted Avalon, 'in Scotland, permission has to be gained from the Judge Advocate to proceed with a private prosecution, and though it was given, the people who brought the case, ran out of money.'

'Yes, but-' began Ross but Avalon interrupted.

'No buts, that trail can be discounted, from our point of view at least,' frowned Avalon, 'the only reason it went ahead at all was because of the magic word ricin.' Ross was quiet. 'Joyce wasn't really acquitted, the trail was essentially abandoned.'

'I'm still not sure why you think it's a good idea to bring Joyce in,' replied Ross, folding his arms in resignation.

'As we heard from the notes we have on Joyce, the dog owners had found that a previous neighbour of Joyce had lost a dog in mysterious circumstances. I can't confirm that, but the date is significant,' insisted the DI. 'If the notes within the investigation are accurate, the other dog died around the end of 2003,' he continued. 'In January 2003, the Metropolitan Police raided a flat in London and arrested six Algerian men whom they claimed were manufacturing ricin as part of a plot for a poison attack on the London Underground. It is worth noting that this was in the news all through that year, long enough to give a disgruntled man time to plan. No ricin was recovered in the London case however, and only one person was convicted. The charge was conspiracy to cause a public nuisance by the use of poisons to cause disruption, fear or injury. The man was jailed for seventeen years.'

'I remember it,' nodded Ross, 'and it was also brought up during training, but the convicted man in that case had previously received a life sentence for stabbing and killing a policeman during the raid as I recall.'

'But my point is,' insisted Avalon, 'the date is significant. Not only that, ricin wouldn't be the automatic choice of poison for most people, would it?'

'I grant you that,' nodded Ross, 'that has puzzled me since it came to our attention.'

'So, there could be some truth in the story,' said Avalon and then continued with, 'we need to track down the veterinary surgeon who confirmed the poison and find out more about the internals of the case. I'll put Megan on it.'

'Do you want me to contact the people who brought the case?' asked Ross.

'No,' Avalon shook his head, 'we need to remain objective about this so let's keep it clean and tidy. In the meantime, I'll see if I can find out who would be in my shoes fifteen years ago, just to see if they can shed any light on this.'

'I can tell you that,' interrupted Ross, 'DI Mowat was still here until 2008. He told me that's when he retired.'

'Looks like I need a talk to Mr Mowat then,' said Avalon, more to himself than Ross. Ross nodded and left to do as he had been asked, and Avalon looked towards the windows. The sky was bright with just a few passing clouds, and he wondered if he should go and see the ex-detective inspector himself. Firstly though, he had to prepare the paperwork, just in case Christopher Joyce proved a little reticent about answering questions.

About an hour later, Frazer came to the booth, soon after she had been tasked with finding the veterinary surgeon.

'Take a seat Megan, what have you got?' he asked looking up from his computer.

'I managed to find the vet who found ricin en the dogs,' she explained, 'or rather I found his wife,' she added. 'Her husband died six years ago, but she remembered the case.'

'Did you get anything?' Avalon asked.

'Aye, a wee bit, but nothing ground breaking,' admitted Megan. 'The wifie says that her husband wasn't all that sure what et was he had found, and so he took et tae an old friend. The friend was a chemist working for a chemical manufacturer en the town, and *he* offered tae check the compound out. Et seems he worked out what et was straight away.'

'What was the name of this man?' he asked. Frazer looked down at her notepad.

'Colin Templeton, he's got a load of letters after his name by all accounts, and es still working en chemicals. He's some sort o' management these days.'

'That name doesn't appear at the trial,' he scowled.

'I know, et was the first thing I checked,' nodded Frazer.

'To be honest, that doesn't mean much in a private action.' He sighed deeply. 'Okay, you better get in touch with Mr Templeton. We need some information from him.'

'Okay Boss,' nodded Frazer and she stood to leave. 'Oh, and I think…' she trailed off and paused for a moment, 'DC White es onto something but he won't say what et es yet.' Avalon gave a quick glance to White who was busy on a phone and then nodded to Frazer. He waited for Frazer to return to her seat and then stood and tapped on the glass. White looked up and Avalon beckoned him into the booth.

'Have you got something?' he asked, even before White was seated. He noticed White's eyes glance to the right, as if looking back to his desk.

'Probably, it's not ready yet,' replied White, slumping into the chair.

'Not ready?' questioned the DI, 'I'm not asking for a report Angus, I just want to know if you have anything yet?'

'No, then sir,' he said with a blank expression. Avalon then realised what White was about. He had an idea about the case, which was probably just guesswork, but due to his past experience, he wouldn't make it known until he had the facts to back-up the idea. Avalon sighed, in some ways he didn't blame White for being cautious.

'I see,' he simply said and then stared at the DC for some moments. 'You know,' continued Avalon after getting no further response, 'keeping an idea isn't a bad thing if you are competing with someone, but as part of a team, I would have thought you would share something that may advance our work.' White took a deep breath and then said,

'I realise that, but as you now know about my time in Glasgow, I'm sure you'll understand if I don't proceed with guesswork,' explained White, and he crossed his arms.

'If you take guesswork out of our toolbox, we would never solve a single case,' sighed Avalon, 'but it's up to you,' and he looked to his computer screen as if to dismiss the DC.

'Well,' said White, and then stopped. He looked off into the distance and unfolded his arms. Avalon suspected he was thinking the situation through. 'I suppose it's almost together now anyway,' he added. Avalon looked back to him and raised his brows. 'It seemed to me,' White eventually said, the first few words spilling from his mouth as if they had been back-logged, 'that the situation at the quarry seemed odd. Yet being odd, it should be easy to work out. When the information came back from Dundee about the bone growth in the child, it all fell into place for me. I just had to find something to verify my...' he paused for a second before adding, 'guesswork.' Avalon leaned back in his chair. He was genuinely interested in what White had to say.

'Go on,' he nodded.

'It seemed pretty obvious that the child was suffering some sort of serious torment and that smacks of abuse, probably the sexual kind. That meant Gibson was the culprit. If the child meant to reveal this to his mother, Gibson may have tried to silence him.'

'Unless the mother knew about it,' put in Avalon.

'Yeah,' nodded White, 'and I think she may have suspected and turned a blind eye to it. That means the child would become more desperate.' White paused for a moment, as if wondering how Avalon would react to the next piece of his idea. 'I think it's likely that the child killed himself.'

'It happens,' sighed Avalon, 'but it's rare at that age.'

'I know,' nodded White and he leaned forward, a little more animated. 'But if for a minute you assume that was the case, it would cause all hell to break loose in that household. If Gibson knew that the mother knew about him abusing the child, he couldn't inform the police about the death, and in a panic, he could have possibly taken the child to a remote spot and buried him.' Avalon nodded slowly as his eyes flitted from side to side, trying to make some sense of the idea.

'So why did the mother end up over a year later buried above him?' he asked with a frown.

'I have an idea about that too, but you haven't asked the question I expected yet,' said White in a rare fit of helpfulness.

'You mean proof?' he asked, 'you have some proof?'

'Oh yes,' nodded White, 'I dug so deep into Gibson's past, I needed a bloody cap-lamp.' Avalon thought this must be a reference to mining, which would have still been in operation in South Yorkshire when White was a boy. 'He has a history. A history which, for some unexplained reason, has never been dug into.' Avalon didn't comment, he just shook his head slowly. 'He was never taken to court before he met Mary Fenner, but a few people he worked with, told the police during the investigation, that they thought he was a pervert. I guess that it never came up at the trial as it was probably quashed by the defence as here-say.'

'That isn't proof,' insisted Avalon. White suddenly stood and went to his computer. He then looked at Avalon through the glass and beckoned him into the main office.

'But this is,' insisted White standing once more and pointing to the screen. Avalon steadily sat and began to read through an email that was on White's computer.

'Jee-sus Christ,' exclaimed Avalon, drawing out the two words. He continued to read and then raised his brows. 'This is good work, Angus. I'm guessing there is more if you said it isn't quite ready?'

'A little,' nodded White, 'but it all brings us to the same point.' Avalon stood and ran his hand through

254

his hair as White replaced him at his own seat. The DI looked into the main office. All work had stopped as they guessed something important had happened. He didn't know if he should tell them yet or wait until White had concluded his investigation. There was a quiet knock at the door. To Avalon's surprise, it didn't open immediately, and when it did, it was slow. The face that peeped around the door was not the DCI, but PC Dowd carrying a box.

'Oh, er sorry DI,' stuttered Dowd, 'it was so quiet in here I wondered if there was anyone in.' A phone rang on Rutherford's desk.

'Hello, DC Rutherford.' His voice broke the hiatus in the activity. Gradually, the others went back to work. Avalon looked to Dowd.

'Come in Neil, what can we do for you?' he asked.

'Did someone just lose their winning lottery ticket?' whispered Dowd.

'No,' not quite,' replied Avalon, 'we just heard that the Queen has died from covid.'

'Jees,' exclaimed Dowd, 'I hadnae heard about that,' he sighed. 'Ah well, they'll be looking for homes for a few corgis I'll wager.' Avalon smiled, either Dowd had realised it was in jest, or he really did have an odd take on life.

'Probably, but that will have to wait until after the big knees up Prince Charles is throwing,' added Avalon as Dowd placed the box on the nearest desk, and pulled out a coffee machine. Avalon smiled wider at the sight of it and immediately removed the sanitiser bottle from the nearby shelf, and handed it to Dowd. He placed the machine on the shelf, stood back and looked at it.

'I tested et, et does work,' explained Dowd, rubbing the sanitiser into his hands and dabbing a little behind his ears for good measure.

'Thanks Neil,' you're a hero,' beamed Avalon, and then added looking back to the machine, 'no matter what the others say.' He turned to the room in general.

'All we need now is-'

'I'm on it,' interrupted Ross, as he stood and pulled his jacket from the chair back, 'I could do with some air.' Avalon looked back to the machine and then over to White, who was once again working. The distraction had given him time to think about the details that White had shown him, and he decided that he would leave it for the time being, as it wouldn't impact on the other items they were working on.

'Any headway on the quarry case?' asked Dowd.

'A little,' nodded Avalon, but he wasn't revealing anything at the moment, and Dowd probably hadn't expected him to, and so he left as quietly as he had arrived.

When Ross had returned with supplies and the coffee machine began chugging into life like some old steam engine, Frazer made her way to Avalon in the booth.

'One thing this virus has done for us,' she smiled, 'es make et easier t' get en touch with people.' Avalon agreed and asked what she had. 'I've been en touch with Colin Templeton, the chemist. I haven't told him the whole story and just told him we were looking at cases involving ricin.' He nodded but Frazer remained standing, which meant she didn't have much to tell him, she was probably just giving him an update. 'He couldn't remember et at first,' she continued, 'which surprised me, as I wondered how many ricin cases he might have come across.'

'I agree, but did you find anything?'

'Not much, he just told me that the substance es reasonably easy tae spot and the vet left him samples t' test. Ricin was found en all the samples.'

'So there's no chance of error?' asked Avalon.

'Doubtful,' replied Frazer with a shrug.

'Okay, thanks. I'll give everyone an update in a minute,' he nodded and Frazer returned to her work. Avalon made his way to the coffee machine after processing the new information and leaned on the booth partition, cradling the newly filled cup, as if it were a long-lost friend.

'Right team,' he began, 'we have some information for you.' He gave them all time to stop their work and relax. 'The first thing I have to say is that we are going to be bringing in several people for interviews and at least one is going to be trouble. I'm pushing for Christopher Joyce simply because ricin was found to have been the poison used to kill his neighbour's dogs. This doesn't mean he did it however, and neither does it involve him directly with the quarry case. I just want information that could put him in, or out of the picture.' He paused. 'Next,' he continued, 'I have applied to bring in Stuart Fenner for questioning. He currently resides in Newcastle, so we will have to send someone down there for him.' He paused again and thought about how to word the next item. He looked to his immediate left and saw the face of White looking towards him. 'Due to some tenacious detective work by Angus,' he began, 'we have a great deal of new information about Geoffrey Gibson. It has come to light, that long before he met

Mary Fenner, Gibson was suspected of being a sexual predator, but nothing was proven and he never appeared in court.' There were audible sighs from the team, a sound that confirmed that some of them, at least, had suspected this. 'Later, he was, however convicted of paedophilia and served time for it. I'll not go into details at this juncture, but I will add that when he came out of prison in 2006, relations of one of the victims found his address, and his house was set on fire. Subsequently, after being pursued, he was given a new identity and moved to Lancashire in England. It seems that either someone got information of who he was, or, he had continued his evils ways. That isn't clear yet, but the outcome was that he fled to Spain, where he is said to reside at the moment. He remains on the sex offenders register and two police forces are applying for extradition due to him breaking the terms of his release, and to answer questions related to an incident while he was living in Lancashire.' Avalon took a deep gulp of the coffee and placed the cup on the table. 'He is now seventy years old, but I have registered our intent to question him in connection with our case, if he can be found and brought back to the UK.'

'But if extradition doesn't happen,' mused Ross, 'that's going to hamper our investigation to a large degree.'

'Yes,' nodded Avalon, 'it isn't a great outcome, but we have to make some headway, just in case we get a chance to interview him.'

'So we need Stuart Fenner to help out a little more,' insisted Rutherford.

'I doubt that will produce much,' added White.

'Why not?' asked Rutherford, 'if Fenner hates

Gibson so much, wouldn't he be ready to tell us what he knows?' White shrugged, Avalon saw that he was reticent to add anything, so he interjected.

'I think what Angus is getting at, is that Fenner may not be innocent in this tale.'

'So, you have something?' asked Ross.

'No,' replied the DI picking up his cup, 'but if Fenner knew something, wouldn't he have been willing to spill the beans during the original investigation or the public trial?'

'Which means,' added White, raising his brows, 'that any information he has, could implicate himself in some way.' Ross creased his eyes. It wasn't a frown as such, more of a look of doubt.

'But, that doesn't add up,' he began. 'If Fenner suspected his son was...' He paused suddenly and looked out of the window. Avalon saw White give a little smile to himself. It was going to be some time before White and Ross were on friendly terms.

'Well, that's a first,' said Frazer, looking across the room, Rossy stuck for words.'

'Not stuck for words as such...' he said slowly and trailed off. He was still gazing out of the window.

'Looks like you have come to the same conclusion as Angus,' said Avalon, taking another gulp of coffee. Ross looked back to Avalon for a moment and stood.

'Not at all,' he frowned and walked towards the coffee machine. He poured himself a cup and then looked down at White. 'You think Fenner killed his wife, don't you?' he said with a slight smile playing on his lips. White gave a little shrug but said nothing, and his expression was calm but blank. 'You think that Fenner somehow found out about Gibson and then questioned his wife to see if *she* knew. She refused to let him see if the boy was safe, so he killed her,' and he took a mouthful of coffee. He then used the cup almost as a pointing tool towards White. 'But, you can't work out why the body was almost in the same grave, because that would mean Fenner knew where the child had been buried.' He then smiled, took another drink and watched White's reaction. 'That's about the size of it I'm guessing,' added Ross.

'Close,' nodded White.

'There's another flaw in that story,' interrupted Avalon. 'If Fenner had found out anything about Gibson, why wasn't it mentioned in the trial? If Fenner had something to discredit Gibson, he would have used it, surely?' It was clear Avalon had a point. There was silence for some moments as Ross made his way back to his seat.

'We still have no connection to the burial site,' added Frazer to break the silence, 'from either of them.'

'True,' nodded Avalon, 'nothing to connect them to the place, or anyone else for that matter.' Avalon looked at his watch but resisted the urge to check it against the clock on the wall. 'I have to go soon, I'm having a word with the ex DI in Nairn,' he looked at Ross, 'about Christopher Joyce this time.' Ross said nothing. He turned back to the window, picked up a biro and began continually pressing the button on the top.

Avalon sat on a wooden seat in the garden of the ex DI, and waited for Mrs Mowat to cease her fussing with the tea and biscuits. When she left them to talk, Avalon asked how he was doing during the lockdown.

'Och, not too bad, we're closed obviously, but it's given us extra time to get the place spruced up,' he smiled, 'how are you lot doing? I bet this lockdown is a wee bit of a problem.' Avalon was taking a sip of the tea, but as he replaced the cup on the table, he nodded and said,

'Yes, it is challenging.' He gave an ironic smile and then asked, 'Do you miss it, the job I mean?' Mowat widened his eyes and replied.

'No, or at least that's what I say when she's around,' he nodded towards the house, 'but if I was honest with myself, yes, I miss it like hell.' Avalon smiled.

'But you have a nice place here.'

'Aye, it's nice enough, but we're both a bit sick of it now,' replied the ex-DI, 'we'd planned to sell up this year but who's going to buy a B-and-B with this lot going on?'

'Oh I see,' replied Avalon, taking his cup once more, 'any other plans?'

'Move back to Caithness where I belong.'

'Back to the Highlands, hey?'

'Back to Caithness, that wonderful county has never been in the Highlands,' insisted the man, and Avalon remembered something Ross had told him. 'Caithness is the Far North. It's a kingdom, not a county. Aye, the Highland council empty the bins up there, and that's about all that shitty government body is worth. I think most of them emptied their heads out with the-'

'So why did you come into Nairnshire?' interrupted Avalon. He had to stop the man ranting.

'This place, it was the right price,' and he took a breather to drink his tea and took two biscuits from the plate. 'But that's not why you came DI Avalon, are you still no further along?'

'We're making progress, but I'm here to ask you about a case that may have crossed your desk about fifteen years ago.' Avalon explained the case involving Christopher Joyce, and Mowat showed some recognition, but there were a few shakes of the head too.

'I remember it, aye. There had been talk of ricin on the news about that time, but we didn't pursue it, as we found no sign of the poison at the property. I think it became a public prosecution, that's all I recall.'

'So nothing sticks in your mind about it?'

'No,' replied Mowat, shaking his head, 'except...' he paused as he tried to bring something from the back of his memory. 'I seem to remember that this Joyce wasn't well liked, and one of my team wondered if he had been set up.'

'Any particular name, come to mind?'

'Sorry, no,' then he reached into his jacket and pulled out an old mobile phone. 'I could give Donny a call. He was the one who dealt with it.' Mowat dialled and Avalon wondered if he and his old team were still friends after all this time. 'He works as a security consultant now,' added Mowat. 'Donny, aye it's Mickey, 'listen, I have a DI here from Inverness, he's...' Mowat broke off and gave a little laugh, 'aye, but I dunna think he'll know that one, as I was saying,' he continued giving Avalon a shifty glance. 'They're looking at that ricin case way back, Chris Joyce, do you remember? Aye, well, can you recall who it was you thought may have set Joyce up?' There was a pause as he nodded several times. 'Aye, I know that, but I can't remember much about it.' Another pause as Mowat's eyes rose.

'Scott? Steven Scott.' Mowat gave Avalon a meaningful nod. 'Aye, well it might help… what? Oh aye, I'm still going if this bloody lockdown is over by then. Okay pal, see you.' He closed his phone and smiled at something he heard during his conversation.

'You still get on with your old team then?' Avalon asked, as he jotted the information into his notepad.

'Some of them, aye,' he nodded. 'Donny just reminded me of what we called DI's back then. Disruptive Influence,' he laughed and then added, 'Is the name Steven Scott any good?'

'Maybe,' Avalon nodded, 'it hasn't cropped up previously, so, it's something to try. We are looking for the ricin connection.' Mowat looked vague at this and so Avalon brought him up to date with what they knew, including the confirmation of the identities. At the mention of Gibson being a sex offender, Mowat sighed deeply.

'There were a few whispers about Gibson being dodgy, but we had no proof on that score,' he admitted, 'but what with Social Services getting it wrong, and dealing with so many lies, we were always pissing into the wind. The pervert stuff was only ever a rumour.'

'DS Ross said you thought they were both heavily involved.'

'That's right,' nodded the man, 'I thought all along that Gibson killed them both until I interviewed Fenner deeply. He was such a bloody liar, that man. I eventually thought maybe *he* had killed them, but with no body, and no evidence to implicate either of them…' He shook his head with a frown.

'You thought Fenner killed them to implicate

Gibson after the fact?' asked Avalon. Mowat nodded,

'Aye, I'm not sure now though, after what you have told me,' he said. 'I expected Mary Anne would have been found with her skull bashed in. Poison? I never expected that.' Avalon stood and smiled.

'Well, thanks for the information and thank your wife for the tea,' he said.

'Will you keep me informed, not about the details of course,' he quickly amended. Avalon nodded and left.

By the time Avalon had returned to the office, there was little of the day left and it didn't take long to realise that the team were somewhat disappointed that they had got no further while the DI had been out. He decided to recap on a few items from earlier in the day with them, and explained what he had heard from Mr Mowat. Though he didn't expect anything to come from it, he suggested that they should explore any possibilities around the name Steven Scott. Frazer soon found him on the database as a petty crook who had been busy earlier in his youth, but for the past decade had kept himself from the courts.

'Any connection with ricin?' was Avalon's obvious question.

'Not as such,' replied Megan, 'Receiving, a minor case of fraud, three counts of drugs found on his person, mainly cocaine,' she then looked up. 'He's been lucky. He did lots of community service but only one term of six months en the nick.' She looked back to the record. 'He was accused of burglary but got away with et due to lack of evidence. Six driving offences, one court injunction due to a stalking offence, and one case of supplying drugs.' She stopped for breath and then added,

'Quite the arse wipe by the look of et, but around 2003, he obviously had been dabbling en the drug industry.' She paused as she read through the rest of his record.

'That doesn't make him a chemist though, does it?' commented Ross.

'No,' was Frazer's quick reply, 'but my limited time en the drug section did teach me that the production of drugs like methamphetamine require some basics of chemistry.' Avalon nodded at this and agreed.

'True, though ricin isn't difficult to produce, someone with an inside knowledge of the illegal drug industry would be a prime suspect,' he acknowledged. Ross shrugged. He could see the point and with nothing better to go on, he began to look at the old records of Scott.

'So what was the issue between Scott and Joyce?' asked Rutherford.

'Unknown,' replied Avalon. 'Mowat didn't know what the feud was about, but he certainly believed that Joyce was disliked, particularly by this individual,' and he wrote Scott's name on the whiteboard. He glanced up at the clock. It was late but everyone was still working as if it was just after lunch. He felt hungry and realised he hadn't eaten all day. He suspected a few of the others hadn't eaten either, but he poured a coffee and put the thoughts aside.

'I know it's early for assumptions,' he began, 'but if this Steven Scott had set Joyce up, Scott may be the ricin connection.'

'Like you say,' frowned Ross, 'it's too early for guesswork.'

'But it could be important,' continued Avalon nodding to Ross, 'so we need to know if Scott had any

265

connection to Fenner or Gibson.' White turned in his seat and said,

'But as ricin isn't difficult to make, couldn't we be making this more difficult than it is?' he asked.

'Possibly,' agreed the DI, 'but he could be the only solid connection to the poison we have. We can't afford to ignore it.'

'Scott is younger than Joyce, he's fifty now,' explained Ross, looking through the records. 'He would be in his late teens, early twenties at the time of the crime.'

'Well,' exclaimed Avalon, with raised brows, 'all the timings fit.'

'All we have to do now is find the connection,' sighed Rutherford. The DI checked his watch.

'This will wait until the morning,' he said, 'let's go home and get some rest.'

Avalon's evening wasn't particularly restful. During these types of cases, when the whole team are eager for a good, strong breakthrough, everyone is constantly thinking through the facts. Not always physically, mostly in their minds. The problem with minds, they are not as easy to switch off as a computer, and though Avalon had eaten, showered and was sitting with a dram, he was still working his way through the case, turning the facts over, sifting them, categorising and dissecting them. He took a sip of the single malt. He wasn't sure why he had returned to the amber spirit once more, it was some time since he had sampled one. Maybe it was this case, and in the back of his mind he wondered if the whisky brought a depth of thought that didn't exist normally. For a moment, his mind came back into the room. Sarah was in the kitchen reading some papers that she had to finish before she went to bed. The rule about work at home would only stretch so far. There were times when it couldn't be avoided and this was one of them, and so Avalon didn't feel too guilty about thinking through the case. He held up his glass to the lamp on the table beside him. The glow of the bulb set the colour of the whisky on fire and brought out hues that he considered were worthy of art. Then, his thoughts gradually drifted back to the case, and why both bodies were found in virtually the same grave. He knew that answer. It was the same man who had placed them there, but why would Gibson kill Mary Anne? Was it just something that happened after an argument? That was likely, but that also put Stuart Fenner out of the frame, and his instinct told him that Fenner had something to hide. Avalon checked to see if Sarah was still busy and then opened his laptop. He was going to find out how easy it was to acquire ricin, and hopefully, that would make a difference to the case. As he read through various sources and some were certainly dubious, he realised that to produce ricin, you had to know what you were doing. There seemed to be three options to its manufacture. One was that you produced ricin. Two was that it didn't work and you would have to get rid of a slightly toxic, slimy mess. And three, you killed yourself trying to produce a poison that is so deadly, even a sample the size of a sugar grain can provide you with a painful death. He closed the laptop and sat on the sofa to finish his drink. The main point that the research had shown him was that ricin wasn't as easy to produce as people had informed him. Yes, it could be made at home and yes, you didn't need fancy equipment to make it.

But, and it was a very big but, unless you knew what you were doing, you could seriously injure yourself at best, and kill yourself at worst. That knowledge meant that at least one of the suspects under investigation could be ruled out. Christopher Joyce wasn't the type of man to undertake something of that nature, but true, he could have acquired it from someone. Joyce's character made that doubtful however, and so now the limelight fell on Steven Scott. He could have had the knowledge to make something of that nature, and it was possible that he, and not Joyce, poisoned two dogs to put the blame on Joyce.

'Did I hear you on the laptop?' asked Sarah. It brought Avalon out of his thoughts and he watched her as she sat opposite.

'Yes, I was just checking up on something.'

'Oh?' she smiled, 'anything interesting?' Avalon knew she was wondering if he had been working, and though it didn't matter if he had, his answer was ambiguous.

'Not really,' he smiled, 'I was just looking up a recipe.'

Chapter Twelve

Ross widened his eyes in surprise.

'Did I just hear you correctly?' he asked. Rutherford simply smiled, and repeated his statement.

'The boss wants us to fetch Fenner up for questioning.'

'Why us? It's a bloody long way to Newcastle. He should know about these things coming from England,' insisted Ross.

'Because DS Wilson and Rory are busy, and I think he wants someone who looks...' Rutherford paused slightly before adding, 'intimidating,' and he smiled. Ross shook his head with distaste. He hated long journeys and particularly hated going so far that you had to cross a national border. He hated crossing county borders, so a trip all the way to Newcastle was immediately resisted.

'Why do we always get the long runs?' he complained.

'We don't,' insisted Rutherford. 'On the last long run, Rory drove, last year when we had to-'

'Whose side are you on?' asked an exasperated Ross, 'anyway, when did he tell you this? He said nothing to me.'

'This morning,' insisted the big man, 'oh, and just to remind you, morning is that time of day when the actual shift starts.' Ross glowered at him.

'What's wrong?' he asked. 'Didn't you get your usual bucketful of Sugar Puffs this morning?' Rutherford ignored him and continued looking at his computer screen. 'Where is he anyway?' added Ross, glancing towards the empty booth.'

'He's with DI Lasiter, a final chat before we bring Christopher Joyce in for questioning.'

'Who's bringing him in?' asked Ross, 'couldn't we swap, Newcastle, for some obscure place up north?'

'Stop whining,' insisted Rutherford. 'I'm not particularly interested in a ten-hour journey, but the DI is trying to swing an overnight stop. The problem is, there's nowhere open during the lockdown.'

'I bet we end up in the bloody cells overnight,' insisted Ross, as he turned his attentions to the window and the sunshine outside.

'Well, at least we'll get all the tea we can drink and a decent breakfast,' mused Rutherford.

'And the desk sergeant at Newcastle nick could read you a bedtime story and tuck you en,' added Frazer without looking over to him.

'When I want input from the social inferior,' growled Ross, 'I'll lift up your stone.' At this, Frazer turned to him, but she wore a mocking smile.

'This trip es really boring into your soul esn't et?' she said. He just frowned, so she added, 'What es et Rossy, are you bothered that everyone will see that you sleep with a teddy bear?' Ross was about to deliver a bruising remark but was prevented by Rutherford who was becoming tired of the banter. He didn't know if it was real or just their way of dealing with each other, but it was becoming tedious to him.

'You know,' he began looking from one and then the other of them, 'I think the boss should send you two to fetch Fenner. It would sort you out once and for all,' and he paused with a deep frown. He then stood and added, 'Aye, that's it, I'll go and see the boss and get it sorted,' and he left without another sound, leaving Frazer and Ross stuck for words and looking at each other.

'That's never gonna happen, you know that,' she said.

'Just ignore him, he doesn't want to go either,' and he turned back to the window.

DI Lasiter had little more advice for Avalon as they sat in the former's office sipping at average coffee. He was, however, interested in the fact that Steven Scott's name had cropped up. Lasiter remembered the name and admitted that there had been some sort of feud, and indeed, Scott was just the type of character to perform such a deed. Avalon had added that the information had come from ex-DI Mowat and could be incorrect.

'I didnae know Mowat that well, but I heard he was a good officer so I would think the information es pretty good.' Avalon nodded.

'He had a good record I admit,' agreed Avalon, 'but to be honest, if there is something in this, it could open things up somewhat.'

'That's ef he'll talk wi' you,' replied Lasiter finishing his coffee. Avalon nodded and sighed. He then thought of something, though it wasn't related to the case. It was more to do with Avalon's personal relationships, and he would have to word it carefully so as to give nothing away.

'You're married, aren't you John?' he began. Lasiter raised his brows a little.

'Aye, but what's that got tae do with anything?'

'Just an observation,' smiled Avalon, 'you must have a magic formula to keep it together.'

'Not I,' laughed the DI, 'no bloody chance, this es the second wifie for me.'

'But you're keeping this marriage going and there are many that haven't.'

'That's down tae the couple,' shrugged Lasiter and he checked that the door to the office was closed. 'The way I see et,' he continued, 'when I'm here, I'm en charge an' everybody has tae jump. At hame, well,' he laughed, 'when the missus says jump, I get my pogo-stick out.' Avalon smiled, he could see Lasiter was probably near the truth. 'But over the years, y' know as you get older, the demands on each other wane a wee bit. Eventually, the bedroom antics make room for DIY instead.' Avalon frowned.

'You telling me that as you get older, sex goes out the window?' he asked.

'Not so much out the windae, more down the drain. The sounds that I used to utter making love, are now reserved for getting on an' off the sofa,' Lasiter insisted. Avalon laughed and said,

'I can't imagine even you getting up off the sofa making a climax noise.'

'No, you're right on that score,' nodded Lasiter with a semi-serious face, 'that particular ejaculation is saved for rare occasions, like when the Scotland fitba'

272

team score a goal.' Avalon gave his own serious look at this comment.

'Not heard a great deal then?' he said. Lasiter shrugged.

'Anyway Jim, why the interest?' asked Lasiter raising his brows, 'you thinkin' o' getting' hitched?'

'Oh,' the question caught Avalon off guard. 'No, not me, I just wonder why some stay married and others don't.'

'Tae be honest Jim, I dunna know,' he sighed, 'I'm a detective not a genius,' and he shrugged deeply, 'you'd have tae direct that little puzzle to the likes of PC Dowd or PC Munton.'

'Maybe it can't *be* fathomed,' smiled Avalon as he rose to his feet. He thought it best to leave before Lasiter asked the question he was dreading. He was too late. As he reached for the door handle of the office, he heard Lasiter make a little cough.

'An' on that subject,' he paused and Avalon looked back. 'I heard somewhere that you were seeing the delicious Miss Underwood on a more than professional basis.

'Oh, really?' said Avalon, as if it was a complete surprise to him.

'I don't know how you made such a good officer,' said Lasiter, raising a single brow, 'I hope your customers can't see through your innocent expression as easy as I can.' Avalon remained silent. Lasiter shrugged and turned back to his computer screen, then added. 'It just makes me wonder what she saw en an ugly bastard like you.' Avalon suppressed a grin and said,

'That's easy my friend,' and he stepped through the door and turned back, 'there's no competition.'

Avalon was barely in his seat before Ross walked into the booth and sat in the spare chair.

'You think I needed a holiday then?' he asked.

'What?' frowned Avalon, not understanding the question.

'A one-night stay, free board and lodging in one of the finest hotels in Newcastle?' explained Ross. 'Namely, North Shields nick.'

'Oh, that,' shrugged Avalon, 'I've got you in a hotel, it's open for key workers so you'll be there for the night,' and with an afterthought said, 'unless you want to drive straight back?'

'The hotel will be fine,' nodded Ross. 'I suppose we have to liaise with the Newcastle mob?'

'Yeah,' nodded Avalon, passing Ross a sheet with notes on it. 'These are the details, but I'll email them to you as well.' Ross looked at the sheet and read the name of the DI he would need to see.

'What vehicle do we take?' asked Ross at length.

'Whatever you need,' answered Avalon, 'if we have it, you can take it. I'll clear it with the DCI.' Ross nodded and walked back to his seat, dropping the notes on Rutherford's desk as he passed. Rutherford glanced at Ross and then read the sheet.

'You see,' he nodded, 'the boss sorted it out.'

'So where did you go then when you went out in a huff?' whispered Ross.

'For a piss, do you want to come with me next time?' hissed Rutherford with an innocent expression. Ross shuddered and dropped the subject.

It wasn't all that long before the team heard Avalon's phone ringing and as he picked it up, he looked into the main room. Everyone was in, except for

274

Mackinnon and White, who were both out separately on other business. DS Wilson was by the coffee machine pouring himself a cup when Avalon's voice could be heard rising in tone. It didn't last long and everyone was expectant and remained quiet. As Avalon put the phone down, there was anger in his face. He banged down on his desk so hard and with such a shout, that more than one person jumped. He leaned on the desk, looking down into the far distance until he glanced back up at the watching faces. He recovered his composure and jotted something on a sheet of paper. He then made his way slowly into the main room.

'I have just had a call from DI Whitton in Preston,' began Avalon in a muted tone. 'He's one of the people who were trying to extradite Gibson. He got an email from a colleague at Scotland Yard informing him that Geoffrey Gibson was found murdered in the Spanish village of,' he paused to look down at his notes, 'Monzalbarba, at twenty-two-hundred hours local time last night. The Spanish police report that his hands were tied and his throat was cut.'

'Shit,' exclaimed Ross, and there were a few sighs over the news.

'That's it then,' added Rutherford, 'not much we can do to a dead man.'

'No, but it's galling that if he was involved in the quarry case, there will be no reckoning,' spat Avalon, the anger still evident.

'Sounds like he might have been up to his old tricks,' comment Frazer.

'Aye,' agreed Wilson getting involved in the discussion, 'they don't piss about in Spain.'

'Is there no doubt?' asked Rutherford, 'no

275

mistake, it's him?'

'No, unfortunately,' sighed Avalon, 'someone from Scotland Yard will be going over to identify him. It's bound to be him as the description fits.'

'So what now Boss?' asked Frazer, leaning back in her seat.

'We carry on, but we might have to tell a bit of a white lie when we get Stuart Fenner up here,' insisted Avalon, 'I don't want him to know that Gibson is dead.'

'He might read about it in the papers,' offered Rutherford.

'Not unless he reads the…' he paused again to look at the sheet of notes, 'Monzalbarba Courier. And I can't see the tabloids over here making a fuss about a seventy-year-old paedophile in Spain.' He looked around the faces gathered. 'Right,' he began, 'we still have to solve the case, even if the main suspect is dead. I better go and tell the DCI about this before she hears of it from some other source.'

Avalon couldn't find the DCI, and so he sent an email as soon as he returned to the booth. He tried to hide his disappointment from the team, but one thing he hated more than criminals, was criminals avoiding justice. True, the man had now paid the ultimate price, and by all accounts, he would have been terrified before that came, but Avalon wanted to add to his despair. He wanted the man to know that they knew he had abused Carl Fenner. He wanted to tell him, he was found out, and the world would know. Did that matter? The man was dead and Avalon knew that was good riddance to an evil man, but it didn't seem to satisfy him. They would soon have to interview Christopher Joyce and Stuart

Fenner, so he had to get his house in order and prepare for the exhausting task of these interrogations. So, for the rest of the day, he made notes and checked his facts so that everything tied together and all the pieces fit. Mistakes during interviews could destroy a case. It would also be the first time he had performed an interview in the upgraded *interview suite,* as it was now called. He paid it a visit, but he didn't see much of an improvement for the vast amount of money it had probably cost, except for there being more space. The two-way mirror was gone and state-of-the-art cameras caught every move and expression. There was a Perspex screen across the table, but that had simply been fitted for the covid crisis. He returned to the office and checked his notes once more. His plan was to interview Fenner himself with the help of Frazer, and let someone else interview Joyce. He had considered Ross and Rutherford, but as they were travelling to Newcastle in the next day or two, he felt it was too much pressure. He decided that he would try out White, under the watchful eye of DS Wilson. Wilson would need a good set of notes, as he had been busy with other business while the quarry case was running. He heard his phone trill, announcing a text. It read,

'*Happy Birthday.*' It had been so long since he had received such a text, for a moment he had forgotten what it was about. It was the cloak-and-dagger way that Anthony Scobie usually got in touch. Scobie was the only so called 'grass,' Avalon had acquired, and being away from the day-to-day business of running a section for some time, he had completely forgotten about the man. He couldn't blame Scobie for caution, if his peers got to hear he was a police informer, well, it wouldn't be good for his health. Avalon thought for a second or two. It couldn't be information about the case they were working on, so it had to be something else. The problem was, with the lockdown, meeting Scobie would be almost impossible. He didn't reply for the moment as he needed to work out how to meet him. Then Avalon got a reply email. For the first time since she had been there, the DCI asked to see him without making her way to the office. That was new. He didn't really have the time to see her, but with the situation as it was, he decided to make a quick visit to explain. He knocked, entered and began to tell her what he knew but insisted that he and the team didn't think it would hamper the investigation too much.

'I see,' she nodded, looking up at him over her spectacles, 'but it's not going to help if he was involved, is it?' Avalon could see that she hadn't softened her approach. She was giving him a doubtful stare that would make lesser officers quake in their shoes. Avalon was not usually aphoristic, but he sought a phrase from the back of his mind.

'Justice delayed, is justice denied,' he said, 'but it's justice either way.' She scowled at him. He knew in that expression she had no idea what he was talking about and didn't quite know how to react. This woman could only react to what she understood. There was no flair, no spontaneity and no shrewd intelligence. He doubted that she had ever been a good officer and how she had risen to her position, he couldn't imagine. 'If you'll forgive me Ma'am, I have a great deal to do,' and he turned to leave before she could speak. She stayed silent and Avalon walked back to The Cave, a little puzzled by the reaction of the DCI. When he sat in his seat once more, he noticed a general memo in his emails. A clue to the DCI's odd behaviour became apparent. DCI Croker was on the mend, and after being isolated, was planning to return to work. It was stated that the DCI may be put on light duties for a week or two, so may not be returning to his post straight away. Avalon smiled. Temporary Detective Chief Inspector Lesley Duncan, could see her tenure coming to a close. This was confirmed by, some seconds later, DI Lasiter entering The Cave, with an expression that looked like he had a four-inch nail sticking through his shoe. Avalon assumed he was smiling.

'And what do y' think o' that?' he announced as he sat, 'The Plague Witch is getting her marching orders.'

'Well,' sighed Avalon, 'you must have a different memo to me, mine just says Croker is well and recovered, and something about light duties.' Avalon feigned looking at his computer screen.

'Et means bonny lad, that very soon, we'll be rid o' her, and oor mannie will be back in place.'

'Our mannie?' exclaimed Avalon, raising his brows, 'that's a change in opinion. I don't think I ever heard the DCI referred to in such emotional tones on previous occasions. Somewhat removed from *The Toad*.'

'Aye,' nodded Lasiter, 'et's true, but when you have tae choose between being attacked by a wolf or a wild dog, I'll go for the wolf every time.'

'I don't recognise the metaphor but I understand its sentiment,' smiled Avalon.

'An' there was me thinking I couldn't speak metaphor,' shrugged Lasiter. Avalon shook his head slowly. The old DI seemed irrepressible. 'But,' he continued, 'I know something that isnae on the memo,' and the resulting grin creased his leather face so much, Avalon thought he could hear it creaking. 'She doesnae *want* tae step down. She likes our little station so much, she doesn't want tae leave.' Lasiter was obviously enjoying himself.

'I've just been to see her,' admitted Avalon, 'and it got me thinking. How did she rise to this level in the force?'

'I did a wee bit o' digging on that score,' confirmed Lasiter. 'She was doing well enough when she was married, rose to DS by the time she was twenty-seven, two commendations by her superiors and solved two major cases in quick time. She was DI at the age of thirty-two, and rising faster than the blood of a Bishop at the sight of a naked nun.'

'I see,' mused Avalon.

'But that's not all the story,' and Lasiter's features contorted even more. 'Her working partner was a DC Mitch Watt, currently DCI Watt down in Perth.' Lasiter leaned back in the seat. 'It has come tae my attention that her divorce with her husband and her working partner happened about the same time. Without the stability of a family life and more importantly, a capable detective to carry her along, her career stalled.'

'So you think she has ridden on the backs of others?' frowned Avalon, 'I would doubt that could be achieved easily.'

'Aye,' that's right,' nodded Lasiter, 'and I think someone saw what was happening and split her partnership up.'

'You mean she and Watt were-'

'No,' interrupted Lasiter with a frown, 'by all

accounts DCI Watt has brains and good taste. I'm just saying that their superior, at the time, may have seen that she was getting a free ticket from the work of Watt. Watt rose quickly himself when released from the vampiric grip of the Plague Witch.'

'You really don't like her, do you?'

'Do you?' was Lasiter's reply. Avalon remained noncommittal and then asked a further question.

'So you think, now that she's got the DCI position, she wants to stick it out?' He sighed then added, 'but she was a DCI at Aberdeen according to legend.'

'Only ever *acting,* or *temporary.* There's a sea o' difference as y' know,' replied the older man. Avalon nodded. It made sense. 'Ef she really didn't have that much skill at her job, a post like this, was her only way tae get a leg up.

'Hang on,' said Avalon, recalling something he read when she took over. 'She was known as a problem solver and I quote from somewhere or other, "but a problem maker to those below her." So where did that information come from?'

'Isn't someone who can be used as a floating DCI useful for solving staffing problems? By all accounts, no one wants her on a regular basis,' replied Lasiter, rising to his feet. 'Not even Aberdeen, and they're pretty much pulled out all the time over there. An' I know.' Avalon recalled that Lasiter had spent time at Aberdeen. 'So you're still bringing Chris Joyce en then?' he added.

'Yes, sometime in the morning,' nodded Avalon.

'Good luck,' replied Lasiter and he headed for the door, 'you'll need et.'

Wednesday the seventeenth of April was a warm morning and held the promise of a warm day in more ways than one. Ross and Rutherford were off to Newcastle to fetch Stuart Fenner north for questioning, White and Frazer went north to bring in Christopher Joyce for the same reason. Avalon was briefing DS Wilson on the background to the case and the suspect so that he could control the interview properly. He also explained that he mainly wanted White to deal with the interview.

'You know Boss,' frowned Wilson, 'you're taking a risk with White on this, I mean, I know he's got two uniform officers to back him up, but don't you think that this es dangerous?'

'He gets paid for doing a specific job, if he can't handle it, I want to know,' replied Avalon.

'At the cost of losing information?' asked Wilson, genuinely worried.

'It's my call, and I want to know if he can do the job or not,' replied the DI.

'Aye, fine,' replied Wilson, holding up his hands in submission, 'so be et.' Avalon understood there was a risk, but White could no longer have a smooth ride in C Section. Maybe DS Wilson was becoming too cautious in his old age, or possibly he just disliked and mistrusted White so much that he couldn't imagine anything but problems. Either way, the team to bring in Joyce had left and he would find out by lunchtime if things had gone to plan. Ross and Rutherford would now be some distance down the A9, heading for Perth and then Edinburgh, before continuing south into North Shields. The plan was then for them to liaise with the local force, who would help them to serve the warrant and secure the man the following day. It was doubtful they would be back at Inverness much before late afternoon, which meant that Fenner would not be interviewed until Friday morning. As he looked through his emails, he saw the image made from the facial reconstruction in Dundee, and except for the wrong hairstyle, it utterly confirmed that Mary Anne Fenner was the body found at the quarry. Her remains, along with those of her son, were being sent back to what remained of her family for burial, though only a distant cousin had any interest in her. Although Avalon knew of her only by her bones, he thought he knew the character of the woman from the many details they had collected. He doubted she was ever fit to be a mother and considered that even if Carl had survived, his prospects hadn't been good. There were many Carl's out there and he wished he could do something to cease their suffering, but he couldn't. The best he could do was dispense justice, or at least what modern society called justice. A phone rang in The Cave and Avalon looked through the glass. Rory stood and moved to another desk. It was Frazer's phone. He heard Rory say hello and then tell the caller that Frazer was out. Avalon stood and walked into the main office.

'Well, I'm DC Mackinnon, can I help at all?' There was a pause and then Rory said, 'She should be back later today, can I take a message?' Another pause. 'Can I ask who's calling then?' He raised his brows and placed the phone back on its cradle. It was then he noticed Avalon watching him. 'Someone for Frazer Boss, female, but wouldn't leave a message or a name. She just hung up.' Avalon nodded and returned to his seat. It was then he remembered Anthony Scobie. How was he going to meet the man with the lockdown in place? Scobie rarely had anything useful anyway, but Avalon couldn't help being inquisitive. He sent a text back to Scobie.

'*It isn't my birthday, but if you have a card for me, I'll be at the multi-story car park off Margaret Street at thirteen hundred hours.*' He was unsure if Scobie would understand the twenty-four-hour time system and added a second text, '*that's one o'clock.*'

He went by car, as time was short, and checked the boot for something he kept there for such occasions. He pocketed a small bottle and slipped it into his jacket before his meeting with Scobie. He doubted that the meeting would produce anything worthwhile, but he considered that now he was back in the driving seat of a section, he ought to show some interest in his only informant. He didn't like criminals, and he didn't trust reformed criminals. Neither did he like Scobie, but he had gained some snippets of information from him in the past, mainly on minor cases. As he crossed the city and made his way to the rear of the train station, he decided to park on the roadside rather than enter the car park. He walked through the bottom level and into the stairwell, then checked his watch. It was one o'clock exactly and one thing about Scobie, he was never late. He climbed the stairs to the second floor and began to wish he had stated which level to meet on. There were very few vehicles, but there were many floors. As he opened the door to the second level, he called,

'Hello, anyone there?' He heard a hushed whistle and then noticed the ferrety face of Scobie appear from around one of the large supporting pillars. Avalon approached and Scobie stood clear of the pillar and walked into the light.

'Hello Mr Avalon,' he said with a forced smile, 'nice tae see you back where you belong by the way.'

'How did you know I was?' asked Avalon.

'I wouldna' be any good as an operative ef a' didnae keep an ear t' the ground,' he replied. It was clear Scobie didn't like the word informant, though that would be better than *grass*, or *snitch*, though both would fit.

'So you have something for me?' the DI asked as he leaned on the wall overlooking Margaret Street. Scobie kept closer to the shadows.

'Aye, I think I do,' he nodded and then looked around the almost empty parking deck. 'There's somethin' goin' on.' He insisted. Avalon gave nothing but a blank stare. 'You heard about the wee fire over at Merkinch?'

'Yes, arson from what I understand.'

'Aye, arson right enough, but what you probably don't know es,' he looked around once more, 'that et isnae the isolated incident you all think et es.'

'If there had been any other fires, I'm sure we would have known about it,' insisted Avalon.

'Not just fires, ef y' know what a' mean.' He paused, still looking for some reaction from Avalon, but there was none. 'You look different ef y' don't mind me saying,' added Scobie.

'Get to the point Scobie, I'm busy.'

'Oh, aye, I'm sure you are Mr Avalon,' Scobie replied sheepishly, 'the point, aye. Well,' he continued, 'there have been a few others who have been troubled Mr Avalon, some more than others.'

'Such as?' asked Avalon, a touch of impatience entering his tone.

'Shop windows smashed, down at Fairways,'

began Scobie, 'a house sprayed with red paint in Milton and two days ago, a car covered en acid on Cauldfield Road.'

'I haven't seen anything like that come in,' shrugged Avalon, 'but in any case, it's not my area. You need to speak to DI Lasiter about it. His team is dealing with the arson.'

'Aye, well,' replied Scobie, looking to the floor and shuffling his feet, 'me and Mr Lasiter don't see eye t' eye ef y' know what a' mean?'

'I'll let him know about it, but if people don't report crime, we can't really react to it, can we?'

'But what ef they don't report et because they have something t' hide?' said the ferrety man. Avalon looked at his watch.

'I don't have time for this Scobie,' he said and felt the bottle in his pocket. 'I can pick up rumours of crime from any pub or betting shop, I need more than gossip.'

'The stuff I know es difficult tae explain Mr Avalon, but I'm hearing words like revenge and vendetta.' Scobie's face showed he wasn't making the story up. There was something he had heard on his travels, which he at least thought was worrying.

'Any names?' asked Avalon.

'No,' said Scobie shaking his head, 'not yet but I'll keep digging.' Avalon brought the bottle from his pocket but held it back.

'So what are you up to these days, Scobie, I hope you are behaving?'

'Aye, Mr Avalon,' he replied with a slight grin, 'I meant it when I said I was going straight.' Avalon knew 'going straight' meant something very different to the

286

likes of Scobie than it did for the rest of society, but neither did the man claim any government benefits that he knew of. He bought and sold, and maybe some of his goods came from unknown sources, but he didn't steal anything himself.

'And are you observing the lockdown?' Avalon asked, placing the bottle on the floor between his feet. Scobie's eyes watched the action and held towards the bottle for a few seconds.

'More or less, but the government doesnea give me any grants or handouts Mr Avalon,' he explained, looking back up to the DI.

'Well, if you don't pay into the system,' replied Avalon, raising his brows, 'you can't expect the system to pay you, can you?'

'True words, Mr Avalon, true words.'

'Keep your ears open and if anything else comes your way, you know where I am,' added Avalon and then he looked down to the bottle. 'Well, bless my soul, look what someone has left here,' he said as if seeing the bottle for the first time. 'You'd better take that and dispose of it before someone smashes it, we don't want anyone to get a puncture.'

'I'll do that, Mr Avalon,' and he bent to pick up the bottle. 'An' look at that, et still has some spirits en there,' he commented, looking at the full bottle. Avalon turned and without another word, he returned to his car. The trip had indeed been a waste of time, but the DI had re-established his connection with his only informant for the cost of half a bottle of cheap whisky.

Avalon was informed by Frazer, that Christopher Joyce had been taken to the interview suite.

'Any trouble?' he asked.

'A wee bit when we arrived,' she replied, 'but when we showed him the paperwork, he seemed to quieten a little. He called us all the black bastards under the sun, of course.'

'How was DC White?' he then asked.

'Fine,' she shrugged, 'he's having a bite to eat and a toilet break at the mo.' Avalon nodded and he turned to Wilson who had joined them.

'I'll go and find him then,' suggested Wilson. 'Do you want us tae start straight away?'

'As soon as Angus is ready,' nodded Avalon, 'I'll come down later and observe.' Wilson nodded and left The Cave with his notes. With the office now empty except for him and Frazer, he turned to her and asked more questions.

'Was he really okay?'

'White?' she exclaimed, 'aye, he's very *by the book* en his approach but he did what he was supposed tae do.'

'You know what I'm asking,' insisted Avalon, raising a single eyebrow. She nodded and then folded her arms in thought.

'He's a bit too starchy,' she admitted, 'I mean, with a character like Joyce it doesn't matter so much but I would suspect that in a more delicate situation...' she trailed off with a shrug. He nodded to her and said,

'Okay, take a break and get some lunch, I'll get off downstairs and see how this goes.'

'Have you heard from Rossy and Martin, Boss?' she then asked.

'No, but then again, I'm not expecting to. I'm more interested to find out what we can from Joyce at the moment.' He then sighed. 'Do you know anything about the arson over Merkinch way?'

'Probably no more than you, Boss,' she replied, raising her brows a little, 'I seem to recall it was a small unit that got torched. Is it important?'

'I don't know,' he admitted, 'it's just something that cropped up in conversation.'

'B Section would know more.'

'Yes,' he replied in some doubt, 'yes, I may stop over there on the way.'

'Aye, two weeks ago,' began Lasiter, 'someone broke en and torched the place. Et reeked of accelerant, and we suspected an insurance job. Why the interest?'

'Just a nod from someone I came across,' shrugged Avalon, 'he seemed to think it was part of a scam or something similar.'

'Like I say,' nodded Lasiter, 'probably insurance, nothin' was stolen as far as the owner was concerned, he didn't even seem that bothered.'

'Who's the owner?' asked Avalon.

'Tom,' called out Lasiter to DS Murrey, 'who owned the burned out warehouse over at Merkinch?' Murrey looked puzzled for a moment, then he remembered.

'I think it was someone called Phillips, Jack or Jake. I didn't do much on that one.'

'Did he have form?' asked Avalon.

'Not to my knowledge,' shrugged Murrey. Avalon turned back to Lasiter.

'What about an incident at Milton?' he asked, but Lasiter shook his head. 'Shop windows smashed?'

'There was a shop window broken. It was in

Queensgate. That was an accident with a delivery though,' explained Murrey.

'Car sprayed with acid?' asked Avalon vaguely.

'Now that does ring a bell,' nodded Lasiter.

'Aye, Cauldfield Road,' added Hamilton, who had been quiet up to that point.

'What came of that?' asked the DI.

'Nothing,' replied Hamilton, 'a neighbour said a car had been vandalised but when we got there, the owner said it was his wife who had done it after an argument.'

'Who was the victim?' asked Avalon.

'I can't remember,' frowned Hamilton, 'I can find it out and mail it to you if you like?' Avalon nodded.

'You have your nose tae the ground on something here Jim,' grinned Lasiter.

'I don't think it's anything, but obviously, the acid attack did happen,' mused Avalon.

'Nobody pressed charges though,' explained Hamilton.

'So, are they linked?' asked Lasiter, his detective gland already secreting ideas and suspicions about a new case.

'I doubt it,' shrugged Avalon, 'conspiracy theorists are everywhere these days.' Lasiter made a sound as if he didn't quite believe Avalon, so the DI decided to change the subject. 'Oh, and I got a copy of a book with all the Para Handy stories in it.'

'And so what do you think?' beamed Lasiter.

'It's, quaint,' replied Avalon, unsure quite how to word his feelings on the spur of the moment.

'Quaint?' frowned Lasiter, and then he thought about it and in a quieter tone added, 'I suppose you have tae have been brought up en that area tae understand the humour.'

'I understand the humour well enough,' insisted Avalon, 'it's just that it's a tale of its time.'

'Aye, well, most of that culture has gone now,' sighed Lasiter deeply, 'who even knows what a Clyde Puffer es now?'

'Isn't it someone from Glasgow who's trying to give up smoking?' offered someone in the office.

'Shut et or I'll gi'e yer a skelped bahoukie y' cheeky bastard,' bawled Lasiter and Avalon smiled at the way Lasiter dropped back into his old tongue whenever he was talking of that area. There were a few good natured comments and then Lasiter added,'Y' can all shut et y' northern teuchter mouths,' he called and then turned to Avalon, 'am I not getting' any moral support from you?'

'Why from me?' smiled Avalon, 'I was born about as far from Glasgow as Boris Johnson is from being an honest man.'

'Och, man, you're a southerner for Christ's sake. Not like all this Heelan scum,' he waved his hand across the room.

'Not any more John,' laughed Avalon, 'I class myself as a Highlander too these days, you'll have to fight them all yourself,' and he headed for the door to the sounds of a rich Glasgow brogue haranguing his team, whilst they jeered back as much as they were given. Avalon had not seen B Section in such a good humour for some time. Was the prospect of ridding themselves of the Plague Witch so joyous? He was wondering if he would ever get that comradery back in his own section.

Chapter Thirteen

By the time DI Avalon got to the interview suite, Christopher Joyce was in room one with DC White, DS Wilson and Joyce's solicitor. The preliminaries had begun. Avalon sat down in the tiny viewing room where he could see images on one of the monitor screens from the three cameras in room one, but there was no sound. He found the controls and turned up the volume.

'But if you have nothing to hide, wouldn't it be easier to cooperate?' he heard White say.

'I've told you, I have nothing to say,' was the flat reply. Joyce was still playing his silence card, and that would stress everyone in that interview room. The solicitor looked as if he didn't want to be there. He was young, too young, and he sat away from Joyce at the rear of the room taking notes in shorthand.

'So,' continued White, 'if we agree that you had nothing to do with any dogs being poisoned, can you tell us who might have done it?' Avalon could see that White was struggling. His intelligence and quick thinking did nothing to enhance his interview technique, and Avalon hoped that Wilson would see it and react.

'That is a police matter, I have no information,'

replied Joyce, and he folded his arms in a defiant nature.

'But Mister Joyce,' questioned White, 'you must see the importance of our need to bring this to a closure, ricin is a very-' Joyce interrupted by banging both fists on the table with such a force that the young solicitor literally jumped in his seat.

'Closure?' bawled Joyce, 'you don't know the meaning of closure, I was innocent, the judge threw the case out and you lot couldn't find anything to pin on me could you?' he stood and looked angry in the extreme. Wilson tensed ready for action but as calmly as he could, he said,

'Sit down Mr Joyce, I urge you tae keep calm.' Joyce looked to Wilson with venom flashing in his eyes but the DS kept his calm and opened his eyes wider, nodding to the seat.

'I would do what the officer requests,' agreed the solicitor, then, he tuned to look at Wilson. 'Is there anything pertinent to my client?' he asked, but Joyce rounded on him too.

'And you be quiet,' hissed Joyce, turning savagely to him.

'Mr Joyce,' insisted Wilson and he placed his hands on the desk, 'please sit down and take a moment to consider. We will have a break.'

'I don't need a break,' growled Joyce looking back to Wilson, 'I want to leave and if you don't agree to that, you either arrest me or by god I'll give you something to arrest me for.' Avalon was about to leave his tiny room and enter the interview room, but he heard Wilson's voice.

'We know about Steven Scott,' he announced. For a second Joyce seemed to stop in his tracks.

'So what?' he asked more calmly.

'We understand that there was a feud between you two.'

'There was, so what of it?' frowned the man still standing, looking less angry but more inquisitive.

'Has et not occurred tae you that you may have been set up over the poisoning?' asked Wilson.

'Of course it has,' hissed Joyce again, 'but it may have escaped your notice that I'm not exactly Scotland's most popular man.'

'Please sit Mr Joyce,' repeated Wilson, and Joyce looked around at the chair as if seeing it for the first time. He sat glancing quickly over to the solicitor who still looked agitated.

'What was your issue with Mr Scott?' asked Wilson once Joyce was in his seat.

'I've no idea, it's so long ago,' replied Joyce with little interest in the subject.

'The issue with the dogs es of little interest tae us Mr Joyce,' insisted Wilson, 'we just need to find who may have access or handled ricin.' He gave a moment for this to sink in and added, 'your name cropped up as et's our only lead to who may have dealings with the poison. You are not on trial here,' he paused, 'unless you did indeed have dealings with et.'

'I still can't help you, and frankly, if I did know, I wouldn't tell you,' insisted Joyce.

'And there lies the problem,' replied Wilson, 'we are stuck unless we know which direction points us away from you.'

'You are all bastards,' growled Joyce, shaking his head, but his body language showed him calmer. Avalon got comfortable in his seat once more, satisfied that

Wilson had the situation under control once again. 'You can't find anyone, so the next option will do?' Wilson didn't react, but he kept his eyes on Joyce. The man sighed and leaned back in his chair, then he began to tap his fingers on his thigh.

'Then we are kind of stuck,' frowned Joyce, 'because of all the people who could have stitched me up, I can't honestly tell you who might have actually done it.' He sighed, and then continued. 'Don't get me wrong, I'd love to have something on that little bastard Scott, and a few of the others, but…' he trailed off for a moment. 'It could have been any of them.'

'So,' began Wilson tentatively, 'what happened between you and Scott?'

'Why does Scott's name keep cropping up?' asked Joyce, 'I could tell you twenty names who had as much hate for me as he did.'

'Chemicals, drugs, he seems the most likely,' offered Wilson, folding his arms.

'Well, aye, he was always taking, or smoking something,' nodded Joyce, leaning forward again. 'It was drugs that got him into trouble with me.'

'Drugs?' asked Wilson.

'Well, in a round-about way,' nodded the man, sounding a little calmer. 'I was in a pub in Inverness, I lived down there then. Scott and his buddy, I think his name was Emery,' explained Joyce.

'Lachtan Emery?' asked Wilson, 'he was known tae us until recently.'

'That was him aye,' replied Joyce, 'so he's gone down?'

'In a manner of speaking,' nodded Wilson, 'he was involved en an accident three years ago, rolled his car whilst drunk and killed himself along with his girlfriend.'

'Sounds like him, a complete waster,' nodded Joyce. 'I'm guessing Scott is still alive if you're trying to involve him?' Wilson nodded and then asked Joyce to continue his story.

'The two of them came into the pub,' continued the man, 'and I saw them watching me. I was with a woman, a married woman.' He paused. 'Even her husband knew about it but Scott was high, he had been taking something and then, with the drink…' he paused, 'it was obvious something would happen. We never got on, and he kept watching me, and so I told the woman to go to the toilet, and then use the back door to leave. I waited and then left myself. They of course followed.' He shrugged as if he had no more to tell.

'And?' asked Wilson.

'They thought they'd have a go. It didn't last long, Emery eventually ran, and with Scott on his own…' he gave a slight smile with a single nod as he remembered the night like yesterday. 'Let's say, I taught him a lesson he never forgot.'

'And that was it?'

'Not really,' replied Joyce, shaking his head, 'I had windows put through, car damaged, but you know what it's like. No one ever saw anything, no one knows anything, but I knew it was him and his gang. In the end, I moved house.'

'There was talk that a neighbour's dog was poisoned previously.' Wilson wondered if the mention of dogs would bring back the anger. It didn't.

'I had words with my neighbour on several occasions, his dog was barking forever,' replied Joyce. 'I don't know if you live near dogs, but their owners really think they are quiet when they leave the house. I even recorded the sound and played it back to him. He told me I could have recorded it anywhere.'

'So you hit him?' asked Wilson.

'Yeah,' nodded Joyce, 'where rational discussion fails, mindless violence wins the day.' Wilson thought he saw a smile on the man's face.

'You were warned about it, I believe,' said Wilson, remembering the details from the notes.

'Yeah, one of your lot came round,' replied Joyce.

'And you told him tae piss off?'

'I don't remember the exact wording, but it was something in that vein,' nodded Joyce.

'So what happened with your new neighbour?' asked Wilson. Even over the PA system, Avalon heard White sigh. He looked surplus to requirements, and both Wilson and Joyce had ignored him. The sigh made them both turn to him, however.

'If I'm boring you, just get off your arse and solve a crime,' scowled Joyce.

'Can you get us some drinks?' asked Wilson to be rid of him. Avalon wanted to leave to have a word with White, but he was interested in what Joyce had to say. He decided to take White's place instead.

'This is Detective Inspector Avalon,' announced Wilson as he entered. Joyce glanced at him, then turned back to Wilson. 'You were saying, about the new neighbour?' added Wilson.

'I wasn't, but I'll tell you.' He then turned around to the solicitor. 'You may as well sod off as well.' The man protested, but when Joyce became irate, he left.

297

Joyce seemed to settle a little more, and as the drinks came in, delivered by a young uniformed PC, Joyce kept quiet. He sipped the tea and studied Avalon over his cup.

'Go on,' urged Wilson, 'about the neighbour.'

'Not much to tell,' explained Joyce, 'he was different to the previous one. This arsehole just turned round and said if I didn't like it, just leave.'

'And you accepted it?' asked Wilson.

'Course not,' laughed Joyce, but there was no humour in the sound. 'Twice we came to blows, you lot came out once, but he calmed down after that. He was a big bastard, but he went down all the same.'

'And the dogs?' asked Avalon. Joyce shrugged.

'The next thing I knew, the police were back round, because the neighbour bricked my windows in and stood in the street with a baseball bat, threatening to kill me.'

'Then what happened?' asked Wilson.

'I'm guessing you read that in the files,' frowned Joyce. 'I don't like baseball, so I took a big tyre lever out, and as I approached him, he ran inside. Then I was arrested.' He sipped the tea again. 'At that point I knew nothing about the dogs.'

'How did you find out?' asked Wilson.

'The copper told me, and that was that. This thing has plagued me ever since.'

'And you never found out who had done it?' asked Avalon. The man shook his head.

'As I said, there was a queue of people who wanted to get at me,' he frowned deeply, 'one of them must have heard about my issues with barking dogs.' Avalon nodded slowly.

'It doesn't help us much,' he shrugged.

298

'I'm not here to help,' insisted Joyce, 'I just want you off my back.' Avalon glared at him. His patience wasn't what it had once been, and he was tired of this arrogant man.

'Well,' he sighed, glancing at Wilson for a moment, 'this doesn't exactly achieve that.'

'Like I said,' growled Joyce, 'I either leave here, or you'll have to arrest me. I'm sick of this and the time has come for action.'

'That's your decision, Mr Joyce,' answered Avalon abruptly. 'We can easily accommodate you if you wish it,' and he stood.

'You lousy bastards never give up do you?' he said. There was menace back in his voice again. 'I have nothing more to tell you, I know nothing about ricin.' Avalon glared back to him.

'Even if I accept that as a fact Mr Joyce, someone set you up and if it was me, I would have found out whom it was after all these years.'

'If I had found a name, do you think the little shite would still be walking around?' insisted Joyce.

'Yes, I do,' replied Avalon, 'because for all your bluster Mr Joyce, I think you are not who you like people to think you are. If you were really as violent as people say, you would have a criminal record longer than Methuselah's beard.' Joyce looked livid, but he remained quiet. 'I think that you live by some sort of perverse code,' continued the DI. 'I think it's the last remnant of morality, not to grass, not to tell what you know. But you are wrong, and it's that fact that keeps us on your case, as you call it, nothing else. We are trying to help you, but you want to play the tough guy.' He looked at Wilson and gave a curt nod then, he looked back at the still fuming man. 'So be it, Mr Joyce.'

'Help? You don't know the meaning of the word,' spat the man. 'There was no help fifteen years ago when I was put under interrogation, first by you lot and then by Special Branch.' Avalon stopped in his thoughts.

'What did you say?' he asked.

'Yeah,' scowled Joyce, 'you didn't know about that, did you?'

'There es no mention o' that en your record,' frowned Wilson.

'Well, am I the only one here not surprised?' he almost laughed. 'They told me they were the drugs squad, but I did my research. Detective Inspector Gouch, and Detective Sergeant Collins I later found out, were both with Special Branch.' Avalon looked at Wilson.

'Et's possible,' shrugged the DS, 'et was the time of the London Attacks.' Avalon thought for a moment. He looked back at Joyce.

'Is that why you didn't pursue anything about this?' he asked. Joyce looked from one to the other.

'They don't scare me,' he eventually said, a little quieter. 'They threatened me with all sorts of repercussions. That's why I tracked down who they were. They even threatened to plant ricin on my premises.'

'Did the Inverness detectives know about this?' asked Wilson.

'You all shit in the same bucket as far as I'm concerned,' insisted Joyce.

'I need to make calls,' said Avalon, looking to Wilson. 'Get Mr Joyce some food, I'll be back soon.'

'I'm not staying, I told you that,' barked Joyce.

'Give me twenty minutes, Mr Joyce. If I have

300

nothing to tell you, you're free to go and I promise that will be the end of it,' said Avalon, and he left.

Frazer watched Avalon enter The Cave and walk determinedly to his booth. There was a look of anger about him but she chose to ignore it for the time being. After he checked something on his computer, she saw him stand and approach her but she pretended to have not noticed him.

'Megan,' he said abruptly.

'Yes, Boss?'

'Get in touch with Mr Mowat, the ex DI, and ask him if he knew that Special Branch had interviewed Christopher Joyce,' he paused. 'I have to make a couple of calls myself.'

'Yes Boss,' and she got to work. Avalon returned to his desk and immediately set to work on the phone. His demeanour seemed to soften as he spoke to someone, then she heard the voice on the other end of her phone. 'Mrs Mowat, I wonder ef I can have a quick word with your husband? Et's DC Frazer from Inverness.' About that moment, Rory returned to the office and wanted to know if DS Wilson was still downstairs, but as the only two other people in the room were on the phone, he went to his desk and began to write up his report. He could hear from Frazer that she was working on the quarry case and looking at the DI he knew there was some sort of issue. As soon as Frazer ended her call, he looked over to her.

'Problems?'

'Aye, I think so. Not sure what, but I would leave the boss for a wee while.' Rory nodded, then asked,

'Has he still got Gordon downstairs?'

'Aye. He and White are still with Joyce, I think something must have happened.' Rory nodded again, glanced toward the DI and continued with his work. As soon as Avalon finished his calls, Rory saw Frazer hurry to the booth and have a quick conversation with the boss. The DI frowned a great deal and then nodded. He said something to Frazer and then he left the office, not even noticing Rory in the room. Frazer returned to her desk and shrugged towards the DC.

'Looks serious,' commented Rory.

'Et's always serious when Special Branch is involved,' explained Frazer. 'Et seems fifteen years ago, they were interested in Christopher Joyce.'

'Because of ricin?' asked Rory. Frazer nodded.

'The problem is,' added Frazer, 'Special Branch has all changed now. It was a secretive club before, et's going to be even more closed shop these days.'

'Aye,' nodded Rory, 'and the boss doesn't get on too well with them either.' Frazer agreed and seemed to be energised as she began furiously tapping keys. Rory sighed and went back to his report.

Avalon was true to his word. He returned to the interview room twenty minutes after he had left. Wilson and White were still in the room and there were a few sandwiches untouched on a plate.

'You can go Mr Joyce,' he announced as he entered.

'That's it? Just like that?' asked the man with a frown.

'You wished to leave, now you can. We won't be troubling you any more.'

'No apology, no explanation?' asked Joyce as he stood.

302

'If you require an explanation, I can tell you that new evidence has been found and you are no longer a suspect,' he explained and then added, 'as to an apology? The situation doesn't require one. We reacted in a proper manner and given the circumstances, we conducted our investigation along set procedures determined by the Home Office.' He turned to White. 'DC White, please escort Mr Joyce to the exit and arrange for him to be returned home.' Joyce stood and glowered at Avalon as he passed, but said nothing.

'So what happened?' asked Wilson as White and Joyce had left the room. Avalon sighed deeply.

'Because ricin was in the news at the time, Special Branch and the anti-terrorism unit became jumpy about mention of the poison,' he explained. 'They arranged with the investigating officers to interview Joyce, mainly to find out where he obtained the poison. They got nothing from him and so moved on to anyone associated with Joyce. Mowat didn't tell us about it as he didn't know there was any outcome from it.'

'That's bullshit,' laughed Wilson, 'he should have known et could be important.'

'Yes, well,' sighed Avalon again, 'there was an outcome.' He paused and sat for a moment. 'I spoke to my MIT contacts. They called in some favours and found out some interesting details. It seems that Special Branch also interviewed Steven Scott, and they must have broken him under pressure.'

'He admitted et?' exclaimed Wilson, 'the poisoning I mean?'

'Yes, he admitted setting Joyce up, but he didn't make the ricin as we thought. He acquired it from a third party. He pointed the finger at a Gerald Doyle. It sounds feasible. Doyle, it seems, is an Irishman and may have supplied the ricin, as he was eventually committed for trial over another incident and spent seven years in prison for possession of dangerous and illegal substances.'

'The name doesn't ring any bells with me,' frowned Wilson.

'I've set Frazer on that task,' explained Avalon.

'And you decided not to tell Joyce about Scott?'

'I thought it best not to,' shrugged Avalon, 'I don't think Joyce would react, but I'll not take the risk.'

'So this puts Joyce and Scott en the clear for the murder of Mary Fenner,' added Wilson.

'True,' nodded Avalon, 'and it could make things much more difficult, unless we can find a connection between this Irishman and either Gibson, or Stuart Fenner.'

'Let's hope we find something before Fenner arrives then,' said Wilson, raising his brows.

The two men walked back to The Cave as Avalon brought up a slightly different subject.

'He's not exactly got the art of interviewing, has he?'

'White you mean?' replied Wilson, 'no, not exactly.' Wilson was quiet until they reached the top of the stairs and turned towards the corridor. 'As much as I dislike him, et's not the easiest part of the job though es et? I mean, he's probably out o' practice.'

'Maybe,' agreed Avalon, placing his hand on the door handle. 'We may have to arrange for him to sit in on the interview with Fenner.' As they entered The Cave, Frazer looked up to him expectantly.

'Found anything?' he asked.

'Something else first Boss,' she frowned. 'I just got the nod that the press knows about Fenner being brought en.'

'I suppose it was going to be difficult to keep it from them,' he admitted, 'it's suddenly become a more newsworthy item.' He thought for a moment. 'Okay, I don't think we need to overreact to it. Maybe it's for the best. It might jog a few memories with the public. Better let Rossy and Martin know, though.' Frazer nodded and picked up the phone as he looked around to White. 'Angus, I want you to monitor the interview with Fenner from the viewing room.' White nodded. He looked as if he understood why, as he presented a look of failure on his features. He turned back to Frazer as she held the phone to her ear and, raising his brows, he nodded towards the booth. She knew the meaning and when she had contacted Rutherford, she made her way to the booth and sat.

'So, what have you found out?'

'Gerald Doyle has quite a record,' she announced. 'He had no known sympathies with either side during the Irish conflict, but he certainly has some very dodgy Irish contacts.'

'Have you traced him?'

'Et seems he's difficult to keep tabs on, but there have been no reports on any illegal activities over the past six years.'

'And what sort of activities was he involved with?' asked Avalon, leaning back.

'He's a dealer mainly. Drugs, weapons, explosives and even information.'

'Nice, so it sounds like he could have certainly supplied the ricin,' said Avalon, glancing up at the coffee machine in the main room.

'Aye, et's the sort of thing he does right enough,' nodded Frazer.

'So, the million dollar question,' sighed Avalon, leaning forward again. Frazer anticipated what the question was and shot an answer straight away.

'I can find no direct route or connection with either Fenner or Gibson, but…' there was a long pause as Frazer looked as if she had a hunch of sorts.

'At this stage Megan, if you have an idea, I want to know, no matter how tenuous it is,' insisted the DI. She gave a curt nod and explained.

'Prior to this, I managed to track down a previous girlfriend of Gibson. She didn't want to talk about et at first, but after Rory told me someone had rung, I followed et up.'

'I think I was in when that call came through,' replied Avalon. She nodded again and leaned forward with an intense expression.

'She wouldn't agree to meet, but on the phone, she answered a few questions. Et seems Gibson was indeed a very odd character. She said that their relationship was never sexual.'

'Maybe she didn't want to admit she had sex with a monster?'

'I don't think et was that,' explained Frazer, 'more that Gibson shied away from et. That would fit with a person with his character defects.' Avalon agreed. 'She told me that at the time she wanted sex, but he refused. Instead, he would drive her to isolated spots and when there, he would just talk, and sometime ask her to remove her clothing and walk around the car in the dark.'

306

'Odd, but go on,' nodded Avalon.

'Their night-time meets became more strange as time went on,' continued Megan, 'until she decided that she had reached a point where she thought he was too weird, and broke off the relationship.'

'I hope this is going somewhere,' said Avalon, looking up at the coffee machine once more. She caught his glance this time and said hurriedly,

'Do you want me to fetch you a brew?'

'No, just tell me the end of the story,' he replied, trying to be patient.

'I asked her where he would take her on these night-time perambulations,' continued Frazer. 'She told me that she couldn't pinpoint the places as et was always dark, but there were three main spots. One was somewhere near Clava Cairns, one was a deserted spot near Cantraydoune, and finally,' Avalon could tell by the cadence in her voice the last one was important, 'she said that he would take her down the A9, and turn off somewhere near Daviot.' She raised her brows. 'That es close to the quarry Boss, and I think for some reason we haven't yet discovered, Gibson knew that area.'

'It seems that way,' nodded Avalon. 'Good work Megan, the problem is,' he said, 'this is heading towards the killer being Gibson.'

'I wondered if they were both involved, but the more I dig into their lives, the more I realise they neither liked each other, or had any connection other than Mary Fenner.' Avalon stared into space for a moment.

'If it was Gibson, how come nothing was found in his car?' he asked to no one in particular. 'You would think that if he had taken two bodies to the quarry, some trace would have been left for forensics to find.'

307

'Maybe the search was bungled?' offered Frazer.

'Either way,' sighed Avalon, 'it's too late now.' Then he had a thought. 'If Gibson had this odd way about him, what did Mary Fenner see in him?' He reconsidered his thoughts. 'I mean, it can't have been a sexual relationship, can it? So what was it that Mary saw in a man like that?'

'Maybe it was exactly that?' offered Frazer. 'If she had been abused by her husband, maybe a man with no demands on her was a relief?' Avalon nodded, she had a point and knowing a great deal about Frazer's past, put that into perspective.

'I suppose so,' he said, 'and by all accounts, she was a chain smoking alcoholic, and maybe Gibson didn't mind that.' He paused. 'But on the other hand, what did Mary have that Gibson wanted?' Even before he had finished the sentence, he knew exactly what it was. 'Carl,' he added.

Avalon began thinking as he was reading, which meant, although the thought had clarity, he had no idea what he had just read. That damn chapter had been started three times, and he had still lost the thread. It was the quarry case. He was at home, sitting reading the adventures of Para Handy but going through the case as the words tripped across his eyes without meaning. He put the book down and looked at the seat opposite. Sarah was bathing, and he wondered if the rule on leaving work, at work, was a good idea. They had nothing else to talk about. He found it hard to believe that two intelligent people couldn't find a stirring topic to discuss in the evening. He had tried. He brought up the subject of the partially mummified body of a dinosaur found in

Canada. Avalon thought it was interesting from the point of view that speculation about the way these animals looked proved to be correct. All Sarah could say was that it probably wasn't mummified at all. It was more likely that it was a fossil of a mummy.

'Is this from a professional standpoint?' he had asked.

'What do you mean?' she had said.

'Well, it could be that you are breaking the rule of bringing work home,' he grinned.

'And,' she replied with a frown, 'I'm betting you were wondering who had killed it.' And that was it. The conversation had stopped before it got started. He looked at the door as it opened, and she walked in. She was dressed in her pyjamas and had her hair wrapped in a towel. She was carrying her phone and sat in the chair opposite, noticing Avalon was not reading his book.

'Have you finished that already?' she asked.

'No, er, no I haven't,' he stuttered, 'I was daydreaming.' She nodded at this and looked down to her phone.

'I just have to text my sister,' and she put the phone down once she had finished. She then went to fetch a hairbrush and returned, removing the towel from her head, and began to brush her hair. 'What is it?' she asked.

'Nothing,' he shrugged.

'You get bored at night, don't you?' she asked.

'A little, particularly with the lockdown,' he admitted.

'And you want to rescind the rule on not talking about work?' she asked, still brushing her hair.

'You should have been a detective,' he smiled.

'I told you once before, I don't mind as long as we're not going to be putting up a whiteboard covered in mug shots, and changing the back room into an interview room.' He laughed.

'Not at all,' he paused. 'It's just difficult to chat about anything just in case it touches on our professional backgrounds.'

'Is this about the dinosaur?' she asked, 'I didn't know you were interested in them.'

'No, not really,' he replied, 'but it seems to me that every subject we try to discuss has to cease because of something or other.' She frowned at this and put the hairbrush down.

'Is that what you think?' she asked, the frown still creasing her brows. He simply shrugged and picked up his book. He could see she was thinking through something, but he opened the pages at his bookmark and looked at the words. He scanned through that chapter again, but once again, he took nothing of it in.

'Well, put the book down and ask me something,' she announced, 'something to do with either of our work.'

'Why?' he asked, closing the book for the second time.

'To get rid of the rule and allow some conversation,' she replied, and he got the impression she was less than pleased about it.

'But that's not what I was trying to say, it's just that…' he trailed off. If he wasn't careful, this conversation could end up as an argument.

'No, I understand,' she smiled this time, 'you're right. It's too much pressure to watch our P's and Q's.'

'So, let's just say, the rule is no more,' he smiled

back, and picked up his book again as if that was the end of the matter. She was silent, she was static, and he wondered what she was thinking.

'What's your opinion on Massively Parallel Sequencing?' she suddenly asked. Avalon almost burst out laughing, but he managed to hold it in with a cough.

'I don't have one,' he replied.

'I would have thought in your line of work it would be highly important,' she added. Avalon threw the switch to the detective part of his brain and tried to work out what she had asked. He wasn't going to give up without a fight. Obviously it was a new technology, and obviously it was to do with forensics. As a great deal of that work was with DNA, and she had mentioned 'his line of work', he considered that she was speaking of something reasonably new in that field.

'If it helps with identification, all well and good,' was his answer. She went quiet.

'Do you really know about MPS?' He looked at her face. He could see she was sceptical but surprised too.

'Yeah,' he nodded, and then paused for a moment, 'after all, I think I really was miss-sold protection insurance.' He kept a straight face, and it was several seconds before she got the joke and thought about throwing her hairbrush at him.

'That's PPI, you fool,' she laughed. He liked to see her smile, though she rarely did, and he returned it with interest. They looked at each other across the room until her phone bleeped. She broadened her smile to him and then picked up her phone. She busily returned a message as Avalon asked,

'Is she well?'

311

'My sister? Yes she is,' replied Sarah, smiling to him, 'just sick of the lockdown.'

'I have to admit,' he shrugged, 'I'm beginning to miss the odd trip to the Castle Tavern.'

'If this goes on for much longer,' she added, placing her phone on the coffee table, 'the whole culture of the UK will change.'

'Probably,' nodded Avalon. He didn't want to go further down that sort of conversation. He was already thinking that the world was about to change for good, or bad, depending which way you looked at it.

'So,' he began tentatively, 'shall we agree that it's okay to mention work as long as it's not *all* about work?'

'Fine,' she nodded, 'but not tonight.' Avalon smiled and went back to his book and that elusive chapter. As he read, he began to see parallels in the stories of Para Handy and his own team. The captain of the Vital Spark had his right-hand man. There was a younger sailor and there was the one no one liked. Did that mean he was Para Handy and DC White was the engineer? He soon realised once more that his thoughts were clouding the chapter, and he finally put the book down and looked around the room.

'Maybe you need to buy a TV,' smiled Sarah without looking at him.

'I'm not a TV person,' he began, but considered that Sarah might be. 'But… if it's… well, something you like to do, I can put one in.'

'I have a TV at home, but I don't watch it much,' she replied unconvincingly.

'It's just that I have a history of TV abuse,' he added with a straight face.

'Do you mean you get abuse from the TV or the

other way around?' she asked, not sure what he was alluding to.

'Oh, most definitely the other way around,' and he gave a little frown. 'I once tortured a TV to death, so it's not a good idea for me to be around them.' She opened her eyes wide for a moment, suppressing a laugh, and then let it go in a loud guffaw, bringing her hand to cover her mouth.

'Sometimes, I wonder if you might be serious about the things you say,' she said, still trying to cease the laugh.

'It's true I tell you,' he explained, still keeping a straight face. 'I painted a cross over the screen so that police marksmen could make a better shot. The only thing that saved it was the tin of spaghetti hoops that appeared at an inopportune moment.' Her laughing stopped and developed into a bemused smile.

'Spaghetti hoops?' she asked incredulously.

'Yeah, in tomato sauce,' nodded Avalon as if the sauce was important. 'There is a time travelling tin of spaghetti hoops,' he paused and looked at the floor for a moment as if considering another plausible explanation, 'or it could be suffering temporal instability or something, but…' He paused again. 'But that story is for another time.'

'Your life is like an episode of the Twilight Zone,' she giggled.

'You mean this sort of thing doesn't happen to you?' he asked with surprise.

'Well, there was that time,' she pondered, 'when the chocolate cake vanished from the fridge,' and she sighed. 'But it turned out that I had forgotten I had eaten it.' She then stood, walked past the sofa and stopped by the door to the bedrooms. 'Come with me,' she smiled coyly, 'let's see if my glow-in-the-dark alarm clock attracts ghosts.' As she disappeared through the door, Avalon shrugged, patted the Para Handy book and stood, saying,

'The Vital Spark is a wonderful thing.'

Chapter Fourteen

Thursday was a big day for Avalon. The morning was sunny and, as he walked across the car park towards the door of the police station, he was thinking through his first actions for the morning. In The Cave, DS Wilson and DC Mackinnon were already there and DC Fraser arrived soon after. With Rutherford and Ross down in England, DC White was the last to arrive. Avalon watched White sit and begin work, and as he did, he wondered how much use White was going to be to the team. He had too many limitations, and he wondered if the man would have to take on Frazer's role in the office and move Megan to a more external role. Maybe it was the case that White was just out of practice in certain areas of the job, and that could possibly mean that in time, he would be capable. His intelligence wasn't in doubt and for sure, in other aspects of police work, he was fine. But, with so few staff in C Section, Avalon needed people who could turn their hands to most things. For now, he would have to concentrate on the matter at hand. Ross and Rutherford would arrive later in the afternoon with their charge, Stuart Fenner, and he and Frazer had to formulate some sort of plan in regards to the interviews with the man. He called Frazer into the booth and she sat with a notepad in her hand.

'So what's the plan Boss?' she asked, knowing exactly what they were about to discuss.

'It's not going to be easy,' he said, raising his brows. 'Fenner seems in the clear as things stand and I'm still not sure how we are going to approach this.' She gave a nod but offered no comment. 'So,' he sighed and began to outline what he had, 'as things stand, we know three important facts.' He looked to his computer screen. 'The two bodies were buried in the same place, which means that the same person must have placed them there, which in itself, points to the same person killing Mary Anne and possibly the child.' He looked back to her. 'The second fact is that Gibson is the most likely person to have committed this deed. It is now known, that he has been a sexual predator and he was cohabiting with Mary and Carl. The third fact is that Gibson moved as soon as Mary went missing. Though there was virtually nothing found at his home or in his car, this really points the finger at Gibson and leaves Fenner in the clear.'

'Makes you wonder ef we are wasting our time with Fenner then,' said Frazer, more as a question than a statement.

'I've thought all along that Fenner is hiding something,' replied Avalon, 'and I'm not the only one. If we are to conclude this investigation properly, we have to try to squeeze out of Fenner what he knows about the crime. It could be nothing, it might be something, but our job is to find the truth.'

'So, how do you want to run this then?' she asked.

'With a bit of luck,' replied Avalon, 'Fenner won't know about the death of Gibson, and so I want to keep it that way, at least at the start of the interview. I also want him to think we know more than we do.'

'That's not going t' be easy Boss,' frowned Frazer, ''cos ef we get anything wrong, he's going to know.'

'I'm aware of that,' nodded Avalon, 'so we have to tread carefully and try to ease information in. At first I think we'll just tell him we have found the bodies of his wife and child, after that, I want to make him think that we're still considering he's our main suspect.'

'I think that's the only way we'll open him up,' she agreed.

'Exactly,' nodded the DI as he looked back to the screen. 'And, I think the easiest way is to break what we know into segments and continue to drop hints as we proceed.'

'I was looking back through the case notes yesterday afternoon,' she began on a slightly different subject, 'and I wondered about the forensic evidence found in the house.'

'Such as?' asked Avalon.

'It says they found a bloodstain on the lounge carpet that had been cleaned,' she explained.

'Yes, I know,' replied Avalon, 'but it does say that they were just two small spots, nothing profound. They could have come from a nosebleed or a cut. No other traces were found.'

'Well, the other thing,' she continued, 'is the fact that no fingerprints of Mary were found inside the car.' She sighed before continuing. 'That's usually an indication the car has been cleaned thoroughly.'

317

'Correct,' nodded Avalon, 'and I'm sure that was the case, but Mary's prints were found on the outside. There had been no attempt to remove them, and more to the point, no other forensic evidence was found.' This time Avalon sighed. 'We can make assumptions, but that isn't fact.' She gave a slight nod and Avalon continued. 'There is so little forensic evidence of a crime here that I have all but discounted the smaller detail. We are almost positive Mary was poisoned. Carl's skeleton shows no sign of injury. The lack of blood at the house or in the car means nothing. We don't even know who the blood came from, as there wasn't enough of it to test at the time. All we can say for sure is that there is no sign of a crime at the house or in the car.' She took a deep breath as he finished. When she let the air from her lungs, she had accepted that Avalon was right. They needed something more to know for sure that Gibson had killed them both. Their only chance, now that Gibson was dead, was if Stuart Fenner gave them something. If indeed, he knew anything at all.

Avalon and Frazer continued to work on their approach as White worked around the edges of the case, checking anything he could find that may have been overlooked. Wilson and Mackinnon were busy on all the other business of the office and, as such, came and went throughout the day. Around lunchtime, Avalon was reasonably happy with what they had formulated and Frazer returned to her seat. Avalon asked White if he had found anything they could use.

'Not really,' he replied in a noncommittal voice. 'I can't find any link between Gibson and Steven Scott whatsoever,' he continued. 'This Irishman, Gerald Doyle, doesn't crop up either. The only link I can find anywhere is tenuous at best.'

'Tenuous is good at the moment,' replied Avalon, 'I'll look at anything.'

'You gave me a name,' and he looked down at his notes, 'Lachtan Emery,' he eventually said.

'Yes, he knew Steven Scott, he was killed in an accident,' nodded Avalon.

'Well,' continued White looking up at the DI, 'In 2004, Emery and Fenner lived on the same street.'

'Interesting,' mused Avalon, 'anything more concrete?'

'No,' replied White, looking back to his notes, 'and it was only for six months or so, but long enough for them to know each other.'

'We need to establish if they knew each other or not. We need to knock on doors. What's the address?' asked Avalon.

'It's in the town, B Section's turf,' replied White.

'Okay,' nodded the DI, 'I'll let DI Lasiter know, then me and Megan will take a drive down there.'

It was proving almost impossible for two detectives to take a car each. The social distancing was having to be relaxed a little, in the office at any rate, so for the first time in a while, Avalon went in his car with Megan in the passenger seat. Ross and Rutherford had gone to pick up Fenner in Newcastle in a single vehicle, and Fenner would be with them at this very moment. The rules couldn't apply all the time. They arrived in Fenner's old street knowing that everyone would be at home due to the lockdown. They started down the street, taking a side each and making their way down, knocking at every door armed with a couple of photographs and a single question. 'Do you recognise either of these two men?' They found nothing from most of the street, but as Avalon knocked at the door where Fenner used to live, he had to converse through the letterbox as the old man inside wouldn't open the door to anyone. He was convinced that everyone outside his house was oozing Chinese flu, as he called it, and the door would remain closed. The photographs were pushed through the letterbox, and after a moment pushed back.

'I don't know the one with a hat on, but the other one used to live on this street.'

'Do you know his name?' asked the DI.

'No, not the sort o' person I would talk to. I lived up the road at number eighty-three then. Ask next door,' he suggested. Next door, knew both faces, but couldn't name them. He then saw Frazer walking towards him.

'I might have something Boss.'

'Go on.'

'I've just been at number thirty-two. The old couple there say that they remember both o' the faces. The woman didn't know their names, but the old guy said the two o' them used to frequent the local pub.'

'Did *he* know their names?' asked Avalon.

'He knew Fenner's name but described the one with the hat as the Irishman,' she replied.

'And could he confirm that they knew each other?' was the DI's next question.

'He thought they did, as the pub wasn't ever that busy, so everyone more or less knew each other,' she explained. 'He also said that there was talk that the Irishman wasn't liked, people said he was some sort of drug dealer.'

'And he probably knew Fenner,' replied Avalon,

more thinking aloud than speaking to Megan. 'Do they have dates for this?' he then asked.

'Yeah,' she nodded, 'they weren't sure at first but tied it down to the dates White gave you. Something to do with a new manager taking over the pub at the time. They worked it back, and it fits.' Avalon nodded.

'Go back to them. Get a statement and get it typed up. Tell them we'll send someone out to get them to sign it once it's done. I'll continue knocking on doors.'

Rutherford came into the office in the late afternoon and looked tired and worn.

'Everything alright?' asked Avalon when he saw him.

'No, not at all, it's been the worst two days of my life,' sighed Rutherford.

'So, he's been a problem?' asked Avalon with anxiousness in his expression.

'Oh, yes,' nodded the big man. 'Nothing but, from the very start to the moment we got back.'

'I didn't think it would be that difficult, I know Mr Fenner would be surprised, but he can't know exactly-'

'Not Fenner,' exclaimed Rutherford, 'he was a quiet as a mouse. It was Rossy, moaning all the way there and all the way back. I think even Fenner was ready to admit everything under such torture.' Avalon gave a muted laugh, then, suppressed his humour.

'I know he can be a bit of a...' Avalon was trying to think of the right word.

'Arse is the word you're looking for Boss,' interrupted Martin.

'I was thinking of prima donna but arse will suffice,' smiled the DI. Ross then walked in.

'Any problems?' asked Avalon with the remnants of a smile still on his face.

'No, pretty easy,' shrugged Ross, then he noticed everyone watching him and Rutherford sighing deeply as he sat at his desk. 'What?' he then asked.

'Oh, nothing,' laughed Avalon and moved to his booth. He then heard Ross asking Rutherford,

'So what have you been saying?' He watched them arguing through the glass and after a few minutes told them to get off home and have some rest. He also told them that they would be the relief interviewers in the morning if the discussion went on through several hours. As they left, Frazer attracted the DI's attention.

'The papers are on the case,' she said. Avalon looked at her screen and saw a picture of Ross and Rutherford escorting Fenner from the car to the police station, the latter with a blanket over his head.

'They got a good one of Rossy,' smiled Avalon as he saw a disgruntled expression on the DS's face. The headline read,

'Man brought from Newcastle in connection with the two quarry bodies.' He read a little further. 'Two CID officers from Inverness arrived at the police station this afternoon with a man brought all the way from Newcastle. He has been brought north for questioning about the discovery of two bodies found in a quarry near Daviot. The man is thought to be the ex-husband of Mary Anne Fenner. Her remains were found along with those of her son two weeks ago. A police spokesman told our reporter that the man has not been charged and is simply helping with inquiries. The mother and son went missing…' he broke off.

'No mention of Gibson yet,' said Avalon, standing straight.

'Not yet Boss, but this will whet the appetites of the tabloids, and you can bet et will be out soon.' Avalon nodded and returned to his booth. It didn't matter now if Gibson's death became public. They had Fenner downstairs and he would hear what they wanted him to hear and nothing else. Avalon had arranged for the man to be fed and have some rest before he and Frazer would begin the questions. Fenner had declined a solicitor as he had said he didn't quite know what the questions would be about. He certainly must have known by now that the police had found bodies, so he was either playing it cool, or he really had nothing to hide.

Stuart Fenner sat in the interview room behind the Perspex shield that ran down the centre of the table. Frazer had introduced herself and the DI and had explained that he still had rights to have a solicitor present. He still declined and asked what the interview was about.

'Have you not heard about the finding of two bodies in a quarry, Mr Fenner?' asked Avalon.

'Aye, I have,' nodded the man. He had an Inverness accent, but with some stray bits of North Shields creeping in now and then. He was dressed very casually in a manner that Avalon did his best not to stereotype, but nonetheless, saw Fenner as unremarkable and ordinary. He had been thirty-five when his wife and child went missing, but he was now sixty-four, and except for a loss of hair, looked very close to his earlier image. He came over as being friendly, if a little suspicious, but given the circumstances, reasonably confident. His manner was relaxed and to the casual observer, this was a man who had nothing to hide, and even less to fear. 'I heard on the news that it could be Carl and Mary.'

'It certainly seems to be them, I'm afraid,' nodded Avalon. He noted that he was the first person to put Carl's name before Mary's.

'I had no illusions about their fate,' the man admitted, 'once they were with that bastard, I knew nothing good would come of it.'

'You mean Geoffrey Gibson?' asked Avalon.

'Who else?' questioned the man, 'I'm guessing it's him you've got for it.'

'We haven't concluded our investigation yet and we have several options in this case,' answered Avalon in a monotone.

'What?' questioned the man raising his brows, 'does that mean I'm,' he paused, 'am I here as a suspect?'

'As I explained Mr Fenner, we are far from concluding the affair. We have several avenues to pursue.'

'Then I need a lawyer,' insisted the man looking indignant, 'I'll say nothing else until I have a lawyer present.'

'So be it,' replied Avalon, standing. He looked at Megan. 'Make sure Mr Fenner can contact a lawyer DC Frazer.' She nodded, and he left to return to the office.

It was so late in the afternoon when a lawyer was finally found, with more time spent on the necessary briefing, that when everything was concluded, Avalon suggested that any further questioning should wait until the morning. He didn't want any accusations that Fenner was tired, or under any particular strain, so it made sense to continue on Friday.

It was typical that Friday was to see Avalon locked away in an interview room when the weather had promised to be a hot, sunny day. He took solace that he was better off than many people, however, as it had been confirmed that over sixteen thousand people had now lost their lives to the covid virus. It was a sobering thought as he entered The Cave and nodded to those already there. He beckoned to Frazer and they went over their notes once more before retiring downstairs to begin the interview with Stuart Fenner. The man still looked relaxed as the preliminaries were, once again, enacted and then Frazer began the questions.

'You mentioned Mr Gibson yesterday, Mr Fenner. Can you explain what you meant?'

'I have to tell you that Mr Reid here,' Fenner pointed to the man sitting behind him, 'has told me about Gibson. I'm guessing you weren't gonna mention that.' Avalon gave the solicitor a blank stare.

'So tell us about Mr Gibson,' asked Frazer once more.

'Not much to tell,' replied Fenner, 'the man was a paedophile and I'm glad he got justice in the way he deserved.'

'Did you know him previously?' she then asked.

'Christ no,' he laughed, 'me and him? In the same place? Only one of us is coming out unscathed,' he said, then, he shifted uneasily as he realised the implication of the words.

'So you had never met him and never been to his

home?'

'No,' frowned Fenner, then he folded his arms as an insistent gesture. 'Never, and to be frank, I wouldn't have anything to do with anyone who knew him.'

'Is that why you severed contact with your wife and child?' she asked.

'Yes, and I warned that bitch about him,' he spat.

'So you knew he was a paedophile before Mary Anne went t' live with him?'

'Yeah,' frowned the man again, 'everyone did.'

'That's not exactly true Mr Fenner,' insisted the DC, 'but you may have heard the rumours about him.'

'So, what's the score here?' and he unfolded his arms and glanced behind him to the solicitor, 'are you thinking I went over to Spain and slit the bastard's throat and then got back in time for tea?'

'How many times did you see Mary Anne after she had left you?' Frazer asked without any consideration to his question.

'I don't know,' he shrugged, 'I went through this at the original trial, twice, maybe three times.'

'One of those times was when you were trying to see Carl, es that correct.'

'Yeah, I was concerned about him.'

'Why the turnaround, after so long,' she then asked.

'I got a letter from the Social Services saying that Carl hadn't been to school for some time.'

'So, as I asked,' she repeated, 'why the change en attitude towards him?'

'You gotta understand my history to know that,' he growled. Frazer sat unblinking, staring straight into his eyes. The man realised she could easily stare him

326

out, so he continued. 'I was from a broken home. I knew what it was like. My dad walked out and then came back some months later. It was like living in a war zone. I spent the rest of my days there just wishing he would leave again, but he didn't. He beat up my mother, she went into hospital, he was arrested and I was put in a temporary home.' He made a snort. 'Temporary my arse.' Frazer didn't want to hear his platitudes. She wanted to keep up the pressure.

'So you decided et was better to stay away?' she asked.

'Yeah,' the man nodded, thinking Frazer understood. Being a woman, she would have all the sympathies for the child.

'So, on one hand you wanted t' do the best for the boy, and on the other, you were fine with him living under the same roof as a man you knew to be a paedophile.'

'That's not how it was,' scowled the man, 'I found out about him later.'

'But you just said you warned Mary about him,' insisted Frazer.

'Aye, I did, a few weeks before that,' and he gave her a mean frown, but this was Frazer. She could out posture a tiger.

'So, when were the other times you saw her?' she then asked. She wasn't giving him time to think, and the man withdrew into himself for a moment. He was thinking through what he remembered he had told them at the original trial. That was very clear, as he gave a slight shake of the head before answering.

'I don't remember exactly, it's a long time ago.'

'You stated previously that you went, once to

convince her to come back to you, and the second to see how Carl was,' she offered, clearly quoting from the original trial.

'That's probably right,' he nodded.

'Where did these meetings take place?' she asked. He sighed deeply.

'Look, if you have the transcripts from the trial, you know what I said, why do we have to go through this again?'

'Answer the question please,' said Avalon. It was his signal to tell Frazer he would take over. This kind of questioning was exhausting, so the pressure would be shared. The man sighed again.

'The first time was on the street. It turned into an argument, as always. She was drunk, or had been drinking. The second time I bumped into her in town.'

'That's when the police were called out to you?' asked Avalon.

'Yeah,' he nodded slowly. 'She was pissed, and I told her to get back and look after the boy. She went for me so I hit her,' he admitted.

'And the third time?' asked Avalon.

'I texted her to say I had to meet her because of the letter about Carl. She said she was too busy. This went on for some time until I threatened to go round to the house.' Fenner reached for one of the small bottles of water that had been provided. He took a large gulp and continued. 'It was only then she agreed to meet. We met in one of the parks, I don't remember which, but she was really against me seeing Carl. She was on edge, I knew something was wrong and so I grabbed her arm and dragged her towards the house. I told her that I was going to kick the door in and see what was wrong. She

328

screamed at me that she would sort it out. She was a mess. Her tears didn't convince me but she said she needed time to sort herself out and get sober. I told her she had until Friday and then I was going to the house.'

'And she didn't get in touch?' asked Avalon, knowing what the original trial notes said.

'No, and after several texts and trying to phone her, I decided to go round to the house,' explained Fenner. He looked to Frazer and then back to Avalon. 'You have the statements of the witness on the street?' Avalon nodded. 'Good, I'm not going through that again,' he insisted.

'You tried to gain access, but neighbours reported you before you got in, is that correct?' Fenner nodded to Avalon's question. 'So, you didn't manage to gain entrance to the house?'

'No, the police came before I got in. There was no point anyway. They had gone,' explained the man, and he leant on his knees in a dejected manner. Avalon wasn't convinced it was for real, but he suddenly had a thought. He quickly picked up some notes, giving Frazer a glance to let her know she should continue the questioning.

'How long was et before you gave her the ultimatum, until you actually went around to the house?' she asked.

'I don't remember,' scowled the man. He was beginning to think that they had something, and it showed. His whole manner was slowly changing. He was nervous, and cautious, and yet if he really had nothing to hide, why was he so evasive? Avalon was beginning to feel more confident as Frazer kept up the questions. Confident to the point, that he was seeing a new possibility in the case. Frazer was pushing him on the subject of the time between him meeting Mary Anne, and the time he eventually went to the house where she and Gibson lived. It rankled Frazer, and it had given Avalon the first clue to his new theory. They both knew the question had been asked at the trial, and Fenner had stated he had been busy, and had things to do. The prosecution hadn't been duped, and neither was Avalon. Had this time been used to formulate a plan? There was no evidence of that, and evidence was what was required. To try out his new theory, he took over the questioning once more.

'When you called at Gibson's house to try to see Carl, were you prepared to force your way in to see the boy?' he asked. Fenner thought for a moment.

'You mean, was I ready to break the law?' he asked and when Avalon didn't react, he added, 'Yes, I was. I had gone to see if he was okay and I wouldn't have left until I had found that out.'

'And so how long were you there before the police arrived?' asked the DI.

'I don't know,' shrugged the man. 'I went to the back door, looked through the windows and looked for signs of life.'

'Ten, fifteen, twenty minutes?' asked Avalon.

'Fifteen minutes, I would think,' he shrugged. For all this time, the solicitor had stayed silent, but now, as if to warrant the wages he would be earning, asked,

'Does this information impact on your case, Detective Avalon?'

'This is my job, Mr Reid. If I asked questions for a hobby, I would probably not consider wasting my valuable time on pointless questions. As it is, you may assume that any question I ask your client will be very pertinent to our investigation.' The man gave Avalon a frown, but the DI ignored him and continued. 'So you waited fifteen minutes without gaining access, and by that time you had assumed that there was no one there?'

'There was no movement, and from what I could see in the house, there was no one in.'

'Yet you remained there until the police arrived?' Fenner shrugged.

'I suppose.'

'And what were your plans after that?' asked Avalon.

'I don't know?' admitted Fenner with another shrug of the shoulders.

'Would you have broken in?' he asked.

'Don't answer that,' informed the solicitor. Fenner stayed silent. Avalon raised his brows after a few moments of silence and then said,

'One minute you say you are going there to find out if Carl was safe, the next minute an empty house halts you in your tracks.' Fenner stared blankly at the table.

'Let's take a break,' sighed Avalon glancing to Frazer, and she announced the details and the time, for the benefit of the recording.

As Frazer joined Avalon outside the interview suite along with White, who had been watching from the viewing room, she raised her brows.

'What do you think?' she asked.

'I think we have some work to do. This morning, I thought Gibson had left us with a minor issue to clear up. My opinion has now changed. Let's get back to the office. Angus, make sure Fenner has food and drink, then join us upstairs.'

Ross and Rutherford watched the recording of the interview that had just taken place. Ross was silent after, but Rutherford announced that he thought Fenner was a complete liar.

'That's more or less what ex DI Mowat concluded,' nodded Avalon. He seemed to be searching through several sheets of notes on copier paper. Rutherford was reading about the case in the newspaper.

'Not a good one of you, Rossy,' smiled Rutherford, 'but I think they captured my attractive side,' and he tossed the folded paper to Ross.

'Jesus,' he exclaimed, 'even my own mother wouldn't recognise me in that shot.' He looked up at Rutherford. 'And take it from me, you don't have an attractive side.'

'Hey,' laughed Rutherford, 'it's not me who's trying to blow bubbles.'

'That was taken as I was talking,' insisted Ross, 'it's a very unfair photograph.'

'What were you saying,' asked Rutherford, 'Hoola hoop, or maybe whoosh?' Ross tired of the conversation and got back to the details of the case.

'So, what angle do you want us to pursue?' he asked, turning to Avalon.

'That depends,' frowned Avalon, 'on what Megan can find out. I put her on tracing the movements of this Irishman,' and he gave a cursory glance to her working at her computer.

'Even if we find him, he's not going to tell you anything,' insisted Ross.

'Maybe not, but I now think that you and Angus

were right,' he said as he examined one sheet of the notes particularly avidly.

'About what?' asked Ross, a little surprised.

'The theory that Fenner was involved in the killings,' explained Avalon. Ross frowned at this.

'But it was you that pointed out the flaw in that theory,' insisted Ross, leaning back in his seat. 'and as I have said previously, how come the two bodies ended up in the same grave?'

'True,' he agreed, 'that is still a problem to sort out, but since speaking with Fenner, I think I can see how it might have played out. My problem is evidence, and a bit of a flaw still nagging at me.' he replied, the last few words of the sentence trailing off.

'Well, tell us then. We're all ears,' demanded Ross as he watched DC White turning to hear more.

'Here it is,' called out Avalon as he slapped the paper with his free hand. 'I knew I had read this somewhere,' and he quickly scanned through it. 'This is from the original trial. Fenner stated that he knew something was wrong when he noticed that even a photograph of Carl had gone missing from Mary's bedside.'

'Not very damning though, is it?' announced Ross sarcastically.

'Not in itself,' smiled Avalon, 'but he was speaking about her bedside at Gibson's house. She had left some time by then so it couldn't have been when she still lived with Fenner.'

'So what?' asked Ross.

'Simple,' interrupted White, 'he said this morning he had never been in that house, so that must be a lie, ergo, there is a reason for the lie.'

333

'No proof,' shrugged Ross.

'No, but it looks like he was in that house at least twice before,' insisted White.

'Why twice?' asked Ross with a frown.

'Pretty obvious,' laughed Rutherford, 'keep up chuckles. If he knew that photograph was missing, he also knew it had been there previously.'

'And here is the second bit of damning information,' added Avalon, reading from the now crumpled notes. 'The report from scenes of crimes says that when they arrived, the rear kitchen window was open.' He looked up. 'It wasn't a large window, but I'm guessing it wouldn't be difficult to get in that way.'

'Okay,' nodded Ross, 'so he could have got in, and let's assume he intended to poison his wife. How would he do that without doing them both in?'

'That one is easy,' smiled Avalon. 'She drank heavily, he rarely drank alcohol.'

'I'm thinking that he wouldn't really care if he killed them both anyway,' insisted Rutherford.

'That's not the case,' put in White once more, 'if this theory is to be taken seriously, we have to assume that Fenner wanted Gibson alive to take the blame for her death.'

'Exactly,' nodded Avalon, pointing to White. Ross wasn't fully convinced, and he glanced out of the window onto a lovely sunny day. Ross interrupted.

'But as you say, you still need evidence, and there isn't a great deal of that as I can see.'

Chapter Fifteen

Avalon looked at the faces of the team. They all doubted that they had any evidence to implicate Fenner in the crime, but not one of them thought he was totally innocent either.

'No matter what's come from this interview, I don't think we have enough to bring this to trial,' insisted Ross.

'I think he's involved too, but I agree with Rossy,' shrugged Martin Rutherford. Frazer shrugged. She wanted Fenner to be guilty of something. She disliked him, and so she kept her feelings to herself.

'It's a challenge,' nodded White, 'but I think he killed his wife. If we don't at least try, the death will be laid at Gibson's door, and Fenner will walk free.'

'Whatever we do, we have to work fast,' added Frazer, 'he's talking to his solicitor about leaving.'

'We simply don't have enough to arrest him,' admitted Avalon, 'and an interview under caution isn't bringing enough out into the open. With no evidence, we're stuffed.' He turned to Frazer. 'Any luck with the Irishman?' She shook her head, but no one considered that particular line of inquiry as being of benefit. 'Then, we let Fenner go. We have no option.' There was a mixed reaction to this. Body language showed frustration from working on a case, only to be disappointed right at the end. Then, on the other hand, there was relief. It wasn't as if justice hadn't been metred out. Gibson had given his life in a terrible and dramatic way at the hands of a vigilante mob. But Fenner? If he had been guilty of anything, then he now knew the police knew. And, if he was innocent, caught up in a situation he was trying to make sense of, he must have anger. Yet, he wasn't angry, he was relieved, and that showed he was culpable in some way. As Avalon drove home that evening, he felt cheated. He knew that building a case against Fenner was almost impossible, and he had been denied the chance to bring Gibson to trial. In many ways, even though the bodies of Mary and Carl had been found, they were still unavenged. There was no justice for either of them.

He was late arriving back at the house. He had driven around before heading home too, which made him even later. Sarah was already there and was seated at the little desk working. She was using his laptop and eating something.

'Oh, hello,' she smiled looking up from her seat, 'looks like you've had a bad day.'

'Sort of,' replied Avalon, as he peeled off his jacket. He needed a drink, but he didn't quite know what. 'Do you want a drink?' he asked.

'Not for me thanks, maybe later. I have a little bit of work to finish.' She then remembered she was using his laptop. 'Oh, I borrowed your laptop, is that okay?'

'Yeah, of course,' he sighed, walking back to the

kitchen. He made himself a gin and tonic, not something he usually drank, but he needed the bitter kick. He returned to the lounge and dropped onto the large sofa which clung around his tired body. Then something occurred to him.

'That laptop was password protected,' he frowned.

'I know,' she admitted sheepishly. 'So you probably need to change your password.'

'How did you work that out? Are you some kind of top international hacker on the sly?'

'I got it on the third attempt,' she admitted with a pained expression, 'second if you consider the first attempt had a possible spelling option.'

'I thought 'Drumnadrochit' was a difficult one to work out,' he frowned.

'Like I said, third attempt,' she shrugged.

'What was the first?'

'Auld Clootie,' she shrugged.

'And the second?'

'Old Clootie, with an English spelling.' She watched him thinking through that answer and decided to try to mitigate the situation. 'But I doubt anyone who didn't know you well, would get it.'

'I better go back to my birthdate,' he said as he sipped the gin. 'What are you eating anyway?' he then asked.

'Tablet, do you want some?' She offered him the bag, and he pulled a square out and examined it. He had heard of Scottish Tablet but never tried any, so this was a first for him. 'It's vegan,' she explained. 'I was told of someone who makes it, so I ordered a bag. I used to love it when I was a child, but since going vegan, I haven't had any.'

'It looks like fudge,' he said as he sniffed at it.

'I've never had that, but I bet it doesn't taste like it,' she smiled. He placed it in his mouth and immediately creased his eyes almost shut.

'My god,' he exclaimed, 'it's pure sugar.'

'Not exactly, but close,' she laughed. As he let it melt in his mouth, he gazed at her. 'What?' she asked, knowing there was something on his mind.

'I was just thinking, how can you eat something like this and not put on weight? I only have to say the word food, and I can feel my trouser belt under pressure.'

'I rarely eat anything like this,' she grinned, 'it's a treat,' and she offered him the bag once more. He refused as she continued. 'Some people can eat more than others. The metabolic rate has a great deal to do with that, I suppose.'

'I'm surrounded by thin people who seem to do nothing but eat, and I,' his voice rose in pitch, 'have to stay with one meal a day and keep to a regime of exercise. Somehow it doesn't seem fair.'

'So who are you talking about? I put weight on very easily. Luckily, I'm not really a foody.'

'For starters, most of my section. They eat so much food, and most are thin, or at least not overweight.' He tried to clean his mouth with a sip of gin, but the bitter after the sweet was almost painful. 'Megan, for instance,' he continued, 'I was once out with her when the team used to go out for a meal. She would eat starters, main, sweet then cheese and biscuits after. She would then call off for a fish supper, and she weighs slightly more than a ghost.' He took another sip. 'Rossy

338

isn't thin, but neither is he overweight. He eats all through the day, and most of it is junk food. I swear he can eat more than a blue whale. Martin is a big man I'll grant you, but not what I would call fat. Yet, his lunch is delivered by a special train.' She laughed at this. 'If I have any extra food through the day, I put weight on.'

'You don't have a bit of fat on you anyway,' she insisted.

'No, because I stopped eating in two-thousand and eight.' She laughed again, and this time turned back to the laptop. 'And now I'm hungry,' he added in a softer tone, taking a sip of his drink.

'I think there's a tin of spaghetti hoops in the kitchen cupboard,' she said without looking round.

'Steady,' he said, 'don't go there. Spaghetti is not for human consumption.'

'So, I'm guessing you're having problems with this quarry case?' she eventually asked.

'Sort of,' he sighed, and this time took a deep gulp of the gin. It seemed to be reviving him.

'Do you want to talk about it?' she then asked.

'No,' he replied, 'but thanks.' He went silent for a minute and then he did ask a question. 'There is something I would like to ask though.' She stopped working and turned to face him.

'Ask away.'

'Something is bothering me about the ricin.' He finished off the drink and looked back to her. 'How come a fast acting poison can be found in the bone tissue? I mean, if it's fast acting, how does it find its way through the blood and into the bone in such a short time?'

'I know what you're getting at,' she replied, 'but

what we are seeing under the microscope isn't always just the substance. There is also residue of what the compound does to the body.' She paused and then added, 'but you have a point. It is wildly possible that small amounts were previously administered, but I would rather guess that the means of it entering the body were responsible for the transfer to the body tissues.'

'And that's another thing that puzzles me,' he frowned, 'could it be administered through alcohol?'

'Maybe,' she nodded, 'but if it was in alcohol for any length of time, or in too little amounts, it would probably degrade.'

'That blows that theory,' he shrugged, and then he had an idea. She noticed the change in expression and asked him about it. 'Oh, nothing really,' he said, 'just something I was thinking.' He stood and took the empty glass to the kitchen. 'Are you hungry?' he asked.

'Not really,' she smiled, 'too much tablet.' He grinned at this.

'Okay, I'll take a shower and then make myself a snack.' As he left, she looked at the laptop and closed the lid. She didn't see herself as the homely, domesticated type, but she thought she would make him something to eat for when he came out of the shower.

Once again, the morning announced itself with a clear sky and the promise of warm sunshine, Avalon climbed into his car and made his way to the office. It wasn't going to be a pleasant day however. He had to think about the wording of his report on the quarry case. They still didn't have enough information to say who was responsible for the death of Mary and Carl, and to Avalon's self-critical eye, they were staring failure in the

340

face. If Gibson had killed and buried Mary and Carl, there was nothing he could do about that now. But, if Fenner still had some connection, and Avalon thought he did, they had failed to bring *him* to justice. His feet felt heavy as he climbed the stairs to the office where he found he was the first to arrive. He began to type up his report for the DCI. By the time everyone was in, the main points of it were finished. It would require another half-hour or so to make it readable, and so he decided to leave it until later. For the moment, he would grab a cup of coffee and see how morale was in The Cave.

'Has Fenner gone back to England?' asked Rutherford to anyone who knew the answer.

'No,' replied Frazer, 'he was put up in a guest house, something about wanting to see Inverness again before he went.'

'How's that work?' frowned the big man, 'there's a lockdown, and he gets to go sightseeing?' Frazer just shrugged.

'I can't help thinking,' said Ross quietly, 'that Mr Fenner is rubbing our noses in it.'

'We have nothing to pin on him and that is that,' insisted Avalon as he leaned on the wall, sipping his drink.

'So, don't you think he's playing with us then?' asked Ross.

'Yes I do,' answered Avalon calmly, 'and the proof of that was clear, every time he contradicted his original story from the trial.'

'So you've changed your mind?' asked White, looking around to the DI, 'you don't think he was involved, he's just playing a game?'

'No, I think he's involved,' insisted Avalon, 'I

still think he killed Mary, but he's wrapped this case up in so many lies, it's no longer easy to see what is fact, and what isn't.'

'Such as?' asked Rutherford.

'Such as the statement about his wife not having a photo of Carl by the bed,' suggested Avalon.

'But, he could have seen that when he broke in to administer the poison,' suggested Rutherford.

'I don't think he broke in. I don't think he ever went into the house. That was all an elaborate story to make us think he knew something. Think about it,' he then said, placing his cup down for a moment. 'There was a window in the kitchen that wasn't secured when the police arrived after he was reported hanging around the house. He could have got in then to see if Carl was safe. But he didn't. He hung around, not for fifteen minutes as he said, but more like forty minutes. I checked the timings from the neighbours who phoned the police. He was hanging around in the hope that someone *would* report him. He wanted the police to enter the house to find Mary's body without any interference from him. A hero, the caring husband who knew something was wrong all along. His problem was that she wasn't there as he had expected.' He picked up his cup and drank.

'And you think that Mary died from poisoning,' began White quietly as he tried to catch up on Avalon's idea, 'to be found by Gibson. He thought she had committed suicide and panicked, so he disposed of the body, which is why it ended up in the same grave as the child's.' White nodded as he ended.

'If Mary had earlier voiced concerns about Fenner asking questions, Gibson would have been

342

shitting himself if he thought she had killed herself,' agreed Rutherford.

'Exactly,' nodded Avalon. 'And it even explains the few spots of blood on the lounge carpet. She would probably vomit, or cough up blood as she died. Fenner wanted the police to find Mary's body at the house. He was probably there to plant the ricin too, as evidence, who knows? When they found nothing, Fenner had to rethink his plan. It could even have been Fenner who continued to hound Gibson over later years.' There was quiet in the room as everyone considered the theory. It was Ross who put the fly in the ointment.

'So how did he get the ricin into her body?' he asked in a casual manner.

'I gave this some thought,' nodded Avalon, 'and after a brief chat with...' he gave a slight pause, he was about to say Sarah but caught himself in time, 'forensics, it is unlikely that booze would make a good carrier for the drug. Therefore, I thought how he could have got the ricin into her body, but no one else's. Mary was a chain smoker. It wouldn't take Fenner long to put grains of ricin into a few cigarettes and offer them to Mary on that final meeting. By his own admission she was in a mess, and was upset, I think he planned it that way.' Avalon finished his coffee and then concluded with, 'and it seems inhalation is a convenient and efficient way to get the stuff into the body.' Ross seemed happy with the explanation and he gave a nod. The room went quiet again. It certainly seemed a plausible theory, but there wasn't a thing they could do, because, just like in the original case, there was no evidence, and no witness to confirm any of the story.

'It fits,' nodded Rutherford.

'Can anyone see any real problems with the theory?' asked Avalon.

'The theory is good,' agreed Ross, raising his feet onto the edge of his desk, 'but not a shred of anything we can present to the sheriff's office.' Avalon raised his brows and then rinsed his cup out. He turned to the team and then spoke with resignation in his voice.

'We need to write up everything we have, there isn't much more we can achieved at this stage,' then he walked back to the booth and pulled his jacket on. Ross watched the DI leave and after a few minutes, followed on. He followed the boss through the rear door where Avalon looked up at the blue sky, pulled in a lungful of warming air and sat on the low wall in the warmth of the sun. He heard footsteps behind him and saw Ross approach, eating an apple.

'That's a bit healthy for you, isn't it?'

'Just something to kick-start my appetite,' replied Ross as he sat a few feet away.

'You're making me hungry,' smiled Avalon, looking at the fresh fruit.

'I'd share it with you, but you know with this plague around…' and he trailed off with a shrug, taking another bite of the apple. Avalon nodded and bent to lean his forearms on his knees. 'You know,' began Ross between chews, 'we still have places to go, we could try to prise something out of Scott, or do some more footwork.' He took another bite. 'There could be someone out there who knows something, they may just need a memory jog.'

'Oh, I intend to keep on it,' replied Avalon, looking at the floor. 'I'm pretty sure that the theory holds water and explains a great deal about the case.' He turned to Ross. 'My only doubt, is why didn't Fenner pursue Gibson more if he knew the truth?'

'Fenner's lazy, you can tell that about him,' nodded Ross as he dropped the remains of the apple in the hedge behind them. 'I would say that once Gibson moved, he more or less gave up. We don't know it was him that gave Gibson away, down in Lancashire.'

'Yeah,' nodded the DI, 'you're probably right.' A car pulled into the car park just as clouds appeared in the utter blueness above. The car stopped and out stepped PC Neil Dowd, a holdall in his hands. He gave a brief smile to the two men seated on the wall.

'So, has 'hear no evil' taken the day off?' he asked.

'At least those monkeys were wise,' smiled Avalon. Dowd stopped for a moment.

'It looked as ef you were waiting for the tide to come en.'

'It would have to be a high tide to reach here,' replied the DI. Ross turned to Avalon and jokingly said,

'It looks like the afternoon shift has brought a change of weather with him.'

'Not quite the afternoon shift, I've just been on an errand, and et's just a wee bit of cloud. Et's still a nice day,' he then paused before adding, 'ef you're not at work that es.'

'There's a bit of a breeze getting up though Neil,' added Avalon, looking back up to the sky.

'That isn't a breeze, DI,' frowned Dowd, 'that's the wind from the beating of the wings of death,' and he continued off towards the doorway. Avalon looked at Ross, raised his brows and said,

'Cheery soul, isn't he?' and he stood as if he was

345

about to return to the building.

'So, what do you want to do from here?' asked Ross, standing to join him.

'I don't know yet. We probably need to look at what we know and see if it's worth keeping people on this for a while,' then he turned to face the door. But as he did, a uniformed PC came through it.

'DI Avalon?' frowned the unfeasibly young officer, 'PC Dowd told me you were out here. DI Lasiter has been trying to get hold of you. Do you want to use our phone?' Avalon nodded and followed the lad, not before he turned to Ross with an expectant look. 'Now, what would Uncle John be wanting with me?' he asked as they walked to the front desk.

'Hello John, it's me,' he said into the phone that was handed to him.

'*Ah, James, you take some finding,*' replied Lasiter. '*I've got someone with me you might be interested en speaking with.*'

'Oh yeah? Who's that?'

'*Steven Scott.*'

'Oh?' was his simple question. He didn't really know how to react. 'Where are you?'

'*Interview room two,*' replied Lasiter.

'I was under the impression that Mr Scott had hung his naughty clothes up for good.'

'*Aye, he has, but...*' Lasiter paused. '*Et's easier to explain et here, are you coming?*'

'On my way,' he replied and handed back the phone. Turning to Ross he added, 'you better come, this might be interesting,' and he explained on the way.

He was at the open door to interview room two in less than half a minute and he entered to see Lasiter with a gaunt faced man who looked in his sixties, but it was clear it was Scott. Avalon had only seen photographs of him in his twenties, but he was recognisable under the wrinkled face. Time had not treated him well, and though he must only be fifty, he looked ten years older at least.

'DI Avalon, this es Steven Scott,' announced Lasiter, Avalon acknowledged the man with a sceptical frown. 'He says he might have something for you.'

'To do with what?' asked Avalon, staring directly at the man.

'I've been following the quarry murders in the paper,' explained the man. He had an Inverness accent but was surprisingly softly spoken, with huskiness in his voice. 'I understand you're looking at Stuart Fenner as a suspect.'

'So you have something?' asked Avalon.

'Maybe, maybe not,' he answered and looked back to Lasiter. That look told Avalon that Scott wanted something. Lasiter sighed a little and looked up to Avalon, who was leaning on the wall.

'Mr Scott's son es en the lock-up,' explained Lasiter. 'He was involved en a warehouse robbery, and we caught them red-handed.'

'As I told DI Lasiter,' began Scott, 'he's not a bad lad, but I don't want him to go down the same route as me.'

'By definition, committing a crime makes him a criminal,' explained Avalon. 'That makes him a bad lad, in my book anyway.'

'But what if I had something that could prove damaging for Stuart Fenner?' asked Scott. He wasn't pleading, but Avalon could see he meant what he said.

He was worried for his boy.

'I will always listen to information that can help with an investigation,' nodded Avalon, but he could feel Lasiter's eyes boring into him for being so matter-of-fact.

'But could that help Josh?' he asked, 'my boy's name is Josh.'

'If I think that a person can be turned away from crime, it would be wrong of me not to consider it. That's what crime prevention is all about, but...' Avalon paused and gave a slight grimace, 'it's the sheriff's decision, not mine.'

'I know that Detective,' nodded Scott, 'I've spent enough time the wrong side of the law, not to understand how it works. But I also know that the sheriff's office take notice of their detectives when considering bringing a trial to court.'

'Sometimes, but your boy was obviously brought in by DI Lasiter's team, not mine.' The man looked across to Lasiter at this.

'I told him,' explained the DI, 'ef he really had something that you could use, I would try tae help.' Avalon drew in air and gave a hint of a raised brow. He looked over to Ross and then back to Scott.

'You had a feud with Christopher Joyce,' he said, and the man nodded. 'You admitted under questioning that you set him up some years ago.' He nodded again. 'So, how do I know this isn't another one of those moments where you just want to pay someone back? To get revenge for something that happened many years ago?' The man seemed to think this through for the briefest moment.

'Because I can give you some information that

will verify that what I say is the truth.' Avalon knew that it would have to be something that couldn't be found in the papers or the news reports.

'Go on,' he eventually said.

'I can give you details of an unsolved crime that the public doesn't know about,' he revealed. 'Details that would only be known if I had been there, or received the information from someone who had helped to commit that crime.' Avalon walked around the small room for a moment and then looked down at Lasiter with a questioning look.

'I'll do what I can for his boy,' nodded the older DI. Avalon looked to Scott and back to Ross. Ross shrugged and so the DI took a chair and sat.

'Then let's hear what you have,' he said, bringing his right leg up onto his opposite knee.

'In nineteen ninety-eight, there was a Post Office hold up in the town,' began Scott. 'A gun was used but not discharged and though no one was ever found for it, I know who did it.' He looked at all those in the room, as if he was thinking through his story. 'It was an Irishman called Doyle, a guy called Emery and Stuart Fenner. At the time, a piece of information wasn't released by the police. That information was that one of the men stuffed his pockets with chocolate bars and an argument ensued between two of them.' He paused. 'Do you want to check it?' he asked.

'We'll do that later,' replied Avalon. 'Continue.'

'It was Emery who stole the chocolate and Doyle who had a go at him about it. Fenner was the one by the door.'

'How do you know this?' Avalon asked.

'Because Doyle told me about it when I got the

349

ricin from him.'

'He just told you?' asked Lasiter.

'No,' replied Scott, glancing over to the other DI. 'He knew that I knew Fenner. He told me he thought the man was a prick. I think Doyle wanted me to think he was a big time criminal.'

'So he was bragging to you?' asked Avalon.

'Yeah, I suppose I was taken in by him,' admitted the man. Avalon looked round at Ross and nodded. Ross understood and left. 'The thing with the Irishman was, he didn't take money. You had to do him a favour.'

'And Fenner's favour was helping him with the Post Office raid?' asked Avalon. Scott nodded. 'So, what did you do for him?' he asked. For a moment, Scott looked as if he wasn't going to say, then he shrugged and replied.

'I drove a van to Ireland for him, and no, I have no idea what was in it.'

'Doyle was involved with something en Ireland?' asked Lasiter quickly.

'Yeah,' nodded Scott, 'that's why the coppers from London were after him. Not for the ricin.' He paused, 'at least, not just for that.' Avalon interrupted him.

'You realise, if any of this is to be any good to us, you're going to have to tell this to a court.'

'I know,' nodded the man. 'Two of them are dead and I'll take my chances with Fenner.'

'Two are dead?' asked Avalon.

'Emery died in a car crash, and Doyle hasn't been seen since the London Police came, so I assume his health deteriorated soon after that.' Avalon considered this. He knew some very dodgy dealings were done

350

within the security services in Ireland, but he would be surprised if it was still the case that late.

'We haven't been able to find him, that's true,' he admitted, more to reassure Scott than anything else.

'Well, Doyle wasn't his real name,' grinned Scott a little sarcastically. 'I doubt he was your normal crook. He wasn't like any of us at the time. I think he came over here, raised cash from heists, then took it back to Ireland for something.'

'Do you know where he got the ricin?' interrupted Avalon.

'No,' replied Scott, 'but it only took him a week to get it. I'd asked what was the best poison to kill a dog. He told me there were lots, but he knew of one that was deadly to everything and couldn't be traced, as it wasn't a known substance.' The man gave an ironic laugh. 'That was a lie.' He looked down to the floor and back up to Avalon. 'You know, at the time, I wanted to get back at Joyce. I never thought about the dogs. That is one of the biggest regrets of my life. I have a dog of my own now. I couldn't bear anything happening to him.' He looked back at the floor. 'I was blinded by my hatred of Joyce.' He looked back up at Avalon. 'Does he know it was me?' he asked. Avalon slowly shook his head. Scott nodded and looked at the floor again.

'What was the feud about?' asked Avalon.

'I really can't remember. I was taking so much shit in those days, it was probably just my paranoia,' shrugged the man.

'Was the visit by the Special Branch the reason you went straight?' asked Lasiter, seemingly interested in that part of the story.

'Yeah,' nodded the man. 'Well, that and the fact

that Josh was born at that time. I thought I had better sort myself out. It changed me a lot.' He looked back up to Lasiter. 'So, you'll do what you can?' Lasiter nodded.

'I can't promise, but we'll do everything we can tae lessen his punishment.'

Avalon had become cynical over the past year. His distaste for the criminal class left him with the idea that once a criminal, always a criminal. He was finding it difficult to believe that someone with Scott's past could change. It was true, he had a clean history since that period of his life, but Avalon didn't feel it could be the case. Lasiter believed it though, and Lasiter had a greater understanding of the local criminal mind than he did. He put his doubts aside and was considering his next move, as Ross returned. The DS gave Avalon a quick nod and leaned on the door frame. That nod meant Scott's story had checked out, and he was telling the truth, at least about Fenner's involvement in a robbery.

'Do you want to question Fenner about the Post Office job?' asked Avalon, turning to Lasiter.

'Do you mean, do I want t' give you an excuse tae keep him here for a bit longer?' asked Lasiter, raising his brows.

'It's just that it was on your turf,' smiled Avalon. Lasiter nodded and then sighed.

'Aye, I suppose I can put Hamilton on et. He loves old cases.' Avalon was about to crack a joke but he decided against it as Scott was still in the room. He turned to the man.

'We need you to sign a statement,' explained Avalon, 'I'll get someone to come down and take the details, you sign it and we'll take you home.' Scott explained that he had come in his car, so Avalon stood and looked back to Lasiter.

'Do you want us to bring him in?' he asked.

'If we do et, you'll miss your opportunity t' gloat I'm guessing?' scowled Lasiter.

'It doesn't matter to me, my gloating days are done,' smiled Avalon, and he meant it. Though, in truth, he would have loved to have been there when Fenner was about to set off home, and the coppers, who he thought were there to escort him, cautioned him and brought him in for questioning on a very different crime. Instead, he would be content with returning to The Cave, and explaining the situation to his team, so that they could see if they had enough to take him to court on a murder charge.

Most of C Section was having a much needed rest on Sunday. Megan Frazer and Angus White were covering duties at the station, but everyone else was at home. Even Avalon, though he was unsure what to do with his time off. If the world had still been a normal place, he and Sarah would have probably gone for a drive north, or down the Great Glen, but with covid? They would be stuck indoors with no chance of anything pleasant to do. Though, Avalon didn't see the prospect of being a prisoner with Sarah a daunting experience. She, on the other hand, seemed totally stuck for anything to do and insisted on finding little chores. Now and then, she would open her own laptop, which she had brought from her house, and spend a little time on it. Avalon knew she was working, but with little or no options to suggest, he let her get on with it. This particular afternoon, she sat reading a book.

'What's the book?' he asked.

'Oh, nothing much, just something a work colleague suggested, but I'm not impressed.' He read the title and the name of the author, but he had never heard of either.

'I'm guessing it's one of those women's novels?' he said but regretted it before he had even finished.

'Women's novels?' she smiled, yet the smile had little humour in it.

'I was thinking of the drivel that my ex-wife used to read. The author's name is always in larger print than the title. It was she who coined the phrase women's books. I thought it was about something personal.'

'I know what you mean,' she comforted him, 'they're not really my thing,' she closed it and put it on a table.

'What is then?' he asked.

'My thing? I don't know really,' she shrugged. 'I like different things. I've tried a few classics and even autobiographies. It tends to change with my mood.' She gave a slight frown and then continued. 'Come to think of it, I haven't seen you read any poetry since I've been here.'

'I think I've gone off it.' He shrugged before explaining. 'I have read everything I can think of that I might like. I've even tried some modern poets, but I think I'm stuck in the past when it comes to verse.'

'Have you ever written any?' she then asked, raising her brows.

'I have,' he laughed, 'but it's very poor.'

'Have you still got it?'

'I'm afraid not,' he replied, 'not the sort of thing one wants other people to see.' She accepted his answer but wasn't convinced it was the truth.

'So, what would you be reading now, if it wasn't for the Adventures of Para Handy,' she grinned.

'Prior to Para Handy, I was reading a book of Scottish Myths.' She looked surprised at the answer.

'I thought you were so much of a realist that myths and legends wouldn't be of interest,' she suggested.

'Far from it. You don't have to believe they exist to enjoy reading about them.'

'I suppose not,' she smiled. 'I suppose it's just another novel.'

'I wouldn't put it so straightforwardly.' He replied. 'I do think that in many tales, there is something remaining of a truth. One of our PC's told me a story some years ago, when I first came north in fact. Being a broad thinking chap, he had his own explanation of a legend he grew up with. It's mainly that story that got me interested in it.'

'Is he someone I know?' she asked.

'Probably, a man of great depth and thinks on a higher level than his outward appearance would suggest. Neil Dowd, he usually works on the front desk.'

'I don't recall the name, but I don't know too many of the uniform people,' she said. 'If he impresses you, I think I need to meet him.'

'He's not your sort,' smiled Avalon. 'He is quite ordinary to the untrained eye.'

'So, what is my sort?' she smiled.

'Oh,' he sighed, 'I don't think I should even think about that. If I get the answer correct, I might get an inferiority complex.' Just for a moment, her smile subsided and her eyes flitted to the floor. Avalon knew a great deal about body language. It was part of his job, yet he couldn't tell what had just flitted through her mind. He didn't consider it too much at the time, but that night, he played that little scene, over and over, and he struggled to find sleep.

Chapter Sixteen

Avalon waited for the whole of C Section to arrive before he began his Monday morning briefing. His first task had been to update the DCI on the quarry case, and though she was more subdued than of late, there was no let-up in her officious nature. He wanted to bring up the fact that DCI Croker would be returning, but he decided not to antagonise the woman, as he had to suffer her for a few weeks yet. For some reason, Croker had sent his heads of section an email to let them know how things were going. An odd approach in Avalon's opinion, but Croker may have thought he had more respect than he really did. The email had, however, brought some good news, which he would impart to the team later.

Back in The Cave, he looked through the windows as they settled in, and saw that although the night had been cool, there was a blue sky and the sun was already marshalling the cold air to the shadows. He stood to the side of DC White's desk and began with a recap of the small details of the issues that were more to do with the running of the section. He also mentioned some of the work that Wilson and Mackinnon had been working on during the past week, and then he brought them all up to date on the quarry case.

'As most of you know,' he began, 'B Section have arrested Stuart Fenner in connection with a Post Office robbery that happened in the late nineties, thus giving us a little more time to build a case against him for the murder of his wife, Mary Anne Fenner. With the help of the statement from Steven Scott and a bit of extra digging, I'm reasonably confident that we will be able to convince the PF office that we have enough to put him away. There's still a great deal of work to do though, so don't breath out just yet.' He paused. 'But saying that, I think you can give yourselves a pat on the back for not losing focus on a case that was confusing at the very least.'

'So, es everything tied up Boss?' asked Wilson.

'More or less, Gordon,' nodded the DI, 'he's denying it of course, but he's denying the robbery too.'

'So, do me and Rory get to hear what happened then,' grinned Wilson, 'some of us have been working for a living?'

'Yes, but there isn't much to it when you know the facts,' nodded Avalon. He leaned with his back on the wall and began to tell the two detectives who hadn't worked on the case, the details, as he knew them.

'Stuart Fenner knocked his wife about, that is clear, and she was a drunk by all accounts. At some stage, she met Geoffrey Gibson who gave her an option to what she had with Fenner. She took it and took Carl with her and, to a certain degree, Fenner didn't seem too put-out by the arrangement. At some time after, Gibson began abusing Carl and that abuse stressed the boy so much, he either threatened to tell his mother or, more likely, his father, and was killed for it. It is also possible

358

he took his own life. Either way, Gibson decided to bury the boy's body at a remote location, and it seems that somehow, he managed to convince Mary to go along with it.' He paused and walked to the coffee machine. He began to pour coffee as he continued. 'They then had a problem. The school wanted to know where Carl was. Social Services were eventually brought in, but through sheer incompetence were unable to see the seriousness of the situation. But,' and Avalon paused to take a sip of coffee. 'A letter was eventually sent to Fenner to ask if he knew where Carl was. Fenner contacted Mary to ask why the boy had not been at school, and when her explanation was unsatisfactory, his distaste of her was reawakened, and he planned a way to get revenge on the pair of them. We simply don't know if Fenner knew Carl was already dead.'

'Yeah,' cut in Ross, 'he's not the most helpful person in that respect.'

'In any respect,' added Rutherford.

'His plan,' continued Avalon, 'was to kill Mary, in such a way that it would implicate Gibson for her murder and throw light onto the fate of young Carl. It didn't quite go to plan as Gibson took Mary's body to the same spot as he had buried Carl, and then left the house and moved south.' Avalon took another drink as Wilson asked,

'So didn't Fenner pursue Gibson? I would have thought ef he was bold enough tae kill Mary, he would have followed up on Gibson.'

'It seems not. Probably because he was now beholden to the Irishman, who had supplied the ricin. If he had left to find Gibson, the Irishman may have thought he was reneging on his payment. That payment was to assist with the Post Office robbery.' Wilson raised his brows. 'After that,' continued Avalon, 'Gibson was watched by the police as it was coming to their attention that he could be a paedophile. Which could be another reason why Fenner didn't continue to pursue him.'

'So what was the connection to the quarry?' asked Wilson.

'It was just a secluded spot Gibson knew of,' explained the DI. 'Back then, the quarry didn't reach that far. The place had easy access, and no one went there.' Wilson nodded.

'Like you say, a wee bit of an anti-climax when you know how et happened,' he agreed.

'What are the odds of him doing time?' asked Mackinnon.

'Pretty high, I would say,' replied Avalon. 'We still have some loose ends to follow up, but as long as a jury doesn't see Steven Scott as unreliable, it should be straightforward. Most of our case is going to rest on his account of both the robbery, and how he came by the ricin.' Avalon waited for a moment and then asked, 'Any questions?' and he was about to turn away, but he remembered something. 'Oh, I nearly forgot. DCI Croker should be back with us in a couple of weeks it seems. He's out of isolation and felling much better.' He looked around the room. The reaction was mixed, to say the least. 'He did email me though and told me we will be getting a new officer in C Section.' Most faces looked towards DC White. Avalon wondered if they were thinking the same as him, but he hoped that the next one wouldn't have the same issues as Angus.

'Do we know who et es?' asked Wilson.

'DC Alan Logan, he's been working in one of the

other sections,' explained Avalon.

'Logan?' exclaimed Ross, 'isn't he the fantasist from Internal?'

'Logan was with D Section last I heard,' interrupted Wilson, 'didn't you work with him for a while, Megan?'

'No,' nodded Frazer, 'I was with him on two surveillance training sessions, that's all.'

'And is he a fantasist as Rossy proclaims?' asked the DI.

'I don't know about that,' shrugged Frazer, 'but he says he was in the army, in Special Forces. He's a good surveillance officer, but...' she looked straight at Avalon, 'he's a bit of a dick.'

'Bound to be if he was in the army,' put in Ross.

'How do you work that out, Rossy?' asked Rutherford with a deep frown. 'Is it because you were refused entry due to psychological issues?'

'Me? Army?' laughed Ross. 'And no, I don't have issues with Logan, and no, I don't know him, but yes, I have heard a few things from people who have worked with him.'

'Such as?' asked the boss.

'He's a risk taker,' explained Ross, 'adrenalin junkie, I would think. But some stories that get around make out he was working for the government after he left the army.' Avalon raised his brows at this.

'He likes to play the game,' added Frazer. 'He drops hints and people make up the bits that they don't know.' She now looked to Avalon. 'He was in the army. I know that is true and he could have been Special Forces for all I know, but a spy? I don't think so.'

'So are we getting?' Avalon almost said

'another', but he managed to drop the word in time, 'someone else's problem or not?'

'I don't particularly like him,' admitted Frazer, 'but as far as I know he's a good copper as long as you pick and choose how you use him.' Avalon nodded and returned to his booth. He watched the team discussing the new man. That's why Avalon had told them about it. He wanted them to converse. He wanted them to form a tighter bond, and bringing another outsider in, could do just that. He looked to his screen. There was now a huge amount of paperwork to write, and even more to check. Yet again, he was a slave to red tape and procedures. He checked the news for information on the covid crisis, but there was nothing pleasant. The death toll had passed sixteen thousand and was predicted to surpass twenty thousand by the weekend. Was this it? Was this the crisis that would see the end of the world? He didn't think so, but he also doubted that any government would be able to react to it. The British Government had stupidly decided to pay an eighty percent of most people's wages, and anyone with an ounce of intelligence knew they couldn't afford to do that. It couldn't last, then what? Avalon thought he knew the answer, and it made him shiver slightly. It was like living on a film set, and he wondered if this was a good time to be a police officer. He looked up. Most people were happily getting on with their work, all except one. Ross was looking out of the window, and there was worry on his face. Was he thinking the same as Avalon? Maybe. Ross sometimes seemed like a wimp. He could be a little unreasonable and he had a side to him that most people disliked, but the truth of Ross was that he was none of those things. His brash side and his other unpleasant tendencies were

362

part of his humour. The truth was, Ross was a thinker. He thought a great deal, and he cared. Avalon knew that, and when he saw Ross gazing out of the window with a glassy stare, he knew Ross was thinking, and he knew he was worried. At that moment, Rutherford made some comment to him and his eyes blinked twice, but by the time that worried expression had turned to face the big man. Ross wore a cynical grin instead and replied with some comment, and then once more turned to the window with that same worried look. Avalon shook his thoughts away from blackness. He still had a job to do and he would do it. He looked at the coffee machine, but he decided that this time, what he needed was air. He left The Cave and headed downstairs and towards the front door. He almost bumped into PC Kirk as he entered the foyer.

'Oh, DI,' she exclaimed, 'I was just on my way upstairs.' He looked down and saw she had a report sheet.

'Is that for us?' he asked.

'I doubt et,' she answered, 'Incident on Lochardil Road.' Avalon took it from her and read the sheet. Several windows had been broken at a property by an unknown party. It was just another minor incident that someone had perpetrated on someone else. He handed it back to Kirk, and she hurried off to B Section and DI Lasiter. Avalon continued to the door and stepped outside as he wondered why someone would break windows. Probably a revenge attack of sorts, but Lochardil Road wasn't exactly crime central. It was then he remembered his meeting with Scobie. He had mentioned a list of incidents that seemed like revenge attacks, and yet Scobie had thought there was more to it than met the eye. But, then again, Scobie was an ex criminal, not a criminal psychologist. Nevertheless, Avalon wondered if there was any connection, at least for just a moment, and then he sucked in a lungful of air and parked his backside on the low wall. He heard footsteps to his right. It was Ross.

'Nothing to do?' Avalon asked. Ross said nothing. He joined the DI on the wall.

'The town is so quiet with this lockdown,' he eventually commented. Avalon nodded.

'So, what were you thinking?' Avalon asked.

'When?' questioned Ross, turning towards him.

'Upstairs,' he replied, 'you were staring into the far distance,' he added and then stood. He set off slowly down the drive, a stretch of asphalt, which was grandly named, Old Perth Road. Ross eventually stood too and followed on.

'How the world is going to change, I suppose.'

'You think it will?' asked Avalon.

'Don't you?' questioned Ross as he caught up. 'At a time we need strong and competent leaders, the UK and the USA have two beings, that have the combined IQ of the Lego, Bob the Builder character.' It was Avalon's turn to be silent now. They reached the end of the car park and Avalon stopped, his hands thrust into his trouser pockets. He looked left and then across to the roundabout.

'I heard Angus making a prediction the other day,' announced Avalon.

'I wouldn't take much notice of Mr Spock,' shrugged Ross.

'But I agreed with his prediction.'

'Which was?' asked Ross.

'That, once the government realises that they have made a promise they can't keep, they will drop the lockdown and everyone will go about their business as usual.'

'It doesn't take a genius to know that,' scoffed Ross.

'No,' admitted Avalon, 'but it's what comes after that. He predicted that covid will spread again and the government will put more restrictions in place. That will cause unrest, and people will begin to take no notice. The government will realise they can't afford to police it, so eventually they will leave the people to die or survive.'

'And chaos reigns,' announced Ross.

'Exactly,' replied Avalon.

'I don't see it quite that way, but I can predict one thing,' said Ross with a sigh. 'There are enough idiots out there to believe whatever the government tells them, just so they can continue on their merry way, burying their heads in the sand as usual. As soon as restrictions are dropped, watch them all scurry off on holidays. I bet some even go to China.' Avalon nodded. Then he turned and looked back at the station, taking a deep breath.

'Whatever happens, we'll still be coming here,' he sighed. 'Come on, let's get some work done,' and he headed off back to the building.

'Are you worried about it?' asked Ross as they walked.

'Yes, but from other perspectives.'

'Such as?' asked Ross.

'This world is changing in my opinion,' offered Avalon, 'things will change in society and communities. That is going to make the future very different.' He suddenly turned to Ross with a smile. 'And I miss our trips to the Castle Tavern, to be honest.' Ross grinned back.

'Yeah, so do I,' he replied then paused for a moment, before adding, 'but I was always taught to think positive.'

'And are you doing?' asked the DI.

'Yeah, I'm positive we're in the shit, and I'm positive I miss going to the Castle Tavern.' Avalon cast him a slight grin before Ross added, 'but I'm also positive I don't miss the poetry.' Avalon stopped and turned around.

'What poetry?' he asked.

'Not that long ago, you would be quoting poetry like it meant something in the world. Not a sniff of it on this case, and that's unusual. But… it suits me,' he added hurriedly, as if it were a serious caveat.

'You're the second person who's commented on that subject,' and he opened the door to the building.

'Who was the first?' asked Ross. Avalon didn't answer. He walked through the foyer and put his memory into overdrive, then said,

'*For Justice, though she's painted blind, is to the weaker side inclined.*' Ross frowned at him.

'And do you believe that?' he asked as they passed the duty sergeant at his desk. The sergeant had been chatting with PC Munton. Munton turned as they passed and said,

'Samuel Butler.' Avalon glanced over to Munton with more than a hint of surprise.

'Yes it is, you're correct,' nodded the DI, 'from Hudibras I recall.'

'Don't know about that DI,' frowned Munton, 'it

cropped up in a pub quiz at Christmas though.' Avalon smiled and began to climb the stairs. Halfway up, he glanced to Ross at his side.

'No, I don't,' he explained in answer to Ross's previous question. 'I believe that justice comes to those who have enough money to buy the best solicitor.'

'No poetry, but the cynic is still there. That feels kind of reassuring,' Ross grinned as they continued to walk. Avalon stopped as they came to the corridor that led to The Cave. The two large windows, the only natural light at that point, looked out over the leafy suburbs of Inverness, where just beyond the line of trees, over forty-six thousand people were observing lockdown, in just eight square miles of space. Over seventy thousand souls, if the surrounding districts were included. Avalon thrust his hands into his pockets and stared out, considering those figures. How many of them would be effected by this horror? How many would succumb to it?

'There are too many people talking about herd immunity and vaccinations for comfort already,' he said at length. Ross stood at his side looking out as he folded his arms.

'So what?'

'I just think a vaccine is a long way off, and as to herd immunity, we have no idea if this thing has some surprises up its sleeve.'

'You mean will it have some long-term issues for those that have recovered?' asked Ross still watching the skyline. Avalon didn't answer. He kept his expressionless face pointing towards the west, watching the clouds saunter by, as if everything below was as it always had been. Ross unfolded his arms and turned slowly to his boss. For a moment he took the man in, but as Avalon sensed him watching, he too turned to Ross. 'You've changed, do you know that?' Ross said and quickly added, 'nothing to do with this virus either. And, I know you won't admit anything, but you've changed all the same.' Avalon kept the blank expression and returned his gaze towards the window. Ross knew him well, well enough to see through any attempt at a lie.

'You're right,' nodded Avalon, 'I won't admit anything.' He pulled his right hand from his trouser pocket and rubbed the back of his neck. 'We're all going to have to change,' he continued, and he turned to walk down the corridor, 'whether we like it or not,' he added in a quieter tone.

The Avalon Series, by Peter Gray.

The Drums of Drumnadrochit

By Peter Gray.

Introducing Detective James Avalon, a man in turmoil. Both his private and professional life is at an all-time low and to make things worse he is seen as a liability to his senior officers. He has to make a change in both aspects of his life, but how? Though he is still on good terms with his ex-wife she is beginning to despair with his lack of compromise in his life until a chance meeting with another officer shows promise of opening new doors to his future.

Auld Clootie

By Peter Gray.

James Avalon faces a new menace in the second book in the Avalon series. Change and upheaval within the police forces sees him struggle with the problems of a reorganisation of the team. Trouble visits once again in the shape of a major crime that seems to have no clues or motives and Avalon has to work with limited resources to solve a crime linked to religion, ritual and legend.

The Brollachan

By Peter Gray.

After just twelve months based in Inverness, Detective Inspector James Avalon now feels more at home than any other time in his career. With his personal life still a shambles, Avalon takes solace in the landscape and his work, but when a woman disappears from her car in plain sight, he wonders about the accuracy of the report.
. When a body is found, the case becomes more serious. Is the woman's disappearance linked to the body or does Avalon need to reassess his methods?

The Black Clan

By Peter Gray.

When Avalon becomes embroiled in secret societies and Masonic rituals he soon finds out how far up the food chain the rot has climbed. Once again the Inverness detective is on the streets and this time he's angry.

Caledonian Flame

By Peter Gray.

Avalon is taking a much-needed rest, his first extended leave since being at Inverness. It gives him time to think, and for Avalon, that isn't necessarily a good thing.

Bored and kicking his heels in Edinburgh, he digs his way through old cases and uncovers much more than a crime, he stumbles on a whole culture of misdemeanours spreading oceans, continents and time.

Avalon scours the streets of Inverness in the last major case of this contemporary series. This time his life is on the line.

Plague Witch

By Peter Gray.

C Section, Inverness CID has continued along without DI James Avalon at the helm.

Now, there is a new killer to be unleashed on an unsuspecting world, and this one can't be stopped by simple detective work. Covid 19, a virus from China, is about to destroy the lives of hundreds of thousands of people, but police business must go on. As usual, C Section are understaffed, with their new DI off sick, and other officers succumbing to the virus, DS Gordon Wilson does his best to run the section until the new DI arrives. The problem is, more trouble waits in the wings.

Also by Peter Gray

A Certain Summer

Sam's Kingdom

With Feeling

New Series

Bethran – Seer of the Picts
A brand new series set in the backdrop of the Pictish
Kingdoms of Scotland.
Set in 690 AD, this story follows Bethran, a well-known
wise man and seer as he travels north on a task he
performs each year. This time, there are surprises.

Please visit:

www.petergrayauthor.co.uk
www.acertainsummer.co.uk
www.avalon-series.co.uk

www.trickyimppublishing.co.uk